Masters' Mistress

OTHER BOOKS BY JAMIE SCHULZ

Jake's Redemption

UPCOMING BOOKS

Masters' Escape: The Angel Eyes Series Book 2
Masters' Promise: The Angel Eyes Series Book 3
Masters' Rebellion: The Angel Eyes Series Book 4
Masters' Betrayal: The Angel Eyes Series Book 5
Masters' Freedom: The Angel Eyes Series Book 6

Masters' Mistress

The Angel Eyes Series Book 1

Jamie Schulz

For my boys with all my love...

DEFINITIONS

Hysterical strength—also known as superhuman strength, is a display of extreme strength by humans, beyond what is believed to be normal, usually occurring when people are in life and death situations. Common anecdotal examples include parents lifting vehicles to rescue their children...The extra strength is commonly attributed to increased adrenaline production...research into the phenomenon is difficult, though it is thought that it is theoretically possible.
Hysterical strength can result in torn muscles due to higher mechanical stress.

- Excerpt from The Free Dictionary, September 2019
https://encyclopedia.thefreedictionary.com

THE BEGINNING

1

Two years after the world war...

SHE STUMBLED THROUGH the punishing rain, running away again. Always running from the horrors she couldn't face and praying they would never catch up with her. The futility of that prayer struck her as a cold chill trickled down her spine, lifting the fine hairs on her nape. She froze, feeling watched by an unfriendly foe. Glancing around, she searched for the eyes that seemed to be drilling into the back of her head, following her everywhere she went. Anyone could be hiding in the impenetrable shadows, waiting to assail her when she least expected it.

No one was there, of course. Her mind was just messing with her again. Still, she couldn't help one last look. Even though the night was too damn dark to see much of anything, it was obvious she was alone. *Who else* but *a crazy person would be out on a night like this?* With a shrug, she picked up her pace, trying to escape her memories once more. But no matter how far she ran, she knew she couldn't outrun the ceaseless torment that trailed her.

The war left its survivors lost and broken. She was no

exception. The strife began with various battles over land and water rights, religious ideation, and other selfish desires too numerous to list, slowly unraveling their world like the torn threads of her tattered jeans. As the hostilities between nations escalated so did the global devastation. The destruction spared no one. Her own personal downfall underwent a similar decline. Now, years later, with her heart fragmented seemingly beyond repair, she no longer cared about civilization's demise. Her sole desire was to curl up and die. Instead, she endured.

She struggled to reach some kind of sanctuary from the pain—the pain she had caused. One slow, staggering step after the other, one more stride to somewhere, anywhere. Her muscles ached from her long, forced march, and her body longed for rest. She shivered with cold, but fear drove her onward. Afraid to stop, terrified of the atrocities she could still see in her head, of the loss that haunted her soul.

Her mind wandered as hours and days ticked by, while she continued her hike through the surrounding forest. Memories fluttered away as quickly as they came, yet, like a moth to an inescapable flame, her scattered thoughts were once again drawn to her personal nightmare.

Forcing the recollections to the back of her mind, she blundered on through the driving rain.

She didn't think about the raiding parties. She didn't think about protecting herself. She tried not to think at all. Reluctant to face coherent thought, she ambled along in a fog of denial, comforted by its blissful haze and lack of…well, anything.

It never stayed that way for long, though.

Every time that old tree popped into her mind, she wanted to scream. Hysteria bubbled beneath the surface, threatening to overflow like champagne from an uncorked bottle, and she wished again that she could lie down and die. Yet, she knew the irrationality of that—if she surrendered, she would fail everyone again. Still, knowing that didn't stop her wishing, but if she didn't find cover soon, it wouldn't matter. She'd freeze to death.

Would I find peace then?

The brown cowboy hat jammed over her ebony curls protected her from the heavy rain, but the harsh wind still wreaked havoc with her hair. Her long black tresses tugged loose from their ribbon so often that she ceased trying to control them. They slapped into her face, blinding her eyes and diving into her mouth. She spit out another nuisance strand and kept on going.

Though dying didn't trouble her, she was deeply concerned about keeping her promise. The promise she'd made only days ago—*was it only days ago?*—to everyone she had failed. Her own desires were no longer important; her pledge was all that mattered. Her vow kept her alive and compelled her to move. Yet, the specifics of how her self-assigned task would succeed were as elusive as catching starlight in a bottle.

She sighed as another shiver shook her small frame.

I am so sick of the cold!

After losing everything—her home, her family, her friends, and the love she'd never deserved—warmth and comfort evaded her. She felt cold to her soul, and she blamed it all on human hubris.

Everything once familiar was gone. Changed. Destroyed. Even interpersonal relationships—those between men and women—had been altered by war. She could almost smell the smoke and burning debris left by the bombs, hear the screams of others running for their lives as the deafening bombardment exploded all around her.

She slipped on the rain-soaked ground and reached for a nearby evergreen, narrowly avoiding a fall into the cold mud. Frozen in place, she slowly began to breathe again, realizing the sounds and smells were just memories that keep popping up. Straightening, she wiped her palms on her damp jeans and stuck her numb hands back into her coat pockets. Tipping her hat into the wind, she continued to amble downhill as more memories crept back into her mind.

After the war ended and soldiers began to return home, they found that many influential women had branded them as criminals. According to them, all men were at fault for the heinous deeds perpetrated by a handful of radical male guerillas and could not be trusted. Tired of being treated like second-class citizens by the women around them, the men who'd survived the world war eventually rebelled against their oppressors. Grossly outnumbered, they quickly lost the Sex War, and the women who feared a repeat of male violence, locked the defeated combatants in chains. Men no longer had a say in their lives, in how they lived, or whom they loved.

The way captured men were treated turned her stomach. Years ago, she used to lay awake at night and often woke sweating and shivering with the fear that what remained of her family would one day be taken by the cruelty of slavery. When that loss became reality, it *was* cruel, but at least it didn't involve years of oppression. Her family was taken under the bright sun of an autumn afternoon and that loss—though quick—destroyed her.

She stopped in her tracks. The night seemed to blacken further as dark, soul-wrenching memories crowded in, crushing her heart and stealing her breath.

I should've done more, she silently railed as the rain poured over her hat and regret clogged her throat. *I should've done something...* She shook her head, once again swallowing her heartache. *Stop it! Stop thinking about it.* She would not go there again, not now. She had tried to save her family and almost died in the process.

Leaning into the wind, she started to walk again, chuckling with derisive mirth as her mind continued along its previous train of thought.

They can't all believe this was the best way to rebuild our society, can they? I can't be the only one who thinks it's ludicrous. Can I?

The world she now knew was filled with selfishness and inequality, fear and pain. She held little hope for a better future for herself, but she had promised to make a difference for others, to change the world, at least her little part of it—a lofty goal that weighed on her shoulders like the mythical burden of Atlas.

She didn't approve of their new society, never participated in any of it. She had resisted the tyranny of the new society for years, but those idiotic, idealistic days had been futile. Now, at twenty-eight, she was weary of it, tired of the constant loss. She wanted to be alone, but she wanted to help people too— polar opposite objectives, but she wanted to try. Those suffering in slavery needed aid, and she wanted to give it. She had a plan. The start of one, anyway.

Do I have the will to implement it? Uncertainty tightened her chest as she trudged through the boot-sucking mud.

A sudden gust of wind surprised her into stillness and she looked up at her surroundings. From what she could discern, she had wandered into a clearing in the center of the forest. It looked like a long-abandoned field with an old, dilapidated barn sitting off to one side, a dark shape in the stormy blackness. Run-down and leaning to the right, the building still had most of its roof. Her lips stretched into a bleak smile. It wasn't much, but it should keep her relatively dry.

Weary, ravenous, and cold, she staggered up to the door. Her numb fingers ached as she searched for a handle. Not finding one, she tugged at the edge of the frame.

Now, if I can just get it open.

The heavy door didn't budge.

Great, she thought with the bite of snide defeatism as her arms dropped to her sides in frustration. *I've found shelter, only to freeze outside the damn door!*

She rubbed her hands together. *Too bad my damn hysterical-strength can't help with this,* she thought irritably as she pulled a lock of hair out of her face and tucked it behind her ear. With a resigned sigh, she placed her shoulder against the edge, and using her legs, she shoved with all her remaining might. The rusty hinges squeaked, and the door eked forward an inch. Encouraged, she kept up the pressure, draining her reserves, her legs shaking with effort. Finally, pushing with the last bit of energy and defiance she had left, the door screeched open far enough for her to squeeze inside. She tripped and landed on her hands and knees, and her hat went flying. Pain shot through her limbs, her freezing hands complaining the most. A moment later, she glanced up through the tangled mess of her ebony curls, searching for her hat, and froze. As her empty belly twisted into knots, she heard the heavy, creaking door slide closed behind her, and felt a powerful urge to run back outside.

She was no longer alone.

Inside, around a makeshift fire pit, preparing to cook their catch of the day, were five strangers—two men and three women. Four of them stood, glaring at her with improvised weapons in their hands, all aimed in her direction.

Fear shot through her and a surge of adrenaline flooded her body, causing her exhausted limbs to shake.

She remained on her hands and knees, trembling but immobile, listening to the rattling of the rain on the ragged roof, distantly noting the louder sound of flowing water splashing to the ground in the far corner. The wind howled under the rickety eves. Shock and fear—and perhaps a bit of good sense—would not allow her to bolt, as everything in her screamed to do.

What are they doing here?

Are they with the Section Guards?

Are they Raiders with a fresh catch of men to supply the auction halls?

Are they friendly?

She held little hope for the last. Few people on their own were gracious to outsiders, and the expressions of the four individuals facing her were anything but friendly. Her second and third queries were more likely, but another swift perusal answered them as well. The men were clothed, not in chains, and appeared to be an equal part of the band.

Not Section Guards or Raiders, then.

They're on the run, too. That left her first question unanswered.

With her initial panic resolved, she sat back on her heels and took in the group's appearance. By the look of them, they fared only a little better than she did. They seemed as leery as she felt, were almost as filthy as she was, but, unlike her, they had started a small fire in preparation to cook a meal.

Just keep going! her traumatized brain screamed as a terrified prickle danced over her skin. *You don't need their food. You don't need them. Just go.*

She eyed the rabbits and what looked like grouse waiting to be trimmed, spitted, and roasted over the tiny flames. Her stomach gave a protesting growl. For the agonizing few seconds she knelt indecisively in the dirt, she couldn't force herself to look away from the bounty by the fire. Only a few seconds, but then her mind wrestled back control and she gradually stood. She was about to turn and run when her eyes locked with the hazel gaze of the pretty woman who had remained seated beside the fire.

The blonde woman smiled, a warm, inviting smile.

"Hello there," the blonde said in a melodious voice that matched the kindness in her eyes. She stood and took a step forward. "My name's Monica Avery. What's yours?"

Still unsure she should scratch the door open and disappear into the night, she didn't respond to Monica's question, only stared at her in silent uncertainty.

"You're welcome to join us if you'd like. Oh," Monica huffed, waving a hand at the others, "Davy. Shawn. The rest of you, put your weapons down and sit. Can't you see she's cold and hungry, and alone?"

"What if she's not?" the one named Davy demanded. "We can't risk her telling anyone about us."

"She's not going to tell anyone, are you?" Monica turned a questioning gaze on her.

With wide eyes watching every move Monica made, she shook her head. She didn't want to hurt anyone.

"You're probably starving," Monica said, taking another step closer. "You are hungry, aren't you?"

Shuffling backward a step, she nodded but remained mute.

Monica halted and tilted her head. "We've met a lot of people in need and on their own. Some of them weren't what they seemed. You're not a Section Guard soldier or a counsel spy, are you?"

Her chest tightened at that question. Had she made a mistake? Were *they* working for one of those organizations?

No, she'd already determined they weren't that kind of threat and she didn't sense any other type, either. Well, at least, not from Monica.

Damp strands of loose black hair stuck to her cheeks as she once again moved her head to indicate a negative response.

"Just proves she's lost," Davy said. "What the hell are you doing out here alone?"

"You are alone, aren't you?"

She glanced at Monica and frowned. She wanted to run away, but she was so damn hungry.

She nodded.

"Apparently, she's doing the same thing we are," the black-haired, olive-skinned older woman said in a soft, accented voice. "Scared of being caught, and looking for shelter and food." She lowered the bow she held but did not remove the arrow from the string.

"Rosa's right," Monica agreed, moving closer still. Apparently, she also didn't detect a threat. "We've seen enough starving wanderers to recognize the look, not to mention our share of spies. Now, will you please sit down,

Davy?"

Unhurriedly, grumbling under his breath, Davy sat by the fire and began to feed it wood from a small pile beside him.

"Don't mind him," the second man said with a crooked smile as he took a seat on the dirty floor. "He's always grouchy."

Both Rosa and the quiet, third woman of the group, Mary, snickered at the comment.

"Shut up, Shawn," Davy growled, throwing a dark look at the other man.

Shawn responded with a cheerful chuckle. "What?" he said, his brown eyes twinkling in the firelight. "It's true."

Ignoring the others, Monica picked up the hat from where it had landed and unhurriedly approached.

Body stiffening, she backed another step away.

"You're safe with us," Monica said, lifting her hands, palms out, clearly trying to appear as non-threatening as possible. "We won't hurt you."

Monica Avery's slow careful movement, her gentle voice, and amiable smile disarmed the shorter woman, and she only gave minor resistance to being escorted to the small fire pit.

Leery, afraid of a trap, she watched the others as they worked together to prepare the meal.

"Ah, damn!" Shawn shouted. Dropping the knife he'd been using to skin the game, he quickly covered the injury.

His low bellow had startled her, but the reaction of the other three women surprised her more.

"What happened?" Monica asked as everyone turned concerned eyes on Shawn.

"Nothing," he replied. "It's just a scratch."

Rosa reached over and gently took his hand to examine the laceration. "A little more than a scratch," she said as she removed a white handkerchief and a faded blue bandana from her pocket. She used the handkerchief to wipe out the wound, using water from a nearby canteen, then bound his hand with the bandana.

"How bad is it?" Monica asked, a note of worry edging the other woman's voice.

"He'll live," Rosa said with a lopsided grin. "You need to be more careful, Shawn, and keep that clean." She pointed at his hand and her voice became stern, like a mother instructing a wayward child. "There's not much I can do if that gets infected. We don't have any more meds and I don't want you to lose your hand."

"Yes, Mom," Shawn replied in a sullen tone, but then a big grin split his face. "I'll do my best."

"See that you do," Rosa replied, but her lips curled up ever so slightly.

The newcomer sat a little distance from the others, but could still hear and see everything. Watching their familiar, comfortable interplay settled something inside her. No woman who truly believed men were inferior barbarians that should be controlled would show that much obvious concern for their physical and emotional wellbeing.

The women seemed to accept that she wasn't a threat, but the men eyed her and watched for sudden movements as they went back to work. Despite Shawn's earlier affability, even he seemed almost as suspicious as Davy. Exchanging pregnant looks and low-voiced comments that were so obviously about her, the men might as well have screamed them in her face. She couldn't blame them. There were women roaming the mountains somewhere who wanted to lock them in chains and force them into servitude simply because they were male.

Some of their mistrust seemed to dissipate, however, when they saw the extent of her hunger.

"At the rate she's downing dinner, we're going to have to go hunting again tonight," Shawn joked and the others chuckled.

Glancing at his dancing brown eyes, she wiped grease from her chin. Her gaze darted around the group, but saw no censure from any of them.

"If you're planning to stick around, I guess we'll have to teach you to hunt," Davy said, poking at the fire with a stick. He glanced at her and one side of his mouth quirked up. "Can't have you wasting away...or the rest of us either. We all," he waved the stick he held inside the flames, indicating the others in their group, "pull our weight."

She met the challenge in his eyes with a hard look of her own.

Breaking the visual duel, Shawn said, "It'll be fun."

She glanced at him and his friendly grin loosened the knot in her chest, but she didn't drop her guard.

"We all need more practice," Monica added, with a smile for the newcomer.

"Yes," Rosa agreed. "It was easier when we had a place and could store up, but this winter's going to be hard."

They all nodded.

She could feel Davy's dark eyes still on her, assessing, questioning, and she turned his way.

"You up for it?" he asked.

Her eyes narrowed at his slightly condescending tone, but she nodded. She would not allow Davy to intimidate her, nor would she refuse the offer. Even though her luck had been mostly bad lately, she was no stranger to acquiring food. Maybe, if she stayed, she would learn something new and teach them a thing or two in the process.

"So, what's your name?" Shawn asked. "We can't just say, 'Hey you!' all the time."

She lowered her eyes to the greasy meat in her hand and shrugged. She wasn't ready to let anyone in just yet, or to speak at all. They could call her whatever they liked.

"O-kay," Shawn said, drawing out the second syllable. "How about..." He paused and she glanced up to meet his thoughtful expression. The moment she met his gaze, he tilted his head and his face lit up with an enormous grin. "Hmm, blue eyes... How about we call you Blue?"

"Shawn," Monica admonished, "I'm sure she doesn't want to be reduced to her eye color." She turned to look at the woman in question. "Do you?"

Breathing out a soft chuckle, even though her chest tightened with uncertainty, she glanced at Monica. She didn't want to know them, didn't want to hang around, so one name was as good as any other. She shrugged again and went back to eating.

"Blue it is then," Shawn said with a laugh and gave Davy a good-natured slap on the back. "You see, Davy? She's got a sense of humor. She can't be all bad."

Davy grunted as he cut a narrowed-eyed look in her direction. "Yeah," he grumbled. "We'll see."

2

FIVE WEEKS LATER, they all gathered around another campfire in a small, snow-dappled glade several miles east of the old barn they'd used as a shelter from the storm. They'd split up earlier to go hunting for the evening meal and everyone had returned, except for Davy.

"We should just get started," Mary said from her seat on a fallen log. She didn't speak often, and Blue recognized the signs of grief and distress in the other woman, but she refused to dwell on it.

"Yeah," Shawn said from beside Mary, "I'm starved, and I'm sure Davy'll be back soon enough. Let's eat."

Monica's eyes swept the darkened shadows beneath the forest that surrounded them. They normally waited for everyone to return before eating and Blue could see the worry on the blonde woman's pretty face.

The familiar clench of anxiety cramped Blue's belly. She wouldn't say Davy had warmed up to her much, but he had been kind at times, teaching her some hunting tricks she'd found helpful over the weeks since she'd joined them. She'd grown to respect him, and when she'd returned his training with some of her own, the feeling had seemed mutual. He still watched her as if expecting some treachery on her part, but Blue couldn't blame him for that. The Raiders and their spies seemed to be everywhere.

"I suppose you're right," Monica murmured. "I'm just a little worried. Davy's not usually this late returning from a hunt. Maybe we should look for him."

Shawn nodded. "Let's eat first. If he's not back by the time we finish, then we can look for him."

"But he may need us now." Monica's voice was hard and worried, and Blue felt cold apprehension gripping her insides. There were only two reasons Davy wouldn't return and both turned her stomach.

"Davy wouldn't appreciate it if we went looking for him after such a short time. You know he thinks of himself as a survivalist, and he's touchy about those type of things."

"Yes, I know, and one day his stubborn pride's going to get him killed or worse."

This is dangerous, Blue thought, sitting off to one side as she normally did, while the others debated. *What am I still doing with them? I should've moved on before...*

She pushed that thought away, unwilling to think about what might happen. Her heart had been torn apart too many times already, and she didn't want to care about these relative strangers.

Yet, despite Shawn's clowning personality, Davy's gruffness, and the women's assorted quirks, a fondness for all of them had grudgingly built up inside her. She'd tried to keep her distance, especially from the men—knowing if anything went bad, they would be the first taken, the first harmed. She only hoped today wasn't that day.

"Maybe..." Blue said, her voice raspy from disuse. She looked up, surprised that she'd spoken aloud—she hadn't intended to. Seeing the stunned faces staring back at her, her shoulders rolled forward and she shrugged. "Maybe we should go check on him."

Monica's mouth snapped closed. Clearly, she was as shocked by Blue's sudden speech as Blue was herself. "Yes," she said, "I think we will."

* * *

A week later, Monica grabbed Blue's arm as she started into the trees once again. The others were out hunting for food. She and Monica had just brought back their two-rabbit-catch and Blue planned to take another trek to search for the still absent member of their group.

"You need to take a break, Blue," Monica said. "We've all been searching for him, but you've been running yourself ragged since Davy disappeared. You're going to make yourself sick."

Blue had tried to remain separate—sat alone during meals, hunted on her own—but somehow, Monica had wormed her way beneath Blue's defenses.

Blue turned to the woman she was slowly beginning to accept as a friend and remembered all the ways Monica had built a place in her heart. Such as how Monica held her whenever Blue woke, screaming from her all too familiar nightmares, which had become a nightly routine, some worse than others, but never pressed her for explanations. Not to mention how Monica had calmed her and then sat up with Blue, telling stories about her family—her mother and father and how much they'd loved each other. "I want to find that kind of love one day," Monica had said the last time Blue had startled them all awake. Blue nodded, but didn't reply—she'd wanted that once too, but things were so different now.

Blue frowned at her friend, but had to admit, if only to herself, that she was exhausted. Worry and concern wrinkled Monica's brow and there was a hint of fear in her hazel eyes.

"Please, Blue," Monica pleaded, a touch of sadness edged her voice. "I know you didn't plan to stay with us, and you don't owe us anything, but we're stronger when you're with us.

And so are you."

"Davy's still out there," Blue said in a flat voice that held none of the terror that had wrapped around her heart over the last seven days.

"And we'll keep looking," Monica replied. "But we both know he wouldn't have left us without word. You should also know the chances of us ever finding him are very low."

Blue looked away. "He's either dead or a slave."

"Yes," Monica said softly.

Blue turned to meet Monica's sad eyes. "And you can just accept that?" Strangely, the fact that Monica had guessed that Blue had once planned to leave their little party didn't faze her, but Monica's apparent acceptance of Davy's fate left a bitter tang on her tongue. She felt the skin around her eyes and mouth tighten as rage boiled up inside her. Anger for Davy, yes, but also for every other loss and every gaping wound that still festered inside her and would never heal.

Monica's hand dropped from her arm. "You know I don't," she said a little defensively. "I just know the futility of searching for him, and so do you. That doesn't mean we'll stop looking, but I don't want to lose anyone else because of it either." Monica kicked a rock in the dirt, then met Blue's eyes once more. "You're my friend, and I value you and your insight, but I've known Shawn since we were kids and Rosa's like a second mom to me. I won't risk them, or any of the rest of you, for something we all know is the far side of useless. Maybe we'll find him again, and maybe by then we'll have a way to save him, but for now, we need to concentrate on keeping ourselves alive. To do that, we need to stick together."

Blue swallowed the lump in her throat. She knew Monica was right, but she hated it. She'd lost again. She was too late again. When would it stop?

Monica's face blurred and images of that old tree popped into Blue's head. The long naked limb swaying in the wind, the coppery tang that filled the air, the arctic cold that never seemed to leave her. Her skin prickled and she felt panic bubble inside as her vision shifted, darkened, and flashed back to that hilltop on the gray, wet morning when she'd been shattered beyond recognition.

No, no, no, she mentally shrieked, struggling back to the present. Her heart rate kicked into high gear and terror crowded into her mouth. She gritted her teeth, sucked in air through her nose, and fought the bitter burn in her eyes, holding back the hysterical scream that threatened to break loose.

The moment passed, and she'd regained her mental equilibrium and control of her breathing. Monica's worried face came back into view; still standing beside her, eyeing her critically as if she'd heard the anguished cries of Blue's splintered heart. Easily reading Monica's questioning look, she straightened her shoulders and sighed. But instead of explaining that Davy's disappearance and their inability to do anything about it only reminded Blue of her inadequacies and losses, she gave Monica a trembling smile and squeezed her hand. "I'm fine."

Returning to the fire, she began to prepare their meal, awaiting the others' return.

3

BLUE LAUGHED ALONG with the others as they watched Shawn's antics while attempting his turn at charades. The five of them had found shelter in this small cave on the edge of the mountain forest for most of the long winter months. It had been cramped, but no one complained. Now, they were passing the time after dinner by playing this old game.

A fire flickered in the shallow pit they'd dug, illuminating the enclosed space and filling the air with the scent of wood smoke. Shawn's shadow danced across the rough walls, distorting his size and shape and making his odd gestures funnier than they already were.

"An old man snoring," Mary shouted.

"An old man counting sheep," Monica guessed.

Shawn dropped his arms and groaned in frustration. A moment later, he started over again.

Blue had given him the phrase to act out—a part of her knowing he would turn it into something to make them laugh. He gave her a quick glare and she smiled at his aggravation. Like the rest of them, he'd become like family to her, the brother she didn't have, and she enjoyed teasing him as much as he seemed to like harassing all of them.

"A rocket man," Monica tried again and Shawn shook his head.

Outside, the spring sun had melted most of the deep snow, revealing large open patches of brown grass dotted with scrub brush. The evergreens were bare of the white and buds had begun to appear on the deciduous trees and shrubs. Blue looked forward to summer. The warmer weather, the better hunting, but mostly, she looked forward to the teeming life that would be all around her. She wanted to feel some hope for a change, rather than the never-ending weight that seemed to crush her into the earth.

"The old man in the moon," Rosa said, her soft Spanish accent filling the small stone room.

"Yes!" Shawn shouted and did a little jig of triumph, kicking up dust from the dry dirt floor. They all laughed as he plopped down on the ground and crossed his legs in front of him. He rested his hands on his knees and gave Blue a dirty look.

"Don't look at me like that, Shawn," she said with a chuckle. "You said you wanted a hard one."

"Yeah, yeah," he replied as if offended, but Blue knew he was anything but. "I'll remember that when your turn comes around."

Blue got to her feet and brushed the back of her tattered jeans. "Sure, you will."

"You think I won't?"

"I don't think you can wait that long." The other women laughed. They all knew about Shawn's penchant for practical jokes and payback.

"We'll see," he said as he tossed another log onto their small campfire.

"Yep, I guess we will," Blue replied then turned toward the cave entrance for her regular evening walk. "I'll be back."

"Mind if I join you?" Monica asked as she got to her feet.

Blue glanced at her with a lifted brow. She liked Monica,

yet she made no secret about wanting her space too. But tonight Blue was feeling the warmth of their camaraderie and spending time with her new best friend appealed to her. She shrugged. "Sure."

They strolled along the rocky hillside, keeping it in view in order to make their way back. The moon was high and full and gave everything an eerie bluish tint. The landscape still looked dead and dreary from the long, cold winter, but Blue refused to let old memories crash her mind. She was getting stronger as time passed and the closer to the new life of spring and summer they came.

They strolled in silence for several minutes, listening to the breeze sweep the treetops. A wolf howled somewhere in the mountains behind them.

"Can I ask you a personal question?" Monica ask suddenly.

She and Monica had shared something of their pasts over the last five months, but Blue had held a lot back too. Monica was aware of that and had never held it against her. This was the first time she had sought to unearth secrets Blue wanted to keep hidden. Her heart stuttered at the possibility, but she shrugged. "Depends, I guess."

"You don't have to answer," Monica said quickly. "I won't press you. I'd just like to know what your plans are."

"My plans?"

"For the future."

Blue tucked her hands into the pockets of her ratty jean jacket and her shoulders automatically curled inward. Of all the things Monica could've asked, what she wanted to do with her life was one secret Blue had kept deeply buried.

"I mean," Monica continued when Blue didn't speak, "we can't survive out here forever. Another bad winter and we might not make it. I want to make something of myself. I know the new society has some bad eggs—"

"Bad eggs?" Blue couldn't keep the incredulity and derision from her voice. She stopped and faced her friend. "They've enslaved men, Monica. They treat them like animals and used them to build their slave stables, to increase their wealth. They claim to be repopulating the earth, only they want all the control and none of the morality. Do you know what they do with the little boys who are unlucky enough to be captured or are born into slavery?"

Monica's expression darkened and she nodded, but Blue didn't stop.

"They're allowed to be raised by a mother—whether she's his blood or not doesn't matter. For six years, they're given a place with people who want them, who care about them, then they're torn from everything they know and told to obey or see everyone they love killed."

Her throat ached and her voice shook, but words kept spilling from her lips. "They're dosed with the fear drug and trained to be slaves! To follow the commands of women, to fear women, and, eventually, they'll hate us all. And when they're old enough and handsome enough those poor boys are trained to breed. Barely old enough to comprehend what's being demanded of them, they're forced to create life knowing what their child will face, male or female."

Blue pinned her friend with her eyes as her hands knotted into fists at her sides. "Can you image being raised from birth to believe that men are inferior? That it's your right, as a woman, to dominate them in any way you desire? How those beliefs could be twisted into the sick displays going on in that town they've built out of the rubble south of here?" Blue waved her arm in the direction of the small town she knew lay several miles away—wishing she could forget it existed—but she didn't give Monica a chance to answer.

"Oh, and then there's the men," she said heatedly, not angry with Monica, not really even seeing her anymore. Her vision had turned inward, to the past. "The men they've broken, the ones they torment, and those they still hunt." She gave a dry, humorless chuckle. "Sure, we outnumber the men who survived the war, but hysterical-strength only gives us an edge in a fight, not any real advantage. If those men who have been enslaved and treated so horribly ever figure that out, we better hope they have more mercy in their hearts than has been shown to them." Blue ceased her tirade as heat suffused her cheeks. Monica didn't deserve a lecture from her.

"I know it's terrible," Monica said softly, her eyes locked on the ground. "I know there's a whole lot I don't know too." She lifted her gaze and Blue saw the stubborn will of the woman before her in the set of her jaw and the glint in her eyes. "But I believe we can be different. We can make a difference."

Blue fought to swallow the ache in her throat, to slow her breathing, to release the tension in every muscle of her body. She'd let herself go too far. The look on Monica's face said she'd guessed some of Blue's secrets. The odd thing about that was, Blue felt Monica would keep them as close as Blue did herself.

Do I trust her?

The answer came immediately. *Yes!*

Monica reached for her hand and held it in both of hers. "You're one of us now, Blue, and I think, together, we can figure out a way to make things better…for everyone. At least, I want to try."

Blue's chest constricted at that disclosure. She hadn't dared to hope any woman would admit to that sentiment.

"I want to create a sanctuary," Blue blurted out. "A sanctuary," Blue paused and looked at her friend, "inside the oppressive society around us. A place where people can live a relatively normal life without fear."

A slow smile curved Monica's lips and she let out a happy chuckle. "You want the same things I do."

"Seems like it."

"You must have some kind of plan then."

"A little. It'll be tricky but not impossible. At least, I don't think it will be. It won't be perfect, but with enough funds, we could buy land, find someone to forge papers naming you as Shawn's owner, and then build something to help others in need."

"That'd be great," Monica said with a joyous laugh, yet her tone betrayed her apparent enthusiasm. "But where do we get the gold to pay for it?"

Blue's limbs started to shake and her heart raced; whether from fear of returning to that awful place she'd left behind or the excitement at the anticipation of Monica's assistance, she wasn't sure. "I'll show you," she said, refusing to let the memories stop her, "but we'll have to travel alone."

"I'm ready whenever you are," Monica said eagerly.

The weight on Blue's heart lightened and, feeling hopeful for the first time in years, she smiled.

*   *   *

A week later, Blue and Monica hiked up a tall hill and stepped under the long, snaky boughs of an enormous, ancient weeping willow. A small white cross was nestled among the pile of tiny leaves at the tree's base. When Monica asked about it, Blue stared at the weather-stained symbol, a shiver going down her spine, and then shrugged indifferently.

Wrenching her eyes from the cross and studiously avoiding her friend's curious gaze, Blue glanced up into the tangle of limbs and then back to her friend.

"Stay here," she said before she disappeared around the huge, gnarled trunk.

A few seconds later, she was up in the branches, climbing into the crook of the willow's thicker limbs. Near the top, straddling a broad, bent spur, Blue reached into a hole where another branch had once been and pulled out a canvas bag. Then, with a piece of twine she tugged from her pocket, she lowered it down. Monica guided the heavy sack until it sat on the ground in front of her. When it landed, a distinct jangle chimed out and she looked up at her friend.

"Open it," Blue said as she descended to the ground. By the time she joined her, Monica's mouth had fallen open and her stunned hazel eyes lifted to Blue's face. Gold coins sparkled inside the plain sack—plenty to initiate their plans, more than enough to do it several times over.

"Where did you get this?" Monica asked dumbfounded by the wealth at her knees.

"It doesn't matter," Blue replied, her chest tightening with discomfort at revealing this much, but she pushed on. "What matters is that we can use it to help people."

"This was your plan?"

"The start of it."

"How long has this been up there?" The higher pitch of Monica's voice conveyed her disbelief that anyone would leave this much gold unattended.

"A while," Blue said in a soft voice. "I've been trying to figure out what to do with it. Now I think I know. If you and the others will help me get started, I'll make sure you have enough to start your own place. I only have one condition..."

"And what's that?" Monica asked, curiosity mixed with sudden caution.

"That you help me to convert others."

"How?"

"We convince the other slaveholders to follow our lead in treating their men like human begins. As many as will listen until we have dozens of them around."

"A lot of them won't go for that," Monica said with a discouraged air. Blue wondered if, like her and so many others, Monica had witnessed the corruption of power and its cruelty firsthand.

"A lot will. Not everyone likes the way things have turned out," Blue said with more conviction than she felt. "We'd be creating a refuge for those we can help, laying the groundwork for change."

"Change will only happen when the councils amend the

laws," Monica countered.

"Then we must get on the section's governing council and start changing the laws ourselves."

Monica stared at her friend in amazement. "Do you think it will be that easy?"

"No, it won't be easy at all, that's why I need help. In return, I'll help you and anyone else make changes from the inside." Blue pointed at the bag of gold. "There's more where that came from."

Monica smiled. "A sanctuary."

"Yep."

"Wow," Monica said, clearly impressed with her friend's ambition. "When you do something, Blue, you go big." Her smile widened and a mischievous glimmer sparkled in her eyes. "Count me in!"

"If we're going to be partners," Blue replied, the corners of her mouth curling ever so slightly, "you should probably start using my real name."

"I didn't think you'd ever tell me your real name."

Blue's gaze twinkled playfully. "You never asked me again."

"Okay, then," Monica said with a conspiratorial grin. "What's your real name?"

"Angel," she said with a full, soft smile that touched her cerulean eyes. "My name is Angel."

4

October 8, midnight, six years later...

BRET MASTERS STARED into the small fire, mesmerized by its wavering glow. In the wet, cold darkness, he enjoyed its warmth and comforting radiance, but he couldn't shake the jittery fear within him. After all, light could be seen for miles at night, and as always, he was on the run.

He'd lost too much in his thirty-five years not to appreciate the things most others overlooked. Living a life on the run made a man painfully conscious of the things he lacked, which was why anytime he had cause, he said a quiet "thank you." Tonight, as on so many others, his only answer came from the rustling of the cold wind through the treetops.

He shivered in the chill of the autumn breeze. Pushing his unkempt, black hair away from his neck and hunching his broad shoulders, Bret drew the collar of his brown knee-length jacket closer, attempting to keep his once-white shirt a little drier and his body a little warmer. A futile attempt, he knew, but he had to try. The alternative was further discomfort, and he'd suffered enough of that already. Bret smiled ruefully at the thought, regretting the loss of his old felt cowboy hat. With the world the way it was, easily acquiring another would be impossible and now, like with so many other things, he'd have to make do without.

Having grown up in the area, Bret was more than familiar with its variable weather—the winds that blew in from the Pacific Ocean and the changes they wrought. Those winds, as autumn progressed, carried in cold, clammy air and rain to the west side of the Cascade Mountain Range. In his current location on the eastern side, temperatures were higher during the day—at least for the next month—and considerably colder at night. But Bret planned to be farther south and into warmer weather again before it could get much colder.

Early last June, a troubled woman persuaded Bret, against his better judgment, to be her guide on a northward journey— toward danger, toward home. For the last few months, he had traveled with the woman and her young daughter, trying to locate her family. As they moved north, they picked up a few stragglers who wanted nothing more than to be a part of a group—safety in numbers and all that. Despite the apprehension their presence triggered in Bret, the newcomers joined their meager band as they made their way through the mountains. To Bret's amazement and relief, they found the woman's husband alive and well on a small homestead in a narrow valley deep in the northern Cascade Range.

They had invited Bret to stay, but he refused. Staying in one place made them vulnerable. Not that roaming lessened the vulnerability, he just felt better on the move—not tied to possessions, emotions, or anything else that could interfere with running when the raiding parties appeared. With those reasons in mind, he had said his goodbyes and headed south.

On his way, he met up with another group, one far larger than the band he'd guided north, and chose to travel with them for a short time. Like Bret, they were migrating toward warmer climates for the winter. Their greater numbers made him nervous—more people meant a bigger trail.

Now, staring at the fire, he decided he'd been with this

group long enough. In the morning, he would strike out on his own once more.

He sat alone on a weatherworn tree trunk a few yards from the fire with the ends of his coat pulled over his patched-up jeans, scrutinizing the shadows outside the fire's glow for possible danger. Seeing nothing, he ran his hands over his face to brush the rain from his bushy winter beard and regarded the rag-tag members of the camp. Some huddled as close to the fire as they could, while others bedded down in more discrete places.

At least they knew better than to make a target of themselves, Bret thought of the latter, knowing Raiders could appear at any time. No one was safe, not anymore.

Bret shifted uncomfortably on the log and swallowed, trying to clear the thickness from the back of his throat. Not far from this very spot he'd lost his closest friend—more like a brother—to slavers five years ago. It had torn Bret apart to lose Jake. His stomach roiled just thinking about what his friend's life must be like now.

Luck, Providence, or God—whatever you call it—awarded him two great fortunes the day the slavers took Jake. First, he had fought back to regain his freedom when he'd thought they were captured, and second, he avoided the trap meant for him. He was a lucky man—his freedom remained intact, but Jake hadn't been as fortunate.

Bret grimaced and his heart clenched as guilt flooded him. No matter how much time passed, it never diminished.

Separated from Bret during the fighting, Jake Nichols was now either dead or a slave. Bret didn't know which was the greater injustice, but either way, the not knowing—and his own culpability for Jake's downfall—nagged at him.

Why did I come back here? Bret mused. *I should've listened to my better judgment instead of that mother's sad story. I should've walked away.*

But he hadn't. He couldn't have left the woman and her

daughter to their own ignorant-of-the-wild devices, not like he'd been forced to do when they took Jake.

☐Since then, he'd taken each day as it came, dodging raiding parties and searching for the insurgents. Everyone had stories about the rebels, but no one Bret had ever met knew how to find them.

Do they even exist? Doubts crept into his stomach and writhed like a pit of angry vipers.

He and Jake had heard about the rebels in fireside stories, and they'd searched, trying to unearth anyone who might know where to find them. They never did, but at least they avoided slavery.

That is, until Bret met Amy Hensford.

Bret raked his fingers through his overly-long black hair and cursed viciously under his breath at the thought of the hated woman. Despising himself more for becoming so infatuated with Amy that he'd entrusted her with not only his life, but the life of his best friend as well.

Jake had tried to convince him that Amy was not what she seemed, but Bret—besotted and blind—refused to listen. That blindness cost him and those around him dearly. To make matters worse, no matter how hard Bret searched for a way— despite the promise they'd made to each other not to try—he couldn't save Jake. Bret never forgave himself for his stupidity and had lived with the crushing guilt ever since.

Never again. I'll never trust another woman!

Yet despite his vows, loneliness wore on him. The desire for human companionship, human touch, burned in his chest. He occasionally succumbed to it, took a lover for a night or two when the rare opportunity arose, but made sure to disappear afterward because he didn't trust they wouldn't turn him in or trap him somehow.

How is it, he thought again, *that I let myself be pulled back here?* But he knew the answer. The woman he'd guided north was only an excuse. Something drew him back. He'd felt the unmistakable pull long before the young mother came along. Some odd compulsion brought him back to this place that held so many bad memories, triggering images of deeply buried sorrow in his mind.

His mother—the first woman who let him down—smiled in his mind's eye, and he could no longer deny that—despite her shortcomings—he had loved her. Maybe she did the best she could. Maybe he hadn't tried hard enough; after all, he'd been just a stupid kid back then.

"You remind me of your father, Bret," she had told him many times. "You look just like him. So handsome…" He could still hear her soft, slurred voice in his head, still feel the ache that accompanied her statement like a fist crushing his heart.

"I hate the way I look," his twelve-year-old self had replied on one occasion when Ruby was especially lost and the tight agony inside him was too much to bear. "I hate that I remind you of him. I—*hate*—*it*! I hate that he left us, that you've left *me*."

"I haven't left you, Bret. I'm still here, and it's a good thing that you look like your father." She tried to smile, to convince him of that fact, but he shook his head sullenly.

"If it was good," he'd said in a shaky voice, his young heart breaking for everything they'd lost, "then you'd still love me."

Bret shook his head and pushed those memories aside. It didn't matter now. Ruby Masters was only the first chapter of unhappiness in a long line of disappointments that had woven his life into the lonely ache it was now.

Near the campfire, an elderly man sitting on a half-buried stump conversed with a young boy of about eight caught Bret's attention. They looked travel-weary and thin, with clothes as worn and dirty as Bret's. The boy sat with his legs folded beneath him, listening at the old man's feet, his upturned face attentive to the senior's story as the firelight turned them both a reddish-orange against the ebony velvet of night.

Bret listened as the elder explained their history and then the rumor they'd all heard that said female supremacy was not a worldwide goal. Bret had yet to find anywhere that was not controlled by women, where men weren't forced into labor of one kind or another.

"If women made men slaves, and we are running and hiding to keep from becoming slaves," the boy asked, "then why do we have women with us?"

"Because, Tommy, there are some who want to help us bring back freedom and equality. Of course, it will never be exactly the same, but at least everyone would be free...including women."

"But women are free, aren't they? The ones we're hiding from, they're free."

"Yes," the old man agreed, "they are, but there are some who're imprisoned by different kinds of chains. All people should be free, Tommy. They shouldn't have to fear their family being taken away and never seeing them again. As I'm sure your mother worries about you. Don't you think?"

"Yeah, I guess so."

"Your mama would do anything to keep you from harm and to make a better future for you. I believe many women feel the same. Some may not even realize it yet. Others may just be...afraid."

"Yeah, right," Bret scoffed in a low voice. In his estimation, women looked out for themselves and weren't worth the trouble they caused. All the women who'd ever been important to him brought one kind of heartache or another into his life. He couldn't think of one—except maybe his mother before his father died—who had ever concerned herself with his well-being.

I finally learned my lesson—use them or be used by them.

Then why did you guide that woman north? He ignored the question, as he always did whenever the softhearted part of him spoke up.

The boy continued to ask the elder questions, but Bret stopped listening, not wanting to think about the past. He had dwelled on it far too much already. All he wanted to do was go to sleep and forget.

But his past and experiences in the wild—not to mention his unwanted feelings of duty to this new group of travelers— made him cautious. He remained awake for some time, watching and listening while the others bedded down.

Heavy clouds rolled in to hide the moon as the cold evening stretched into night. The wind whispered through the nearby forest and the cry of a mountain creature occasionally rang out to chill them further. Strangely, the sounds comforted Bret and reminded him of better days in a happy home. Days that had turned bitter after one rainy night, when an out of control car unexpectedly took his father's life.

"Why won't you look me? Why won't you talk to me, Mom?" Bret's younger self had cried one night out of frustration and resentment. His father's accident had left them deep in debt and, a few short weeks later, Ruby had given up. Her emotional deterioration had only made Bret more determined to take on additional responsibility to save the home he'd loved. "We can turn the ranch around, why won't you help me? Dad would want us to make this work. Why don't you?"

"Oh, Bret," she had said sadly with a bleary-eyed smile and a slight slur to her words. "You're so young... You don't understand."

"I understand that you don't care about me anymore!" Fear and anger had burned hot in his chest and it had been all he could do to keep tears from his eyes. "You don't care what I want. All you care about is getting drunk!"

Bret remembered several similar exchanges, where he had always ended up running to the barn, knowing she wouldn't follow. There, amidst the hay and the one horse they still owned, he'd cried out his hurt and despair, and rebuilt his innocent resolve to hold their home together.

He had tried every day for nine months to do his father's job, working himself into the ground between chores, school, and looking after Ruby. Not yet thirteen years old, tired, frustrated, and miserable, he had put his heart and soul into saving their home.

He'd been stupidly naive.

A groan of annoyance for dredging up the past again rumbled in his throat. Bret swept his hand over his face and focused on the present. He stood and stretched his tired body, glancing around the camp, picking out the scattered, still forms of sleepers among the shadows. He turned to the forest, about twenty-five yards to the east of their camp. That would be his escape route if a raiding party should find them. They had assigned guards and their replacements, but Bret wanted to reassure himself with a quick survey of the campsite, and then kicked out the fire.

He lay on his back, his side against a huge log, and tucked his left hand behind his head. His stomach growled and he rubbed his belly. He'd been saving a portion of his rations in preparations for his departure, which meant he was often hungry, but that was life in the wild. Thankful he'd had anything to eat at all, he ignored the gnawing ache in his middle and stared at the sky. The murky clouds churned like a boiling cauldron backlit by the moon. He knew he should be struck by the night's fierce splendor, but he was unable to relate to the beauty of the scene. All he could think about was staying alive, remaining free, and how, in the morning, he'd be on his own.

5

October 8, 4:00 AM

BRET WOKE ABRUPTLY, clawing his way out of restless dreams. His eyes popped open. His breath came in rapid beats. His heart stuttered in his chest. Glancing around, he wasn't sure if his fear was because of his dreams or something he had subconsciously detected.

Something in the real world. Something close to him. Something dangerous.

He gave the camp a furtive once-over from his concealed hiding place.

Nothing.

He propped himself on his elbow to see more clearly.

Still nothing.

But *something* had roused him.

He looked at the moonless sky. Dawn was still an hour off yet, but gray signs of its impending arrival filtered through the tallest treetops to the east. A low-lying, murky fog had drifted over them while they slept, and a mist dampened everything.

A heavy raindrop splashed on Bret's cheek and he wiped away the moisture. He could smell the coming storm and was once again thankful for something—his long oilskin coat.

He sat up and stared into the blackness of the old forest. Last night the nearness of the trees had comforted him for their shadows and shelter. Now, something about the foggy darkness bothered him.

Bret forced his strung-out nerves to calm as he stretched out once more, but a few seconds later his eyes snapped open. Fear crept into his mind and slid down his spine like ice cubes down a shoot. His ears strained for any tiny sound as he lay motionless.

A second passed. Two. Then he detected it again. Something pounding the ground, something getting closer. It sounded like...horses, running horses. The sound of the galloping hooves matched his racing.

"Horses!" He shouted the dreaded word as he sat up, hearing other voices take up the cry. "Horses!"

Bret caught movement out of the corner of his eye and turned his head. The Raiders were already upon them. He ducked back behind the log to evade the flying hooves of the first jumping horse and rider.

He wasn't quick enough.

A hoof slammed into his shoulder, leaving what felt like a deep laceration in his flesh and hammering Bret into the ground. Agony assailed him, radiating through his arm and chest. The back of his head throbbed from hitting the ground, but there was no time to dwell on his injuries. He immediately rolled toward the log for protection, but banged his head against it, hard. Stars danced before his eyes, and something warm and sticky oozed over his forehead and down the inside of his shirt.

Don't worry about it now. He tucked his body against the log and covered his aching head as several other horses followed the first. He opened his eyes in time to see the last rider in her uniform of a dark green shirt and black pants, sail over him. She let out a high-pitched howl for the hunt like the tiny Amazon-wannabe she was.

The other members of his tattered camp scattered at the sound of his cries, but he hadn't been swift enough to save them. A group of fifteen or so were already captured. The Raiders, with the Venus-symbol insignia embroidered in red on their uniform's right arm, continued to skillfully whirl their whips, rounding up the dozen or so remaining men, women, and children still trying to flee through the forest on the opposite side of the meadow. Sympathy pinched his heart, knowing all of them would be imprisoned and sold as slaves— the men because they were men, the women because they were considered traitors, and the children for the next generation of slaves. He couldn't help them; he knew that better than anyone after what had happened to Jake.

He pushed the feeling aside and concentrated on his situation.

Jumping to his feet, Bret ran for the trees, away from the dozens of horseback women combing the forest behind him. The surviving tendrils of fog whirled around his legs as he risked a quick glance over his shoulder.

None of the Raiders had noticed him yet. He redoubled his efforts. The forest was his only chance. His one shot at continued freedom. His only way out.

He didn't want to be sold and used, only to be sold and used again.

He wanted his luck to hold.

Rain fell harder, the heavy drops pelted him and soaked his clothes, the water icy, but not as cold as the fear in his gut.

His mind filled with vivid images of his other escapes from women on horseback. The memories encouraged him and fueled his efforts. His heart hammered against his ribs like a trapped animal trying to escape. The vital blood and oxygen pumping into his limbs aided his frantic desire to run faster.

He was close to the concealing brush beneath the trees, the distance only fifteen yards, the huge log in the open glade where he had slept getting smaller behind him.

Not much farther, he told himself as he jumped an old fallen tree, slipped on the wet grass, and dropped to one knee. Rattled, he lunged to his feet and kept running, dodging rocks and deadfall as best he could in the dim morning light.

Absurdly, as it always did when he was running for his life, a very old song played in his head, and the upbeat tempo matched the beat of his boots.

Six yards.

Almost there. I'm going to make it!

His heart leaped with joy at the thought.

Then it dropped like a boulder.

From out of nowhere, a peach-colored appaloosa crossed into his path, blocking his way. Bret skidded to a halt, his well-worn boots sliding in the wet grass, his arms pinwheeling to keep from going down in the mud. He cast a wild gaze over his surroundings, trying to identify another route to the freedom he so desperately craved. When he found none, he focused, panic-stricken, on the rider in his path.

She was off her steed and ready to fight before Bret could even think.

The music in his head died, along with all thoughts of freedom, so clear only moments before.

Desperate, he overcame his lifelong disinclination to hurt women and threw a punch at her chin as she raced toward him. She fell, but to Bret's amazement and frustration, she was on her feet again in the blink of an eye. The heightened levels of adrenaline pumping through her body ensured that her nerves wouldn't register the damage to her jaw for several hours.

Because his frontal attack had so little effect, he took the next best course of action—he ran. But as he moved to dash past her, she tripped him with her ankle, sending him sprawling face first into the mud. She laughed as he rolled to his feet and faced her again.

Having never encountered this specific problem before, he didn't quite know what to do. He just needed to make it to the underbrush and he'd be scot-free, but he had no way of knowing if any more like her lurked in the shadows of the trees. Climbing to his feet, he searched his surroundings, wide-eyed and foolish, trying to ascertain his next move, but he should've been watching his opponent.

Pain radiated through his jaw, and he tumbled backward from the force of her punch. She advanced on him and he prepared to defend himself, but she didn't give him the opportunity.

Bret reached his hands and knees and scrambled away, but she leveled him with a kick to the ribs and a blow to the back of his neck which dropped him to the ground. She continued her assault, striking him in the body and head so aggressively that he was unable to rise and fight back. A boot to the side of his head shot pain through his ear and caused blackness to narrow his vision, and he struggled to remain conscious, to keep fighting. At least if she killed him, he wouldn't have to suffer the humiliation that followed capture.

Her assault unexpectedly ceased and after several frantic attempts, Bret managed to roll over and prop himself up on his elbows. His head swam and his heart thrashed in his chest, bruising itself against the prison of his ribs. As he glared at his assailant with the sweat of fear and exertion coating his body, he was so chilled, so unnerved by his circumstance, he shivered. The woman smirked down at him and chuckled, her long golden hair spilling over her shoulders, her dark, amber-colored eyes flashing at him.

He stared at her, unable to reach his feet, blinking and biting back pain as she landed one final blow. The last sound to reach him as blinding agony turned everything black was her chillingly triumphant laughter.

6

BRET MASTERS WOKE with an aborted scream lodged in his throat. His gaze darted to every corner of the gloom-infested room expecting to see beautiful monsters looming over him preparing to attack. Panic pumped ice into his veins as he struggled to free himself from whatever held him immobile. His mind lurched into the present as the aches and pains of his battered body registered.

The Raiders captured me. The dismal thought settled over him like a lead cloak and he exhaled a long, stuttering breath. *I'm in prison.*

For the last God knows how long, he'd been interned in this place of humiliation and pain. The fear he felt was real—though chemically amplified by the drug the guards used to control the men they incarcerated—but his terror-filled reaction upon waking had been caused by nothing more than a dream. A nightmare, actually, but one based on the reality of his captivity. As his mind shed its fog of sleep, he breathed a sigh of relief that he was alone in his cell.

The heavy weight of the cold steel shackles encircling his neck and wrists held him secured to the stone wall behind him.

The short chain between his ankle restraints bound his feet to an iron ring in the floor. This position forced him to sit straight-backed and uncomfortable on a rough wooden bench in his dark, filthy dungeon, where he had rotted for what seemed like forever.

By his crude estimates, weeks had dragged by since he'd arrived in this place, and his imprisonment worsened with each passing day. His eardrum, ruptured in the fight during his capture, was now infected. The low, constant ringing on that side annoyed him and threw off his equilibrium. His clumsiness and helplessness exasperated him even more.

Demeaning abuses were a daily occurrence, the shame and fear he felt were heightened by the drug they injected into him several times a day. One such experience occurred only the day before and he still attempted to forget the humiliation of being showered like a dog. The only pleasant part of the whole bathing process had been encountering the kindly barber who'd put him at ease, if only for an hour.

God, I look awful, he remembered thinking after the guards had dragged him into the barbershop last night. Filthy and leaner than normal, barely recognizable as the man he remembered, Bret had been shocked by his altered appearance reflected in one of the long mirrors lining the shop's walls. His long, tangled hair hung lank and dirty around his bare shoulders and his overlong beard looked more unkempt than ever.

Despite his overall ragged condition, the injuries he'd received during his capture were healing well. The gash on his forehead had left only a tiny scar and though the deep purple bruising on his shoulder and chest from the horse that kicked him still ached, the discoloration had diminished to almost nothing.

When he'd first arrived at this prison, the guards had taken all of his clothes, leaving him exposed and vulnerable to their hungry eyes and greedy hands. The reflection he'd seen last night mirrored the red welts and bruises that crisscrossed the length of his naked body—rewards for his repeated refusal to obey. His keepers made no qualms about using physical punishment. They also insisted the prisoners only speak when spoken to. To aid in this, the captives were kept isolated and, what the confines didn't separate, the drug did well to keep divided. Bret suspected they maintained this practice to prevent the inmates from conspiring to escape or retaliate, since they outnumbered the guards by a significant amount. Unfortunately, for Bret anyway, his current prescription of fear didn't adequately affect his troublesome attitude, which the marks of abuse covering his body readily avowed. He was afraid—the minimal dosage ensured that—but he could not hide his contempt.

As a result of his relatively hostile attitude, the metal shackles he wore hadn't been removed since his capture. They chafed his skin raw, and in the mirror's reflection, his broad shoulders drooped from the combined weight of the chains and his growing despair.

His imprisonment accounted for the changes in his appearance, but not for the change in his eyes. Sunken, with purplish circles underneath, they darted everywhere before focusing on the mirror as if they belonged to a terrified stranger and not the strong, confident man he knew himself to be. *Those can't be my eyes...*

That had been last night, and the memory still disturbed him.

He woke this morning freshly bathed, his black hair shorn short, and his long beard clean-shaved. The change made him feel more like himself than he had in a long time, but the drug's constant fear rumbled through him and kept the pleasant sensation from growing too strong.

The guards' arrival a short time later doused any contentment over his improved condition. His heart thumped in his chest and anxious sweat dotted his hairline as they approached. Fingers closed into useless fists, his body tensed for another round of humiliation or pain. To his surprise, all they did was bind him and lead him from his cell on his first and only outdoor excursion since they'd locked him away in that dank, tiny room.

A cool breeze caressed the long length of his nude body. The fragrant scents of pine and frost tickled his nose and shocked him so much that he stopped in his tracks. He took a deep breath of the crisp autumn air and turned his face up to the sun. The light shone through his closed lids, almost unbearable to tolerate, but he didn't turn away. It had been too long since the sun and wind caressed his face, and feeling them lightened his spirit. The warmth of irrefutable hope suffused him from the inside out and, knowing it wouldn't last, he wanted to savor the rare sensation.

His escort, annoyed at his impromptu halt, hauled on the lead chain, jerking Bret forward by the neck. He grunted and gasped as his eyes popped opened and his knees collided with the cold, hard-packed ground.

"Get up, slave," the woman growled. "You should know better than to stop without orders."

The chill of the air around him registered and his heart dropped back into the well of despair, but Bret didn't respond. He knew from painful experiences to remain silent. Instead, he stood and, unable to resist, allowed them to lead him into a large enclosed area with other fettered men. About two hundred haggard men stood in a long, single-file line, and not one of them, Bret noticed with a grim frown, was as heavily chained or guarded as himself.

Bret recognized a few faces as his guards ushered him forward, but he didn't make the mistake of acknowledging any of them. Hoping to avoid another beating, he kept his eyes down the way his guards continuously demanded of him, but that didn't mean he wasn't aware of his surroundings.

A twenty-foot chain-link fence skirted the perimeter of the

yard, and numerous women with whips in their hands and clubs at their waists stood guard. The windowless building where the slaves spent their time until they were auctioned off stood behind him, and another structure with balconies and sliding glass doors that overlooked the yard, rose up to his right. Several other unspecified buildings littered the grounds, but none of that interested him. What drew Bret's attention was the forest. The evergreens outside the enclosure towered into the sky. They cast a long silhouette in autumn's morning sun and gray shadows lived beneath the boughs.

I'd disappear in those woods if I could just get over the fence, Bret thought. But his chances to escape this place were almost nil. Even if he got out of the building, how could he scale the mesh-link barrier without either being caught or—considering this was a prison—electrifying himself? Trying to climb would be useless, but if he got the chance, he would attempt it anyway. He might get lucky—it wouldn't be the first time.

Last in the long line of frightened, unclothed men waiting to be inspected by a tall redheaded woman who had approached from behind the buildings, Bret shuffled his feet and tried to hold the rising fear inside him at bay.

The inspector's bright gray eyes raked over them, and Bret fought the sudden urge to hunch and grovel. He kept his eyes on her, though it made his stomach feel like acid was burning a hole through it. Even from a distance, he could see the cruelty in her expression and it sent a jolt of dread through him as he automatically dropped his gaze.

She stood in front of the line for several minutes, allowing her narrowed eyes to drift over the helpless and uneasy men. When her scrutiny fell on him, Bret felt it like a wave of icy dread. Once again battling the drug, he lifted his head and met her stare, then the chemical in his system took control of his reluctant will and his eyes dropped to the ground again.

She remained before them for another long minute, her glare

sweeping over the men once more. Then, with one last, long look in Bret's direction, she moved to the first man at the opposite end of the line.

Damn, he thought, fighting the terror bubbling in his chest. *What the hell are they going to do to us now?*

7

ALTHOUGH BRET DIDN'T KNOW what they had planned, he was sure it would be unpleasant. Assorted scenarios floated through his mind as he watched the redhead approach the man at the other end of the line. She ran her hands and eyes over him like a farmer examining stock, then told his guard to take him to an area she indicated and moved on without so much as a passing glance. She performed the next inspection more thoroughly, particularly when it came to the more private areas of his body. Poking, pulling, and stroking with utter disregard for the man who cowered before her, she smiled while she molested him. When she finally finished her eager petting, she sent the unlucky man to another location. The third individual joined the last, the fourth started a new row and so on as she continued down the line, treating the men like animals, inspecting them like beasts at auction.

Are they culling us somehow? The thought frightened him, but he was certain their captors wouldn't kill them—they were valuable, as livestock if nothing else.

After an interminable, nerve-wracking wait, the redhead reached the man who stood beside Bret. Uncomfortably aware that her gaze considered him far more often than the man she inspected, Bret struggled not to fidget.

When she stepped before him, Bret met her pointed stare, but his will left him within seconds. She stood unmoving, looking him over with a salacious smirk. Bret somehow found the nerve to lift his eyes and her gaze locked with his. It surprised him to find she was older than he'd first thought. Approximately fifteen years older than himself, she was an attractive woman, except for the cold rancor emanating from her. She held his gaze and her smile widened as her expression flashed with greedy lust. She touched his chest and broke the spell—his eyes dropped, and he heard her snicker.

Rage, that he could do nothing about, boiled through him only to be battered into nothing by a surge of fear as her nails dug into his flesh. Not enough to damage, just enough to get his attention. Her fingernails trailed over his skin, leaving thin, red welts as she sauntered around him. Stopping directly behind him, she placed both hands on his hips before they slid down over his buttocks and each leg.

Her touch made Bret's skin crawl, and he shuttered. She laughed as her hands moved up his long legs with deliberate slowness, caressing each muscle until she stood upright again. She performed an almost tender inspection of the shallow lacerations and bluish-purple bruises left by the whip on his back and thighs. He stiffened at the minor pain it caused, and her examination intensified, but he refused to move or show any more signs of discomfort. At least those he could control, the tremors the drug-induced never seemed to leave.

Apparently satisfied, she circled around to face him again.

"Look at me," she ordered, waiting with an amused grin while he fought the chemicals in his system and met her eyes. "What's your name?"

"Bret," he answered warily.

"Bret what?"

"Masters… Bret Masters."

"Well, Bret Masters, you're a very handsome man. Did you

know that?"

He clenched his jaw but didn't respond, only forced himself to meet her eyes.

"I asked you a question," she said, her voice low and dangerous.

"I've been told so before," he replied, managing a cool disdain even though he avoided her eyes.

"I told you to look at me, slave!" Her harsh voice, too much for his frayed nerves, made him jump. After a moment, she captured his gaze once more and continued, "Yes, very handsome. And sexy, too. I'm almost tempted to keep you for myself." She reached down to fondle him. He flinched from her rough caress but somehow found the will to stand still and meet her eyes. His jaw clenched as she played with him, eliciting a response he didn't want. Smiling up at his strained expression, she took her time stroking him to attention. Bret squeezed his eyes shut, tried to focus on something else, but she didn't give him a chance.

"Open those pretty eyes of yours, handsome," the woman said and, unable to stop himself, he did as she ordered. She smiled a calculated, lustful grin that made the hair on the back of his neck stand on end. She looked like a predator, and he felt like her prey.

Too many minutes later, she released him with a sigh and her eyes raked over him one last time.

"Take him to the breeder's line," she said to the guards, and they ushered him away.

Bret refused to feel embarrassed by his erection, though that didn't stop his muscles from quivering with fury over the throbbing irritation the woman caused. How could he allow her to touch him so intimately? Why hadn't he at least tried to keep her from using him like a toy, to enjoy and toss aside when she had finished with him? But he knew why.

His jaw ached from clenching it so hard as the reason pumped more anger through his veins. *What could I have done?* he asked himself again as the knuckles of his fists turned white. *Nothing, that's what.*

He hated to be played with, especially that way, but he couldn't do a damn thing about it. His only recourse was to walk proudly while ignoring the stiffness between his legs. So, he shuffled along and—head up, back as straight as he could make it—listened to the clanging of the chains and desperately willed his unwanted arousal away.

When Bret reached the end of his designated line, the men stood quietly in anxious anticipation while the guards connected a small, colored tag to the steel band around each man's neck.

Like cattle, Bret thought as he watched. The one his guard attached to his collar was deep red. He wondered what it indicated, what the significance of the color was. An instant later, he decided he didn't want to know.

8

December 30

"DON'T TOUCH ME," Bret growled as menacingly as the drug would allow at the most recent of his many daily visitors. Forced to sit upright, chained to the wall, Bret fought the urge to pull away from her. She sat far too close and didn't seem to care that he wanted nothing to do with her.

Several times a day, a guard like this one would arrive to bring him food or to recite the daily brainwashing on how they expected him to behave now that he was property. At first, when he had acted out against those tenants, they resorted to beating him as they had so many times before. But since his inspection in the yard and the subsequent visit from the little gray-haired doctor—who'd treated his injuries but done very little to ease his aches and pains—the guards had limited their abuse to the soles of his feet and confining him in stress positions to make his muscles ache and cramp. He still fought them any way he could, but apparently, his lack of enthusiasm for this woman's attention didn't faze her in the slightest.

"Why not?" the short-haired brunette guard asked innocently as one of her hands and both eyes slid slowly down his chest, causing him to shiver with dread and revulsion.

In the weeks since his one and only trip outside, women regularly stopped by his cell to ogle him with lust in their eyes. Like many of the others, this one clearly wanted up-close-and-personal time with him and, after feeding him his afternoon bread and broth, decided to take what she wanted whether he complied or not. The gawkers didn't bother him much, though he disliked being stared at, but his discomfort far worsened when they touched him without his consent.

"Because I said no!" Experience told him she wouldn't listen, but despite the tremors of anxiety running through him, he couldn't accept her unsolicited advances, either.

"I can make you feel good," she said, a knowing smile on her thin lips and a note of warning in her voice as she pushed his knees wide. "Most of the men here enjoy my attention."

His hands balled into fists and he inadvertently jerked at the shackles that bound him to the wall as her palms slid up the inside of his thighs. He drew his legs together, but her nails dug into his flesh as a warning and he ceased.

"Get your hands off me!" he tried again, though, thanks to the drug surging through him, his command wavered into a plea.

"I want to see you. I want to *feel* you," she told him unapologetically as she reached the apex of his legs. "It will go easier if you don't fight me, but either way, I don't need your permission."

Knowing he had no alternative, Bret clamped his jaws shut and closed his eyes, trying to ignore her eager touch and concentrate on anything else hoping to frustrate her. He also prayed she didn't intend to coerce him into more than an unwanted arousal. So far the majority of the women who came to fondle him hadn't pushed him that far, but they had become angry when he spoke or behaved in anything less than a polite, submissive way. This guard seemed to take it in stride that she would have to use pain to compel him, and that sent ice through his veins. He preferred to avoid more punishment, but he still hated that he had no choice.

"What are you doing in here?" a second woman barked, interrupting Bret's concentration. The stroking hands flew away from his body and the woman beside him lunged to her feet, stumbling through an excuse.

"I don't want to hear it," the authoritative voice interrupted. "You're not supposed to be in here. Get out and don't come back."

When Bret opened his eyes, he was unsurprised to find Sara Barret gazing at him from the cell entryway. Short blonde hair frizzed around Sara's head like a bad perm, and her muddy, hazel eyes were avid when they admired him—which she did often. Bret found her lean, bony frame less than feminine, but not exactly off-putting to a man who hadn't been with a woman in so long he'd lost count of the months. Yet, aside from being a head guard, there was nothing overtly special about her. The influence she wielded was minimal but would be enough to suit the needs he secretly harbored.

"Your admirers grow more brazen by the day," she said as she entered his cell and sat beside him.

"Guess you'll have to keep a closer eye on me," he said with a slow smile. Sara had visited him many times over the last several days, always hinting at the possibility of much more intimacy to come, as if to ascertain his willingness to comply. He endured her advances, even responded positively to them, because Bret recognized Sara's authority and growing obsession with him as the opportunity he needed to flee. His determination to get away before the auction scheduled for the next day was like a rock lodged in his throat.

He knew what she wanted from him, could see it in the way she bit her lower lip as her eyes hungrily moved over his body, but he intended to be long gone before that happened. Not that the prospect of being with her was totally unappealing; he simply wanted as much time as possible to run for his life. If it turned out he had time for sex too, well, then so be it, but it wasn't his priority.

The humiliation he had suffered at their hands was horrible enough without going through what he feared most—the auction itself. His heart and mind, his compassion and intelligence would count for nothing when they dragged him out on that stage to be sold like an animal. He would only be another piece of chattel for them to use and abuse as they saw fit. He could not abide that. He had to escape.

"Time's running out for us, handsome," Sara whispered in his ear, flicking her tongue along the edge. He stifled the cringe of revulsion that struck him as he leaned closer. He met her smiling gaze with another lazy grin and stamped down the anxiety and disgust roaring through him.

"That would be a shame," he murmured with as much seduction as he could muster. "What're you going to do about it?"

*   *   *

Late that same night, two women arrived to take Bret to Sara. Awakened from a restless sleep, they bound him as usual, hustled him through the lower levels, and then up through several stairwells. The chilly air and slimy dampness of the stones beneath his bare feet caused goosebumps to blanket his skin. Since his last trip outside for the inspection, Bret knew that he and the other more difficult acquisitions were kept in a deep dungeon. The long, echoing hike from his cell made it feel as if they were climbing out of the depths of hell. Occasional hoarse cries of other men pounding against the walls and the soft sobs of the already broken souls added to the authenticity of them all suffering in perdition.

All we need are the scorching flames, Bret thought morosely. Thankfully, the despondent sounds faded as they mounted the seemingly never-ending steps.

Heavy iron bound with chains still restrained Bret's limbs and even without them, he was in no condition to subdue his captors. He needed to keep his wits and stick to his plan if he was to have any hope of escape.

After passing through several locked gateways, they came to one made of wood rather than metal. The hallway on the other side was richly decorated with ivory walls, gold detailing, and burgundy carpets. They passed several mahogany-colored doors before they reached their destination and one of his escorts rapped once. A few seconds ticked by before she opened the door wide and motioned for Bret to enter.

Crossing the threshold, he hesitated in the near complete darkness after the bright hallway lights. Without warning, the door closed behind him, and he was left alone in a stranger's unlit apartment, still bound in his full set of heavy chains and shackles. Standing motionless, Bret waited for Sara to come to him or give some sign of her presence, but after a minute or two of listening, the only sound he heard was the crackling of the dying embers in the hearth across the room. The flameless fire gave off no light and the clink of chains filled the disturbing silence as Bret fisted his hands and shifted his feet. They had administered his last dose of the drug before dinner several hours ago and though its effects had diminished somewhat, it pulsed through him anew as he endured the unknown environment. He fought it, knowing he must not give in, not now when his freedom was within his grasp.

Suck it up, man. You can do this. You must!

Fear was an emotion he had mastered long ago. But that was before the wars and before the drug that made his sturdy limbs tremble and his stomach knot with nausea. When he sensed more than saw someone enter the room several minutes later, the sickening weakness took control and an icy wave of dread crashed through him. He broke out in a cold sweat and his clenched fists tightened further as he attempted to reign in the torrent of terror bubbling to life inside him. He managed to whisper Sara's name but received no response, and another bone-chilling rush of the drug's effect assailed his system.

Damn it! he thought, his fury battling the fear. *Why won't she answer?*

She's playing with you, his cynical mind replied in a voice he recognized though it wasn't his own.

He stood motionless, each nerve in his long body tense and alert to any movement, noise, or touch.

The unknown person came toward him but stopped short of contact with him and he called himself every name his addled mind could think of for a coward as he barely repressed the immediate urge to crumble to the ground and roll into a protective ball.

Cool fingers on his chest sent a strange mixture of alarm, lust, and anger through him. The sensation, and her touch, chilled his bones. He shivered, but the distress that had assaulted him in the silence slid away. The person before him couldn't be anyone else but Sara and, as his fear subsided, he became more aware of the woman standing there. The heat of her body hovered inches from his own and he wondered if she was as cold-blooded as all the other women he'd known. Or would she be different?

He doubted it. Years ago, the doubt that any benevolent women still existed in this new society had begun—and that doubt had grown ever since.

Sara might be different, the obstinate side of him argued. *After all, she's been good to you.*

That much was true. She had snuck him extra food and massaged his sore neck and shoulders, always careful not to hurt him, whenever she visited. She'd even brought him medicine, which did more to ease his aches and pains than the pitiful medication the doctor had supplied.

But when you asked her to stop them from giving you the fear drug, she refused, his pessimistic side retorted in that same hated yet familiar voice. *She won't give up her cushy position for you.*

What about the risks she's already taken? his stubborn

optimism replied, but it wasn't strong enough to drown out his past, especially after Amy's heart-wrenching betrayal. He would not allow Sara or any woman inside the protective walls he had built around his heart. Not now, not ever again.

"Bret," Sara whispered, her voice making him jump.

He tried not to sound irritated, but his reply still came out short. "Yes?"

"Hold me," she sighed, but it sounded more like a whine.

"I can't," he responded, feeling ridiculous for whispering, but, thanks to the drug and the lack of sufficient light, the situation made him uneasy.

"Why not?" she asked too stridently for his nerves not to rattle at the high-pitched annoyance that crept into her voice. He took an involuntary step away from her, as the nervous tension, conquered only moments ago, flooded into him once more.

Damn you, he berated himself. *Don't be afraid of her. She doesn't want to hurt you; it's just the drug freaking you out.*

"I'm still chained," he said, his manner apologetic.

"Damn them. I told the guards to unchain you." She stepped away and he heard her fumble with a drawer and then the jingle of keys. A moment later, a soft light from a small table lamp weakly pushed back the shadows. She smiled as she returned to him and, after trying two, found a key that worked in his shackles. Brief minutes later, the restraints were on the floor and Sara was in his arms, stroking his chest while he rubbed the chafed skin around his wrists behind her back.

Her naked body felt smooth against his as she pressed her small, high breasts against the broad expanse of his chest. Then, when she got a whiff of his unwashed state, she wrinkled her dainty nose, gave a disapproving hiss, and pushed him away. He frowned, somewhat offended by her show of distaste—if for no other reason than it had never happened before—but she covered her insult with a quick smile.

"Follow me, Bret," she crooned, tugging on his hand. "I'll

give you a hot bath and a massage to soothe every muscle in your body." She winked and a lascivious grin told him exactly what was on her mind.

Curious where she would take this, he followed as tendrils of hope curled around his needy heart.

She might be a friend. One could never tell.

9

SARA SOUNDED SO SWEET, he almost believed she had intended to pamper him from the start, but reminding himself of where he was quickly swayed him from that idea. She planned to fall into bed with him, thinking he would satisfy her fully before she sent him—hours later, chains and all—back to his dark and dirty cell. But he would not dutifully play the part of her boy toy; it hadn't been *that* long since he'd lain with a woman, or so he told himself. On the other hand, his mistrust of women didn't placate his body's the needs and urges. Still, if anyone would be used tonight, it would be Sara Barret.

"This is just what you need," Sara said as she led him from the foyer. "It'll make you feel like a new man."

"I'm sure *you* will," he said with a suggestive curve to his lips. Sara giggled and flashed him a broad, flirty smile that he returned but dropped the minute she turned away.

Bret didn't dispute the bath partly because he wanted to be clean again, but also to give himself a chance to case her apartment and devise a plan. As he trailed her through the living room, he noticed the sliding glass doors along the opposite wall. They led onto a small balcony and the velvety black night beyond. Hope trickled to life inside him but dwindled quickly when he realized, judging by the flights of stairs he'd climbed, he was at least four stories up. Far too high to jump, but he had little choice. Trying to gain his freedom along the course he had traveled to arrive here would be useless as his escorts still guarded the hallway. The balcony appeared to be the only other viable way out.

Details and options churned in his mind as he followed Sara through her apartment until he saw the golden cord decorating the heavy curtains surrounding the glass doorway. It may not be long enough, but the nylon cable would get him much closer to the ground.

If he could detain Sara long enough to reach the forest, he would be free. If only they hadn't started beating his feet rather than his body. His soles were almost healed from the last pummeling he received, though they were still uncomfortable to put weight on, and he tensed in nervous expectation of the pain he would suffer to reach the ground.

Sara led him into a tiled bathroom with an oversized porcelain bathtub, illuminated by eerie moonlight flowing in through three long, high-set windows in the east wall. The coarse sway of Sara's narrow hips as she strolled straight to the tub to turn on the water struck a chord in Bret. The steam swirled around her naked body, making her seem ethereal but pretty in her own way. That she chose to do this for him was a kindness, a privilege not offered to him in a very long time, and the simple fact she was doing it made him oddly grateful despite his lack of interest.

Bret stood in the doorway as Sara grasped a bottle among the many decorating a small table nearby and poured an ample amount of greenish liquid under the spray. Almost instantly, the room filled with a fragrant odor so heady it made Bret's head spin. Tiny white bubbles emerged on the surface of the water as Sara bent to test its warmth—giving him a generous view of her backside in the process. He admired her feminine curves with sex-deprived masculine interest, but she did nothing for him. No longer staring when she motioned for him to enter the water, he grinned in anticipation and stepped forward.

He eyed her thin form and noted how the strange light radiating off the gray-blue tile and her translucent white skin made her look more like a ghost than a flesh and blood woman. The odd picture she presented in the spectral glow roused unwanted memories of another time and another woman— Amy by a mountain hot springs in the moonlight. A momentary tightening in his loins rocked him and he shook his head while averting his eyes, trying to forget what that image had once meant to him. He pushed the sensation aside and stepped into the warm, fragrant water. Groaning with long-absent pleasure, he eased his filthy, aching body into the bubbly depths. The heat soothed the pain in his limbs and tingled along his cool skin as his head fell against the rounded edge of the porcelain rim, and he tried to relax.

Sara's cold fingers on his shoulders a few seconds later startled him.

He had forgotten she was there.

"It's only me, Bret," she said, massaging the tight tendons in his neck. He took a deep breath and tried to relax.

As his muscles unwound, his mind turned over all the possible ways to distract Sara while he escaped; yet every scenario seemed to end with him resorting to violence he would rather avoid. He could snap her thin neck like a twig before her adrenaline kicked in, but he knew what would happen if he did—she would be dead and he would feel guilty. He had enough remorse to carry already, but if he had no other choice...

I'm not a murderer, he thought, *but I'll do what I have to do.*

He sighed as Sara worked the muscles of his shoulders before she began to scrub him clean. She started by giving him a shave. Quickly mixing suds in a mug, she smoothed the white foam over his cheeks, jaw, and neck, but when he balked at the straight razor in her hand, she allowed him to shave himself while she watched.

When he'd finished shaving, Sara massaged shampoo into his hair, kneading his scalp, and then ran her fingers through the short, inky strands as she let the rinse water wash away the suds.

Her soft touch soothed him. His muscles slowly loosened and he melted into the round curve of the tub.

Lathering a washcloth with soap, Sara rubbed it over his body. Scrubbing upward from his sore feet, she inched her way to his thighs and, encouraged by his silent compliance, stroked higher. Soon the cloth disappeared, and she took him into her hand, caressing him with knowledgeable fingers. He opened his eyes and found Sara's hazel gaze darkened with desire. He gave her a crooked smile, savoring her hands on him, but only tolerating her to achieve his goal.

To get out of this prison, he would go along with whatever she wanted.

It hasn't been that long, he reminded himself. *And if you expect to escape tonight, you better not hang around for dessert.* He smiled at his analogy while he lifted her hand to his lips and brushed a kiss against her knuckles.

"May we finish this elsewhere?" he asked, locking her gaze with his. "This water is filthy. I don't want you to have to touch it." He knew his words produced the desired effect when a sweet smile pulled at her lips and she got to her feet.

"Of course, Bret," she replied as she returned from the linen closet across the room. "If you'll stand up, I'll dry you off and then we can find a more comfortable place to get cozy and have a toast." She smiled up at him as she dried each of his legs, lingering on the task longer than needed; her comment gave him more excitement than she did.

Does she mean alcohol? A plan began to take shape in his head.

Tossing the damp towel aside, she led him into an adjoining bedroom. Pink satin covers, pulled back in invitation, covered a full-sized bed and several lace-edged pillows were stacked against the plain, wooden headboard. Matching nightstands bracketed the bed, with matching table lamps turned on low.

"Sit down," she said and he complied without argument. She sat next to him and snuggled up close, stroking his chest. "Would you like a drink?"

The only alcohol Bret had imbibed since the end of the war was usually a bitter and very stout, homemade brew. The high-quality stuff was lost—or at least he'd assumed it had been. Maybe, like with most luxuries in this broken world, the very wealthy hoarded the good stuff.

"What do you have?" he asked, expecting some sort of moonshine.

"Is old Tennessee whiskey okay?"

Tennessee whiskey? Okay?

His taste buds tingled, but his tone was even. "That'll work."

She giggled and got up to bounce on her toes across the floor. "Good."

"On the rocks," he added when she reached the door.

"No problem." She smiled and left Bret alone in the semi-darkness. He ambled to the entry, where he leaned against the frame and gave in to an urge to observe her. He admired her slim shape as she glided across the floor, and again he was reminded of a ghost—a thin, bony ghost. He shook his head and closed his eyes to disperse the image of spectral skin from his mind as she flipped on the kitchen light. He debated making a dash for the balcony and decided against it.

"Sara?"

"Hmm?"

"Bring the bottle, would you?"

"Sure." Her answer was sweet, and she smiled over her shoulder at him as she took the bottle down off the shelf, doing her best to show off her reedy figure. He returned her smile, a reward for her display, but he was still unimpressed. He went back to the bed and sat with a sigh as he swung his long legs onto the mattress and reclined against the stack of cushions.

On the brink of freedom, he was keen to be done with Sara, but didn't want to rush her for fear she would suspect something. He liked her enough not to want to hurt her, but his anxiety to be gone was growing.

He heard the clink of ice cubes in a glass and tried to remember the last time he had ice that didn't involve chipping it off a snow covered rock or frozen river, or electric lighting for that matter. The abundance of energy in this place, when there were so few modern conveniences everywhere else, astounded him.

The glow from the kitchen vanished and her light footsteps brought her back to him. She halted in the entryway. Thanks to her pale skin, he could just make out the shape of her skinny frame, and for some reason, her pose elicited an unexpected burst of lust. His blood heated and a familiar ache began in his groin.

He smiled. *Maybe I can wait a few minutes.*

Once again acting coy, she whispered his name and glanced around as if unsure of his location.

"On the bed," he said, playing his part. She followed the sound of his voice and set the glasses on the closest nightstand, before switching on the small lamp sitting on its polished pine surface. Peeking at him with a sly grin, she poured the brown-colored liquid into each glass.

"You look better," she observed. "Not so bruised and swollen."

"They've been ignoring me lately," he said.

"Enjoy it while you can," Sara told him while tracing a finger along his jaw, apparently missing the scorn in his remark. "Darla, and many more I'm sure, will be after you tomorrow. I know Darla has no shame in using a club or a whip, and neither do most of the others."

Something undefinable glimmered in her eyes as she spoke. Lust was obvious, but something darker lingered in the hazel depths, too. Bret wondered if the inscrutable flicker was remorse for the pain he might suffer or an avid desire to watch.

"I intend to enjoy myself a great deal," he said, changing the subject and trying to sound amorous. He casually brushed his knuckles over her thigh to take the glass she offered him. At his touch, her hazel eyes lit up and twinkled. She met his gaze and her lips split into a broad smile as she sat down next to him.

"I intend to enjoy tonight too," she retorted, clinking her glass against his before taking a quick sip. She set the flat-bottomed tumbler down to fluff some pillows behind her back and then picked up the drink once more. "Who knows," she smiled, "maybe your new owner will be generous and share you with me. It would be such a waste to lose you to a selfish woman who'd keep you all to herself. Darla's too mean, though."

She sipped at her whiskey unmindful of Bret's stiffening body or the righteous fury burning in his silver-green eyes.

"She's jealous too," Sara continued. "I'd never get to see you again if Darla bought you...I wouldn't be able to afford her fees. Maybe one of the others will acquire you. Carrie Simpson would be decent to you, I think...and me too." She turned to him with a brilliant smile and it took what remained of his self-control to return the gesture though his mind was seething. She talked about him as if he were a toy to be passed around from one woman to the next! She didn't care about him. She only wanted to satisfy her lust before he was sold off to some other heartless bitch without a second thought about what he wanted or how he felt.

Despite all that had happened with Amy, he was still too sensitive. She'd often laughingly told him he was sentimental, but he had believed she cared for him and thought nothing of it.

As a boy, Bret had learned how dangerous being tenderhearted was. He'd forgotten for a while, until Amy's betrayal reminded of it. Unfortunately, he hadn't lost his habit of trying to read between the lines—that and his stupid, lonely heart—and both had lied to him again. This time he went in with his guard up, but he'd let it slip somewhere along the way.

The realization that he had held a secret hope he might gain an ally in Sara stung. Now he discovered, once again, how ridiculous he was to hope for anything.

He needed to be harder, colder. To live in this new society, Bret knew he must be cruel—and he could be—but it chafed him mentally and emotionally; he'd seen enough savagery as an adolescent. But he was determined this evening would be his final lesson in the basic art of survival.

Bret squelched his burning indignation and smiled at her upturned face. He emptied his glass with one quick swig and reached over her to grab the liquor off the nightstand, then refilled both their glasses.

"Oh, not so much," Sara laughed, unaware of his dangerous mood change.

The thought of her comeuppance when the guards discovered him missing was enough to bring a genuine curve to his lips. He knew he must look somewhat savage in that moment, but Sara thought he lavished affection on her and returned his smile. Her reaction almost made him laugh.

Half an hour later, Bret replenished Sara's drink for the seventh time. Dizzy drunk, she seemed not to care or discern how much he encouraged her, while Bret still nursed his second refill. Leaning into him, giggling, and delighting in his presence, she gazed into his face as she raised her glass for another toast to them and their evening together. In so doing, she sloshed an ample quantity of the potent, brown brew over the rim and stared transfixed as it spilled onto Bret's chest and trailed through the curling wisps of chest hair that arrowed into his lap. The cool liquid cause goosebumps to raise on his skin, and he shivered as it trickled over his genitals.

He held back a curse as he looked down at the mess in his lap. When he met Sara's gaze, her glassy eyes were smiling.

"Oops." She snickered, then gulped the remainder of her drink. Setting the glass aside, she slipped her hands over his thighs, eased his legs farther apart, and unsteadily repositioned herself between them. She bent over him and began to lick the fluid from his skin. The action surprised him. He hadn't expected any woman in this place to be interested in his pleasure. But then again, maybe she just meant to speed the way to her own.

He inhaled sharply and the sound seemed to encourage her. She giggled again as she progressed downward from his chest, her tongue tasting every inch of masculine flesh along the way. Her languid pace was so excruciating, so deliberate, that by the time she reached his belly, Bret's breathing was ragged and sweat had started on his brow. His blood raced. His heart slammed in his chest. Hot, urgent need pulsed between his thighs. As she traced the tip of her tongue around his bellybutton, he decided he was willing to give her everything she wanted in order to get the physical release that had been out of his grasp for what felt like an eternity.

It's been long enough! his body screamed at him and his mind, overstimulated by her mouth on his flesh, was unable to argue. Laying back against the pile of pillows, he reveled in the pleasant cravings she stirred within his sex-starved body.

Sara pushed his thighs farther apart to nestle herself between them, and then rested her head on his chest as her fingers wrapped around the silky iron rod of his erection. A contented sigh emanated from her as she gazed at his long length in her hand. She lowered her head as if to service him, but instead, she rested her cheek on his muscled abdomen, his skin still damp from her mouth, and promptly passed out.

When she didn't move for several seconds, Bret peered down at her and called her name, but his attempts to wake her were futile. She would not be coherent for quite a while, and nothing he did would change that fact.

This was how he wanted her. Wasn't it?

So near to that pinnacle of pleasure, he almost wanted to assume she was teasing him. But he couldn't lay claim to his supposition knowing the amount of alcohol he'd practically forced down her throat. She was not used to the strong drink, that much was clear. Yet, after coming so close to the long-absent sexual release through the yielding warmth of a woman's body, it was acutely distressing to realize the ultimate moment of carnal ecstasy was not forthcoming.

She could've at least finished, he thought with a bitter frown.

None too gently, he rolled her off his lap and onto the bed. He got to his feet and stood, watching as she wiggled into a ball, a smile curling her thin lips. Disgusted, he tossed the edge of the comforter over her naked form and shook his head.

"Still the same guy I've always been," he muttered and turned to search the room, once again intent on his freedom.

10

BRET SEARCHED HER CLOSET for something to cover his nakedness and found a pair of gray sweatpants and a long-sleeved black T-shirt. Both were tight as he pulled them on, but they would provide at least a modicum of protection from the elements. He knew exactly how cold the mountains were in the winter and that if he hiked into the higher elevations without something more than his skin, he would succumb to hypothermia before he got very far. Unable to locate any suitable shoes, he pulled a pair of wool socks over each foot. Finding nothing else he could use, Bret crossed the floor to the bed and, casting Sara one last repugnant look, switched off the bedside lamp, picked up the spare blanket he'd also found, and left the bedroom.

Traversing the shadow-draped living room, Bret carefully avoided the furniture as he made his way to the sliding glass doors. He hesitated when he reached for the handle. What if there were guards watching the balconies? What if someone saw him? What would they do to him? More questions swept through his mind and a chill of foreboding raced over his skin. Then he straightened his shoulders and lengthened his spine. "It can't be worse than what they've already done to me."

The entry easily slid open and the icy breath of winter blew in through the opening. Skin prickling from the sudden chill and residual fear, he stepped onto the balcony and shivered as he surveyed the auction yard stretched out before him. He frowned at the eerie stillness and a cold tingle swept down his spine. He saw no one and nothing indicated he should be alarmed, but the lack of sentries or guard dogs or anything resembling security started an uneasy flutter in the pit of his stomach.

What looked like several feet of snowfall covered the ground outside the perimeter fence and nothing moved—though Bret watched the grounds for several minutes.

They're awfully confident, he thought. *Must not have many escapes…or attempts either.*

That didn't surprise him considering their liberal use of chains, drugs, and pain. In any case, he'd apparently have little trouble once he reached the ground. His biggest problem was Sara. If she woke and found him missing before he made it over the fence and well away, they would catch him.

The possibility, no matter how unlikely, tightened his chest.

Still, he had expected more opposition to his flight for freedom than an empty yard. *Lucky again, I guess.*

Another long, slow look around convinced him the way was clear and though nerves still jumped in his gut, he began to feel a desperate urge to move, to run, to climb, and run again. He needed to move quickly, get over the fence and away before someone decided to check the clearing.

Eyes darting between his trembling hands and the still empty yard, Bret tied one end of the golden rope he'd pulled from Sara's curtain rod to the balcony's black post. He then tossed the other end over the rail and the blanket followed right after. He peered over the side and saw the cord did not quite reach the second floor.

"What the hell," he muttered and, after another survey of the deserted grounds, willed himself to move. Tremors shook his body as he stepped over the metal barrier, but he would not stop again.

The task was more difficult than he had anticipated. Severely weakened by too little food and too many beatings, he struggled to lower himself down the rope. His arms trembled with the effort. His palms began to sweat, and he slipped more than once as he made his way downward, the slick rope burning and cutting into his hands. Somehow, he managed to hold on long enough to reach the end of the line. His aching fingers clamped desperately around the cord as he prepared to shift his hold. In a quick lunge, he grabbed for the third-level balcony's lower gusset, grasped it, and clung. He breathed a sigh of relief as he released the cord and used the metal bracket to shakily climb the rest of the way.

His toes touched the handrail of the second-floor balcony, but he slipped when he attempted to maneuver himself to the floor and his arms were too spent to correct his fall. He landed on his side with what sounded to him like a loud thump. He scrambled up and plastered his back flat against the wall. Standing in the darkness to the right of the glass doors—the same as the ones in Sara's room—Bret waited, held his breath, and prayed. Several minutes passed while he stood in the freezing cold, but no one appeared at the door. When nothing happened after another slow count to sixty, he moved to the railing and the tricky part of his descent.

Though he now stood only one story up, he saw no way to reach the ground without jumping. Bret winced just thinking about landing on his sensitive soles, but there was no other choice. He crawled over the rail once again and lowered himself until his long fingers were all that held him to the base of the last balcony. His wool-covered toes dangled about two yards from the earth, which, in the dark, appeared to be only snow-dappled grass.

Bret took a deep breath, reminded himself to stay quiet, and then let go. Pain from his abused soles shot up through his legs when his feet connected with the frozen ground. Somehow, he limited his reaction to a single, soft grunt. He rolled when he landed taking some of the pressure from his feet, and he stayed where he fell for several seconds, breathing hard and waiting for the throbbing to cease. The snowy ground was a balm for his aching soles while he took a moment to catch his breath. Not wanting to waste too much time, he got up, grabbed the bedding he let fall earlier, and pressed his back up against the building. A sense of foreboding grew steadily in his belly, but Bret saw nothing to hinder him as he stared into the oppressive night. Despite the lack of opposition, the fear pulsing through him and the ice-cold air were conspiring to make him shake.

He would make it.

He would be free again.

Bret gathered his courage and slowly crept through the darkness. With every step toward the fence, an increased feeling of dread weighed on him, turning his sore feet to lead. Then something made the hair on the back of his neck stand on end. He instantly dropped into a crouch and everything in him went on high alert. He stood motionless, watching, listening.

At first, he berated himself for allowing the drug to take control again, but then his frightened mind understood. After being imprisoned in the dark for what must've been months, the sudden warning from his rusty instincts momentarily overwhelmed him.

When no suspicious sound or movement reached him, he crept forward again. When he crouched in front of the last barrier to his freedom, he twisted and gazed over his back-trail.

Nothing.

Bret refocused on the chain-link in front of him. He didn't hear the telltale hum of electricity, but he tested it for voltage anyway.

Again, nothing.

He took one last hasty look around and then began to climb. His arms felt like over-stretched rubber and his feet ached more with every upward step, but thinking about the forest beyond and with his need to be free surging through his veins, he focused on the top and forced his exhausted body to keep going.

Apprehension gnawed at him as he neared the top, and fear, not quite terror, bloomed to life once again. He fought the drug still surging through his veins, battling the desire to collapse onto the ground and hide. His arms and legs trembled. He repeatedly glanced over his shoulder, expecting to see an army of guards in the yard behind him.

He kept climbing. He would not stop.

Less than two feet from the top, he smiled as a joyous rush of freedom burgeoned to life in his chest.

Then something happened.

A stinging tingle shot through Bret's entire body, numbing his senses and stunning his brain. His eyes and teeth clenched. His muscles contracted and his fingers clutched the steel fencing, unable to let go as he convulsed from the electrifying force now flowing through the metal. A part of his shocked mind knew what had happened—someone had seen him and then thrown a switch.

Had Sara warned someone and thwarted his escape?

As abruptly as the electric flow started, it stopped.

His fingers relaxed and released the heavy mesh.

He felt himself fall as if in a dream.

He hit the hard-packed snow with a hefty thud. His instincts screamed for him to run, but his limbs would not move. Not quite conscious, his mind faded and he couldn't focus. As he drifted into darkness, Bret knew if they didn't kill him, the miserable life he'd been leading would be nothing compared to what they'd do to him now.

I failed! It was his last thought as the guards made their way toward him and before everything went black. *Oh, God, please let them kill me. I failed...*

THE AUCTION

1

December 31

BRET MASTERS AWAKENED to a sharp prick in his hip. Groggy, his whole body aching, he attempted to pull away from the minor pain, but the concrete wall next to him his confines held him firmly in place. It confused him for a moment, until his gritty eyes finally focused on the two women looking down on him. It was then that he realized his morning booster of the drug caused the pointed sting in his side. The chilling effect coursed through him and its hold on his senses increased, putting his nerves on edge. His skin became sensitized—hyper-aware of everything around him—and every sound boomed in his ears. He groaned as his stomach knotted and his heartbeat picked up. The strength of the sickening concoction always surprised him, but not so strong this time as to incapacitate him; only enough to make him lay motionless as the guards released the chains from the floor rings that held him stretched over his old wooden bench.

When he had regained consciousness after being electrified on the fence the night before, he found himself stripped naked and strapped to the floor of the hellishly hot chamber where they had tortured him so many times before. And somewhere nearby, he heard a woman screaming. He didn't recognize the voice at first, but when the shrieks ceased and her curses began, he knew to whom the cries belonged—Sara Barret. Apparently, she'd been punished for allowing him to escape.

Lying there helpless, Bret overheard a heated conversation between Sara and another woman he'd never met before. Most of the words were unclear, but the tone of their voices told him that a high level of animosity existed between them. The parts of the conversation he did hear made little sense to him.

"You know your place now, Sara," the new woman said. "Make sure you remember it."

"Fine, but I want justice," Sara hissed back.

"Don't worry, you'll get your chance," the stranger replied as the women entered the room where Bret was tied down.

Though much more attractive than Sara, this new woman had an undeniable cruel streak. She'd whipped the soles of his feet mercilessly with a thick, two-inch leather strap until he was writhing and fighting the chains that bound him. But he denied them what they wanted—the pleasure of hearing him scream. When he'd clamped his jaws tight and stubbornly refused to give in to the pain she inflicted, she allowed Sara to enact her final, brutal vengeance. By the time they'd finished with him, he was covered in sweat, too weak and in too much pain to walk. Two guards had then dragged him downstairs to his cell where he slept poorly after they chained him on his back with his arms above his head and his knees bent over the end of his makeshift bed.

That must've been hours ago. He had no idea what time it was now.

His mind cloudy, utter enervation stripping him of his will to fight, Bret kept his eyes closed as a guard lifted his bound wrists to secure them to his waist. He hissed at the stiffness in his back and shoulders, and, surprisingly, she paused, allowing his muscles to become accustomed to the change of position before moving them again in slow increments.

"Thank you," he whispered in a raspy voice only she could hear, and then peeked at her from between the slits of his lids. She glanced at him. Her eyes flicked worriedly toward the other guard then back to his face. Her lips tightened, but there was kindness in her eyes. She gave a quick, polite nod, accepting his gratitude, but didn't respond otherwise. It was enough. At least one of them didn't want to torment him further.

The second woman at his feet, fighting with the lock that held his ankle manacles, took a little longer to free him of the restraint. Once she did, however, she was less patient with his slow response to her commands.

"Sit up," she said in a harsh tone. He tried to comply, but after his first abortive attempt, she grabbed the metal collar encircling his neck and hauled him upward.

Bret grunted but didn't struggle.

Still, with no resistance from him, the pitiless guard restrained him as usual. The length of links secured around his waist dug into and pinched the flesh at his sides, but he made no comment. He'd become used to this routine when they took him from the cell—shoot him up with the drug to make him too afraid to resist then chain him so he could hardly move.

Finished securing his bonds, the second woman dragged him off the bench by the metal shackle around his neck. He complied without thought, only wanting whatever they were going to do to him over as quickly as possible. The minute he put pressure on his abused soles, however, his eyes flew open, his legs buckled, and he dropped to his knees. Losing his balance and deprived of his arms to right himself, he tumbled forward. Panicked, Bret's fingers caught in the long links of chain connected to his neck, attempting to keep the guard from strangling him further.

"Wait," he croaked, gasping to catch his breath.

"You're going to walk this time," she said irritably. "We

may have dragged you down here last night, but I'll be damned if we're going to carry you *up* those stairs."

"Okay, okay," he breathed, "just give me a minute."

He struggled back to his knees and rested his forehead against the coolness of the dirty, stone floor, preparing himself for the pain of walking. He still clenched the lead chain tightly and he knew if he held it too long, she'd break his fingers yanking it out of his grasp. He took a deep breath and then made his awkward way onto his swollen feet. He groaned as the hours-old scabs cracked open, and he almost fell again. He swayed and the more compassionate of the two sentries surprised him when she appeared at his side. She wrapped her arm around his waist and steadied him.

"Okay?" she asked, and when he nodded, she released him. He let loose his tether as, with a look of disgust for the kind guard, the crueler woman turned and walked away. He stumbled after her as she quickly led him through the door of his cell. In the hallway, the kind guard took the lead and set a slower pace as they made their way up the steps. Bret didn't care where they were taking him, he couldn't. He fought to stay upright, just followed their lead, his mind flinching at every stab of pain his body felt. He couldn't do anything else. Despite his best efforts, however, he collapsed several times on the stairs only to be yanked upright and berated by the malicious guard before being hustled forward again. They guided him through the halls and onto the grounds outside. This time, however, instead of the men standing in one long line, they stood blindfolded and gathered into several color-coded groups based on the tags attached to their collars.

The scene set off alarms in Bret's mind. His muscles tensed as every instinct he had told him to run the other way, but the drug kept his will at bay.

His guards halted outside the door and he shivered in the cold morning air. They led him to the group facing the large open yard and then commanded him to stop and stand still.

Unable to do anything else, he did as ordered, and the kind guard quickly tied a blindfold over his eyes while the other woman secured him with chains from his neck shackle to three steel rings anchored in the ground. He couldn't move far in any direction. The extra precautions only made his rapid heartbeat thump harder and brought a sheen of sweat to his brow. They could do anything to him bound like this and being blind only made his anxiety worse. An involuntary shiver shot through him and he prepared for another round of torment…or worse.

A moment later, their footsteps faded and Bret breathed a sigh of relief. At least they weren't going to torture him again. The sun on his skin felt good, but the air was too chilly to feel warm and cold prickles broke out all over his body. *How long are they going to leave us out here?* It was the middle of winter, and if they stayed outside after dark, they'd all freeze. *They won't do that,* he reminded himself. *You're worth too much to them alive.*

That eased his tenseness a bit, but just as he relaxed a little, he sensed someone approach him.

"Hello, handsome," Sara's voice purred as she stroked his chest.

He sucked in a startled breath and flinched at her sudden caress. Her touch made his skin crawl, but with his arms bound as they were and with the tethering chains, there wasn't much he could do. Thankful that he had himself under some control, Bret concentrated on the intense dislike that flooded him.

"What do you want?" he asked through clenched teeth, focusing all his attention on the threat before him.

"Oh," she crooned elongating the vowel. To his ears, she sounded thrilled and his senses went on high alert. "I just came by to give you a little gift."

"What?" Bret hissed, but she didn't answer. She moved to his right and he waited nervously as seconds swept by, her movements muffled by the fuzzy, ringing noise in his ear— which had been reinjured when she kicked him while he was bound to the floor the night before. He was about to repeat his question when a familiar sting pierced his hip. The chains clanked but held him in place when he tried to pull away from the offending prick. He didn't need to see to know what she had done; the large quantity of liquid being forced into his body was difficult to miss.

"What the hell are you doing?" he asked, trying to make it sound like a demand, but it was very hard as dread over the possibilities quickening inside him ran rampant through his system.

"It's just a little something to help you enjoy your day." Sara giggled. "You didn't think I'd let you get away with making a fool of me, did you?"

A wave of fear and nausea struck him and he clamped his jaws together, fighting the urge to cringe at the bite in her tone. Instead, he forced out a stinging retort. "You didn't need me for that."

Her fingers knotted in his short-cropped hair and wrenched his head to the side. He wanted to pull back, but the chemical pumping through his veins conspired against him.

"I lost everything I've worked my whole life for because of you," Sara hissed as she held him at the awkward angle. He could feel the warmth of her breath against his cheek and icy prickles danced over every inch of his skin as he struggled to remain upright. "You will regret betraying my trust."

"It wasn't trust," he murmured and, through panting breaths, only just managed a disgusted chuckle. "It was l-lust."

"Whatever," she replied, giving him a rough shove that put him off-balance. The chains rattled and he shuffled his feet to keep from going down, then groaned at the resurgence of pain shooting up his legs that shifting his weight caused.

Sara laughed. "I see my lesson is still a grim reminder for you today," she said. "Good!"

His body shook violently and he thought he might vomit. "W-What did you d-do to me?" He already had a pretty good idea, but he couldn't stop from asking.

"I told you, just a little payback."

Another frightening thought caused a sheen of sweat to coat his body. Last night, she'd been blind with rage over what she called his treachery. The way she'd attacked him, and with him unable to protect himself, she might have murdered him if her new superior hadn't been there to stop her. Now, they were alone and she'd had time to plan this attack. Is this when she got her final revenge?

"Are you... Wi-Will it...k-kill me?" he stuttered, unable to keep his voice or breathing steady.

"Oh, no, no," she laughed again, clearly enjoying his distress, "I would never do that. I'd get in real trouble for that. No, this is only a little extra of the drug, 'cause I know you like it so much."

He groaned. She wouldn't kill him and she couldn't hurt him the way she wanted, but she could terrify and humiliate him beyond enduring.

He cursed her through his teeth. The uncontrollable quivering growing.

"T-They already g-gave me some," he told her. "Ho-How much more did you g-give me?" Panic engulfed his senses, threatening to overwhelm the small amount of self-restraint he barely clung to.

"Don't worry so much," she said slapping his cheek, the act less than playful.

He recoiled. Almost fell.

"I know they already gave you some," she mimicked his serious tone, and then she snickered. "This stuff is more concentrated and, knowing your pride, should make you wish you were dead rather than having to stand there and take it. But to answer your question, you'll jump at every sound, flinch at every touch, and there'll be at least a couple *hundred*," she dragged out the last word for emphasis, "women here today. And though most won't be able to afford you, I can't imagine any of them not wanting to touch you." She traced her finger down the middle of his chest, making him cringe and tremble.

Nausea gurgled and churned in Bret's belly. His heart hammered unnaturally in his chest. Sweat beaded his brow and his breath came fast and shallow. His legs trembled worse than before and his hands balled into impotent fists as the drug wreaked havoc on his self-control.

"Added to what you've got in you," Sara continued as she moved away, "this ought to make for some great entertainment. For me, anyway. A much better revenge than the meager amount Kelly allowed me last night, and this won't damage your sale value. Of course, it might stop your heart, but that's only in rare cases. It will make you sick, but…well, either way, I'll have my revenge, and you'll have been punished for your lack of proper gratitude and blatant disrespect."

He could hear the shrug of indifference in her voice.

"By the way," she said, apparently unable to resist one more taunt, "how are your feet?"

Bret swore at her and thrashed against his chains helplessly.

She cackled with glee. "Not good, huh? Well, try to have a nice day, Bret. I'll be watching."

*   *   *

Less than half an hour later, the yard was filled with horses, some saddled, others pulling two or four person buggies or carts. The animals were kept in the holding pens to the north of the Auction Hall while the women they had conveyed here milled around examining the merchandise.

It didn't take long for the effects of the extra drug to seize hold of Bret. Almost immediately after Sara administered the injection, he started to tremble inside. Now, every movement, every noise frightened him so badly that he worried he would disgrace himself. He feared he was going insane as he struggled with his body's desire to flinch at every approach or shy away from every touch, fighting the chains that bound him, keeping him in place.

Sara's estimation hadn't been an exaggeration. Each woman who approached him wanted to fondle him in one way or another and, to his growing dismay, she'd been right about his popularity with the throng milling around him. In his current state, their presence was like fire ants crawling across his skin.

Bret struggled to stay on his tender feet, despite the surging dread driving him crazy. *This is the worst humiliation yet,* his mind seethed. To be put on display like some kind of prize was the most dehumanizing thing he'd ever suffered. But his fury and frustration didn't lessen his alarm or his body's response to the drug. With his mind in a frenzy, cold sweat covered him, and, like a strung-out druggie looking for his next fix, he shivered and shook uncontrollably.

The blindfold made it impossible for him to make out any part of his surroundings. Not the faces of the women who swarmed around him. Not Sara, who laughed at him from her perch on the platform near the Auction Hall. And not the tall man in a black pea coat who regarded him with stunned familiarity from across the crowded yard.

2

ANGEL ALDRIDGE LEANED against one of the corral posts near the Auction Hall's crowded display yard. The cold wind stirred her black curls as she observed—with growing distaste—the melee going on around the merchandise on display across the wide, snow-dappled enclosure. Disgusted by the scene, she turned toward where the attendees' horses were kept, and where her own horse—a large, black stallion named Ebony—stood alone not far from her. Angel smiled as he tossed his head in the air then broke into a short run, kicking up clods of dirt and frost as he crossed to the other side of his private pen.

"Show off," Angel murmured with an affectionate smile. Chilled, she pulled the collar of her long, black wool jacket closer around her neck and snugly rewrapped her ivory scarf. The sun was up, but crispness lingered in the air, and, being the middle of winter, it would not get warmer anytime soon. It was only a matter of time before clouds rolled in with more snowfall to bury them once again in another layer of the icy, white blanket. They'd be lucky if the temperature reached ten degrees above freezing before March.

Finished adjusting her scarf, she returned her attention to the bustling spectacle in front of her. Across the yard, women raved over the new prizes up for sale, deciding upon which one they would bid. Angel would never understand why they made such a fuss. The prizes were only men after all, but the prevailing opinion among the majority of affluent women completely disagreed with hers.

"Slavery isn't the answer," Angel had argued at the governing council meeting a few months ago and not for the first time either. "You've just exchanged one broken system for another." Her best friend Monica, had given her a supportive smile, and several of the less influential women had tentatively nodded their agreement, though none of them but Monica ever verbalized their thoughts. Over the years, too many who had once spoken out had fallen victim to unfavorable consequences that often followed their complaints. The worst was a suspicious death that occurred years ago. A woman, who'd vehemently argued against Darla's leanings toward corporal punishment for slaves, was found dead on the side of the road. Supposedly, she'd broken her neck falling from her horse when the animal had spooked and bolted in his panic. Most of those on the council at the time hadn't believed that report, but they had no way to refute it, and Darla's power increased . It had continued to grow exponentially as she recruited other women who held similar beliefs and found ways to get them a seat at council. She also gave out loans to many of the less wealthy women and then demanded favors—and obedience. By the time Angel had joined the council, most of the other members had ceased trying to stand against their more powerful counterparts, and now Angel constantly fought an uphill battle just to keep the balance in check.

"Men must be strictly controlled," one of her fellow council members had said. "Their unchecked aggressive tendencies are the reason we lost everything in the first place. And the vile, base atrocities they inflicted on female prisoners during the Sex Wars only proves they can't be trusted."

"Those were the actions of a few renegade groups, not all men," Angel replied, but she'd known it was a lost cause. She'd already made these arguments dozens of times and nothing had changed.

"They tortured and killed *hundreds* of women and recorded their crimes for us to see," another woman had practically screeched, clearly outraged by Angel's defense of the male gender. "Who knows what the rest of them did behind closed doors or what other atrocities they would've unleashed if we hadn't stopped them. They destroyed our world, but they'd also enslaved *us* in so many different ways for centuries and they would've continued to do so, and you think we should just let them go?"

Angel's heart had clenched seeing the tears that spilled from the woman's angry eyes. The fact that horrors had occurred on both sides during that war was on the tip of her tongue but saying so would do no good.

"I will *never* agree to freeing them," the woman had continued, and the other affluent members murmured their agreement. "I had sisters that men debased and murdered; I will not allow another man, any man, the freedom to do it all again."

The tense discussion that followed had been long and useless and Angel had eventually relented.

Remembering the argument, she pushed her hands into the pockets of her long coat, leaned back against a corral post, and sighed. Too many women harbored a bitter grudge for what happened during the wars. She had a few of her own, but those were not something she would discuss...not with anyone. But as a wealthy landowner, Angel had the means and influence to oppose the lawmakers who were far more aggressive in expressing their opinions—and sometimes deadly in defending them. They still tried to find ways to thwart her, but, so far, though she knew she had a target on her back, she'd kept out of their line of sight.

What the rest of the world thought about male slavery was difficult to discern. They no longer had the advantage of instant communication—a benefit taken for granted before the wars. Instead, they relied on the news and rumors of couriers who were occasionally sent to exchange information. Yet, from what Angel had learned in the last six years as a member of the governing council, life was much the same in the few towns that they communicated with as it was here.

Staring at the women fawning over the male slaves as if they were some pretty new trinket or accessory reinforced Angel's belief that a battle against slavery was unwinnable. At least, not until attitudes changed, and not through any action requiring strength or numbers. She feared some kind of split was coming though—a war between the opposing female factions or between the more avid slaveholders and the rebels who still occasionally made a nuisance of themselves. But, though rumors about the rebel bands running occasional raids abounded—as they had for years—Angel didn't hold much hope in their cause.

She shook her head. An agreement between all the parties didn't seem likely in any case, especially when those in power liked having men at their disposal and at their mercy. They would fight to keep that supremacy. Personally, Angel had experienced enough strife and she did her best to make changes without getting anyone killed or imprisoned, but change moved slowly.

Standing under an early January morning sun, cynically surveying the milling women across the yard, Angel's stomach churned. Taking part in an auction always made her feel sick. Seeing the men treated like toys to be played with or like wild animals to be broken, made her ashamed to be part of it. But the only way to get a man out of here was to purchase him and, despite her wealth and her wish to do so, she couldn't buy every slave up for sale.

She was here for one reason. To purchase a doctor named

Hillman. The last general practitioner on Angel's Lazy A Ranch, Dr. Beck, had passed away almost two years ago. Since Dr. Beck had taught Angel about medicine and how to care for the sick, she'd taken on his duties after his death. Some injuries, though, like fractured bones, internal injuries, and the like still required a trip to the small hospital in town. After an accident a few months ago that almost proved deadly because of—as she saw it—her lack of knowledge, Angel was willing to pay a substantial amount to acquire Hillman. That was her main reason, but there was another.

"No, no, no...not again!" Peggy's anguished cries after her last miscarriage still rang in Angel's head and weighed on her heart. Even now, standing in the winter sun, a chill ran through her, remembering the horrors of that day and how she'd failed another person she cared for. There had been so much blood and if they hadn't gotten Peggy to the hospital in town, they may have lost her too.

"I can't go through this again, Angel," Peggy had softly sobbed a week later, while Angel sat beside her bed holding her friend's trembling hand. Her usually smiling face had been deathly pale and so drawn that Peggy's partner, Theo—who had gone to work with the other cowhands—had been reluctant to leave Peggy alone. Angel and several other women took turns watching over her to alleviate his fears.

"I know, honey," Angel had consoled as guilt for not doing more to help her friend gnawed a hole in her gut.

"I know there are other children out there," Peggy murmured, her swollen, red rimmed eyes pleading with Angel to understand. "Theo and I are happy to help any of them, to love them and care for them, but...I want a baby of our own, formed by our bodies and our love. Theo may be leery of getting pregnant again, but I want to keep trying. All I've ever wanted was to be a mother to my own child, and, now, being with Theo, I...I know it's selfish, but..." Peggy sighed and lifted shiny eyes to Angel's. "Do you know what I mean?"

Angel nodded. She knew too well, but her losses didn't matter anymore. She was here for these people, to make their lives better, not to whine about her own. Not right then, at least.

"Yes," she had said, giving Peggy's hand a comforting squeeze. "I understand and I'm going to make sure it never happens again."

She probably shouldn't have made that promise, but Peggy was a friend. The least she could do was make sure there was a competent, trained medical doctor nearby in case anything else should occur. She owed the people in her care that much. She'd been a fool to think she could do it all herself.

Now, here she stood in the Auction Hall compound, sadly amused yet thoroughly disgusted by the inane females in their gaudy seasonal clothes wandering about the grounds gawking and gossiping.

She remained by the corral for some time, taking in the scene until she spotted the tall man making his way toward her, a serious expression on his normally happy face. She smiled and thought again how appealing Jake looked in his dark suit and the stylish, black pea coat he wore, despite his grave manner whenever they came here. This place made him anxious and angry, and Angel couldn't blame him.

Jake's height and broad-shouldered build coupled with his short, dark-blond hair and trimmed mustache and goatee only added to his imposing appearance. Up close, his expressive hazel-green eyes sparkled when he smiled and turned to ice when angry, but despite his daunting appearance, Jake was a very nice man. Nearly three years had passed since she'd rescued him from Darla Cain. A few months later, Jake repaid that service by saving Angel from a late-night assault, and, afterward, they grew very close. He often worried, hovered, and mothered her and, though annoying, she loved him all the more for it.

She tilted her head and smiled at him as he approached.

"You look so handsome, Jake. Anyone here today you might want to impress?"

He grimaced at the compliment. "Thanks," he muttered in a gruff voice, "and you know the answer. But that's not important." Before she could harass him further with more sisterly teasing, he abruptly shifted the subject. "I need to talk to you."

She straightened away from the fence post at his serious tone. "What is it? What's happened?"

He shook his head. "Nothing's happened. I just want to...ask a favor."

Her brows went up. "What kind of favor?"

He shook his head again at the concern in her expression. "Don't worry, I'm fine. But there's someone who isn't."

"What are you talking about?" Angel asked with a frown.

"Do you remember that friend of mine...the one I told you about?"

Something tender and hopeful fluttered in her heart but she pushed the little annoyance away. "The one you traveled with? The cowboy?"

"Yes."

Her breath caught as memories, and a deep, yet forbidden emotion, once again bubbled up within her. Warmth flashed over her skin and her heart rate picked up. She sighed and buried the dangerous feelings she could never admit to. "I remember. What about him?"

"I think he's here."

"Where?" Her smile returned and she shifted her eager gaze behind him, telling herself that particular man's importance to Jake was the only reason for her excitement. But no one was there. Refocusing on Jake, she frowned up into his steady gaze.

"Over there," he said, nodding toward the display area. "The one in the crowd."

She inhaled sharply when her eyes fell on the man Jake had indicated. He stood in the breeder's section—*add another zero to his cost*—and by the look of him, even at a distance, she understood why. Her smile faded and a sense of apprehension constricted her chest.

She remembered every story Jake ever told her about his friend—from childhood, through adolescence, to adults living in the wild. Everything from Bret's sometimes-quick temper to his cautious, tender heart and loyal friendship through all the trial's he and Jake had faced. To the mysterious bits of history Jake would never wholly explain, Angel had heard them all numerous times and they had settled in the empty places of her heart. They stayed with her, kept her company when she was lonely, and to her, Bret Masters had become more than a faceless name on cold nights or in the darkness that often consumed her. He'd been a safe harbor she'd never have to admit to, and she couldn't get him or those tales out of her head. But an absent fantasy hadn't been a problem. Now here he was, in the flesh—a good thing for Jake, but maybe not such a good thing for her.

"Oh, Jake." She sighed and her shoulders drooped as she turned back to him. "Are you sure?"

"No," he said, hunching forward a little and shaking his head. "It's been five years…I can't be sure. But, if I'm right, he hasn't changed much. He's a little thinner, but this place can do that to a man."

Angel nodded but her mind was running a mile a minute.

"What's his name again?" Not that she needed him to tell her; she couldn't forget the man's name.

"Bret Masters," Jake replied.

"Right…Well," she said, once again gazing toward the display yard. Then her eyes returned to Jake. "I'm not promising anything, but I'll find out if it's him or not."

"Thanks," he said and his face lit up with a grateful smile.

Angel frowned. "I said I wasn't promising anything. You know why we came here, Jake, and a man like that could cost more than I intended to spend. The doctor will be expensive as it is, and we *need* him." Her silent implication screamed, *We don't need another breeder!*

"I know, I know," he mumbled, shifting his feet. Digging his hands deeper into the pockets of his pea coat, he went on in a clearer tone. "If you'd find out if it is him and where he ends up, I'd appreciate it. I'd like to see him, talk to him again."

"I know you would." She reached out to touch his arm as the wretched expression on his face broke her heart and guilt tightened her chest. "Don't worry, Jake," she said with a soft smile. "I'll see what I can find out."

3

WHEN SHE REACHED her destination, Angel stood back beyond the mob of women while they finished their protracted inspection the man Jake thought to be his long-lost friend. While she waited, she studied him, unable to keep from recollecting everything Jake had told her about Bret Masters.

From what she could see of this man's face, he was handsome in what would have once been called a classic, Hollywood-type of way, but with a masculine ruggedness that made him even more attractive. In the old world of TV and movies, advertising and consumerism, he could've easily been a top-rated model or movie star with that straight nose, strong square jaw, and perfect masculine lips. His tall, athletic body only added to his appeal, but in this world, his good looks were not a bonus, not for him anyway. His attractiveness only meant he'd be sought out by more women to use him for their breeding purposes, or worse. But right now, Angel could see there was definitely something wrong, something besides his discomfort at being handled by strangers.

Sweating profusely, his skin glowed in the cool morning sunlight, but he seemed unsteady on his feet, twitching and jumping at every touch or noise. His extreme distress tugged at her heart and stoked flames of anger for his mistreatment, but his condition didn't surprise her. All slaves were dosed with the fear drug before sale. Angel was familiar with the method and its effects, yet this man seemed more agitated than the others. No matter how valiantly he tried to hide it, the torment he endured was painfully obvious—not that the women ogling him would bother or care about his misery.

Tired of waiting for their intimate inspection to end, Angel finally intervened. "It's time to move along. Now."

The man whipped his head in her direction, his jaw clenched and his whole frame trembled like a leaf in a storm. His impressive chest heaved with rapid breaths as if he'd been running for his life. *Maybe it felt that way to him.* Her chest constricted. *Can't they see how he's suffering?*

"Why? Do you want him all to yourself?" one woman demanded in a sour tone.

"I believe you've all pawed at him enough," Angel replied, a little of her anger breaking through her calm. "Put some gold down and you can do all you want later."

"Just because you have money doesn't mean you can tell us what to do," a blonde, stylishly dressed woman said. Angel sized her up with a glance; she was young, proud, and not as wealthy as she wanted her overpriced clothes to imply.

Angel smiled and met the younger woman's eyes with a hard, determined stare. "If you don't have a lot of money, you shouldn't be looking at him." Angel tilted her head toward the man in question, while her gaze included them all.

"She's right," a voice said from behind Angel.

The man's sharp intake of breath drew Angel's attention. He stood rigid, every muscle taut as if expecting an attack. Angel frowned and suppressed an annoyed sigh as she turned her attention to the frizzy-haired blonde guard who strolled toward them.

"If you don't have a lot of money," Sara Barrett repeated Angel's words as she came to a stop beside the man, "you shouldn't be looking. He's going to be expensive."

"Well, I have plenty enough for him," an older woman Angel didn't know said. The woman's lust-filled brown eyes glittered as she studied his tall frame. "What do you think of him, Sara?"

Sensing a battle coming, the rest of the female mob beat a hasty, though none too happy, retreat.

"Well," Sara lowered her chin and leaned toward the older woman, a smile pulling at her lips, "he's in the proper section for sale, that's for sure."

"Right." The other woman elongated the word as her eyes raked over the man again. "I heard a rumor you'd been with him. Is he as yummy as he looks?"

"Oh, most definitely," Sara said, her eyes settling expectantly on his face. In a deliberate rather than affectionate move, she reached over to caress the man's buttocks.

He recoiled and, baring his teeth, growled low in his throat like a cornered wolf.

Sara jerked her hand back as if he might bite and played off the scene with a forced giggle. "He *is* yummy, isn't he?"

"That's not the way I heard it, Sara," Angel said crossing her arms over her chest, the barest of smirks curving her mouth, remembering the rumors she'd overheard earlier.

Sara's face went blank and then her brows knitted together. "What do you mean?"

"You snuck him out of his cell without permission and got caught. Then found the whip on your back instead of having a good time on it."

Sara's wide-eyed, stunned expression did more than substantiate the insult.

The man's quiet chuckle confirmed it.

Hatred contorted Sara's face as she turned to him. "Shut up!" she screamed as she struck him across the face with her open palm. The resounding smack echoed through the yard and drew several gawking eyes.

Angel winced as his head whipped to the side. He stumbled, the metal links of his chains clinking, and he groaned as he strove to stay upright, but his awkwardness seemed to have little to do with Sara's slap. The chains anchored to the ground jerked him up short and he grunted at the sudden stop. His knees sagged and Angel reached for him, afraid he would fall. But, at the last second, his legs straightened and he stood as if nothing had happened. She admired his determination to appear calm, but also saw how hard he struggled to remain on his feet.

The older woman blinked in surprise at Sara's violence and crept off without another word.

"How dare you repeat such lies about me," Sara hissed at Angel, her hands balled into fists at her side. "I'd be within my rights to charge you with slander."

Angel arched an eyebrow. "Only if it isn't true and, judging by your reaction and his," she nodded toward the man, "I'm sure it is. You know how rumors always grow worse as they spread. So, why don't you just leave? Now."

Sara glanced at the man with malice in her eyes then leveled a sour look at Angel before she finally retreated, cursing Angel under her breath.

Finally alone with the slave, Angel lifted her eyes and studied the man's face. She'd noticed before that he was tall, but up close, he towered over her smaller form. He stood well over six-feet in his bare feet—at least two or three inches taller by her estimations. His shoulders were broad and, though she suspected he was thinner from his stay here, his body was heavily muscled in all the right places. A dusting of curling, black hair covered the temptingly sculpted contours of his chest, adding to his virile splendor, and she couldn't help but follow its tapered path downward over a work-hardened abdomen, and lower still as it narrowed further below the hollow of his innie belly button and…

Stop it! She jerked her eyes back to his face. *Damn, you're as bad as all the rest.*

He was attractive, no doubt about that. Standing close to him, she could make out his features a little more clearly through the blindfold the men always wore when on display. His nose appeared long and straight between high cheekbones, and his square jaw and strong chin were stubbled with blue-black whiskers. His mouth was wide with what she could only qualify as sexy lips, the lower slightly fuller than the upper, and chiseled with a masculine beauty she found distracting…

What are you doing? she asked herself, her fingers only inches from discovering the truth about the texture of his lips. *You're not here for that. You're never here for that.* She forced her arm back to her side. *What's wrong with you?*

"Hello," she said, but he didn't respond. He acted as if her voice didn't register. She crossed to his other side and repeated her salutation. This time he twisted his head toward her, a frown creasing his brow and a tremor running through his body.

"Can you hear me?" she questioned.

Again, he didn't respond, but this time he seemed to hear her speak.

She stepped closer to him and, seeing his body stiffen, she reached out to reassure him, but thought better of it and dropped her hand.

"I'm not going to harm you," she said, and he tilted his head as if confused. "I just want to see if you're injured." As she spoke, she noticed a swollen redness around his right ear. "What happened to your ear?"

"It's infected," he said in a deep raspy voice that rose goosebumps over her skin. Her heart stuttered at his unexpected reply and she pressed a hand to her chest, staring up at him for a breathless second. Then, berating herself, she collected her scattered emotions and quickly asked, "Has anyone looked at it?"

"Just you."

Red slashes marred his face and covered the rest of him as well. She touched one on his cheek to determine the depth of the bruising and he jerked away. Off-balance again, he stumbled and started to fall, but she stopped his downward motion with a hand on his arm. His limb was hard and warm despite the chill of the air, and the minor contact sent tendrils of tingling awareness shooting through Angel's body. She gasped softly but took a ruthless grip on her self-control and pushed the sensation away.

"I told you," she said when he stood on his own again, "I'm not going to hurt you. Please, just hold still." She released his arm and absently wiped her trembling palm against her coat.

He didn't comment. But when she touched his side—again, ignoring her somatic response—he flinched and shivered without pulling away. His strength of will astounded her, but Angel grimaced at his mistreatment as she marked the bruises on his ribs.

She stood so close to him that the heat of his naked body warmed her even through her clothes. She admired the corded muscles of his arms, the long fingers of his masculine hands, the classic V-shape of his brawny torso, and the swarthiness of his flesh—male flesh, toned and chiseled and magnificent...

My God, is there anything about him that isn't *distracting?* she thought, annoyed with herself for contemplating his nakedness again.

The tingles were back in spades.

Inspecting the welts defacing his skin, she attempted to ignore her increasing sensitivity to him, when, without warning, he abruptly swayed toward her. Startled, she drew back and glared at him, a sharp word coming to her lips, until she realized his sudden movement was unintentional. While she watched, he made an adjustment and stood straight.

Lowering her chin—and being careful to avoid the more private areas of his body—she peered down at his legs, searching for a reason for his inability to stand without wavering. Looking farther, she saw his feet appeared swollen. She crouched down for a closer inspection. Barely visible around the edges were the indications of red sores.

She tilted her head up. "Would you lift your left foot please?"

He shivered but complied. Unstable on his own, she took hold of his ankle and told him to lean on her if he needed to do so. A few seconds ticked by, but he did as she said, and Angel looked down.

Her stomach clenched at what she saw.

The skin on the sole of his foot blazed an angry red from toes to heel, the flesh bleeding in places, and in the center a cracked, blistered burn. She guessed his other foot would be the same, but she checked anyway. It, too, glowed a furious scarlet and the burn matched as well. The damage appeared to have happened as recently as last night and his injuries had gone untended.

Angel clenched her jaw and shook her head. *They didn't even make an effort to safeguard against infection.*

Gently, she released him and stood.

I'm amazed he can stand at all.

"Why did they do this?" she asked.

"I tried to escape."

She nodded. An attempt at freedom explained why they would risk damaging him so close to the auction. "And your ear?"

"It happened during my capture," he said. "Sara kicked me last night and reinjured it."

"And they didn't send anyone to tend to you?"

"There was someone, but she didn't do much." He sounded bitter and she didn't blame him.

"Are you okay otherwise?"

"Why do you care?"

"I don't necessarily, but I know someone who does."

He obviously wanted to ask who would be interested in how

he felt, but he didn't. Instead, he responded curtly to her previous inquiry. "I'm fine."

"Good," she said. "Now, will you tell me your name?"

His brows drew down beneath the blindfold and she saw a muscle twitch in his cheek. A long pause followed and Angel waited, giving him the time he needed. He shivered and his jaw clenched tighter in irritation. Most likely all he wanted right now was to go somewhere less frigid, more quiet, and to be left alone.

"Bret Masters," he finally replied.

Angel smiled and inhaled deeply, feeling lighter as if a weight had been lifted off her chest. "Thank you," she said, far happier than she had a right to be.

His head drew back as if startled.

"I'm sure all these questions are annoying. And, just so you understand, I think what they do here is wrong, and I'm sorry you had to go through it." She wanted to tell him to sit down, to take the weight off his injured feet, but from what Jake had told her about him, she was positive that suggestion in this situation would not be well received.

He frowned in her direction and she almost wished he wasn't blindfolded. Maybe then she could tell how angry or terrified he really was.

She considered telling him about Jake but decided against it. No sense getting his hopes up when they might never see each other again. Until she knew he and Jake could be reunited, passing on the knowledge would be cruel.

"I wish you well, Bret," she told him and scowled with concern when another tremor shook him. "I'll leave you alone now."

He acknowledged her with an impersonal nod and she shrugged, wishing she could do something more for him. Knowing the impossibility of that, she swallowed hard, averted her eyes, and, despite the tightening in her chest, forced herself to walk away.

Angel went back to where Jake waited for her "Well?" he questioned, as she leaned against the same fence post she'd used earlier. "Is it him or not?"

The eagerness of his question and the look of desperation on his beloved face squeezed her heart. "Yes, it's him and he says he's okay, but I have my doubts. He's definitely in need of some first-rate medical attention."

Jake's fists came out of his pockets and he leaned toward her, a frown darkening his brow. "Why? What's wrong? What did they do to him?"

She placed a consoling had on Jake's arm as she gave him a quick rundown of Bret's ailments. "Besides that," she said, "he's pumped so full of the drug I'm surprised he's not on the ground curled into the fetal position." She frowned as her gaze drifted back in Bret's direction.

"Angel," Jake said and she looked up at the huskiness of his voice. "He's my best friend. I…I have to help him."

"How?" Her heart constricted again and her limbs went suddenly shaky.

He avoided her gaze. "I'm almost afraid to bring it up."

"What is it, Jake?" Her heart racing now, she tried to slow her rapid breathing.

"You won't like it."

She narrowed her eyes and the hard thudding of her heart slowed but didn't lessen in potency. She knew what he was doing, dragging it out to elicit her emotions. He knew her too well, and she knew him well enough to know where this was going, but she helplessly followed along. Isn't that where she wanted to go anyway? "I won't like *what*?"

He paused and looked down, shifting his feet, as if deciding whether or not to speak. Apparently making his decision, Jake straightened his shoulders and stood tall. "You won't like that I'm going to ask you to buy him."

"You're right," she huffed, crossing her arms and scowling back at her friend's hopeful expression, "I don't like it."

"You know what he means to me, Angel." Jake's tone, his eyes, his whole demeanor, beseeched her and the desolation in his voice broke Angel's heart.

How could she even consider letting him down?

"He's my brother by choice if not by blood."

She nodded in understanding, but still frowned. Bret was Jake's family, and Jake was hers. She couldn't say no to him after all he'd done for her. Yet, Peggy was also her friend and her continued happiness, not to mention her health and the wellbeing of the rest of the ranch, meant they must have a doctor. Angel wasn't willing to leave anyone's life in question because of her lack of knowledge. She wouldn't risk it again.

Then there were the unmistakable feelings Jake's stories about Bret Masters had awakened inside her.

"What about Peggy, Jake?" Angel asked, shoving the burning need which suddenly churned in her chest into the dark abyss from which it had come and grasped at the only hurdle she could think of. "She needs that doctor. What am I going to tell her when we come back with a breeder instead?"

"Does that mean you'll do it?" he asked, a smile curving his lips.

"I don't know."

"You need someone who understands ranching, too. Someone better than me," Jake said, working a different angle to convince her Bret was worth more to her than she thought.

She opened her mouth to tell him it wasn't necessary. She couldn't let the same thing happen to Bret as had happened to Jake, but he didn't give her a chance.

"And like I told you," Jake hurried on, "Bret grew up on his parents' ranch, helped run the place until they had to sell it. He worked on another one later as a foreman. He taught me everything I know, and he's more knowledgeable than all the rest of us combined. That kind of expertise would have a huge impact on the ranch's production. It might take a couple of years, but he's capable of doing it. He could make our operation more profitable than we ever imagined. We wouldn't have to worry about how to feed everyone or the finances. We'd be set." He paused. "I know the money's an issue, but isn't there anyone who could buy the doctor for you today?" he questioned as if the thought just occurred to him. "Someone who'd share his services until you could pay for him later?"

Brows lowered, suspicious, she tilted her head. "Like who?"

"Well," he said while he looked over the horde of women and rubbed the back of his neck. Then he smiled again. "How about Monica? Doesn't she owe you a favor?"

"More like I owe her," Angel mumbled then raised her voice and her eyes, pinning him with a shrewd glance. "She might do it, but I bet you already knew that."

He shrugged, but seeing the excitement on Jake's face, she reinforced her statement.

"I said "might," Jake. She has to be careful with her money too, even more so than we do. I *will* remind her of that."

"The only way you're going to find out is if you ask," he said in his big brother voice.

"All right, but now you really are going to owe me…big time," she said with a teasing smile. "You do realize that, don't you?"

"Yeah, I know," Jake said returning her grin, but his eyes were grave. "I already owe you my life."

Angel shook her head and opened her mouth to negate that statement, but Jake didn't give her a chance."

"I owe you everything, but if you do this for me, I'll owe you far more than I can ever repay."

A lump settled in the back of her throat and she fought the burn of tears in her eyes. How could he not see that she owed him?

"I haven't done anything yet," she told him. "Give me an hour or so and I'll see what I can do. You want to come with me?"

"Into that crowd?" he asked glancing at the women who

mingled not far from the slaves on display and gave a theatrical shudder of disgust that made her giggle. "Hell no!"

4

JUST OVER AN HOUR LATER, Angel made her way back to meet Jake where he waited for her by the fence line.

"Will she do it?" he asked with an eager smile and then answered his own query. "She will, won't she."

"Yes," Angel replied with a raise of her eyebrows, not surprised that he'd guessed the outcome of her conversation with Monica. "She'll do it, but she told me to tell you, you're lucky she likes you." She smirked and then, taking his arm to head into the hall together, she gave him a rundown of Monica's singular demand. His non-stop grin, lack of questions, and the unusually rapid way her proposal came together with Monica made Angel certain that they had planned the whole thing together. The realization made her feel even more guilty than she already did for Jake's continued stay at her ranch.

A companionable silence dropped between them as they traversed the courtyard. Lost in her thoughts, Jake's abrupt stop wrenched her to an unexpected halt outside the Hall's entrance.

"What?" she asked peering up into his set features. She knew that look.

"I'll stand in the back."

"We've had this discussion, Jake," she said. "I don't care what they think is proper, I want you by my side."

"I'm not worried about them." His tone and the concern in his gaze made her bite her lip and rethink the irritation she felt for the repeated argument she had anticipated.

"Then, what?"

"I don't want anything to interfere with Bret's purchase," he said, reinforcing how important this was to him, not that she needed the reminder. "If I go down to the seats with you, there'll be an argument, yes, but it's more than that."

"How so?"

Jake glanced around at the empty space surrounding them before meeting her gaze with a serious one of his own. "Bret'll be expensive, as you said."

"Yeah, and?"

"I won't be able to hide my feelings about this. If anyone notices my reactions during the process, they'll know why you're bidding on him. Darla, especially, would do her best to keep us apart."

Angel couldn't help a grunt of disgust. "She'll probably do that anyway."

"Yes, but she's not the only one you'll be bidding against."

Angel pressed her lips together and lifted a questioning brow, wordlessly willing him to get on with it.

"Look, I'm aware of how much this is going to cost you. Far more than you intended, I'm sure, and...I know *you*."

She gave him an I-don't-know-what-you're-talking-about stare.

"They piss you off," he told her and smiled into the scowl she bestowed on him. "Don't glare at me, sweetie. They do, and we both know it. I don't want you to go crazy and impoverish the ranch to win a bidding war because they make you angry. And you will, I can see it in those pretty blue eyes of yours. I've seen you do it before." He sighed. "I know you're determined to do this for me, which is why I don't want to make this harder than it's already going to be."

She stared up into his hazel eyes and melted at the affection and fear she read there. Jake loved her, she knew that, but he also loved his friend and was terrified that Bret would suffer just as horribly as Jake had if they didn't save him today.

Jake was right about the rest too. She hated to lose, and she would hate losing this time even worse. Particularly because of what it meant to Jake—who'd been so much more to her than just a confidant over the last three years. And after seeing what they'd done to Bret, she was even more motivated to win.

"All right," she said, once again curling her arm around his, "we'll do it your way, but you can at least escort me inside."

"Thank you." He smiled and patted her hand as he led her into the building without another word.

Once inside the round room with its enormous domed ceiling, she left Jake in the roped-off area in back where several sentries were positioned to guard them and headed into the audience to find a seat. Halfway down the aisle, Angel glanced back at her friend and Jake gave her a reassuring smile.

I'll be fine, that grin said.

She purposely sat alone, not wanting anyone to realize she and Monica would be working together, which some may expect. Her stomach fluttered and her muscle twitched with eager anticipation as she made note of her competition and waited for the repugnant proceedings to begin.

"Welcome, ladies," a female emcee said over the loudspeaker. "We have quite a wide range of offerings for you today. So, without any further delay, we'll get started."

The educated men, like the doctor, were slated for auction right before the breeders, who occupied the last place on the schedule. Hours and two intermissions lay between now and the moment Angel and her friends awaited. She sat through all of them trying not to bite her lip nervously, portraying a level of calm that she didn't feel.

As the time dwindled, she grew more anxious and thoughts

about Bret troubled her. She sympathized with his situation as she did with all the men who ended up in this place, but something else wiggled its way in with those feelings—something that had been living inside her for years. A deep yearning that, now, unexpectedly and unwantedly swelled within and crashed down into her like a tsunami. The enormity of it frightened her.

For years, she had told herself she didn't need a man. Well, she didn't need this man she only knew third-hand either. Despite his attractiveness and her secret feelings about him, she would not allow sentiment to confuse this event and turn it into something more than helping reunite two friends. Shaking her head in self-reproach, she told herself the apprehension twisting in her gut was her fear of disappointing Jake and breathed a little easier.

Monica's acquisition of the doctor went far better than either of them believed it would and Angel wondered why the bidding wasn't fiercer for an experienced physician. Not that she would complain, three thousand was a bargain, but it made her nervous too.

Maybe they're saving their money for one breeder in particular. The thought made her heart pound.

Five minutes after the second and last intermission, another icy finger of anxiety crept up Angel's spine as the mistress of ceremonies walked back onto the stage.

"Well, this is it," the tawny-haired woman said. "The time many of you have been waiting for…"

Angel straightened her spine and shifted in her seat. *Here we go!*

DARLA CAIN LEANED FORWARD in her seat and her heart rate increased. She'd been waiting for this day for two long months. She hadn't been able to get him out of her head ever since the yard inspection where she'd first set eyes on the slave who called himself Bret Masters.

Masters, she thought with a smile. *He will never be a master of anything again.* She crossed her legs as anticipation burned through her body. She couldn't wait to get him back to her training room. Considered this section's foremost expert at training slaves, she was anxious to test her skills on Bret's long, luscious body. To see his arrogant green eyes lower, his proud head bowed in defeat. Prickles of anticipation and excitement danced over her skin.

"Are you making a purchase today, Darla?" one of her many acquaintances inquired, clearly hoping to draw her into conversation, probably attempting to gain greater favor.

Darla's lips thinned with annoyance for the interruption of her thoughts.

"Yes," she said succinctly, her discerning eyes never straying from the first slave sold as he descended from the stage.

"Let me guess…" the other woman chuckled as if she joked with a close friend, which, of course, they weren't. "The tall, black-haired one, with the stunning green eyes and gorgeous body?"

Darla inclined her head, uninterested in any further conversation. She tolerated these women for the sake of the council but didn't engage with them unless it would gain her something. She especially didn't want to be distracted while the breeders were on stage.

"He *is* attractive," the woman said with enthusiasm, and every one of Darla's muscles stiffened at the woman's next words. "I think I'll make a bid for him myself."

Heat flashed through Darla's body and her eyes narrowed to dangerous slits as she turned to the other woman with an icy-calm expression. "He's mine." Her tone brooked no argument.

The woman's gaze went wide with surprise and quickly looked away. Darla exuded confidence and intimidation, knowing the power she held and using it.

The other woman said and slouched in her chair. "Of course."

A soft but urgent murmur broke out around them, but Darla didn't pay any attention. She knew her followers were passing the word. None of the women with her today, or any of the others, would dare go against her.

Lips curling upward, Darla settled back in her seat. Today her dark fantasies about the tall, raven-haired slave would come true. It didn't matter what the silly women bidding now did, she could outbid them all.

Well, most of them anyway.

The smile slipped off her face.

Darla had seen Angel Aldridge in the audience and noted her lack of determined action. Angel had made a couple of cursory bids earlier, but didn't appear to have much interest in the breeders.

Good, Darla thought. If she bided her time and didn't appear too eager, Darla would be taking her prize home tonight.

And he *was* hers. She'd already accepted that, had repeatedly pictured it in her mind until it felt like reality and, now, her plans were about to come to fruition.

She wasn't sure what it was about this slave that had captured her so completely. He was an attractive man, but there was more to her obsession than that. He'd met her gaze, almost challenging her as she examined him weeks ago. No one had done that in a very long time. She loved a challenge, especially when it came to breaking a defiant man to her will. She was good at it, thanks to her long-dead husband. Years ago, he'd taught her about fear and pain, humiliation and submission. He'd changed her, but, eventually, she'd grown stronger.

She frowned at the unwelcome memory, but then her smile returned as she recalled how she'd made him pay for everything he'd forced upon her—all the agony and violation, the unending expectation of total obedience. She'd proven him wrong in the end, just as she would prove to Bret Masters that *she* was his Mistress and belonged to no one else but her.

5

AWAKENED A SHORT TIME AGO and led from his cell once
again, Bret stumbled along at a pace too fast for his fettered
ankles to keep up. Escorted by the same malicious guard who
had directed him earlier, she took him to God-knows-where
and he prayed something would slow her down as she hurried
him forward despite his clumsiness.

After his conversation with the unusual woman out in the
yard, unwanted female attention had once again teemed around
Bret like swarming bees. He'd fought the drug and to stay on
his feet, but twenty minutes later, his legs buckled and he
curled into a cringing heap. On his knees, he barely held in the
keening wail that threatened to burst from his lips. But the
women surrounding him didn't seem to care that he'd
collapsed or that his body visibly shook—their hands still
caressed every part of him they could reach.

To his relief, two guards had finally dragged him back to his
cell a short time later, where the doctor paid him another visit.
The tub of ice water she'd ordered to soak his feet felt like
heaven, but all she gave him for the pain was more aspirin
before leaving him alone. Then, too exhausted and sick with
fear to care what might happen next, he'd fallen into a restless

sleep.

Now, blindfolded again, the callous woman steered him across the courtyard and into a building. From atmosphere, however, he guessed the structure was a large warehouse of some kind. The floor, like the steps they climbed to his current location, was metal, cool and smooth, and although the air was not warm, the cold was not as chilling as standing outside.

More things to be thankful for.

Now, he stood in line again, the drug making him shiver inside and the nausea growing increasingly worse as the minutes dragged by. After his respite from the crowd and his short nap, however, his hold on his courage was less tenuous. The only sounds were those of panicky men breathing, the light clanking of their chains, and a distant murmur Bret couldn't place. The unusual hum grew in volume and a few minutes passed before awareness of voices—talking and laughing somewhere nearby—struck him. Then the chains rattled as the line ahead of him moved and drowned out the sound.

He wished for the umpteenth time they would remove the blindfold. He hated not being able to see or make sense of the odd things he heard. Maybe then, the waves of fear and doubt assailing him might not be as strong.

The sound of the chains dwindled as they came to a halt once more. Then Bret almost jumped out of his skin and, for a split-second, he swore his heart seemed to stop when a woman's voice suddenly blared over a loudspeaker.

"Well, ladies, this is it. The time many of you have been waiting for," the bellowing woman said while Bret gasped for the breath he'd lost. "The next section up for auction is…the breeders!" A deafening cheer filled the air like a crowd of sixty-thousand-strong at one of the old professional sport stadiums rooting on their team to victory, and followed it up with a round of overeager applause.

Bret's mouth went dry and a wave of dizziness struck him. "Oh, God," he moaned quietly. This was what he'd feared from the moment they took him.

A wave of disgust pumped through his veins as the bidding began and increased quickly before the auctioneer shouted, 'Sold for eighteen hundred,' and then a minute later, the chains rattled and the process began again.

Limbs trembling, an insane urge to bolt swept over Bret, but he fought it, struggling to cling to the lucid part of his mind that told him he couldn't see, the chains hindered him, and his feet still ached too much to flee.

Growing weaker and sicker as he stood listening to the auctioneer's banter, his legs shook and his tender feet throbbed painfully.

The guard thrust Bret down a step with an unexpected shove, and he groaned as he landed hard. In a heartbeat, he was rammed against the railing, the bar grinding against his lower back as a hand clamped over his mouth.

"Shut. Up," the woman holding him hissed. "You've caused enough problems." She removed her hand and with a rough tug, jerked him into line. "I won't put up with your crap, and if you fall again, I'll make sure they whip you before you leave. You won't make a fool of me too."

A vulgar response automatically rolled onto his tongue, but telling her what she could do to herself and her threats wouldn't be the wisest thing for him to do, even if the drug allowed him to say it.

Bret remained silent, his stomach twisting and his heart beating faster with every step he took. He could feel sweat soaking into the cloth tied over his eyes and trickling slowly down his chest, but cold enfolded him like a heavy frost.

After what seemed like hours, the stairs finally ended and Bret's guard ushered him forward. He wanted to resist, but the fear and his pride wouldn't let him.

Something soft brushed harmlessly against him, but its unexpectedness sent Bret over the edge. He whirled around, dislodged the guard's hold on his arm, and prepared to confront an aggressive opponent.

"Now," the auctioneer's voice boomed over the loudspeaker in a pleased tone that turned Bret's heated blood to ice and stilled his frantic scuffling, "here's what most of you have been waiting for, and a fine breeder he will make! What shall be the starting bid?"

With a stunned mind and hesitant feet, he stumbled forward as the guard towed him toward the sound of the crowd. She brought him up short and fastened his leash to a bolt in the floor, all while the auctioneer spoke. The guard removed the blindfold from his eyes and, as he blinked in the brilliant light that filled the Auction Hall, he heard a rash of astonished female exclamations.

"Oh my, he's beautiful!"

"Is he as good as he looks?"

"Put your money down and find out."

A brief spattering of laughter echoed around the room.

Bret shifted uncomfortably and bared his teeth in fury, disgust, and embarrassment. He pulled on the chains with an inadvertent yank, wanting to run so badly he could taste it—a bitter, coppery flavor, like blood on his tongue.

Wide-eyed, he took in the crowd of faces leering up at him. He forced himself to look away, to take a deep breath, and tried to relax before he collapsed and embarrassed himself further.

"Twelve hundred," one woman shouted above the others, unwilling to wait for the auctioneer to begin.

"Twelve! My, that's a heavy starting bid, but start with it, we will," the auctioneer said in a happy, greedy tone before she began her banter.

Bret only listened with half an ear as the price multiplied. Instead, he attempted to ignore the sea of faces staring at him by gazing around the glamorous room.

He stood on a stage-like dais with a set of wide stairs running down either side to the audience floor below—both glowed a satiny silver and sparkled under the bright lights. The luminous color repeated itself in the silk curtains that draped the back of the round room. Rows of silver chairs lined the full length of the black and white checkered floor below where Bret stood. Women filled the seats, and they were staring up at him with hungry eyes. His skin tightened and bile burned the back of his throat as those eyes raked over his naked body without so much as a thought about him. It made no difference who won him. He wouldn't stay long, no matter where he ended up.

Yanking at the chains again, Bret looked away and wished in vain that he could cover himself from their avid stares. Instead, he gazed toward the men in the far back. All dressed in black suits and under heavy guard, they waited patiently for their owners. Bret searched the crowd in the rear, not expecting to identify anyone; yet, contemplating the small sea of male faces, he stopped short to stare in disbelief. One individual stood out like a flashing beacon in the dead of night. The face was unclear, but the man he scrutinized possessed the same stature, the same appearance, the same stance. Bret's breath caught in his throat.

It can't be...

"Forty-five hundred," someone cried as if in triumph, but Bret barely heard.

As he stared, the too-familiar man in the back of the room nodded to another person in the crowd. Bret combed through the fervent faces closer to the platform and caught the slightest indication of acknowledgment from a tall woman, her vibrant blonde hair pulled into a high ponytail. Without a glance at Bret, she looked toward yet another woman on the opposite side of the room and lifted a hand to her simple coiffure. The second woman gave an almost indiscernible response before lifting her gaze to him.

Her eyes impressed Bret. They were the brightest, the darkest, the deepest, most heavenly blue he had ever seen. They were an ocean for a man to get lost in, alluring with just enough wariness to spark his need to rise to the challenge.

Slowly, his vision pulled back enough to see her eyes were only the beginning of her beauty. Her sun-kissed skin appeared silky smooth. Her nose was straight, above a luscious mouth with full, pink lips. Her ebony-colored hair framed a fine-boned oval face and hung past her shoulders in a mass of gently curling waves. She wore no makeup, which made her seem a little plain compared to all the flash and glamor around her, but Bret found her appearance wholesome and stunning.

He sucked in a breath and berated himself. *She's just another woman who'll hurt you. Stop hoping for the impossible.*

In the middle of the shouting bids, Blue Eyes stood up, showing a short, curvy figure, which Bret, despite his inner chastising, examined with male appreciation. Lifting her chin in what looked to him like stubborn determination, she addressed the auctioneer in a loud, demanding voice that brought everything to a stumbling halt, "What's wrong with his feet?"

Her unexpected question plunged the room into silence.

The auctioneer glanced at a group of women sitting off to the side and cleared her throat before she answered. "Nothing." Her composure was clearly shaken. "Why do you ask?"

"Because," Blue Eyes retorted while crossing her arms, "there's something wrong with them, and his ear too. Did any of you notice his ear's infected?"

The auctioneer flicked another swift glance toward the same woman to her right. "Well, no," she replied as her gaze refocused on the blue-eyed woman. "How do you know it is?"

Those heavenly blue eyes turned cold and her jaw hardened. "Because I asked him."

So this was the woman he spoke to outside earlier. Bret almost wished he hadn't been blindfolded during that conversation. He would've enjoyed seeing her up close. He also now understood her concerns about his health and chuckled in silent scorn—the stingy bitch wanted to depreciate his value.

Heat flashed over Bret's skin and his body tensed. He lifted his chin and glowered at the audience, his blood pounding rage through his veins. They wanted his body, but they only saw a breeding slave standing naked on a stage, not a man with a heart and a mind. And one of them thought his price was too high? Shaking his head, shame joined the fury that swept through him, momentarily blocking out the fear, as he yanked at his chains again. He was worth a hell of a lot more than forty-five hundred!

"Are we done, or are we still declaring?" the last bidder asked, eyeing him as if she wanted to retract her bid.

He caught her gaze and his lips curled in his nastiest smirk.

"No, we're not," the blue-eyed woman said and broke his menacing glower at the other bidder. He focused on the small woman with the same malice, but his glare didn't appear to bother her. In fact, she didn't even look at him.

"If anyone bothered to ask him about his health," she continued, "you'd have known of his injuries as well, but then I suppose that's too much to hope for."

Bret frowned, confused. She sounded bitter, but he couldn't understand why. She wasn't chained up and forced to stand naked in front of strangers to be sold like an animal.

"And, Darla," she said, twisting her stiff posture toward the same group of women the auctioneer had glanced at, "if your guards talked to these men instead of beating them all the time, they might be a little more responsive, not to mention *obedient*."

The scorn that infused her last word deepened Bret's frown.

"Not this one," a young guard who stood near the stairs leading down to the checkered floor said. "Why do you think he's chained so heavily?"

The auctioneer's glare silenced the chatty guard in an instant. An uncooperative slave would bring a much lower price.

Blue Eyes lifted a pointed eyebrow at the guard's comment and tilted her head. "Because most of the guards here are sadists who enjoy beating the spirit out of men."

"No one forces you to come here to get your slaves," an audience member chided her.

"It's not like I have much choice though, is it?" Blue Eyes shot right back.

"That's some heavy criticism, Angel," the auctioneer said with a slow shake of her head and another quick glance to her right.

Angel... Bret thought, savoring her name in his mind as his eyes scanned over her. The name seemed to fit her outward appearance, but he doubted its implied connotation extended to her heart. *Don't be a fool,* his inner voice rebuked him again. *She's just like all the rest.*

Straightening her shoulders, Angel replied, "I only criticize what needs changing."

The auctioneer bit her lip. Her eyes shifted to Darla, who nodded her head and spun her fingers in a quick get-on-with-it motion.

The auctioneer, rubbing her palms on her black slacks, refocused on Angel and said in a calm voice, "The bid is forty-five hundred. If you wish to make a bid, then make it. If not, please sit down."

"Yes," Angel said, her blue eyes as cold as ice and hard as granite, "I wish to make a bid: Ten thousand, gold."

Several spectators gasped at the size of her offer, while the rest of the room went deathly silent. She met Bret's eyes as stunned whispers filled the air, and he shivered with trepidation as a caustic smile curled her pretty pink lips.

6

GLARING OVER AT DARLA, who sat calmly in her owner's box with her closest allies, Angel sighed and struggled to keep her rigid posture. She wanted to slouch against the back of her chair, sag under the weight on her shoulders, but she couldn't. No matter how drained she felt, or how tired of the games she was, she must appear strong and confident, even if all she wanted was for the auction to end so she could leave this awful place. And she knew Darla Cain. This battle had just hit a crescendo, and Darla wouldn't give up easily.

The room remained almost deathly quiet as long seconds ticked by. No one seemed to breathe as they waited for a response.

Darla nodded, the price increased, and a buzz of whispers filled the room.

"Angel can't afford to bid again. Can she?"

"She's crazy to make an enemy of Darla Cain."

"They're already enemies...can't you see that?"

"Fifteen," Angel shouted with a lift of her chin and, again, the room went silent while Darla's expression hardened and her shoulders bent just a little.

Heat swept over Angel like a billion tiny pinpricks and she

did her best to regulate her breathing, despite her rapid pulse. She pressed her hands flat against her thighs to keep her fingers from balling into anxious fists and her knees from bouncing nervously. Darla wasn't stupid, but she was ruthless and greedy, especially when it came to the men she purchased. Still, she wouldn't put it past the redheaded woman to make another bid just to cause Angel to spend an even more ridiculous sum.

Doing so, however, would gain Darla nothing but scorn. It would make her look weak and desperate, which, being proud of her position and the power she wielded, Darla would never risk in such a public way. At least, that's what Angel hoped.

By the look on her face, Darla had clearly made big plans for Bret and she was furious that Angel was once again interfering in her schemes. She could only imagine the dark fantasies the cruel woman had built up over the weeks Bret had been imprisoned here. Angel only hoped he hadn't been forced to submit to them before now.

Angel held her breath as the challenge hung in the air, hoping, praying, there would be no counter-offer. Fifteen thousand was an unheard-of amount for any slave, but Angel was determined the other woman would not take Jake's best friend.

Several agonizingly long heartbeats later, Angel sighed as Darla reluctantly shook her head. A huge burst of relief loosened the bands of tension around Angel's chest and her mouth curled into a glowing grin of triumph. She'd never experienced anything like it. Normally, she was just thankful the whole bidding business was over and she could go home. But this time, she felt joyous, energized, almost weightless. She couldn't stop smiling, unwilling or unable to acknowledge that the warmth spreading through her chest had nothing to do with her victory and everything to do with the man on the stage.

A nasty, calculating smile suddenly brightened Darla's

brooding face and Angel stared in stunned disbelief. *She lost. What does she have to be grinning about?* Frowning, fearful of what Darla's smirk might foretell, Angel shivered.

It doesn't matter, she thought, shaking off the curtain of dread that had closed in around her. *He's safe from her now and Jake will get his friend back.*

And what are you getting? She ignored that sarcastic thought just as she ignored Darla's games and decided to enjoy the moment.

At least Darla didn't force my hand, she thought, and her heart fluttered as she turned toward Jake. *Fifteen thousand, good grief! That's enough for three men like Bret.*

Heading toward the aisle, Angel once again ignored the little voice in her head that whispered, *You would've spent far more than that to save Bret Masters.*

She shuffled through other buyers and nodded to Monica as she made her way to where Jake awaited her with a strange look on his face. She didn't need to ask what he was thinking; she knew her behavior surprised him. But Jake never asked her for favors, and she would've done almost anything to ensure she did not let him down.

They had treated Jake's friend abominably and it had stoked her fury while tugging at her heart. But she denied any possibility that her actions resulted from her own feelings about the man she'd just saved. *I didn't do it for me,* she thought. *I did it for Jake.* His kindness over the years fueled her desire to protect the friend Jake cared about and guarantee the man's future safety. If that meant paying more than she planned... *Well, to hell with it! I'll worry about it later.*

STANDING IN THE CENTER of the shining silver stage, head down, eyes squeezed shut, and his wrists aching from the tension he placed on the chains that bound him, Bret's heart had sunk with the first "Going."

Then it thudded painfully with horror at the word "Gone."

"Sold" left him mortified. His face tingled with heat, his knees felt weak, and a thickness filled his throat making it hard to swallow.

His freedom was gone. He was now considered property.

His mind screamed with disbelief. Nausea threatened to overcome him.

He was no longer the master of his own life. He was owned...by a blue-eyed Mistress who claimed she didn't approve of the practices they utilized here. Yet, she had happily participated in purchasing him like stud for sale—in making him a slave.

Would she treat him like a man or torture him instead?

Would she demand things from his body he was not willing to give?

Would he ever have any control over his life again?

He doubted it. He doubted all of it.

He hung his head and closed his eyes, trying not to panic. The thought of another person owning him—a Mistress *owning* him—would drive him crazy. He couldn't think about the ramifications, what this event just turned him into.

A sob tickled the back of his throat and he jerked at his chains once more. He knew he couldn't escape, not yet, but his time would come. The thought made him feel a little better but didn't alleviate the pulsing shame that slammed through him.

As a guard led him down the silver stairs to the checker floor below, he lifted his head and tried to find the blue-eyed woman, but she was no longer in her seat. He searched the room, frantic to catch another glimpse of his new Mistress. When he found her, another shot of hope warmed his chest.

His Mistress—Angel—ambled down the aisle toward the rear of the room. She didn't look back, but Bret's jolt of lightheartedness came as she exited through the double doors with her head up and shoulders straight, followed closely by the man Bret had seen earlier. The one who looked exactly like the one man he'd never expected to see again—Jake Nichols.

A New Home

1

January 1

SPRAWLED ON THE FLOOR of the Action Hall's transport van, Bret's stomach rebelled at the vehicle's endless rocking. He groaned and pressed his bound wrists against his belly, fighting the need to unload what little remained of his pitiful breakfast. He lay still with the heavy steel shackles still in place and dressed once again in his old clothes. With no heat in the rear section, his worn-out rags barely kept him warm and his bare feet added to his chill. Yet the nausea and icy cold did nothing to rouse him or help him keep his eyes open for more than a few seconds.

Where the hell am I now?

After they sold him to his blue-eyed Mistress the day before, they took him to an area behind the stage where Darla Cain had appeared to demand his loyalty and his vow to be her spy. Bret didn't want to tie himself to Darla nor aid in her plans—whatever they may be—and when he refused, she'd ordered her guards to beat him. One of her employees eventually shouted the words, "lose everything to Aldridge," which had a sobering effect on Darla, and his beating abruptly ceased.

Now, once again dosed with fear and riding a tidal wave of illness caused by the drugs, he was on his way to God-knows-where, but all he cared about was reaching their destination soon so he could exit the swaying conveyance and throw up.

He surveyed the dim compartment and the other men who sat on benches along either side of the cargo area brief glimpses. None of them were interested in him or his plight, and not one appeared to be as sick as he felt. They looked awake and alert, unhappy but not ill.

At least we're all miserable, he thought with grim satisfaction and squeezed his eyes closed once more.

They had traveled for several hours, making frequent stops. A woman's muffled voice shouted above the motor and they slowed to make another.

The roiling in his belly had grown worse, sweat rolled off him, drenching his clothes and chilling him further.

The van inched forward, and his mind drifted as inane thoughts of how strange it was to be in a motorized vehicle struck him. When was the last time?

The vehicle came to another stomach-lurching stop and jerked Bret back to the present. The cab doors opened and banged shut. A moment later, the bright, early afternoon light flooded into the hold. Bret averted his eyes from the sudden blinding brilliance, groaning as the throbbing in his head increased. Unsympathetic to his pain, the guards grabbed each of his arms and dragged him through the opening. They dropped him on the wet, ice-cold ground, and slammed the rear doors. Loud footsteps crunched over something as they walked away, but another voice halted their retreat.

"Stop right there! You don't just drive in here, dump him in the snow, and drive off without a word."

One guard said something about making other deliveries as another set of crunching footsteps brought a third person cringingly close to Bret's side.

Snow... That's why I'm so cold. The chill provided relief for his bruised and swollen face but caused his violent tremors to increase.

He groaned again as someone rolled him onto his back.

"Oh, God," the unknown woman whispered, so close that he jumped and tried to move away. A gentle hand on his shoulder kept him in place.

"What happened to him?" Her voice was louder and sounded strained. A hand brushed his face, dislodging the snow stuck to his cheek and forehead. Though everything about the touch was tender and unthreatening, he recoiled from it. Again, mild pressure kept him still.

"Sara got ahold of him," the driver said. "She wanted some revenge for losing her position."

Bret wanted to correct her lie, even opened his mouth to tell the newcomer that Darla Cain had done the damage, but his throat tightened and nothing came out.

"Well, you can tell Darla her negligence will cost her half," the unknown woman beside him said in such a hard voice that Bret's stomach roiled and his fear amped up again.

"Miss Cain sends her regrets," the guard replied, "but says she'll deduct no more than three thousand."

"I don't care what kind of phony regrets she sends. She won't receive a penny over seven and she'll take it, or she'll be paying me a lot more."

"Of course," the guard said almost as if she had expected the threat. "I'll give her the message. The refund will be returned to you tomorrow. Will there be anything else?"

"The key for his chains?"

Bret heard shuffling sounds and then one of the guards stepped forward, he assumed to hand over the key, though the movement made him cringe.

"You may go now," the new woman said sharply, dismissing the driver and her partner.

The guards got back into the van and drove away.

Bret's condition had improved with the fresh air, but he still felt vile and continued to shiver uncontrollably. Someone lifted his head into their lap and his heart fluttered, but he didn't pull away. The same person reached over him and her clothing tickled his face. It held a faint scent that reminded him of spring and flowers—*Lilacs? In the snow?*—but his stomach was in no condition to appreciate it. He groaned a third time, wriggling away from the warm, fragrant softness, and fought to keep from embarrassing himself.

The front of his long coat pulled away from his chest and a woman's shocked inhalation sent ripples of terror up and down his spine. He froze, and his gut clenched once more, expecting the worst.

"Oh, my…" she said in a hushed voice as she touched the ugly slash that ran across his chest. He flinched and her fingers instantly retracted. "Can you hear me?" Her voice was heavy with concern as her hands cradled his achy jaw.

He wanted to open his eyes, but it was too bright.

"It wasn't Sara," he mumbled. "It was—"

"I know," she interrupted. "Don't worry about that right now. Are you all right?"

"I'm sick," he muttered, scarcely understandable. "They gave me something…to make me…sleep and be…afraid."

"Do you know what they gave you?"

"No," he groaned. The pounding in his head felt like someone was beating on his skull with a hammer. "I'm going to be sick."

"Try to hold on," she murmured as her hand brushed his cheek. "I want to get these chains off you."

She quickly removed the shackles and threw them aside.

"Someone get rid of those," she said with disdain as she pulled one of his arms over her shoulders. "Help me get him into the bathroom." Another person, a man, took Bret's other arm and together they carried him into a large, white house he only glimpsed before they rushed him inside.

Minutes later, Bret vomited until there was nothing left to

expel. Even then, his body continued to convulse until he felt too weak to remain on his knees.

Now, slumped on the floor with his forehead resting on the cool surface of the toilet, he reveled in the relief the porcelain awarded his throbbing head. Waiting for the nausea to dissipate, he held his forehead against the ceramic bowl and tried to breathe evenly. When the woman came into the room, he rolled his cheek along the rim to squint up at her.

"Are you all right?" she asked, gently placing her hand gently on his shoulder.

"Maybe...will be...after...a while," he said as his heavy eyelids drooped and unconsciousness threatened. "I'm so...damn...sleepy. Can't—keep—eyes—open..."

"Bret?" He didn't answer. "Jake," she said over her shoulder, "he's passed out. Come help me move him."

2

"HE'S STILL STAYING WITH ME, RIGHT?" Jake asked as they hauled Bret's heavy, unconscious body up from the floor.

"You're the one who wanted him here," Angel said with more bite than she'd intended. She wasn't thrilled with the situation, but she'd already admitted letting Darla Cain have Bret was not an option.

"Good," Jake said as they half-carried, half-dragged Bret out of the bathroom and into Jake's apartment a few yards away. Once there and Jake had undressed him, Angel examined the damage done to his body.

Angel winced at the pain he must've gone through. Fresh bruises and lacerations covered him from head to knees, overlaying others that looked days old. His assailants had been vicious, but also careful. She suspected he'd suffered a minor concussion from blows to his head, but the swelling and discoloration on his face, though grievous to look at, were superficial. His ribs weren't as lucky. After running her hands over his torso, she surmised at least two were fractured, but surprisingly, considering the amount of battered flesh, she found no other broken bones.

She gently touched the torn flesh on his chest and her heart twisted when he groaned in complaint. *How could they do this to another person?*

She sent Jake to get some warm water and towels while she finished her examination.

Too distracted the day before, she'd failed to notice the smattering of other injuries now evident under the newer ones. This type of mistreatment at the Auction Hall was not unusual, but Bret's condition was far worse than commonly seen after sale. Cringing at the dark splotches of blood pooling under his skin and the thin slashes caused by a barbed whip, her eyes welled up and her breath stuttered through a constricted throat.

You're lucky, she thought as sadness and anger tightened her chest. *I've seen a lot worse.*

Sitting on the bed beside her patient, her eyes drifted over his tall form, noticing—despite his ailments—how swarthy his skin looked compared to the white sheets. She took in the broad shoulders and wide chest, his muscle-ridged belly and trim waist. His narrow hips were hidden by the sheets pooled below his navel, and his long, powerful-looking legs stretched restlessly beneath the bedclothes. She could easily fathom what other women would appreciate in him. He was far too thin, but aside from that, and even with his face bruised and swollen, he was an attractive man.

☐Recoiling from the thought, she swallowed hard and closed her eyes. She opened her eyes and her gaze slid over the contours of his long body.

Stop it! Stop staring at him, stop thinking about him... Too much danger lay in allowing herself to be attracted to anyone, let alone a man in her care. Yet she'd already let Jake's stories and her own imaginings give this man—this stranger—too much meaning to her shattered heart. Now that Bret was here, she could no longer allow herself to ponder the fantasies she had once conceived just to escape the pain of her miserable reality.

She shivered and cold crashed over her in a sudden deluge

as the memory of another horribly injured man obliterated everything else. Her heart sped up, pounding hard against her breastbone. She pressed her fingers into the sharp ache and looked away from Bret, her lids sliding closed again. Her shoulders curled inward as she massaged the painful throbbing in her chest, knowing it would never truly leave. Inhaling a shuddering breath, she tipped her head back and stared at the ceiling, struggling to dissolve the disturbing recollection.

There was so much blood...

More tears stung her eyes, hear head ached, and she trembled almost as much as the man who lay inches from her side.

I can't go there, she thought, and her eyes drifted back to the battered man beside her. *I can't go there anymore either...*

When Jake reentered the apartment, Angel still sat at Bret's side, staring down at him and gripping his forearm. With his entry, she self-consciously jerked her hand away from Bret and lunged to her feet. She rubbed her damp palms along her thighs and stared back at her friend's curious expression. His eyes shifted to Bret and he shook his head.

"Even beat up and passed out..." Jake mumbled and smiled.

"What?" she asked, unsure if she had heard him correctly.

"Nothing," Jake said, giving her a fond smile. "I just didn't think you'd succumb so quickly." He set the towel beside the bowl on the nightstand.

She sucked in an unsteady breath as her fingers brushed her neck and her head snapped up. She blinked at the sudden burn in her eyes and Jake's teasing grin instantly disappeared.

"You okay?" he asked, placing his hand on her shoulder. "You look upset. I didn't mean anything..."

She shook her head gloomily. "I know. It's not you. I'm just...sad," she said as she picked up the washcloth he'd brought in and dunked it into the warm water. "It'll pass."

Jake frowned but let it go.

"How about him?" He nodded toward Bret, his crestfallen

look revealing the level of shock he suffered over the thrashing his friend had taken.

"Given a little time I think he'll be fine." She gave Jake a quick rundown of what she'd learned during her examination and what she suspected. "The drug is still in his system, so he'll be sick until that's gone. The rest will take time."

"Are you going to confront Darla?"

Angel snorted and tilted her head. "How much good do you think that will do?" She smiled to lessen the sting of her words. "No," she said softly as she glanced at Bret again. "I've demanded a discount, but the rest isn't worth it. I'd never be able to prove Darla was responsible for hurting him, so a confrontation would be a waste of time. Besides, he should recover, and if he's as knowledgeable about ranching as you claim..." She raised an eyebrow.

"He is," Jake said with a nod.

"Then he'll have a place here. Just like you."

Jake smiled.

Angel turned away and, using the damp towel in her hand, began to wipe the blood from Bret's chest.

"Is there anything I can do?" Jake asked.

"Grab a towel and help me clean him up."

A little later in the kitchen, they emptied the water bowl and tossed the bloodstained towels into the laundry before heading out again.

"He's going to need more medical attention," Angel said as they left the room together. "I hate to wake him though. The rest will do more for him now than I can, and it'll probably be the best he's had in weeks."

"I'll take care of him."

"I know you will," Angel said, patting his arm. "And when he's stronger, you'll teach him what he needs to understand about living here. Just make sure he stays out of trouble. I don't want a repeat of Toby."

"Will do, but Bret's not like that in any case."

"I hope so." Angel sounded tired as she stared at the floor, her hands pressing against her stomach. "I'm going to have enough difficulty explaining to Peggy that the doctor's going to be living with Monica for the time being."

"You haven't told her yet?"

"No," she said, shaking her head, her eyes glued to the floor. "I knew the agreement would cause her to worry, so I kept putting it off. I can't put it off any longer."

"Do you want me to come along?"

She met his concerned gaze and saw the guilt he felt for the situation painted plainly on his face. She gave him a wan smile. "No," she said, once again patting his arm consolingly. "There's nothing you can say. It was my decision. I'll just have to convince her there was no other way to help you both."

Angel turned to leave, but Jake stopped her with a hand on her arm.

She turned her head and lifted her brows.

"Thank you, Angel," he said after a slight pause. "I know how much this cost you, and the possible ramifications for Peggy, but..." He sighed, shifted his feet, and shrugged. "I can't say I'm sorry I asked. This means a lot to me."

Compassion clogged her throat and she threw her arms around him. "You're more than welcome, Jake," she said as he returned her embrace. "I'd do anything for you." She pushed back, tilted her head, and gave him a teasing smile. "Don't worry so much."

3

TREPIDATION CHURNED IN THE PIT of her stomach as Angel crossed the snow-covered lawn of her dooryard headed toward the row of small townhomes where Peggy and Theo lived. She rubbed her arms in deference to the chill and reminded herself—yet again—that her motives at the auction were right and good. Still, a part of her wondered if, maybe somewhere deep inside, she'd made the decision to help Bret Masters for purely selfish reasons.

"No, no, no...!" Peggy's cries of pain and fear from three years before echoed in Angel's mind once more. "I can't lose him. I can't, Angel. Don't let me lose my baby!"

Angel saw the blood soaking through the bedsheets as she did everything she could to stop the flow. The scene reminded her of another horrible sight that froze Angel in place and struck terror through her soul. Horror had gripped her heart at the realization that she might fail Peggy too. That her friend might die because Angel thought she could actually take the place of a real doctor.

The panicked drive to the hospital in town had seemed interminably long that day, but they'd managed to get there just in time. Theo had been a pale-faced wreck, his heartache and fear for his partner plain on his suntanned face as he held Peggy close in the pickup's rear seat.

"She's going to be okay," Angel had told him, hoping to reassure him—and praying she was right.

He glanced at her bloodstained hands and then lifted red-rimmed blue eyes to hers. "I can't go through this again," he'd said in a pained whisper. "She's my life..."

Angel swallowed hard and nodded. There was nothing else to say.

The doctor in town had been able to stop the bleeding and, physically, Peggy recovered, but her resolve hadn't changed. She was afraid, but she wanted to try again. Angel had promised to help, but now the situation had changed.

The news about the delay in obtaining the doctor would be a blow to Peggy's fragile confidence—not to mention causing her serious anxiety that the doctor wouldn't be on-hand for during the early part of her planned pregnancy. Angel was certain, however, that she could convince her friend it would all work out, but she expected Peggy's initial reaction to be anger and panic, neither of which would be good for her.

Nothing I can do to change it now, Angel thought as she reached Peggy's front door. *The deal's done.*

After Angel's soft knock, the door swung open and Peggy gave her a pleasant grin. "Hi, Angel." Her dark chocolate-colored eyes twinkled with excitement as Peggy waved her inside. "Come in, come in. Did everything go all right?"

Angel cringed but plastered a smile on her face as she eased onto the couch in the small living room.

Revealing what had happened at the auction the day before went just as Angel had predicted. Running the gauntlet from disbelief to disappointment, Peggy rapidly turned spitfire mad.

"You bought a breeder?" she screeched and jumped to her feet in a sudden rush, her straight brown hair seeming to bristle like an angry cat's tail. "How could you do this to me, Angel? You said you'd take care of things. I trusted you!"

Her last poignant declaration struck Angel straight in the heart as Peggy plopped back into her seat with a quiet sob.

"I made an arrangement with Monica," Angel said and filled Peggy in on the rest of the story.

With her eyes on the floor, Peggy's hand unconsciously reached up to twist a lock of her dark hair. "What's the catch?" She looked up with a frown wrinkling her brow.

"What do you mean?"

Peggy rolled her eyes. "I mean, there has to be some sort of catch. Monica isn't stupid. She wouldn't spend money on a doctor she couldn't really afford without a good reason. And the fact that she's your friend isn't enough—that luxury is beyond her wealth."

"She wants Jake," Angel said bluntly.

"To live with her?"

"Yes."

Peggy straightened. "And you agreed to that?"

"Yes."

"Permanently?" Her voice rose in disbelief.

"That's up to Jake, but I'm sure that's what he wants."

Peggy tilted her head, confused. "Why? I thought…"

Angel smiled. So many people made the same mistake.

"No, Peg." Folding her hands on her knees, Angel leaned forward, gauging her words—not everyone knew the particulars surrounding Jake's tenure with them. "Jake and I are just friends…close friends, but that's all. He and Monica have always had a connection."

"But he does so much around here, and you…depend on him…a lot…sometimes…"

Angel heard the implication in her friend's keen observation and felt the heat of shame and embarrassment flash through her. At times her weakness left Jake no other option but to take care of things. It was also the reason he felt responsible for her.

"I know I rely on him," Angel said, plucking at the sleeve of her lightweight jacket. "I need to stop doing that so much." She took a deep breath and met her friend's gaze. "If the situation was reversed, he'd do the same for me."

"When will he leave?"

"When the doctor comes to live here."

☐Familiar with the regulations of buying and trading slaves, Peggy nodded. Jake moving to Monica's without some gold and the trade of the doctor would send up red flags Darla and her ilk would attack as quickly as anything else that might give Angel or her friends additional leverage.

Eventually, their conversation turned into a discussion about the future and Peggy beamed with excitement for the possibilities. Envy tugged at Angel's insides and the muscles of her neck and shoulders bunched as the shattered pieces of her heart twinged with the regret she could never escape.

A harsh knock at the door interrupted them. Jake stood on the threshold rubbing at the back of his neck when Peggy answered it. His arm instantly dropped and his eyes darted behind Peggy.

Recognizing his troubled expression, Angel jumped to her feet and hurried over. "What's wrong, Jake?"

"Bret's sick and I don't know what to do."

* * *

"What are his symptoms," Angel asked as they hurried up her front porch steps.

"He's in and out of consciousness, yelling, muttering, tossing and turning, and violently trembling."

"How long has he been like that?"

"Since shortly after you left."

They entered Jake's apartment through the outside door. A decent-sized room, it housed two beds, a large, six-drawer chest-of-drawers, a small desk, a wood stove, a closet, and a connecting bathroom. A picture of his parents—both of whom died before the wars—sat in a handmade frame on a small bedside table. On one white-painted wall, a matching set of compound bows hung, loaded with hard-to-get aluminum arrows. Angel glanced at those as she crossed the room. Jake was proficient with them and, over the years, had taught her how to use them, too. During those lessons, he had also told Angel about the hunting trips him, his father, and Bret used to go on.

Jake shut the door as Angel jerked her eyes from the bows and her mind from Jake's tales, and she crossed to the bed.

Her heart twisted the minute she saw Bret's restless form. He looked awful. Under his naturally bronzed complexion, he was paler than before and sweat drenched his face, hair, and neck. He mumbled repeatedly, but she couldn't make out the words.

"The last time he opened his eyes," Jake said, coming up behind Angel as she laid a hand on Bret's fevered brow, "he threw up and complained about a headache. When I checked, his head was hot. That's when I came for you."

"He's still hot," she muttered, the ache in her chest intensifying. Removing her hand, she turned to Jake. "Sounds like they gave him too many drugs."

It wouldn't be the first time she'd seen that. But, aside from running a blood test to determine if her diagnosis was correct—which they were ill-equipped to do—there was no other way to narrow it down. The small hospital in town had some medical gear and could perform a simple blood sample analysis, but Angel didn't want to move Bret if they didn't have to. Transporting him, even in the old gas-powered truck Angel kept in a lean-to behind one of the barns, would cause him a lot of discomfort she'd rather avoid if possible.

Angel pulled back the covers and rested her ear against his damp chest. His heart and breath rate were far too high and, even though he was sweating and burning up, his entire body trembled as if freezing cold. All were side effects of too much of the fear drug. Combining that with the sedative he said they'd given him, caused his shaking and flu-like symptoms.

"He'll have to ride it through," she said as she replaced the blanket.

"Isn't there something you can give him?" Naked fear for his friend showed plainly on Jake's strong face. "He seems to be in pain."

"Unfortunately, no. Anything I give him now would only make the effects of the other drugs worse. He's been on them for a while and you know how they work."

Jake nodded knowingly. The longer a person was on the drug, the longer its affects would take to dissipate.

"I don't think he'll have any lasting effects, but we'll have to wait for his body to expel them before I risk giving him anything else. It could be a few days, but he should be calmer by morning." A pang of doubt made her bite her lip. "If not," she said, "we'll take him in."

"What can I do now?" Jake asked as he stared down at Bret's restive form, stark lines of worry etched on his bearded face.

"Make sure he drinks a lot of water. He's going to throw up a lot more before he's done, but the water will help rid him of the drug and keep him from getting too dehydrated. Cool him off, if he'll allow it…there's plenty of snow outside for that. It'll hurt but do what you can. Once his fever breaks, be sure to keep him warm until his chills stop. When they do, and he's calmer, let me know and I'll check on him again. Maybe then we can treat his other wounds more aggressively. For now, though," she said as she went to the door, "that's all I can do for him."

"Are you sure?"

"As sure as I can be," she answered, though her uncertainties about her healing skills pecked at her confidence. Still, Bret was not the first man she'd treated for this exact ailment. "I know it seems bad, Jake," her tone was gentle, "but he'll get better. Just give it a little time."

4

January 3

BRET MASTERS BLINKED at the bright afternoon sunlight that streamed in through the lone window across the unfamiliar room. He turned away from the brilliance and groaned. His whole body ached, his mouth was dry, and he felt as weak as a day-old kitten. Thankfully, his stomach, though still a little woozy, had lost most of its recent nauseous tendencies. Unfortunately, that didn't help the God-awful pounding in his head.

Quiet movement beside the bed drew his attention and he peered through slit lids while an anxious shiver danced over his skin.

His vision was a little blurry at first, but once it cleared, he focused on a man, who, oddly—and a bit unnervingly—looked an awful lot like Jake Nichols.

The Jake-look-alike gazed down at him from beside the bed and gave Bret a lopsided grin. The apparition—*this must be a hallucination...Jake's long gone*—hovered over him like a mother over her sick child; looking as if he hadn't slept in days. *Just like Jake would. Am I dreaming? This seems so...real...*

"Hey, brother."

He sounds like Nichols too.

"Jake?"

"Yeah, it's me," his old friend said with a chuckle Bret remembered fondly.

Bret's throat suddenly felt thick and he blinked, his eyes burning, utterly stunned to be looking up at his long-lost friend. *I never thought I'd see him again.*

Still smiling, Jake turned to say something to a man behind him, but Bret was too shocked to hear what he said.

Jake's here? His mind whirled as he stared in wide-eyed wonder. *Either I've gone crazy or this is one hell of a coincidence.*

"How're you feeling?" Jake asked when he returned his attention to Bret.

"Terrible," Bret said in a croaky voice. Trying to sit up, he groaned at the tenderness of his aching ribs and fell back onto the pillow again, his arm pressed to his side. The fingers of his other hand came up to rub his forehead as if massaging it would ease the throbbing and somehow stop the spinning inside.

Then his memory came back to him in a rush.

They sold me...as a slave.

Dread and anger pulsed through him and he forced himself into a sitting position. Swaying slightly, Bret pressed the heel of his hand to his forehead and groaned as dizziness assailed him.

"Whoa there, Bret." Jake placed a steadying hand on his shoulder. "Just relax. You need to rest for a few more days."

"No, I don't," Bret said as his eyes quickly surveyed the unknown room, looking for the guards who must be close by, waiting to chain him again. "I need to get out of here."

"You can't."

"The hell I can't," Bret said. "Watch me." He slowly tried to rise, gritting his teeth to keep from groaning again. After two tries, and waving off Jake's objections, Bret swung his legs over the side and pushed away the blankets. He stared down at himself, stupefied to find that all he wore was a pair of navy-blue boxer-briefs. His eyes narrowed as he looked up at his friend. "Where are my clothes?"

Jake only gave him a wouldn't-you-like-to-know glare.

Bret glared right back. He was familiar enough with that look. Jake would not help.

Ignoring his friend's deepening scowl, Bret struggled onto his sore feet and felt the scabbed-over skin split with the pressure. He stifled a hiss and pulled the comforter from the bed, disregarding the small stabs of discomfort shooting up from his feet—and the stronger ones in his side. He wrapped the coverlet around his shoulders and holding it together in front of his chest with one hand, he made his way to the door.

"Where are you going?" Jake sounded harassed.

Bret smiled to himself. The old Jake often sounded that way when he was annoyed…or worried. "Out."

"Like that?"

Bret heard the humor in Jake's voice and glanced over his shoulder, a black brow arched mockingly. "Give me some clothes and I'll be happy to be more appropriately dressed." Without waiting for the reply he knew he wouldn't like, Bret shuffled toward the closest exit.

"Bret, wait," Jake called, chuckling softly. "That door doesn't lead outside."

Bret ignored him, concentrating on reaching the doorway without falling. His head pained him, almost as much as his ribs did, and dizziness made him even more unsteady, but he kept going. He put out a hand to lean against the frame. Panting with exertion, he rubbed the back of his neck with the other hand, trying to catch his breath. The heavy blanket on his shoulders shifted and slithered to the floor while he stood swaying. Not about to reclaim it with his head swimming like it was, he let it go. When the spinning eased, he straightened, intending to continue through the door. When he raised his head, however, the cerulean eyes that had haunted his disturbing dreams stared back at him.

"What're you doing?" she asked, her brows pinched over her small nose. Without waiting for an answer, she drew him back into the room. "You should be in bed."

He stared at her as she ushered him the few steps back into the room and gently yet firmly pushed him down onto the mattress. "You need to stay in this bed for a few more days before you go running around."

Overcoming his surprise at her sudden appearance, Bret frowned and his shoulders tensed. "Who the hell are you?"

"My name's Angel," she said as she picked up the comforter he'd dropped on the floor. "I own this place."

"Ah," Bret nodded, then tilted his head and dusted off his nastiest tone. "So you're the one who thinks she paid money to own me."

"I did." She threw the thick comforter over the bed, apparently taking no heed of his hostility.

"Nobody owns me," he said defiantly.

"I never said I did. Nor do I believe I do," she said, sounding amused as Jake lifted Bret's ankles and maneuvered his legs onto the bed.

Bret stared at her, mute and rebellious.

"You really shouldn't be up yet," she said as she pressed him back onto the mattress and pulled the blankets over his chest.

"I tried to tell him that," Jake put in, and Bret scowled at him for his trouble.

"Well, make sure he stays in it for at least three more days and continue with the liquids." She headed back toward the door. "You can give him a little solid food if he wants some." She pinned Bret with a pointed look.

He narrowed his eyes and remained speechless. Annoyingly, his insolent behavior had no effect.

She shrugged. "If he can keep it down, he can have whatever he likes."

The prospect of decent food made his mutinous stomach growl. Heat suffused his neck and he immediately schooled his eager expression into an arrogant mask of disdain, his insolent act spoiled only by his fingers massaging his temple.

"He does seem to be feeling better," she mused, and to Bret, she add, "You should be on your feet in a few days. And don't worry about your headache, it's a side effect of the drugs. It'll go away after a while. Until then, you're going to need all the rest you can get. I can get you some aspirin if you'd like."

Bret frowned at her and closed his eyes, still rubbing the side of his head.

"Suit yourself." He could almost hear her shrug before she said goodbye to Jake and left the room.

"Who's she?" Bret asked and, irritated with himself, his frown deepened. *And how the hell did she maneuver me back into bed like that?*

"That's Angel. She owns this place. Runs it, too," Jake said distractedly as he began to cleaned up the small room. "She bought you at the auction, but you already knew that."

"What do you mean, 'bought me'?"

Jake's lips thinned at Bret's dangerous tone but gave his friend a flat look before he sat down on his own bed across the room. "I asked her to buy you." He tilted his head. "Think of it as gaining your freedom."

"Freedom?" Bret shouted, jerking upright. A heartbeat later, he thought better of it and stayed where he was, glaring at the older man while holding his side and rubbing his temple. "Are you crazy?" His tone lost some of its volume and its bite.

"You'll understand once you've been here a while," Jake said. "Besides, it's not her fault. I asked her for a favor."

"What favor?"

"To buy you. I asked her to buy your freedom as a favor to me."

"What do you mean for you?"

Jake swiftly detailed the circumstances behind Bret's purchase. "I didn't want you to suffer through the same kind of experiences I did."

Bret heard the forlorn note in Jake's voice, but the wary look on his face said he wouldn't explain any further.

"Why would she do that?" Bret asked, unwilling to believe a woman would be so generous to any man. "She must have some other motive."

"No, she doesn't," Jake said. "She did it because I asked her to."

"Yeah, right," Bret scoffed and rolled his eyes. "She's a woman, Jake, and no woman is going to do a man a favor for any reason."

"She's not the same as the ones we've met before," Jake said, rising and coming to stand beside Bret's bed, "especially not like those at the Auction Hall. She's…different."

"Different?" Bret's black brows climbed toward his hairline and then snapped back down like a broken rubber band. "Sure, she's different; she's just more subtle with her brainwashing. I see she's got you twisted around her finger." Palpable disgust tainted his voice. "Nothing could make me live like that. You used to feel the same way. What happened to you, Jake?"

A muscle twitched in Jake's cheek and the tension in the room seemed thicker than split pea soup. "Evidently, a hell of a lot more than what happened to you."

"I've dealt with my share of bullshit," Bret said bitterly. He took a deep breath and sat up, intending to stand, but Jake pushed him against the mattress and held him down. As he did, Bret caught a glint of something so dark and granite-hard in Jake's eyes that he wondered if his friend actually hated him.

He certainly has every right to…

"You have," Jake replied to Bret's comment, his voice rough with suppressed emotion. "But right now, if you don't stay in that bed, I'm going to tie you to it. I don't care what kind of chip you have on your shoulder. You may not think much of me anymore, but I can still handle you, injured or not."

Taken aback by Jake's heated outburst, Bret wondered what nerve he'd struck. "Okay, okay," he forced a laugh and threw his hands up in a placating gesture, hoping to tease a smile back onto his friend's face, "I'll stay. Just don't hurt me."

"Shut up, you little shit," Jake said with a strained chuckle. He straightened and the tension in the room eased slightly.

"You're wrong, Bret," Jake said, breaking the awkward silence.

"About what?"

"About Angel. She's different. She doesn't use the controlling tactics the others do—no drugs, whips, torture, or anything else. She treats us like people and there are more just like her."

A curious grin pulled at his lips and Bret once again wondered what his friend wasn't saying.

"Believe it or not," Jake said with a short chuckle, "there are a few decent women left in the world."

Bret sighed and dropped his eyes to the dark green comforter that covered his legs. He didn't want to talk about this right now, and he definitely didn't want to argue with Jake. Five long years had passed since he'd last seen his best friend and the guilt over what had happened still weighed heavily on his heart. He owed Jake a lot—he had for most of his life—and he wanted to spend this second chance getting to know him again, not fighting.

And, maybe, find a way to make up for his mistakes too.

"Sure, Jake, whatever you say," Bret said tiredly, lifting his gaze once more. "But right now, what I really want to hear about is food."

A corner of Jake's mouth quirked up. "Hungry?"

"Yeah."

"I'll get you something from the kitchen. Sandwich sound

alright?"

Bret's stomach growled and he chuckled self-consciously. "Sounds great."

"I'll be right back." Jake opened the entry door but turned with a final warning. "I better not catch you up when I get back."

"Yes, Mom," Bret joked with a grin.

"You haven't changed much have you?" Jake sounded almost pleased by that.

Bret's lips curved up roguishly and Jake laughed, shaking his head in grudging tolerance.

"Just go, will you?" Bret said. "I'm starving."

"Sure thing," Jake replied and closed the door behind him.

5

January 4

BRET HAD SPENT most of the previous day and this morning sleeping, he still felt the need for more rest weighing down his body. But after missing dinner last night, the hunger that now gnawed at his insides kept him awake. Propped up in bed, waiting for Jake to return with his breakfast, Bret stared at the patch of sunlit blue sky through the window across the room as his mind wandered through the sorrows of his past.

It had been more than thirty years since his father Anthony had been killed in the accident that had left Bret and his mother devastated and their ranch in dire straits.

As Bret had been told, Anthony was hurrying home through a raging storm when he'd lost control of his truck and crashed over an embankment. The vehicle rolled several times into a ravine and thrown from the cab, Anthony had been crushed and died instantly.

Bret's chest tightened when he remembered the sheriff's officers who had shown up at their door with the news. That had been hard enough, but the sadness and torment that followed only grew worse as the months passed.

His life turned graver living with his uncle. Not a day went by that Vince didn't find a reason to berate and beat him. In fact, being locked away at the Auction Hall hadn't been all that different from living with his uncle—except with chains and a lot of unwanted female attention.

"What did I tell you about touching things that don't belong to you?" his uncle had bellowed more than once, always blaming Bret for anything that was missing or misplaced. "Where is it?" he'd demanded, often slurring his words. "Where did you hide it?

It didn't matter what the item was or whether Bret had any idea of its location or not, he was always at fault. Because Vince often drank himself into a righteous fury, and sometime even when he hadn't, he took out his pent-up aggression on his nephew.

"I'll teach you to steal from me." That declaration—or one very much like it—was usually followed by Vince's fists.

Recalling the colorful array of bruises he'd carried during his early teens and how he'd gotten them, Bret sighed. Being on the receiving end hadn't been bad enough, though. His increasingly anti-social attitude, combined with his tendency to attract trouble from his peers, led to other problems for Bret. Problems that later encouraged assorted rumors about his character that he didn't bother to contradict.

He'd never understood how Vince could be related to his mild-mannered father, but their strikingly similar appearance left no room for doubt.

Hearing footsteps in the hallway, Bret pushed aside his gloomy ruminations and straightened up to adjust his pillows. A moment later, Jake open the door from the kitchen and the smell of sausage, eggs, and bacon wafted into the room.

"Is that really bacon?" Bret asked, not quite believing his nose.

"Yeah," Jake said with a smile as he closed the door and set the serving tray on the desk.

"Do they have pigs here too?" he asked, amazed at the

luxuries they had so far from town.

"Nah," Jake replied as he dished out their fare. "There's a farmer about ten miles from here who raises them. We do some trading throughout the year for the meat."

He brought Bret his meal and then sat at the desk to devour his own breakfast. Pancakes also adorned his plate and the sweet maple syrup was a treat for his tongue, the food, in general, amazing.

They ate in comfortable silence, falling into the companionship they'd always shared once they'd overcome their original animosity more than two decades ago.

He asked for seconds, which Jake provided with a soft laugh. "You're going to be right as rain in no time," he joked.

Bret smiled, his mood dimmed by the memories of his unhappy childhood that had pushed their way back in during their quiet repast.

His uncle's violence didn't stop with Bret. Vince's aggression also favored Bret's mother, though not as often. Ruby rarely carried the bruises or injuries Bret did. Because, just as Bret had tried to protect her and himself from losing their old home—even though he still harbored some animosity toward her for her lack of aid in that endeavor—he did his best to shield his mother from Vince's wrath.

"You owe me," Vince bellowed one day as he grabbed Ruby's arm and jerked her toward him.

"No, I don't," Ruby replied, pulling away from him. "You said you'd changed, that you'd help us, not demand—" She stopped abruptly when she noticed Bret enter the room. Her gray eyes had been sad and frightened and, despite the heartache she'd caused him, that look had been enough to spark Bret's protective instincts.

At fifteen, Bret had been a tall, lanky kid, nowhere near the size he'd grow into, but big for his age. Still, he'd been no match for his uncle.

"What's wrong?" Jake asked, startling Bret from his dark

recollections.

Bret met his friend's concerned eyes, and his stomach tightened at the sharp scrutiny he saw there. He shrugged, unwilling, as always, to discuss the part of his life that had scarred him the most. "Nothing."

"Then why do you look like someone just shot your favorite horse?"

Slanting a piercing look at Jake, he grunted a disbelieving chuckle and looked away. He hadn't intended for his unease to show, but he'd forgotten Jake's ability to read him so well.

Bret kept his head down, averting his face as he squeezed his eyes shut.

In the darkness, he saw his mother fall to the ground, blood oozing from a split lip. He heard her scream for him to stop as he launched himself at Vince. Unbridled hatred had burst inside him like a poison-filled balloon. It had raced through his pulsing veins, turning his vision red with rage as he unleashed an ineffective attack.

"Bret?"

He heard the worry in Jake's voice and pulled a curtain in his mind, temporarily blocking that scene and all the others like it.

"I'm all right," he said, lifting his head, meeting Jake's anxious gaze.

"Are you in pain?" he asked, leaning forward slightly, his eyebrows drawing together.

Bret shrugged. "A little, but not too bad."

"Then what was that?"

He studied Jake for a long, silent heartbeat. Jake had been his best friend for years, the brother he never had. He knew more of Bret's story than anyone, and he'd always had Bret's back. Despite their five-year separation, there was no reason to hide his thoughts.

"My mom and...Vince," he finally admitted.

Jake exhaled a long breath. "About that last fight?"

Bret nodded. "And others."

"You know that wasn't your fault."

Bret glanced at his friend but didn't reply. He hadn't been strong enough that day, but the last fight between him and Vince, two years later, had been different.

"You were still just a kid," Jake said, "and you were protecting your mother. Vince deserved what he got...and more."

"Yeah, maybe," Bret murmured, remembering the scene he'd walked into after returning from a camping trip when he was seventeen. The one where he'd discovered his mother's lies and the truth in Vince's vicious revelations that had shattered his heart and left him lost and adrift in a murky sea of deceit and doubt.

"If you hadn't hit him and fought him off," Jake said, his voice soft with understanding, "Vince wouldn't have quit. He would've come after you; he may have killed you and your mom."

"I know," Bret said, staring at his hands where they rested on the emerald comforter in his lap. "I just can't help but wonder what happened to him."

That wasn't all he wondered about. So many questions had been left unanswered. Well, Ruby had explained her version, but Bret didn't believe her. She'd not only broken his heart with her deceptions—no matter how well-meaning they were—she'd broken his faith in her too. It didn't matter that they'd eventually rebuilt their relationship—that she'd pulled herself together and became the woman, the mother, he remembered from his childhood. Because no matter how much he had wanted her love, and to believe in her once more, he could never bring himself to completely trust her again.

That was a whole other kind of pain.

The desk chair squeaked as Jake shifted. Bret could see him from the corner of his eye, elbows on his knees, his head hanging low, and he wondered what his friend was thinking.

"He wasn't dead," Jake said softly, and when Bret looked up in surprise, his friend's eyes looked wary.

"Who?" Bret asked.

"Vince. You didn't kill him that day."

The old bands of guilt and fear over what he thought he'd done tightened around Bret's chest. "And how do you know that?"

It had been a fear that had worried him for months after their final battle in Vince's living room. That the police would show up at the apartment Jake had graciously offered to share with Bret and Ruby, and arrest Bret for Vince's murder.

"I saw him at a hardware store," Jake said, "three months later, just before your mom and I moved over the mountains."

Bret remembered that day. He'd been surprised when Jake arrived with his mother and assumed he was only there to help Ruby move. But the amount of gear loaded in Jake's truck bed and the uncertain look on his friend's face told a different story.

"After all your talk about country life," Jake had told Bret with a lopsided grin as he stood beside his truck that sunny afternoon, "I decided to check it out for myself."

"I thought you liked construction work?" he'd asked, still a little stunned.

"I do," Jake said, "but with the war getting worse and more people crowding the streets, even the suburbs were starting to feel...oppressive."

Bret had happily put in a word with his foreman and soon, Jake joined him on the ranch, and Ruby had moved into a small apartment in town not far away.

Bret didn't tell Jake everything about that night with his uncle. For a while, he'd kept Ruby's lies to himself, but he'd never disclosed her disgusting relationship with Vince, or the ugly scene Bret had walked in on that night to anyone. Despite Jake's obvious concern when he'd correctly interpreted the tension between mother and son, he'd asked only once and then let the question go unanswered when Bret refused to discuss it. And Bret was thankful his friend never pushed the issue.

"Are you sure it was him?" he asked, staring into Jake's resigned gaze.

"Yeah, I'm sure. His nose was bent and he had a scar on the side of his face that hadn't been there before, but it was him. He recognized me too. Made some nasty comment I didn't quite hear and told me to stay the hell away." Jake scoffed, "A part of me wanted to rip him apart for all the shit he put you and Ruby through."

"It wouldn't have changed anything."

"No, but it might've made me feel a little better."

Bret grinned, but it slipped away. "Why didn't you tell me? Why did you wait all this time?"

Jake shrugged and sat back in the chair. "I don't know. Back then, I thought it would be better to just forget about him. He got what was coming to him, should've gotten more in my opinion. You were finally free of him and I didn't want to dredge up painful memories by mentioning his name. You never brought him up, so I left it alone."

Bret sighed. He wasn't sure how to feel about that. He knew Jake and how protective he was of his family—Bret and Ruby included. It was one of the reasons they'd become such close friends. But to let him think, after all this time, that he might've beaten a man to death in a blind—albeit righteous—rage bothered Bret. "I wish you'd told me sooner."

"And remind you of all the abuse that bastard rained on you?" Jake asked. "You and your mom needed to heal, not think about the past."

Bret narrowed his eyes as he stared back at his friend, wanting to argue, but he couldn't find it in him. "I worried about it for years," he said, then shrugged at the wretched expression that fell over his friend's face. "Not all the time, but I still...I wondered."

"The cops would've found you right away if he'd died that night. It's not as if either of you had a lot of places to go when you left Vince's."

"Yeah, I know. That's what I kept telling myself." He turned away, his memories tumbling around in his head. Too much to remember. Too much bad had filled his life, but he'd never regretted his friendship with Jake.

He shifted on the bed and glanced at his friend. "So," he said, "how did you end up here?"

Jake sat back and crossed his arms over his chest as he looked away. Bret read Jake's sudden discomfort in his body language.

"Well," Jake said slowly as he faced his friend, "after I was taken, I was held at the Auction Hall and sold, same as you."

Bret nodded, he'd known that much.

"The Auction Hall owner bought me and she was..." Jake sighed as a pained look crossed his face. His jaw clenched and a muscle twitched in his cheek before he reined in whatever emotion had stirred inside him. "Cruel," he finished.

Bret's stomach tightened as the weight of guilt and regret crashed into him. He remembered Darla Cain, the red-haired owner of the Auction Hall, and the depraved game she'd played with him during her inspection of his body on the grounds outside. He dropped his eyes and ran a hand over his face.

"I should've tried harder," he muttered.

"To do what?"

"To get you out," Bret said, meeting Jake's bewildered gaze. "I followed the trail to the Auction Hall. I waited a few days, hiding mostly, trying to find a way to get to you. Almost got caught twice while I prowled around. The third time they kept after me. I ran, and I never stopped."

"You followed the trail?" Jake sounded stunned.

Bret nodded. "When you didn't show up at the rendezvous, I went back to check."

Jake's face turned white and he shook his head in disbelief.

Bret turned away from his friend's expression as shame squeezed at his heart. "I'm so sorry, Jake," he said and when he looked up, Jake was frowning.

"For what? It wasn't your fault."

"I left you there," Bret said, his voice turning raspy with emotion, "in the mountains with the Raiders. I ran like a coward and left you behind."

"No, you didn't." Jake shook his head. "It was chaos, all those people were running and screaming while we fought the Raiders. There's no way you could've known where I was or what had happened to me."

"I should've checked," Bret said through the thickness that had gathered in his throat. Out of all his mistakes, leaving Jake in the hands of the Raiders was one of his deepest regrets.

"And done what?" Jake asked, leaning forward and resting his elbows on his knees. "Been captured with me? That would've killed you, Bret."

"You turned out all right."

Jake lowered his head and scoffed. "I'm lucky to have survived at all." He lifted his gaze. "I owe my life to Monica and Angel."

"Monica?"

"She's a friend of Angel's," Jake said, as he leaned back in the chair again. "She needed help building a house and got me out of Darla's dungeon to do it. I threatened to run when the time came to go back and, somehow, Darla heard about it. She came for me, intending to punish me, and Monica sent me here. Angel made sure I could stay, and I didn't care how." His eyes turned dark and serious. "If not for them, I'd either still be locked up in a cell rotting away or dead."

Bret heard the message Jake didn't say—that he should let go of the past and find a way to accept his position now. Only he couldn't do that, not as a slave.

"I'm glad you're happy, Jake," he said as he turned onto his side and pulled the comforter over his chest.

"It's more than that," Jake said, straightening away from the chair's back. "I love Monica. I care about Angel too. They're both good women and they'd do anything to keep the people around them safe."

Bret's jaw tightened, holding in his skepticism, but Jake's frown said he'd read Bret's reservations as easily as a neon sign at night.

"I know you have your doubts, Bret," he said slowly, "and I know why."

Bret's brows drew down and his mind immediately returned to the awful scene between his mother and Vince all those years ago. He opened his mouth to ask what exactly Jake thought he knew, but Jake didn't give him a chance.

"I know you don't believe it," Jake said again, "but it's the truth. I only hope you'll give them a chance so you can learn that for yourself."

6

January 5

BRET LAY ON HIS SIDE resting with a pillow hugged to his chest, a knee bent over another, and the blankets bunched around his hips awaiting Jake's return from his ranch duties. Half asleep, he'd dreamed about riding fences with Jake before the war when a knock on the door across the room startled him awake.

"Yeah," he mumbled and heard the door open behind him. Slowly, he turned over on the bed, expecting to see Jake. Instead, he found Angel standing in the open doorway, a small wooden crate held in her arms while a cold draft rushed in from outside. He hadn't seen her since he first woke two days ago. He'd been hoping not to see her again for some time.

"Hey! Grayling, get out of there," Angel scolded the gray blur that slipped through her legs and darted into the room to disappear under Jake's bed.

"What was that?" Bret asked, propping himself on his elbows and peering at the shadowed area below Jake's mattress.

"Just a young stray we picked up a while ago," Angel told him. "He's a great cat, but he thinks the whole place is his personal domain. I'll get him out of here so he doesn't bother you."

"Just leave him be," Bret said as he dropped onto his back again. "He'll get bored and leave on his own. No need to stress him out by trying to drag him out from under there."

"You know about cats?"

"A little," Bret said with a frown as an old pang struck his heart. "I've been around a lot of animals. Don't like to see any of them traumatized for no reason."

A small smile curled Angel's lips and an odd look of approval shined in her eyes—which made him uncomfortable. Despite Jake's urgings, he didn't want to make friends with this woman, and he certainly didn't want to encourage her to attempt it either.

"Shut the door," he said a little more gruffly than he'd intended as he tugged the blanket over his bare chest.

Glancing back at the open doorway, she apologized as she quickly closed it with her foot, locking out the chilly breeze.

"What do you want?" he asked when she turned back toward him with the wooden container still in her arms.

"I brought some salve and bandages for your injuries," she said as she crossed the room. "You needed to sleep more than anything yesterday, and I didn't want to disturb you. So, I thought, if you don't mind, that I'd take care of them since you're awake."

He eyed the box in her arms, unsure if he wanted her anywhere near him. He'd had enough of women pawing at him for a while, and he didn't believe she would treat him any differently. But then again, Jake seemed to trust her.

"I'm glad you decided to stay in bed," Angel said, setting the box on the nightstand and striking a match to light his bedside lamp.

"I didn't do it for you."

Shrugging, she reached inside the wooden crate. "It doesn't matter. You'll get some of your strength back soon, but the more rest you get, the faster you'll heal." She turned to him with a small towel in her hand and a polite smile on her face. "Will you let me take a look at your back?"

"I'd rather Jake did that," he said, watching her through narrowed lids.

She glanced around. "Where is he?"

"He had some chores to do...said he be back for dinner."

She nodded. "He'll probably still be a while then." She tilted her head. "Would you please sit up and let me help you? I promise I won't hurt you."

He hesitated, debating the possibilities, but his aching body won out.

Guarded at first, Bret's muscles bunched beneath her hands as she began to examine his wounds. Despite his wariness, however, his taut neck and shoulders began to relax under her soft, deft touch and a heavy sigh escaped his tight lips. Then, inhaling deeply, he noticed an unmistakable fragrance. It tantalized his senses, and warmth flooded his over-aware body, giving him a sense of peace and safety that he didn't understand. He frowned and inhaled again.

Some kind of flower, he thought. *Lilacs? Yes, that's it. Lilacs.*

He remembered that scent from the day he arrived.

Realizing the delicate perfume emanated from the woman beside him made Bret's shoulders tighten again.

This was the lilac-scented woman who had lain his head in her lap and removed his shackles while he lay sprawled in the freezing snow. *This* was *that* woman?

Back then, the flowery perfume overloaded his drug-affected senses and made him sick. Now, the alluring fragrance reminded him of spring and stirred something in him he hadn't expected—desire.

While he sat silently brooding on his body's reaction, she carefully cleaned his wounds that needed attention, and then, tossing her towel aside, she plucked a container from her box of supplies. She opened it, dipped her finger inside, scooped out a small amount of what looked like some kind of cream, and reached to apply it to a slash on his arm.

He caught her wrist in a lightning-quick movement, startling a gasp from her.

Their eyes collided.

"What's that?" Bret asked, nodding toward the cream.

"Medicinal ointment," she said, her tone slightly husky. "It'll help prevent infection. It might sting a little, but it won't hurt you." Her startled expression shifted from his eyes to his mouth and back again.

She was attracted to him.

Well, too bad, he thought. He was one breeder she would never get to play her games with.

A calm mask fell over her expression and her gaze drifted to his fingers still wrapped around her arm. "Do you mind?" she asked with an arched brow.

He released her and rested his elbows on his knees, his eyes still locked on hers.

She bit her lip, quickly lowered her gaze to his injuries once more, and began to apply the salve in generous amounts.

Despite his misgivings, Bret curious about her and studied this woman who'd paid a great deal of gold to procure him— supposedly for altruistic reasons. At first glance, she appeared plain, but her short stature with womanly curves in all the right places definitely had a feminine allure that had captured his attention at the auction and stirred his interest—though reluctantly—as he sat watching her now. Her long, ebony hair shined in the lamplight, the unbound curls bouncing and swaying as she stirred. The scent of lilacs surrounded him and his lids closed more than once just so he could focus on the fragrance, while his fingers unconsciously rubbed together as he imagined running them through the sweet-smelling, silky strands.

A frown creased her forehead as she worked, her smooth,

black brows pulled into a determined V over her elegant nose. Full, pink lips adorned her wide mouth, currently pressed together in a concentrated line as she tended to his wounds. To him, they looked soft and very kissable. Long, thick eyelashes of the same shade as her hair framed the most striking of her features, big cerulean eyes that smiled at him shyly whenever their gazes met. She wore no makeup, but to him the lack only made her more appealing. She seemed fresh and innocent and, had things been different, he would've wanted to lose himself in those eyes, to kiss those tempting lips, and bury his face in her luxurious, sweet-smelling hair...

Whoa! His relaxed posture suddenly stiffened. *Where did that come from?*

She glanced at him with uncertainty in her eyes, and he stared back at her blankly but softened his rigid muscles. She went back to work and he mentally shook his head. After his time at the Auction Hall, he shouldn't be interested in any woman, no matter how soft or sweet-smelling. After everything he'd suffered there and before, he'd promised himself no woman would breach his defenses again. He needed to remember that.

"Why are you doing this?" he asked as she tossed the salve and bandages back inside the box.

She picked up a small roll of medical tape and frowned at him. "Because it needs to be done."

"What're you going to do with me?"

Her frown deepened. "Help you get better."

"No, I mean when all this is healed." He waved a hand over his torso. "What then?"

"You'll work around here like everyone else does," she said, applying tape to the bandage over the long cut on his chest. Her brows drew together suddenly and she looked up. "Why do you ask?"

"What, exactly, will I be doing?"

She shrugged. "I don't know exactly." She stepped back and

tilted her head, scrutinizing him as if trying to determine how to best use him. "What can you do?"

Bret's jaw clenched and his fingers curled up at his side. *Why won't she answer the damn question?*

"Look, lady," he said in a raspy, barely controlled voice, "I was sold as a breeder. I want to know when I'll be expected to provide sexual services? 'Cause, I've got to tell you, you're going to be very disappointed."

She avoided his direct stare by fiddling with the tape in her hands.

"Never," she murmured, her voice so flat and emotionless he almost felt insulted. She shook her head. "I don't expect anything like that from you."

"So, who'll be taking advantage of my *services* then?" His sarcasm snapped like a whip and she met his gaze with another frown.

"Whoever you choose," Angel replied before refocusing on her clenched hands. "I don't allow women to exploit men here. You choose who you sleep with, not me."

"Then why am I here?"

She looked at him, her head slanting to the side as if confused by his question. "Like I said, to heal and to work. Either around the house or in the fields, you'll help raise the food we eat—crops or cattle." She stepped away and hurriedly gathered the rest of her things, prepared to go. "I'll leave you alone so you can rest. Jake should be back soon."

Directly on the heels of her statement, Jake entered from the kitchen with a heavy serving tray in his hands. He still wore his boots and a farm jacket, but the savory smell of beef overrode any other smells his clothes might've picked up while working. Taking in the bandage on Bret's chest, he smiled at them both.

"Looks good," he said, nodding in Bret's direction as he set the tray on the desk beside the door.

Angel smiled, and the twinkle in her eyes when she looked at Jake sent a stab of irritation through Bret he didn't quite understand.

"Thanks," she said as she placed the last of her medical supplies in the wooden crate. "He put up a fight, but I wrestled him into submission."

Shrugging out of his jacket and tossing it over the desk chair, Jake laughed at the joke, but Bret recoiled.

Maybe it was because of his conversation with Jake the day before that her lighthearted remark unearthed memories of pain and misery he wished he could forget. Maybe it was just his mistrust and suspicion of manipulation...he didn't know. But that comment, coupled with her evasive answers to his questions and his unwelcomed reaction to her nearness, caused his annoyance to blossom into full-fledged fury, and, not thinking, he instantly lashed out.

"I only let you touch me because of the pain and the possibility of infection," he said in a rough, dangerously low voice. "Don't pretend there's more behind why I allowed you near me."

Lips slightly parted, her big blue eyes widened as if stunned. He had no idea why he was suddenly so outraged, only that the idea of her having any control over him triggered something inside him he hadn't felt in years—fear. Nothing like the dread he'd experience at the Auction Hall or with the drug, but something older and far more personal. A vulnerable, intensely emotional, save-yourself-from-the-worst-experience-of-your-life kind of fear.

So, the hated voice of his Uncle Vince whispered in Bret's mind, elongating the word and bringing the recollection of a long-ago battle with it, *has my boy been in another fight? Or has some girl been slapping you around again?* Vince had chuckled at his own dig and lifted his hand to meaningfully rub his chin, preparing the insult that would cut deep. *I've told you and told you, boy, those little bitches'll never want to keep you once they find out what a useless piece of shit you are. They wouldn't want you now if not for your pretty face...*

Bret sucked in a steadying breath as he glared at Angel's startled expression, trying to push the memories back into the room in his mind from which they'd unexpectedly erupted. But now that they'd broken free, he couldn't bury them again.

Angel shook her head slightly. "I'm sorry. I didn't mean to—"

"I don't care," he growled, attempting to block out his uncle's words and the pain that accompanied them. *Truth hurts, don't it boy?* His hands felt clammy and started to shake. He clenched them on the sheets beneath the comforter to hide his unease. "I don't need your help. Get out."

"But I—"

"I said, get *out!*"

"You're in no position to be giving orders, Bret," Jake said as he stepped forward, his voice a husky warning and his eyes hard and flinty as he glared at his friend.

"It's okay, Jake," Angel said holding up her hand as if to stem his brewing anger. Jake stopped where he was. "He just needs some time to get used to us."

Bret snorted. "Fat chance."

"Knock it off," Jake cautioned again.

"I'll see you later, Jake." Angel moved the box of meds to the desk and called to Jake over her shoulder, "You should check his dressings in the morning and change them if needed. You remember what to watch for, right?"

"Yeah," Jake said, slanting another dark look in Bret's direction.

"Good. Oh," she said as if just remembering something, "Grayling's under your bed. He snuck in when I arrived."

"I'll let him out when he's ready."

"Thanks." She glanced at Bret but quickly turned back to Jake. "Well, goodbye," she said, giving them both a tight smile before she left through the porch door.

As soon as her footsteps disappeared down the walkway outside, Jake turned on Bret. "You shouldn't have done that.

She was only joking."

"She doesn't own me," Bret replied evenly, "and she *will* not control me."

"She's not trying to control you," Jake said frustrated, and then tilted his head, regarding his friend with a curious frown. "Is this about your uncle?"

Bret looked away and shifted against the pillows he'd stuffed behind his sore back. He'd forgotten how well Jake had known him and the agony of his past.

And you, you little bastard, Uncle Vince's voice ranted in Bret's mind and he remembered how his limbs—despite his resolve to be brave—had shaken in terror of the glaring, giant of a man towering over his twelve-year-old self the day they'd met. *You'll work around here until you're old enough to get a real job and pay your way. I won't have any lazy freeloaders living under my roof.*

That had been Bret's first experience with the uncle he hadn't known existed until he and his mother moved into Vince's home. If Vince's little speech that day hadn't revealed precisely how much he reviled his estranged relatives, his treatment of Bret and his mother everyday afterward had declared his unwarranted animosity.

Jake sighed and his shoulder slumped. "Angel is not your uncle, Bret. Vince is long gone, probably dead by now. Why can't you let all that go?"

Bret's eyes snapped up as heat flashed through him. "You know damn well why."

"Your mother loved you, Bret," Jake said softly, "and you're not Vince. You're nothing like him. Don't let what happened back then, or the lies he told you, continue to taint your life."

Bret ignored the part about his similarities to Vince. He'd long ago accepted his connection to that despised man and everything that might mean. "I tried that once before," he said. "And you know how *that* turned out."

Jake shook his head sadly. "Amy didn't deserve your trust or your love. I tried to tell you that."

Bret's chest tightened at the mention of the woman he'd once loved—the one who'd betrayed him and enslaved Jake. The heavy weight of shame settled in his gut and his clenched hands tightened on the sheets. "You just had to remind me of that, didn't you?"

Jake turned back to the serving tray. "I'm not trying to pick a fight," he said as he quickly dished up their food.

"Then what *are* you doing? 'Cause it sure as hell sounds that way to me."

Jake paused, and Bret saw his shoulders rise and fall in a heavy sigh before he picked up Bret's dinner and turned around. "I'm just trying to make you understand that you're safe here. Angel won't have you beaten or locked in a closet."

Bret eyes darted uncomfortably to the blankets, his stomach twisting at the allusion to some of what he'd tried to forget, but Jake didn't stop.

"She won't lie to you or stab you in the back either. She only wants to help, and if that little outburst you just showed is how you treat someone who really wants to help you," Jake said sounding equal parts exasperated and outraged as he crossed to Bret's bedside, "then you've changed more than you realize."

Jake placed Bret's meal on the nightstand with a little more force than necessary. "Eat," he ordered and, picking up his own dinner plate stacked with food off the tray, he exited the room in an indignant rush, leaving Bret feeling furious, hurt, and more than a little ashamed.

7

January 6

A KNOCK ON ANGEL'S bedroom door drew her attention from the ranch ledgers spread out in front of her.

"Who is it?" she called wearily as she rubbed her tired eyes.

Jake poked his head around the door. "May I come in?"

"Yes, Jake, come in," she said with a chuckle at his animated facial expression. Having become the big brother she never had, Jake made her laugh a lot, and she loved him dearly for it. She also trusted him more than anyone, except Monica.

Shutting the door behind him, Jake crossed to the wing-backed chair sitting before the hearth at the end of her bed. Quickly, he spun it around and collapsed onto its pale lavender cushions with a sigh. In the few moments it took him to sit, his happy expression turned grim and Angel sobered. As she watched, he leaned forward, rested his elbows on his knees, and looked down at his clasped hands. "I need to talk to you," he said slowly.

A shiver of dread tickling the back of her neck. "What about?"

"Bret," he said, meeting her anxious gaze. "I wanted to apologize for his behavior last night."

Relieved it wasn't something worse, she shrugged. "Why? He's not you, and it's not your problem."

"Yes, but he's my friend and he wouldn't be here if I hadn't convinced you to help him." He sighed and his shoulders drooped. "I…I want you to know how much I appreciate what you did for him…even if he doesn't."

She leaned forward, her elbows pressing into her thighs. "I didn't do it for him, Jake." She smiled and raised her eyebrow to emphasize her meaning. When he returned the gesture she continued, "I don't know him, and he doesn't know me. If he doesn't care, it doesn't matter."

Liar! She ignored the voice in her head.

"I'd still like to apologize."

She smiled again. "Apology accepted. Now, is there anything else you need?"

"No, nothing in particular. But I am curious about what you're working on in here. Wouldn't you be more comfortable in your office with those?" He nodded toward the open ledger at her knees.

"I didn't feel like sitting in the office," she said, "but I needed to go through the books. It shouldn't have taken long, but…" She sighed as she picked up her pencil once more. "I think I've done some bad accounting."

"What do you mean?"

"I mean, somehow we're losing cattle, and last summer's corn and hay crops should've yielded better results than I'm able to account for now. It's starting to look as if a sizeable portion of our hard work and livelihood is being stolen."

Jake's eyes widened. "How?"

"I don't know," she said softly, a concerned frown wrinkling her brow. "I'm thinking of implementing a regular headcount and more frequent fence checks to try to stem the tide. I'd like to post guards as well, but that might cause trouble." She looked up. "What do you think?"

He nodded. "Sounds like a good idea. You said the losses

started last summer?"

"Might be longer, but the numbers indicate the losses began slowly and have steadily grown. They've increased over the last few months."

His eyebrows drew down. "How many animals are missing?"

"By my rough estimate, almost two hundred."

Straightening up in the chair, Jake gave a sharp whistle of astonishment.

"That's a lot."

"Yeah. Either someone can't count or something's terribly wrong in these records, and I just can't find it."

"Maybe both?" Jake suggested.

"Possibly, but the steadily increasing losses don't feel coincidental to me."

Jake shook his head. "Me neither."

Silence descended while Angel stared at the columns of digits. Outside, she could hear the ranch kids shouting and laughing in the yard, apparently deeply entrenched in another snowball battle.

"I want you to go out and monitor the herds for a few days," Angel said. "Get a headcount for a baseline to track changes and look for any further evidence of what might be happening. Take some others with you to help and let me know what you find when you get back."

"All right," he said, though she sensed hesitancy.

Normally, he'd already be out the door with a plan on how to complete the task.

"What is it?"

"It's just..." He took a breath and continued in a nervous rush, "What about Bret? He'd be perfect for this type of thing, but he can't ride yet—he's still too weak. And I can't very well take care of him if I'm not here."

"Don't worry about Bret," she said, dismissing the issue with a wave of her hand. "I'll make sure he gets what he needs until you come back. Even if I have to do it myself."

"Are you sure?" Jake asked, raising his eyebrows. "The summer pastures are *huge*. The cattle will be spread all through the hills out there. It's going to take us days to find them all and check the fences. Can it wait a few weeks for the fall round-up?"

"No. I need this checked out now. I don't have the time and I don't trust anyone else but you. I've put it off long enough. If our food supply keeps disappearing at this rate, we'll have issues next winter. I don't want anyone going hungry because we didn't do our due diligence."

Her description of future dangers should've convinced him, but his expression said he still had doubts.

"Don't worry, Jake, I can deal with Bret."

"Okay," he said, but he didn't seem convinced. "When do you want us to leave?"

"As soon as possible," she said as she glanced at the old grandfather clock across the room.

"All right," he replied, rising from his seat. "I'll let you know when we're ready to head out."

An hour later, Jake appeared at her door and Angel followed him outside. She watched from the front deck as he and seven other riders—five workers and the two required guards who doubled as cowhands—mounted and turned to ride toward the gates.

"I'll see you in a couple days," Jake said as he steadied his gray gelding with ease.

Angel nodded, smiled, and waved as they left.

Returning to the house, she made a detour to check on Bret. When she reached the entry to the men's apartment, she paused to gather herself before she knocked.

No one replied.

Concerned about her patient, Angel cracked open the door and peeked around the edge.

Bret was in bed, fast asleep.

At least his stubbornness hasn't gotten the better of him...yet, she thought, relieved to find him sleeping.

Not wanting to disturb his rest, she quietly closed the door and headed upstairs to finish what she'd started with the bills and inventories.

Two hours later, she had finally packed everything up and put the box of ledgers and receipts beside her door to return to her office. Standing, she shivered and rubbed her arms. She'd been so wrapped up in her work that she'd forgotten to light a fire in the hearth. She went to her closet to find a sweater to ward off the sudden chill. Tugging one free from an overhead shelf, Angel jump aside as another small box came out with it and tumbled to the floor. She gasped as its contents spilled, not needing to see the objects scattered across the hardwood to know what lay in the heap. Pictures and letters, a few other things from her past—all reminders she didn't want to look at and memories she didn't want to recollect.

I should get rid of that stuff.

She winced at the piercing ache in her chest the thought caused. She had told herself a million times to throw away those mementos, but she never did.

She dropped the sweater from her trembling hands and crouched down, not intending to sort through the box's contents, but began going through the items anyway. They were all that was left of her old life, all except what she carried inside her.

So little left, and so much broken or lost...

A crippling weight settled on her chest and her vision blurred. Images and words of those once dearest to her adorned the paper in that box. Photos slid out of the pile and a pair of deep cobalt blue eyes grabbed her attention. The world around her slowed and her hands halted their sorting. Those twinkling eyes stared out at her with a brilliant smile that made the image come alive.

I always loved his smile...

Reaching out, she lifted the fading snapshot from the small pile, allowing herself to slide into history...

The room around her receded, replaced by a wet autumn landscape. She sat under the old tree as a cold wind worked at blowing in a storm and small leaves swirled around like tiny tornadoes. She looked down at a mortally injured man. His dirty-blond head rested in her lap and his startling dark blue gaze stared up at her.

She could smell the blood.

His blood.

"I love you," he whispered. *His lips quirked in that half smile that always made her heart stutter. Only, this time, the casual confidence that usually accompanied that mischievous grin was unconvincing.*

A sharp pain lanced through her chest...

Squeezing her lids closed, she shook her head. When she opened them, the world had returned to the present, only her lingering heartache remained. Her gaze focused on the old picture in her hand, the face blurring as tears filled her eyes and spilled down her cheeks.

He used to tease her about her unruly hair, calling her "Curly Q" or "Curls". She hadn't minded, not really. Even when she was annoyed with him, his crooked, teasing smile somehow always made her laugh. The warmth in his eyes let her know he would stand by her, no matter what.

And that's what killed him... That and my stupid, sanctimonious need for retribution...

Her hands shook as she held the photo a moment longer, then she took a shuddering breath and threw it and every other piece of memorabilia back into the box. She scrambled around for the lid, slapped it on, and stuffed the whole thing onto the closet's top shelf. She stepped out and slammed the door. Leaning against it, tears slipped from her eyes.

I can't let them go...

Sliding to the floor, she sobbed uncontrollably. Curled on

her side, she tried to stop but couldn't. Her mind filled with haunting memories and she cried until her head ached, until her eyes puffed up and burned. The razor-sharp ache in her chest cut wide and deep and she cried until the pain had hollowed her out completely and exhaustion mercifully took her.

When she awoke, the room had dimmed considerably. A definite chill permeated the air, or maybe it was from the enormous, icy hole inside her.

She shivered.

Get up off the damn floor, she scolded herself.

Slowly, she pushed up into a sitting position and sighed, rubbing her aching head and gritty eyes, telling herself she couldn't keep doing this.

I should just burn those photos and get it over with. Jake would help her with the task if she asked. She knew he would, but... She shook her head. She wasn't ready to explain the details to Jake.

She envisioned his worried hazel eyes silently begging her to talk to him as he had so many times before. She'd told him as much as she could, but she hadn't been able to talk about her darkest memories. Only once had she been able to share a tiny portion of that pain. She didn't regret telling Monica, but— though she suspected Monica had shared much of the tale with Jake—Angel still didn't want to discuss it again. Not with anyone. Not even Jake.

Already feeling guilt-ridden for Jake's protracted stay at her ranch, Angel didn't want to add more worry to his already considerable apprehension where she was concerned. He felt obligated to her and responsible for her, and she trusted him with the ranch and her life. But she couldn't open the heartache again, and she could not look into Jake's kind eyes and refuse once more. She couldn't face his disappointment or the gut-wrenching guilt.

Pushing those thoughts away, she got up off the floor and headed for her bathroom. She washed her face and the cold water felt good on her gritty, puffy eyes. She fixed her hair, then, with a shrug for the marginal improvement to her appearance, she headed downstairs to gather some dinner for herself and Bret.

Heat spread rapidly through her chest at the thought of seeing Bret again. A flush swept her skin as memories of the hours she'd spent envisioning the man Jake had told her so much about danced through her mind. She'd never expected to actually meet Bret, so she'd let her dreams run wild. And for years, the idea of him had been her crutch—a way to avoid her pain and do what she must without distraction. Strolling down the hall toward the stairs, a part of her thrummed with eagerness to see him again, to find out if the real Bret was more than the wary, obstinate man he seemed to be. Could he be as wonderful as the man she'd imagined?

No. No one's that *perfect.* Besides, this Bret Masters was nothing like the one she'd imagined. For one thing, he was far better looking that she'd ever dreamed...and far more angry. She understood his wariness—his recent experiences alone would explain that—but his anger came from something far deeper. From bits and pieces Jake had let fall over the years, Angel knew Bret had a troubled past. She didn't know what had happened—Jake would never explain—but she'd guessed it had something to do with Bret's family.

Shaking her head, she banished her growing eagerness. *Stop it,* her mind scolded her rapidly beating heart. *Getting warm and fuzzy over Bret Masters is the last thing we need right now...* She had too many enemies and too much heartache to allow that to ever happen again.

8

DESCENDING THE STAIRS into the large open foyer, Angel met Carl on his way to notify her that evening meal was served. Tall for sixteen and awkwardly lanky, Carl spent most of his time in the kitchens training with their resident grandmother and head-cook, Esther.

"Dinner's ready, ma'am," the young man said with his sandy-brown-haired head angled downward. His cautious brown eyes flicked up to her face, then slid back to the hardwood beneath his feet.

"Thank you, Carl" Angel said in her friendliest voice as she stepped down onto the foyer floor. "I was just coming down."

Carl shifted his feet, uneasy in her presence. "Esther wondered, Miss, if you would be dining with us this evening?"

She smiled, trying to put him at ease. "No, I won't, but I'll tell Esther. You go sit and enjoy your meal." The sound of clanging dishes and ringing silverware came from the dining area at the rear of the house.

He stepped back almost bowing. "Thank you."

"You're welcome, Carl, but please, call me Angel."

"Yes, ma'am... I mean, Angel. Thank you."

She sighed as he shuffled down the hall. Carl had been with

them for six weeks and that was at least her twelfth reminder for him to use her given name. She shook her head and followed him to the large kitchen where she found Esther cleaning while the others ate.

"Esther, have you eaten yet?" Angel asked as Carl continued into the spacious room at the end of the passage. Esther stood at the stainless-steel sink, and she jumped at Angel's query. The newly washed dish dropped from her fingers and plopped back into the soapy dishwater.

"Goodness, girl, you're going to give an old lady a heart attack sneaking up on her like that," the gray-haired woman said with a hand pressed to her chest.

"Right…" Angel laughed. "You'll outlive us all, Esther."

"Maybe so." The cook smiled, but then her face straightened. "Did Carl get you like he was told or did my good cooking bring you out of hibernating in your room?"

"I met him in the foyer on my way down," Angel answered, ignoring the gentle gibe. "So, both, I guess."

"Aren't you sweet." Esther grinned. "You saved that boy from a scolding he wouldn't forget and paid me a compliment at the same time."

"You're welcome," Angel said, her lips quirking upward. "But don't be too hard on him. He's new and not used to our ways yet."

"Ah, you're kind-hearted, but Carl needs someone to straighten him out, not baby him. Don't you go undoing all my hard work."

Angel laughed. If anyone would spoil the young man, the head cook would do a fine job on her own.

Esther cocked her head. "Are you alright, Angel?" she asked, cutting off Angel's mirth, and ending the topic of Carl.

"Yeah," she answered a little too quickly, hoping the house grandma, as Esther had been dubbed, didn't see through her white lie. "Just a little tired. Going through the accounts is not my favorite thing." She tried to smile.

Esther's frown eased a bit but worry still filled her eyes.

"All right," Esther said as she set down her washcloth and dismissed the awkwardness that filled the room. "What would you like tonight, my dear?" She headed over to the stove where pots containing the evening feast sat waiting to replenish the warming pans on the banquette tables in the other room. Several servers moved in and out of the kitchen, taking items out to the population in the dining room. The staff would sit down for their meal as soon as everyone else was served.

Angel sighed, relieved Esther let her probing question go so easily.

"What have you got? It smells fantastic!"

"Roast beef, mashed potatoes, gravy, and country veggies. There's also some salad and chocolate cake if you want some."

"Sounds great! Dish up a serving platter with everything and I'll grab the plates. I'll need enough for two and one is very hungry."

"Two?" A discordant note rang in the head cook's voice.

Angel's shoulders tensed, knowing Esther's thoughts had returned to her previous concerns. She pretended not to notice. "Yeah, two. One for the man who arrived a couple days ago, and the other is for me."

"Oh…" Esther released a sigh and her rigid stance eased as she turned to her task.

They placed everything on an oversized serving tray and Angel carried the heavy platter to Jake's apartment. She knocked lightly, hoping to catch Bret awake.

"Who is it?" he called.

"Angel," she said. "I've brought you some dinner, if you're hungry."

A slight squeaking came through the door. It sounded like he had moved on the bed. She hoped he hadn't been up on his still-healing feet.

"Come in," he said tiredly, and concern for his well-being flooded her mind.

Angel clumsily turned the knob and pushed open the door. Her gaze sought him out and found him still in bed. He had piled the pillows against the headboard to lean against and the blankets were pulled over his belly. His whole being seemed beyond exhausted, but there was something else haunting his eyes when he met her gaze. She knew he'd been sleeping, so she feared something worse than weakness and fatigue was troubling him.

She did a quick visual inspection as she kicked the door closed and crossed the room with the heavy tray in her hands. "Are you all right?" she asked a little worried about the strained expression on his face. "You seem..." She was at a loss for what to call the misery she sensed radiating off him in mood-dampening waves.

He glanced at her, suspicion clear in his narrow-eyed look, but there was something else she couldn't put her finger on. He seemed...sad, almost needy, but she didn't say so, quite sure he wouldn't appreciate her observation.

"Just tired," he replied and dropped his eyes to the forest-green blanket covering his lower half.

"Did you sleep well?" she asked, standing beside the bed and holding their dinner tray.

His head snapped up. "How did you know I was asleep?"

"I checked on you earlier," she answered, shifting her feet, feeling uncomfortable under his direct stare. "You appeared to be sleeping soundly."

His frown deepened some, but he shook his head and lowered his eyes. "I'd prefer it if you didn't come in here without my permission."

"I-I'm sorry," she stammered, stunned by his calm response—she'd expected a little more heat. "I didn't actually come in...I just peeked around the door. I knocked but you didn't answer and I wanted to make sure you didn't need anything."

He nodded but didn't say more. A tremor shuddered through

him and he inhaled sharply.

"Are you sure you're all right?" she asked, wondering if he was suffering some negative side effects from the drug.

"I'm fine," he said, his voice raspy and he glared up at her this time. Then he glanced at the tray she held and his face softened. Another shiver swept over him and he met her gaze once more. His stomach growled and his mouth curled up at the corners in a heartbreakingly self-conscious grin that set off a hint of dimples in his lean cheeks.

Her traitorous heart fluttered at the sight.

"Are you going to stand there holding that all night or did you actually intend to feed me?" His tone held a teasing note which surprised her and the glint in his clear green eyes sparkled warmly.

Her heart thumped a little harder.

She stared back at him, breath halted, stupefied by that smile. Reminded that despite his injuries, the man was a gorgeous sight. His utter maleness and over-the-top handsomeness stirred a primal female awareness in her that she hadn't acknowledged in years. But something else struck more deeply. Something aside from his obvious good looks thrummed and sparked in the space between them, calling to her like a physical need.

His stomach growled again, breaking the odd spell he'd put her under. Suddenly recalling his teasing words about the meal she'd brought, embarrassment colored her cheeks for staring so blatantly.

"Oh, yes," she fumbled her words and the tray as she set it on the dresser by his nightstand. "I thought you might be hungry."

He huffed out a breath. "I am."

Transfixed, she watched as he carefully adjusted his pillows, clearly unaware of the broad expanse of masculine torso and tempting play of flexing muscle his movements displayed.

"What've you got?" he asked. "It smells wonderful."

Jerking her eyes away before he could catch her gawking again, she repeated the menu Esther had given her while she doled out his food. She picked up the dish and turned a questioning glance toward him. "Sound good?"

"Bring it over."

"Yes, sir," she teased as she handed him a napkin and his dinnerware. She paused as he stared hungrily at the food, and a little pang squeezed her heart. She wanted him to be happy here, but his stubbornness and obvious animosity worried her.

"Enjoy," she said, turning on her heel and ambling back to the dresser.

"Where are you going?" he asked as she gathered her plate and utensils and started for the door.

"I was going to dine elsewhere."

He frowned. "Why?"

"I didn't think you'd want me here."

He glanced at the still untouched plate in his lap, then looked up at her as curiosity filled his expression. "You could've had someone else do this."

"Everyone else has other things to do. I told Jake I'd take care of you in his absence."

"Sorry to put you to so much trouble, but I'll be fine on my own."

She ignored the bite in his tone. "I'm sure you will, but you need food and you need to stay in bed. I'll leave and return for your dishes when I'm done. I'll bring something for your ear too."

He lowered his gaze with a sigh and stared at the fare in his lap. He shrugged, seeming to come to some kind of conclusion, and moved a little farther back on the bed. His stomach growled for a third time and she peered at him inquiringly. He mumbled a curse, grumbled something she couldn't make out, and picked up his utensils as she turned the doorknob.

"You might as well stay," he said stabbing a piece of meat with his fork. She glanced at him over her shoulder as he popped the morsel into his mouth, his eyes closing in silent appreciation.

Marveling at his invitation, her jaw nearly dropped to the floor. "Thank you." Trying not to allow her surprise to show, she mentally shook herself as she returned to the desk.

"Welcome," he replied with another charming smile that made him look more attractive...and dangerous.

"Why the sudden attitude adjustment?" she asked as she set her food on the desktop. She pushed aside the medical supplies from earlier and sat down to eat.

He took a deep breath before he spoke. "They had me locked up and isolated so long, I...I guess I just need some human interaction." His voice was soft and low as if ashamed to admit his weakness. "A few days can be a very long time to spend alone after enjoying good company again."

Hanging her head, she pushed her food around with her fork. "I'm sorry about Jake having to leave," she murmured with remorse tugging at her heart.

Bret nodded. "Jake told me about the missing cattle." He paused, as if considering his next words, and she looked over at him. "Did you ever think that one of your neighbors might be stealing them or that the animals might be sick and dying off somewhere?"

"I thought they might've contracted something, but we checked and couldn't find any obvious signs, and we've found no bodies. Still, there's a lot of empty land around here, we might've missed something. But rustlers? Here? I don't know." She shook her head. "We're quite a ways from anyone I'd suspect of doing that."

"It was just a thought," he said with sudden apathy. Something in his tone brought Jake's earlier comment to mind.

"Jake thinks you'd be the perfect person to look into our cattle problem."

Bret arched an eyebrow. "Does he?"

"Yes. Do you have any idea why?"

"No." His answer was muffled by a mouthful of roast beef. He swallowed and, while soaking up the brown gravy with a thick slice of buttered bread, he continued, "You'd have to ask Jake."

Angel stared, mesmerized by the flex of his biceps and the muscles of his chest and abdomen. Her body leaned toward him, an intense desire to run her fingers over those flexing muscles sent a shiver down her extremities. Her tongue darted out to lick her suddenly dry lips and her heartbeat thudded in her ears at the open display of manly flesh.

If anyone had told her three days ago that she would be gawking at a man eating his dinner with a sudden, undeniable heat burning between her thighs and a wholly different kind of hunger scorching through her vitals, she would have told them they were crazy. She was beyond those distractions now.

Yeah, right...

Knock it off! she told the sarcastic little voice in her head. *He's just a man and the only reason he's here is because of Jake.*

She averted her gaze and straightened her posture, then went back to her previous questioning. "Jake said you're better at raising and caring for cattle than he is." She waited for a reply, but none came. "Do you know about ranching?" She couldn't keep the slight irritation out of her voice, though it was more for the effects of her lingering stray emotions than his avoidance.

"A little." His marathon feeding halted, and he stared down at his half-finished meal. "I worked on a ranch before the wars," he said somewhat reluctantly.

Her eyes snapped back to him. "You did?" Jake had mentioned Bret's previous occupation, but she didn't want Bret to feel cornered—better to let him tell her himself.

"Yeah..." Staring at his plate, he sounded almost defeated.

"Did you like the work?"

He shrugged. "I guess. Why?" He frowned at her.

"I need a rancher. Someone who knows about cattle, horses, crops...everything." She waved her hands to encompass the entirety of her holdings. "We've been doing okay for ourselves with hands-on learning, but to be honest, no one but Jake knows all that much. We've learned a lot the hard way and paid the price for it. We need someone with the skills for the job, and soon, before we lose everything we've gained."

"From what little Jake's told me, this is a big place. Are you telling me you've been running it all this time and you don't know anything?"

"I got this far with books and word of mouth and what expertise we had available, but the ranch has only been profitable for the last two years with Jake's help. And he says his skills are limited. As I said, I've learned quite a bit from him, but I'm not as knowledgeable as I'd like, at least not as much as someone with previous experience."

"So you think I can fix all your problems?" She heard the edge in his voice, but she couldn't stop now.

They needed him.

"When you're feeling better, of course."

"Of course," he mimicked.

"We could really use your expertise," she said, hoping to appease his suspicions and overcome his reluctance. When he was silent for several seconds, avoiding eye contact, she tried a little mild prodding. "Will you help me?"

"No." His response was instantaneous and cold. He started to eat again.

"Why not?"

He took a sip of milk to wash down his last bite before he turned his indignant silver-green eyes on her and answered in a soft yet menacing tone, "Because I won't help you make me into a slave even if you paid money to make me one."

"Bret," she started gently while attempting to rein in her temper, "I didn't mean to imply you were, or ever would be a slave. I'm asking if you can do the job"

He didn't speak, only stared at her with stony eyes and a blank expression.

"Every person here works to keep this place running and the income flowing so we can stay here without interference—it's the only way we can survive. If not, everyone would wind up with their prior owners or worse, and no one wants that."

"I don't have a prior owner," he said, unmistakably offended. "What's my incentive?"

"You'd go back to the Auction Hall to be resold, and this time you'd end up with the woman who tried to outbid me at the auction."

She let her comment sink in and he looked away, shifting against the pillows behind his back.

"Do you want that?" When he didn't reply, she pushed a little harder, this time struggling to maintain a calm, level voice. "Wouldn't you rather help me keep this place running so these people could stay here with their families? Families that, without a doubt, would be broken up if not for this home. Which is the worse evil, Bret? You tell me."

BRET SAT MOTIONLESS staring down at his empty plate, contemplating her words. He remembered the dark filth of his small cell, the drugs, the fear, the chains, the pain, and most of all, the humiliation. The cold gray eyes of the woman who had him whipped and beaten out of spite floated in his mind. Then the dark amber-colored ones of the lovely blonde who had pummeled him into unconsciousness at his capture.

He hated losing his independence more than all the rest.

Bret scrutinized the woman next to him—the woman who had bandaged his wounds and offered him some sense of his lost freedom. He stared into the eyes of an angel—his experience telling him she was anything but—and wished he could make himself trust her. He had to admit that so far, she was different, and he did want to help. He missed the work. He missed the animals. Taking her offer would be a brief reprieve from the constant fear; at least he'd have steady meals and a warm bed. If running the ranch meant he could ride a horse again it would be worth the small price she asked of him now.

Hell, I might even be able to use the position to regain my freedom. That thought decided the debate.

"All right," he said. "On one condition..."

"What?"

"If you want this place to run smoothly and be profitable, I need complete control over operations and access to all the information necessary to learn what's been happening and how to fix it."

"There are rules, Bret, and limits to what you can do."

"I'll follow your rules if they don't interfere with what needs to be done."

She shook her head. "They're not just my rules. There are outside influences that could hurt you and the rest of us if you go against them."

He sat lost in thought for a long, silent moment. "I have my own limits," he said, "but I'll do whatever's required to keep everyone safe. As long as you back me in what I'm trying to accomplish."

"You'll have my full support," she said, "as long as you don't do anything dumb."

His eyebrows went up in silent question.

"I mean," she elaborated, "anything to endanger you or me or anyone else here. We don't live so far from everything that the council wouldn't hear about it. What you do will affect us, but it'll also affect all the other homes out there as well."

How could anything I do affect any of them? Bret silently wondered, but he kept it to himself.

"Agreed," he said, playing along; knowing that when the time came, he'd run and never look back.

Still seated in the desk chair, Angel leaned toward him, elbows on her knees and her eyes direct. "I want your word, Bret."

His face showed nothing, but he cringed inwardly. Such a simple thing, but did she know how much giving his word would bind him?

Did Jake tell her to force him to give it?

How much did his friend reveal to her anyway?

His fingers clenched around the sheet in his lap

"I agreed," he said, hedging. "Don't you trust me?"

"Not as far as I could shove you," she said and shrugged before she sat back in the chair. "But then again, I hardly know you. Maybe I can and maybe I can't, time will tell. For now, though, I'll take your word."

Staring back at her, Bret hesitated, unwilling to imprison himself all over again. His desire to do something beyond sitting in a dark room alone for an unspecified amount of time warred with his need to escape from this new prison, but he knew attempting to run in his current condition would be ridiculous.

"Fine," he said, "you have my word. For now."

"Which means?"

"It means I reserve the right to change my mind."

"As long as you tell me beforehand."

"Why? So you can lock me up?"

"So I can talk you out of it."

He shook his head. "You won't."

"I'd still like the opportunity to try."

"It won't make any difference."

"I'm aware of that possibility," she replied and her eyes turned sharp. "But, for now, do you promise to follow the rules?"

His grip on the sheet tightened and he sighed. "Yes," he answered, but the word, spoken in a voice as hard as granite, tasted like the bitterest brew in his mouth.

9

"GREAT," ANGEL SAID with more enthusiasm than she felt for his reluctant capitulation. *Maybe he'll at least give us a chance.*

Standing, she removed his empty plate from the bed where he'd left it and set it on the desk with hers. Then she fished out the medicinal salve, a container of saline, and bandages from the box she'd left there earlier.

"If I remember correctly," she said when she returned to the bed with the bottle and a couple of towels tucked under her arm, "your feet still need some attention." She lifted an eyebrow and glanced between his covered feet and his wary eyes. "Do you mind?"

A grunt was his only reply. Taking that as approval, she pulled the blankets back and knelt at the end of the mattress. She inspected his injuries, tucked a towel beneath his heels, and unscrewed the lid from the bottle.

"This'll hurt," she said, looking up at him holding the saline in one hand and a dry cloth in the other.

He grunted though he sounded less sullen and more resigned this time. When she'd soaked the injury and wiped away the gore that remained, he flinched but didn't say a word.

"Do you know who did this to you?" she asked, surprising herself. The question had been bouncing around in her head for several minutes and it just seemed to pop out on its own.

"One of the guards," he answered and shifted slightly.

She glanced at him, hoping his apparent discomfort was not because of her ministrations. He frowned at his feet and his face looked hard as stone. She wondered if he was reliving the horror they'd unleashed on him.

"Was it Sara?" she asked to draw him out of his reflection.

He looked up and she saw that his normally clear green eyes had turned to a stormy silver-green. She'd noted the color change before and had suspected it was linked to his darker moods. Seeing it now, and knowing he must be angry over what they'd done, she knew she'd been right.

"What do you care?"

Yep, definitely angry.

"I care that someone hurt you," she said, giving his injuries one last look.

"Why? You don't know me, and if I'm not to be used then why do you give a damn at all?"

"I'd hoped we could be friends," she said, standing and tossing the blankets back over his feet. "But that's not the only reason."

"Yeah, sure..." He looked away and she wondered what he thought she meant.

"You're also a person, and Jake says you're a good man," she said as she moved to put the medical supplies away. "Why wouldn't I care about someone hurting you?"

He didn't reply, but the glare he'd locked on her again softened to a confused frown as if she'd given him something to think about.

"Your feet aren't bleeding anymore," she told him, "so I didn't reapply the bandages. If you stay off them, you should be able to walk in about a week, though they'll still be sore."

He nodded as she picked up their now empty dinner tray.

"If there's nothing else you need for tonight, I'll leave you alone," she said she pulled open the inside door.

Grayling darted through the narrow opening with a chorus of meows and leaped onto Bret's bed. The cat marched across the mattress as if it were his own and nuzzled Bret's hand.

A soft smile lit Bret's pensive face and he reached to scratch behind the cat's ears. "Hey there, buddy," he said warmly, focusing his attention on the loudly purring Grayling.

Angel couldn't help but grin. Bret had been so moody when she'd arrived and irritated only moments ago, but seeing his undeniable affection for the cat's company brought a grin to her lips.

Intending to leave him with his new furry friend, Angel held the tray closely and turned to start out the door.

"Don't go," he said and she looked back at him. He met her questioning gaze and shrugged, looking more than a little uncomfortable. "I won't be able to sleep for a while and I don't want to sit here alone."

"All right," she said and shut the door before she returned the tray to the desk. She sat in the straight-backed chair and turned to him.

Stroking Graylings sleek head, the soft smile was absent from Bret's lips. His brows were drawn as if concentrating on something that didn't please him, but his hand moved gently over the cat's gray fur. Grayling's purr rumbled fast and loud from his small body. Angel admired Bret's raven-haired head as he stared at the swishing tail of the contented feline.

Watching the scene, Angel's smile returned. She liked this side of him—the quiet, gentle man who found pleasure in the company of an animal.

"How long has Jake been here with you?" he asked without taking his attention from the cat.

"Didn't he tell you?"

He met her eyes and sat back, resting against the pillows and crossing his arms over his chest. "He told me about being sold to Darla Cain," he said before he repeated the pertinent points Jake had told him earlier. "He told me all that, but he didn't give me a timeline."

Angel nodded in understanding. "He was with Darla for not quite two years. Monica's house took about six months, and he came to me for help about three years ago."

"I see," he muttered. "Who's Monica?"

Angel smiled. "She's a good friend of mine who lives on the other side of the ridge behind us." She pointed in an easterly direction.

Bret nodded.

"Anything else you want to know?"

"No, I guess not," Bret said softly, smiling as Grayling climbed into his lap and settled in.

"Okay. Then I have a question."

He peered at her with suspicious eyes. "What?"

"How did you and Jake meet?"

His shoulders tensed. "Why are you asking?"

She shrugged. "I'm curious."

"Why didn't you ask him?"

"It came up once. He said something about being school buddies, but not much more." She neglected to mention the other stories Jake had told her, but that wasn't the question.

BRET SIGHED. He didn't want to talk about his youth or the other topics that conversation could lead to, not with this woman. But he didn't see any reason not to tell her that part of the tale. Besides, by giving in to the loneliness that had been growing inside him, he'd opened the door by asking her to stay.

"We met in junior high and become friends later."

"Why later?" Angel asked, standing to drag the chair closer to the bed. With her heels hooked in the chair's lower rung and her elbows on her knees, she leaned forward and rested her chin on her hands. The way she gazed at him with her big, innocent-looking eyes, waiting for the story, did strange things to his insides. He felt himself being drawn into those fathomless blue pools, wanting so much more.

I could get lost in those eyes...

His gut clenched. Confusion and doubt flooded his mind. The last thing he needed was another woman in his life screwing with his head.

Averting his gaze, he put a stranglehold on the sensations her pretty face unexpectedly awoke in him. He shifted, disturbing the cat in his lap. Grayling's head twisted around to glance up at him with his amber-green eyes as his claws dug into the thick comforter. Bret reached down to sooth the startled creature and let the sensation of the cat's smooth fur and rumbling purr calm him.

Angel's nearness made him uncomfortable—as did his unwanted reaction to her. He kept staring at her mouth whenever she spoke, wondering what it would be like to kiss those tempting lips. He flicked a peek in her direction. She was frowning at him expectantly and he remembered she'd asked him why he and Jake hadn't become instant friends. He cleared his throat and willed his body to settle.

"We didn't like each other at first," he said, still petting the cat in his lap, "and we'd fought more than once. One night, we ran into each other at a movie theater. I don't remember exactly how it started or who did what, but the confrontation escalated into a huge brawl. We caused a lot of damage and we'd both been in trouble a few times before, so when the cops broke up the fight, we ended up in juvie."

"Oh." Angel said sat up as if surprised, but sympathy filled her gaze. "Well, that's awful."

"It wasn't great," he agreed, "but it was a wake-up call...for both of us. After a few days, we soon realized the only way to survive jail—even kiddie jail—was to know someone. Since the only person either of us knew was each other, we formed a grudging truce. And we've been friends ever since."

"What started the animosity between you two in the first place?"

"Something stupid, I'm sure," Bret said, refusing to disclose the pain they both had suffered at the time. "The biggest kid on the block kind of thing. I don't remember anymore."

"Did you ever go back?"

"Back where?" Bret asked, glancing into her big-eyed gaze. His gut clenched again and that same magnetic draw pulled at something inside him, but he ignored it and the heat suddenly rolling through his body.

"Back to juvie?"

He shook his head. "No. Once you've been there, and if you have half a brain, you make sure you never go back. And neither of us is stupid."

She smiled. "Good."

"I'm glad you approve." His tone was wry, but a grin tugged at his lips.

He glanced down at the cat, patted Grayling's head gently, and then rested his hand on the animal's back. "Well, now you know my story, what's yours?" He winced inwardly, thankful not to be looking at her just then. He hadn't meant to ask that question.

From the corner of his eye, he saw her sit back, bite her lip nervously, and drop her gaze. *What's that about?* he wondered, intrigued despite himself.

Shifting in her seat, she glanced at him, and then stared at her hands clasped in her lap. Something about her position, the way she seemed to curl in on herself, bothered him. She looked so small and fragile all of a sudden and the tender part of him, the one he shielded from the hurtful world, rushed forward. He frowned, startled by the strength of his reaction.

She sighed as if coming to a decision and then slumped a little more in the straight-backed chair. "There isn't much to tell," she finally said. "My family lived in the suburbs north of Seattle. Then, when I was still a young girl, we moved over the mountains. We lived close to town, but it was a far more laid back, country way of life."

Oddly pleased by how much she valued the change to a country lifestyle, he nodded as his slow grin returned. But then her voice became almost emotionless and she seemed to shrink into the chair, and a part of him sunk with her.

"We were already living in the mountains when the war came." She bit her lip, glanced at him warily, and shrugged. "That's it. I told you it wasn't much."

"Then what did you do?" Bret asked, curious about the signs of discomfort she displayed.

"Nothing much," she said avoiding his gaze, "mostly just tried to stay alive like everyone else. Then I came here and bought this land."

He frowned and suspicion washed over him. She was lying; at least, he sensed there was something she obviously didn't intend to share with him.

Why would that bother me?

Outside the room's lone window, the weather had picked up. Bret saw small snowflakes swirling in the wind. The sight brought back his arrival here and his supposed place on her ranch. Then another thought struck him.

"Why don't you use your breeders?" He winced inwardly. What was wrong with him? He usually didn't let his mouth run wild like this, especially around people he didn't trust—or women in general. But after the words were out, he realized the part of him that had been so moved by her sadness—maybe all of him—really wanted to know.

Angel straightened in her chair, squared her shoulders, and the clear azure of her eyes turned a stormy bluish-gray. "That's none of your business," she said with more bite than she'd shown so far. She wiggled back in her seat and crossed her arms over her chest.

Unrepentant, yet intrigued by the sudden fire he'd seen in her eyes, he chose not to pursue it. He could tell by the stubborn lift of her chin that she wouldn't tell him anything and he wasn't in the mood to fight. Instead, he shrugged and changed the subject to something less personal. When he asked about Darla, Angel groaned and rolled her eyes.

Surprised, he tilted his head and lifted a brow. "What's that about?"

Angel shook her head. "Darla and her cronies use their power to hurt and humiliate, rather than to help and heal. This mess of a society we live in," she waved her hand in the direction of the small town where the Auction Hall resided, "was all their doing. They don't want it to change, they like everything just the way it is."

Bret eyebrows climbed higher. "And you're nothing like them, right?"

"No, I'm not," she said, sitting a little taller.

"We'll see," he mumbled loud enough for her to hear, but she didn't respond. Then something she'd said replayed in his head and his curiosity resurfaced again. "Tell me about her 'cronies.'"

Angel sighed and her lips tightened but she didn't refuse to answer, though she didn't tell him much. The only exception was a woman named Carrie Simpson.

"Carrie claims to be a friend," Angel said, "and uses it as a pretense to come here once a year for an inspection and always causes problems. Then she acts all putout when I make her leave."

Bret frowned, having trouble following. "And she's a…friend?"

"No, she's definitely *not* a friend. But letting her say what she wants is better than an all-out dispute. Arguing with her about it wouldn't do any good anyway."

Bret didn't understand that any better than the rest, but he let it go.

The wind whistled under the eaves outside, reminding Bret of wintery days on the ranch before the war.

"Do you have any family?" Angel asked, breaking the quiet that had descended around them.

Bret's head came up and his eyes narrowed, mistrust and the pain of his hurt-filled past hurriedly reconstructing his defensive walls. "No, I don't. They're all dead." His answer was terse and a bit snappish, and Angel shifted uncomfortably under the glare he leveled on her.

"I'm sorry," she said softly, and for some reason that made him feel like a bully. He relaxed into the pillows behind him and shrugged again, purposely softening his retort.

"It was a long time ago," he said, managing to sound less cantankerous. Then, to make up for his gruffness, or perhaps just to move on to a less painful memory, he talked about his parents' ranch. At first, he carefully avoided revealing too much about himself or his family, but as he got lost in the memories, bits and pieces of his life's disappointments came rolling out like water from a burst dam.

Out of all the things he could've chosen to discuss, the subject of his mother was one topic Bret hadn't meant to breach. After all these years, her faults–and his own—still stung too much to feel good about airing them out, especially with a virtual stranger. Yet, with little encouragement from Angel and for some reason he couldn't fathom, Bret found himself expressing his sadness over losing his mother. In a hoarse. but low voice, he described the hurriedly dug grave and the sorry excuse of a funeral they'd held for her. Gazing down at the slumbering cat in his lap, Bret continued, his mind sliding into memory, having forgotten Angel sat beside him.

Bret hadn't been sure of his feelings the whole time he and Jake had been searching for Ruby. The only thing he'd known for sure was that he had to find her. Later, the same unsettling thoughts and emotions had churned inside Bret as he and Jake stood beside Ruby's open grave. He had carried her from the ruins of her bomb-concussed apartment where she'd been crushed when it collapsed. It had taken them hours to find her, but Bret refused to leave until he knew if his mother was dead.

She'd seemed so small and frail in his arms, the weight in his chest weighting him down far more than her slight body. The early spring wind had felt arctic as it tugged at his farm jacket and nearly dislodged his old black Stetson, but he hadn't paid it any attention. Back then, he'd been too distracted with his feelings of loss and grief—and utter disappointment in himself for everything he should've said—to notice the chill.

He and Jake interred her in a meadow of wildflowers not far from where she'd lived, and with every shovelful of dirt they moved, Bret regretted not bringing Ruby to live at the ranch. They'd only had minutes to say their goodbyes before they hastily departed as the war crashed in behind them.

He and Jake had started running that day and never stopped.

A gentle hand resting on his arm startled Bret out of the past and he turned to look at her.

"I'm sorry, Bret," Angel said, her eyes soft with sympathy he didn't want. He didn't need her pity!

Suddenly furious at the thought of why this woman was so interested in his past, he stiffened and swiftly responded with the self-preservation he'd learned to exert in his youth.

"Oh, you are a piece of work," he said in a hard voice and yanked his arm away from her touch. "You come in here, all sweet and soft, and start digging for things to manipulate me. Well, you won't get anything more from me. I won't let you use me, and I won't be a slave!"

Angel recoiled from the fierceness of his unexpected verbal attack as if he'd slapped her. Instantly, he regretted his harsh response. His chest tightened as a part of him wished he could take back everything he'd just said, but his pride and wariness wouldn't let him.

Their eyes clashed as she slowly stood and silently turned to gather their dishes, her back straight and head held high. He admired her for that show of quiet dignity.

"I was only being a sympathetic friend, Bret," she said in a tight voice as she faced him again. "I was *not* trying to manipulate you."

*   *   *

Over an hour had passed since Angel's regal departure and Bret now lay on his back with his hands folded behind his head and the cat curled up at his side. He stared at the evening-shadowed ceiling and mulled over their exchange, mentally kicking himself for letting his guard down so quickly.

But why did I do it? And why with her of all people?

Did it have something to do with the undeniable attraction he felt for her?

He did have to fight the thoughts that filled his mind whenever Angel was around. He tried to deny his fascination, but no matter what he did, he kept wondering what it would be like to kiss her, to pull her close and find out if her skin was as soft as it looked. To discover if every part of her had the same sweet-smelling fragrance as her lilac-scented hair.

Aside from being alone too long, he didn't know why those thoughts kept hounding him. She was his Mistress; she had paid money to own his body, to use him in whatever way she saw fit. She was definitely now someone he could trust or find attractive.

Besides those infuriating facts, however, he found her to be cute in a short, curvy sort of way. Not the type of woman he normally went for. The tall, trim, but undoubtedly female guards from the Auction Hall were better examples of what he was normally attracted to. Still, as Jake had often told him before, and probably would again, he didn't have much luck with the women he chose.

A softly purring Grayling heaved a sigh beside him and Bret glanced down as the dozing animal. Glad for the cat's quiet company, he slid his palm over the sleek gray fur and smiled as Grayling's purrs instantly turned rapid and loud.

"What do you think, buddy?" he asked as he continued to

idly stroke the cat. "Should I go for it?" He chuckled at his idiotic question. After all the pawing and unwanted attention at the Auction Hall, it's a wonder he didn't try to hide whenever Angel entered the room.

Not that being around Angel didn't cause him some unease—it did, just not as much as he had thought he'd feel around a woman after nearly three months as a terrified, chained, helpless prisoner. Yet, despite the women who'd actually imposed their will on him with physical caresses, he'd not been forced into anything more intimate. Other men hadn't been as lucky.

Remembering those intolerable liaisons in his cell, Bret wondered if Angel might find some fault with him—such as his unwillingness to provide the sexual services expected of a breeder—and either return him to the Auction Hall, sell him to someone else, or punish him the way Darla had before he came here. Jake claimed that wasn't Angel's way, that she brought people here to save them and help them recover, to give them a home and a purpose.

Bret wasn't sure if he believed that.

Life had taught him to guard his heart and fight when he had to. Arguing with or even shouting at Angel probably wasn't such a good idea, but he couldn't accept what she'd done to him. Whether she did it for Jake or not; whether to save Bret or help herself to his body, he didn't care. He would not be her slave—not a breeder or any other kind. He'd agreed to help on the ranch, but only to aid his cause, not whatever hidden agenda Angel may have. Because no matter what the cost, he would do whatever it took to regain his freedom.

10

ANGEL FELT HIS BODY heat radiate over her flesh before he touched her. His arm slipped around her waist, tugging her gently across the bedsheets toward him. The next thing she knew, his mouth nuzzled her neck as his weight pressed her into the mattress. All she could think about was how much she loved this. Loved having him near, having his hands, his mouth, his everything touch her. But something about this—about him—seemed wrong. His body was bigger than she remembered and the scent she'd always associated with him was...different.

"Mmm," he murmured, his lips pressed against her throat, and she felt the vibration in the deepest parts of her. "You taste wonderful."

He'd said that before, but something wasn't right. His voice wasn't right.

His mouth nibbled along her throat, her earlobe. Heat shot through her and she giggled softly as her fingers traced the valley of his spine and the firm muscles of his back—but even that felt erroneous. Her body trembled and his arms tightened around her.

"I'm so glad you're mine, Angel," he whispered in her ear, and her misgivings faded away as a little shiver of excitement danced along her nerve endings. "All mine. My Angel..."

She loved when he murmured to her like that. Loved it more when his words turned dirty. She loved feeling every hard inch of him surround her...but something was wrong. His voice sounded deeper, and the way he moved, the way he touched her, held her, caressed her, was different.

His tongue slid around the edge of her ear. "I want you, Angel..." His warm breath tickled the flesh he'd just dampened. "I want to be inside you."

She froze.

That was not his voice!

Raking her fingers into his short hair, she instantly knew she was right to be alarmed. Even in the darkness, his hair should've been a lighter shade and slightly longer. It should've curled around her fingers as she clutched the strands. But this man's hair was jet black and cropped short.

Startled by that realization, she tugged until he lifted his head and looked down at her.

For a heart-stopping moment, his face was the one she remembered so well—his sweet, contagious smile curving his lips and his dark blue eyes looking deeply into hers. Then she blinked and everything blurred, changed, and coalesced into... another man!

The eyes she stared into weren't blue; they never were. They were green...

No! Oh, no... No, no, no...

Clawing her way back into reality, Angel's eyes popped open to darkness and she lunged upward. Sitting in the middle of her big bed, her heart thumped against her ribs like a jackrabbit trying to escape and her hands fisted in the sheets. She tried to slow her racing breaths and calm the riot of shudders that shook her.

Regaining some control, she kicked back the blankets and dangled her legs over the edge of the bed. Her hands clutched the mattress' edge.

"What was that?"

But she knew.

She'd had that dream and others like it many times over the years, but before they'd always starred the same blue-eyed man. Her reckless and wayward daydreams of the last three years had bled into her unconscious.

Despite all the fantasies she'd entertain about the man from Jake's tales, Bret had never entered her dreams. Maybe because she didn't have a clear image of him, or maybe because her dreams, like her heart and soul, were reserved for someone else.

An invisible vise gripped her chest at that thought.

Darkness enshrouded her room and a glance at the curtained French doors told her it must be very late, or very early. Either way, after her long day helping on the ranch, she was very tired and tomorrow would be just as busy.

She needed sleep.

Inhaling and rubbing at her breastbone with shaky fingers, Angel stood and slowly ambled toward her bedroom door. She wouldn't be able to go back to sleep now, not for a while anyway, and not without something to calm her amped up nerves.

Some herbal tea should help, she thought as she shuffled from her room and down the stairs.

After helping with the morning feeding on the homestead earlier that day, Angel had gone out to the lower fields to check in with Jake. She'd ended up spending several hours helping repair a downed fence line and then searching for the cattle that had wandered off. As a result, her muscles were sore and she was exhausted, but it had been a good day. Jake filled her in on what they'd discovered so far—which wasn't much aside from the fact that they were nearly done with the head count and he expected to be back at the homestead the next day. A little pang of disappointment had struck her with that. Not because she didn't want him and the others to come home, but she knew that meant she wouldn't be eating her meals with Bret anymore. But then, the fact she'd had that disturbing feeling at all meant Jake couldn't return soon enough.

Bret's only here because of Jake, she reminded herself.

In the kitchen, still a little groggy from lack of sleep, Angel lit the lantern on the wooden plank dining table in the corner, then dug a teapot out of the cabinet nearby and filled it with water at the sink. She lit the wood-burning stove and set the pot on to heat, then gathered the makings for her herbal tea.

With her cup prepared, Angel sat down at the long dining table in the corner and, resting her head on her folded arms, waited for the water to boil. As she sat, her mind drifted a bit and her body finally began to settle from its agitated state.

She heard soft cries of distress somewhere in the distance and, at first, thought them a part of her dreams, but then something loud and more intense awakened her fully. She straightened, cocking her head, listening, but whatever she thought she'd heard had disappeared.

Shaking her head at her uneasiness and her wild imaginings, she stood and went to check on her water. The pot was barely warm and the water only tepid. She couldn't have been dozing for more than a few minutes. With an impatient sigh, Angel returned to the dining table, but just as she went to sit, another string of pitiful murmurs came from the hallway.

Though it rarely happened, she knew the threat of intruders or even Rebels was very real in their remote location, which caused the muffled sound to strike fear in Angel's heart and sharpened her senses. Adrenaline pulsed through her veins and she began to shake and sweat broke out all over her body. As much as she hated the sensation and the weariness it inevitably caused, she was thankful for the extra benefit of hysterical-strength as her trembling hand grabbed the lantern off the table and rushed to the kitchen's doorway. Cautiously, she glanced down either side of the hall, but no one was there.

"No!" The one-word roar came from the room across the hall—Jake's apartment.

Fear for Bret brought her to the closed door. She knocked, but there was no response. Another shout exploded from inside and anxiety shot through Angel's tingling limbs. Alarmed for her patient, she turned the knob and went inside.

Pulling back the winter curtain that shrouded the bed for warmth, she winced at what she saw. Bret had kicked off most of the blankets in his fretful tossing, his fists were twisted in the sheets, and he seemed to be fighting something in his dreams. Sweat beaded his body and matted his hair to his head. Panting breathlessly, his eyes were squeezed closed and his face appeared flushed beneath the shadow of his lengthening whiskers. Worried that his fever had returned or something worse, Angel gently pressed her hand to his damp forehead. He felt warm but not feverishly hot.

"No!" he bellowed, followed by a rash of mumbled words she couldn't make out. His back arched and his body flexed, thrashing against the sheets as he struggled in his nightmare.

"Bret?" she called, trying to rouse him without startling him, but nothing happened. Raising her voice, she tried again. "Bret?" Still no response. Concerned his frantic movements would tear open his healing wounds, Angel leaned across the bed, gripped his shoulders, and shook him. "Bret!"

His eye snapped open and locked on her. One instant she was staring down into his wild gaze, the next she found herself flat on her back with the crushing weight of his body on top of her.

He'd moved so fast that she hadn't registered his hands on her arms or that her feet had left the floor until she was on the bed with him. Now, she lay trapped beneath his broad chest, with his lean hips cradled between her thighs, and his arms caging her in. Though the sudden change had surprised her and her new location made her slightly uneasy, she wasn't afraid.

"Bret," she said softly, her shaky fingers brushing his ribs. "Bret?"

His body stiffened and he shuddered. "Did I hurt you?" he asked, his voice muffled by the mattress as he lay with his face pressed into it, trembling.

"No. You startled me, but I think you hurt yourself worse."

Propping himself on his elbows, he lifted his head, his face mere inches from hers. Her stomach fluttered, suddenly unnerved by their position and his nearness. Impulsively, her eyes dropped to his mouth. His handsomely chiseled lips were slightly parted, and so close she could feel his breath on her face. Her skin prickled and her mouth went dry. Dragging her gaze back to his, she nervously ran her tongue over her parched lips. The small movement caught his attention and his eyes followed it before returning to hers. Something flashed in those crystalline jade depths, but so briefly, she couldn't tell what. Still, it made her shiver.

An anxious frown creased his brow. "I'm sorry I frightened you," he said, his deep voice somewhat hoarse as if his throat had been blasted by desert heat. "I didn't mean to…"

"I know," she replied with a soft smile once his words faded and he didn't continue. She understood the power of dreams.

His frown deepened and his body stiffened, clearly suspicious. "What're you doing in here anyway?"

She hated that he thought she would sneak in on him. "You were screaming in your sleep," she said and his brows shot up in surprise. "I just came in to check on you."

Even as the adrenaline that had flooded her system faded and exhaustion brought on by the rush of hysterical-strength threatened, her body came alive with the nearness of his. Breaths came way too fast and shallow, her breasts tightened beneath the hard warmth of his bare chest, and she stared at him as if frozen in a predator's clutches. Tingles raced over her skin and a shiver rocked her to her toes as memories of all the scenarios she'd fantasized about over the years filled her head. They'd been nothing compared to this—to the real Bret Masters.

He was a large man, very tall and broad shouldered. Every hard line of his body cut into her softer one in the most appealing ways, especially the hot bulge nestled along her thigh. Recognizing that for what it was, her insides clenched in eager expectation. It had been a long time since she'd felt the deep ache of desire, but she didn't let herself think about that. Doing so would ruin this fiery buzz that swarmed through her veins.

Her fingers unconsciously slid over his biceps, admiring the corded muscle beneath his warm, satiny skin. Unable to stop herself, she stared at his mouth, wondering how it would feel on hers. Instinctively, her head lifted a fraction as his lowered toward her. She didn't think about the past or her promises...didn't think about the danger. Too wrapped up in the lost sensations this man stirred inside her, she didn't think at all. She felt his body tighten around her and her heart slammed in her chest. Heat spread through her tingling body as she closed her eyes, anticipating the inevitable.

11

UNABLE TO LOOK AWAY, Bret stared into the fathomless depths of Angel's eyes. The softness of her body had registered even before he settled over her, but by then it had been too late to stop the course of his actions. Moments ago, he'd wanted to groan with the pain that had ripped through his back as his partially healed wounds tore open. Now, with Angel's lovely face so close and her lilac scent filling his senses, he couldn't stop thinking about all that delicate femininity beneath him. Every tempting curve called to him, and his body's baser needs demanded he explore each and every peak and valley.

Her eyes dropped to his mouth and her pupils dilated. He could already feel her rapid breathing and the pounding of her heart. She was attracted to him. Not that he was surprised by her reaction; he'd seen it many times before. He'd just never enjoyed strangers looking at him like that. It reminded him of his uncle and all the cruel, hurtful, and ultimately true—as far as he knew—things Vince had tormented him with for years. Unfortunately, though he'd finally escaped his uncle's hate-filled wrath, the memories continued to haunt him.

His body responded to Angel; his heart hammered away in his chest just as fast as hers and heat pounded through his veins. Everything in him cried out for her, but he tamped down the need thrumming through him. He'd been celibate for too long, but this wasn't the time, and Angel wasn't the woman with whom to end his sexual dry-spell. At least, that's what he told himself.

Then she licked her lips and an electric spark set fire to his insides, and he forgot that she'd made him a slave.

Her eyes widened slightly and she shivered.

Was she afraid of him? Did his reckless—albeit justifiable, considering the nightmare he'd been having—actions harm her somehow?

No, she'd already said she wasn't hurt. He frowned, remembering that she had also said he'd startled her. The idea that she must be afraid of him didn't sit well with his self-imposed moral code. He didn't hurt women...at least not unless he had to, and even then, reluctantly.

"I'm sorry I frightened you," he said, his voice hoarse from the strain of the physical and oddly emotional sensations pumping through him. "I didn't mean to..." He wasn't sure how he intended to end that sentence, but luckily, he didn't have to.

"I know," she said, a tender smile curling her lovely lips.

Shit, he thought, jerking his gaze back to hers, *now I'm thinking about kissing her again.* Then another thought occurred to him and the heat dimmed as suspicion narrowed his eyes.

"What're you doing in here anyway?"

Her head titled and she gave him a look that said his mistrust hurt her somehow.

"You were screaming in your sleep," she said quietly. "I just came in to check on you."

He shouldn't have been surprised by that, the dream had been a mixture of life with his uncle and the chains of the Auction Hall. But her explanation and his crying out in his sleep wasn't what occupied his mind.

The fact he was naked, his hips between her legs, wasn't lost on him. Neither was how the thin cotton of her sleepshirt did nothing to prevent her hardened nipples from poking provocatively into his bare chest. His body, acutely aware of every inch of her, reacted appropriately, the lust pounding through him, pushing everything else out of his mind. Yet, he held back.

Staring up at him with a mixture of fear and desire swirling in the blue pools of her eyes, her fingers slid over his arms and her irises darkened further. But he was way ahead of her—he'd felt the allure from the moment he first felt her beneath him. It didn't matter who she was or what she'd done; he wanted her. Wanted to kiss those temping lips only a few inches from his own and run his fingers through all those silky, ebony curls. Wanted a lot more than that, but, right now, kissing her was the most pressing of his wants.

His body tightened and his head lowered slowly.

Are you really going to do this? He winced at the sound of Vince's damn voice in his head again. *You're more pathetic than I thought. But then again, I guess she paid enough for your services, huh, boy.* Sharp, mocking laughter cut through the need that had taken control of his common sense. But this time, the hated voice was right—this was exactly what he didn't want.

Angel sighed softly, her breath warming his lips and stoking the flames inside him. Heat washed over his skin like a tidal wave and reignited the hard pulse between his thighs. It would be so easy to kiss her, but he didn't trust himself not to get wrapped up in her—in her taste, the feel of her lips, and the sultry softness of her body. It had happened before, and his stupidity had cost him—and those he cared for—dearly.

Stifling a groan and taking firm control of his senses, he rolled away from her, pulling the comforter over himself, effectively putting as much distance between their bodies as he could without getting off the bed. He'd expected her to be upset by his sudden departure or at least question what he was doing, but she didn't say a word. She didn't move either.

Turning his head, he found her still on her back, her face averted and her body trembling. He felt her quaking more than saw it, but it didn't make sense. She seemed to be breathing hard too, but more as if in a state of distress rather than turned-on.

Her odd behavior disturbed him.

"Angel, are you all right?" he asked, moving to take her hand. Before he could reach her, however, she sucked in a deep breath and sat up abruptly. Letting out her air in a rush, she scooted toward the end of the bed.

"I'm fine," she said as she stood and turned toward him, though she didn't meet his eyes.

"Are you sure?" he asked with a lopsided grin. "You weren't expecting...something?"

Now why did I say that?

Brows lowered, she tilted her head and met his gaze. "Like what?"

"A kiss, perhaps?"

Her lips thinned as she pressed them together, then she tugged her sleep shirt into place and crossed her arms over her chest. "I expected no such thing."

Her cheeks turned rosy in the lamplight and his grin broadened.

Why am I enjoying this so much?

"It certainly seemed that way to me," he said as he slowly sat up and tried not to wince at the twinges in his back. "And you definitely looked like you wanted one."

"Well, I don't. I'm perfectly fine..." She frowned suddenly, her head slanting as if something puzzled her. "But you're not." She pointed at his side. "You're bleeding."

He looked down at himself and, sure enough, bright red smudges adorned his side and the sheet just below his ribs had turned crimson.

"If you turn around," she said grabbing some medical supplies from the box she'd left on the desk, "I'll take a look."

"I'll be fine," he said, not ready to have her touch him again.

She gave him an exasperated look. "You're *bleeding*, Bret. Please, just let me look?"

Despite grumbling again that it wasn't necessary, he obliged.

She tsked sound as she set the supplies aside and examined his injuries. "Well, this must hurt."

He grunted an affirmative reply.

"And you've made a mess of these dressings. I'll need to replace them."

As she removed the damaged bandages, he couldn't help but wonder about her again, and he spoke without intending to. "Where did you learn all this?"

"All what?" she asked, distracted.

He glanced at her over his shoulder. "First aid."

She smiled and met his gaze briefly before she went back to replacing the dressings. "We had a doctor live with us for several years when we first moved here. I'd thought it was important to know how to help care for people, so I asked him to teach me."

"So, you're a doctor now?" Something about that didn't seem right.

She chuckled. "Far from it. I'm more like a nurse without the degree."

He nodded. "I see."

"There," she said as she smoothed out the last piece of tape, "good as new." Picking up the supplies, she quickly returned them to the box and then turned back to him. "You should try to get some more sleep."

He groaned and ran his hands over his face and then up into his hair before dropping them to his side. "I don't think I can sleep anymore right now."

"You need rest."

"Yeah, tell that to my nightmares."

She gave him an odd look that made him want to question her again, but he didn't get the chance.

"I can make you some herbal tea. That should help you relax."

He frowned. "You don't need to go to any trouble."

"No trouble," she said. "I was making myself some when I heard you scream."

He squirmed a little, not liking that she'd seen him in such a vulnerable state.

"It'll help you sleep," she said as she headed for the door. When she pulled it open, they both heard the soft whistle of a too-long-on-the-burner teapot in the distance. She glanced back at him and grinned. "Be back in a jiff.

12

ANGEL OPENED HER EYES and, for a moment, didn't know where she was. Then her groggy memory returned. She was laying on Jake's bed with the comforter wrapped around her and the early morning sun lighting the room.

Last night, Bret had grimaced after taking his first sip of the tea she'd brought him, even with the honey she'd put in to make it less bitter. But he had liked the splash of homemade whiskey she'd added to it.

"You could've just brought the moonshine," he'd teased with a crooked smile that brought out a dimple in his whiskered cheek.

"This is better for you," she said, sipping from her mug.

"Maybe, but I bet the moonshine would accomplish the same thing and taste better by itself."

She didn't reply. He was just teasing her, but she didn't feel like exchanging witty banter. After her long day and the burst of hysterical-strength that had surged through her body when he grabbed her, she was too tired.

Despite his grumbling, he'd finished the last of his drink in one large gulp then set the mug on the nightstand. By the time Angel returned from taking their mugs back to the kitchen, he'd fallen asleep. Curled on his side, he'd appeared to be resting quietly, no mumbling or thrashing. Angel had stayed for a while to make sure he didn't cause any more damage to himself should the nightmares return. She succeeded in staying awake for a while, sitting on the edge of Jake's double bed with his navy-blue comforter draped over her shoulders. But it hadn't lasted long before her eyes drooped. Angel had added some fuel to the room's wood-burning stove, then pulled the blanket tightly around her and laid down on Jake's bed.

If Bret wakes again, she'd reasoned with herself, *I'll be close by to help him.*

Thankfully, she hadn't needed to.

Turning away from the bright morning light coming through the window, she crawled out of the blanket and glanced at Bret's bed. He lay on his side, one arm under his pillow and the comforter pulled up to his shoulder. He looked peaceful and vulnerable, and so damn handsome he nearly stole her breath just looking at him.

Stop that, she scolded herself as she turned away and began to make Jake's bed. *You don't need a man. You don't want one either, remember?*

Then why did you stay with him? another voice in her head asked.

Because he might've needed me, she argued.

Right...

She shook her head and ignored that sarcastic thought. She may be attracted to Bret—she'd have to be dead not to be—but she certainly didn't want him.

But she had wanted him. Lying beneath him on the bed, staring into his changing eyes, she had wanted him *badly.* Wanted his kisses, his hands on her, reveling in the weight of his much bigger, broader body as he crushed her into the mattress. It had seemed so much like her dream that she'd almost felt as if she *was* dreaming.

His hard bulk had felt wonderful, and she seemed to fit

against him just right.

It was intoxicating.

It was wrong.

Thankfully, he'd pulled away when he did. She'd like to think that her better judgment and common sense would've reasserted itself before she did something utterly stupid, but she had her doubts. She couldn't deny, even to herself, that she'd only realized her mistake after he'd rolled onto his back. Then all she'd felt was mortified by her lack of restraint and overcome with guilt. It had been all she could do not to embarrass herself further by running from the room. Somehow, she'd held in the tears of shame and gained control of her shaking. She hadn't been able to look at him at first, but then he'd hinted at knowing what she'd felt in his arms.

She couldn't let him think that.

She would not go down the path of love again—not with him, not with anyone. In their society, caring for a man was too dangerous in too many ways. She could never let him know that, for years, just the idea of him had been an antidote for her loneliness, a safe diversion when other more personal and infinitely more painful memories invaded her mind and heart. Luckily, she'd been able to divert his teasing. She'd hated to see the blood on his back, but it had been a good distraction all the same.

"Good morning," Bret's smooth, deep voice greeted from across the room.

Tugging down the last corner of Jake's comforter, she looked over at him with a smile to hide her sudden discomfort. "Morning. How did you sleep?"

"You tell me," he said as he stretched on his back. The blankets slipped precariously.

Heat swarmed up her neck and she looked down. Unnerved by his unconsciously sexy display, she fiddled with the end of her nightshirt. "What do you mean?"

"I mean," he said slowly, "you're still here."

She peeked at him and, seeing he was decently covered, she lifted her head. "I thought you might have another nightmare and I didn't want you to rip open any more of your wounds. Some of those lacerations are deep. As it is, the scars may take a very long time to fade."

By his sudden frown, he didn't like that. Maybe he hadn't thought about them scarring. Or, maybe, he had.

"I slept fine," he said, tucking his hands beneath his head. "I could use something to eat now though. Unless you have other ideas?"

His grin said he was teasing her again, but there was something in his eyes that made her stomach twist. To distract herself from the power of his charming yet suggestive grin, she ran her fingers through her still ruffled hair—not that it did much good with her wild mane of wavy, bouncy curls—and then unnecessarily straightened her top.

"I'll send Esther in with some breakfast," she said over her shoulder as she crossed to the door, "but I won't be back until later this evening to check on your bandages."

His smile never faltered. "I guess I'll see you then."

13

An hour after Angel's departure, the house cook arrived with a heavy platter of eggs, sausage, a cup of fruit, waffles, and—to Bret's wonder and gratitude—coffee. The short, gray-haired woman in her late fifties introduced herself as Esther before she cheerfully went about putting Bret at ease. She fluffed and stacked his pillows behind him, prepared his plate, and set it in his lap all before he could object, while her endless stream of friendly chatter never stopped.

"Oh, I need to sit for a minute, if you don't mind," Esther said as she plopped down in the desk chair with an exaggerated sigh. "These old legs are getting too tired for all this standing and running around."

"Fine with me," he said with a wink and a playful grin, though his experiences kept him wary. "I could use a little good company." Bret took a bite of the syrupy waffle and moaned with pleasure as the sweet maple flavor exploded on his tongue.

Esther smiled. "Well, you're a real charmer, aren't you?" She surprised him by returning his wink. "My husband was the same way. I've always had a soft spot for charming men."

While Bret dug into his breakfast, Esther proceeded to make

him chuckle with stories about her husband. She even threw in some dirty jokes he was surprised she knew, and quickly had him feeling like a long-lost grandson.

"Well, I best be going," she said as she stood to collect his empty plate and utensils. Placing them on the serving tray, she picked it up and headed for the exit. "I'll see you again at lunch, Bret."

"Esther?" he called as she swung open the door.

She turned to face him in the entryway. "Yes?"

"Where's your husband now?"

"He's dead, my dear…has been for many years."

Sadness for her loss settled in with the breakfast in his stomach. "I'm sorry to hear that."

"Thank you, Bret," she said. "You're a nice young man. You be sure to stay in bed now. You're not strong enough to be traipsing around yet."

"Yes, ma'am." He gave her another wink and a good-natured smile. "I'll do my best."

"See that you do," she said and pulled the door closed.

* * *

A few hours later, barefoot and dressed in a pair of Jake's jeans and an open white shirt that dangled from his broad shoulders, Bret stood at the room's lone window. Sick of lying in bed, he'd risked the short walk to the closet to scrounge for something more to wear than boxer-briefs. The trek had been painful but less so than he'd expected and, once dressed, he hadn't been able to resist a gander outside.

Laughter and shrill shouts of happy children playing had lured him to the window. The animated scene in the snowy dooryard kept him there, watching the kids enjoying a fun-filled snowball fight under a sunny, winter sky.

With one hand tucked into his jeans pocket and the other holding back the cream-colored curtain, Bret leaned a forearm against the wall and grinned at the lively game of tag the kids played. He didn't know how long he'd been standing there when a knock sounded behind him and the inside door opened. Glancing over his shoulder, he found that Esther had returned with his lunch.

"What are you doing out of bed?" Esther scolded as she set the tray down on the desk and walked over to stand beside him at the window.

"I heard the kids and wanted to watch," he said, giving her a quick smile before he turned to the crazy melee outside once more. "It's been a long time since I've seen children laugh or play." He turned his head to meet her gaze. "Most of the ones I've seen in the last few years had been frightened and unhappy."

She sighed and pulled back the other curtain. "It's so sad they have to pay for our mistakes."

"Yeah..." Bret murmured as he watched the boys and girls running around the dooryard. "I don't understand how they can do it."

Esther looked up at his profile an inquisitive glint in her eyes. "Do what?"

"Have kids. How can they bring them into a world like this?"

"Didn't you ever want children?"

Tensing, he glanced at her. His wariness warned him to be careful as he turned back to the window. "Yeah, I suppose I did. Once, a long time ago, before I realized where the world was going. Now," he shook his head, "I don't want any, much less the hassle of trying to raise them in this mess."

"You might change your mind."

"Why do you say that?" Suspicion spiced his tone.

"There's no forced breeding here."

Bret's eyes widened. He hadn't known about *that* practice, but he didn't get a chance to ask her to elaborate.

"There are no rules meant to keep men in their place," Esther continued. "Here, everyone has the right to choose what to do with their life. Angel only imposes penalties when someone endangers our safety or the prosperity of this ranch."

Letting the curtain drop, Bret scoffed, "And I'm sure she delegates their punishment personally." Lured by the scrumptious smells awaiting him on the desk, he partially buttoned his shirt as he hobbled across the room to his lunch.

"She's fair, Bret," Esther said, perching on the edge of Jake's bed and turning toward him. "She's been known to lose her temper at times, but she's never been cruel. Not like the other landowners or the inspectors with their love of the whip. They'd be the only reason she'd ever enforce one of their gruesome punishment laws, but so far, she's never allowed it here. No matter how much they threatened or complained."

His eyes narrowed in disbelief. In his recent experiences, the women were more likely to beat a man than speak to him.

"It's the truth. I have no reason to lie to you."

Bret shook his head, the tension in his shoulders easing a bit. "No, I guess you don't."

Pulling out the desk chair, he sat down and lifted the platter lid from his lunch and inhaled the tempting aromas. A thickly piled ham and cheese sandwich sat on the plate. Beside it, a side of macaroni and cheese, a small green salad, milk, and chocolate cake. *Chocolate!* The sight made his mouth water and his stomach growled. He'd dropped a lot of weight during his imprisonment, but if they kept feeding him this well, he'd soon be as strong as he used to be.

Flashing Esther a hearty grin, he picked up half the sandwich and dug in, closing his eyes to savor the sweet and salty flavor of the meat.

"How long have you been here, Esther?" he asked between bites.

"Me? Oh, let me think…" She wiggled her fingers as if counting. "Six? Yes, six years now." She sat up taller. "I've been here from almost the beginning. Anything you want to know, just ask."

"Okay, then, I'm curious, why doesn't Angel use her breeders?" He wasn't sure why he cared, but something about the way Angel had reacted to him made him curious.

Her brow furrowed and she cocked her head. "Where did you hear that?"

"Everyone at the Auction Hall seemed to think it was a fact. Is it true?" He didn't know why he didn't just say Angel had all but told him so.

"As far as I know it is, but I don't know why."

He nodded, but something in his expression must have hinted at his thoughts.

"Don't misunderstand, there have been many who were interested. One of them was bad, but none of them ever turned her head."

Bret frowned. "One was bad?"

"Yeah… Toby." She sighed. "He was a problem from the start. Angel, being the sweetheart that she is, still tried to keep him here. But after he attacked her—"

Bret coughed to clear the macaroni and cheese that had lodged in his throat. He took a drink of milk and swallowed hard before he repeated, "He attacked her?"

"Yes, late one night in her room."

"What happened to him?"

"She sold him to Carrie Simpson, and I'm glad she did."

"I thought she never sold anyone." The knowledge made him nervous. Even if he'd never physically harm her, maybe his refusal to act as a slave would get him sold anyway. He'd lose Jake all over again if that happened.

"She doesn't, but Toby was a violent man. Angel wouldn't accept his advances, so he tried to rape her and hurt her badly in the process. But it would've been worse if Jake hadn't been in the kitchen with me."

"Jake stopped him?" Bret's brows climbed upward, even more curious now. "Couldn't she do that herself?"

"Normally, if she'd had the chance, but he broke her arm."

Heat flashed through his body and every muscle tensed, disliking that someone had hurt her.

"Jake broke into her room and beat the man unconscious," Esther continued, unaware of Bret's growing disquiet. "He might've killed the bastard if Angel hadn't stopped him. It took a bit of persuading, but Jake and her friends finally convinced her to sell Toby."

"So, she sold him off to someone she doesn't like. No doubt in retaliation for hurting her," Bret said after unclenching his jaw.

"Not exactly. Carrie had been after Toby for months. After he attacked Angel, she agreed to the sale. From what I understand, he and Carrie got along famously...until she got bored with him. Last I heard, she sold him, but I'm not sure where he is now."

"Hmm," Bret muttered, lost in thought until she stunned him with her next question.

"Why do you ask?" Esther smirked and Bret got the impression she wanted to play matchmaker.

"No reason," he said and studiously ignored the discordant voice inside his head. *Liar. Liar. Liar...*

"Probably for the best. Most rumors say she and Jake are an item," Esther said with a sideways glance toward him. "I don't put much stock in it myself, but I've been wrong before."

"Jake?" Bret's belly knotted up as he pictured Angel with Jake. He nearly growled as anger crawled up from his gut and slammed into the back of his throat. He caught it just in time. Then wondered at it.

"Yes, they spend a lot of time together. Of course, Jake works the ranch, but he also helps manage the daily household duties, issues with the staff, and the other workers too. He's often in and around the house and works with Angel daily, but they socialize as well."

"Socialize?" The word seemed to burn his throat.

"Yes, I've seen them with their heads together chatting and

laughing, like best friends."

"Maybe more than friends," Bret mumbled as he looked down at his nearly finished meal.

"Maybe. Maybe not." Esther gave him a sly smile he didn't like at all.

"What're you grinning at?" he asked after swallowing the last of his salad.

"No one can be strong all the time, Bret. We all need someone. She does, whether she admits it or not...and so do you."

His back stiffened. "You barely know me."

"You're different." She gave him a thorough once over as he tossed his napkin on his now empty plate. "You'd stand up to her when she's wrong, but still be there if she needed you. I think you'd be good for her."

"Me and—"

"Angel. Yes." Her eyes were serious. "I think you'd be worthy of her and I'm sure you could use a decent woman too."

Irritation burned in his chest, but he curbed his tone. "You don't know anything about me. And neither does she."

"She might know more than you think." Esther got to her feet and gave him a smug smile. "I do."

A glare knit Bret's black brows together.

She chuckled as she rounded Jake's bed. "Don't look so annoyed." She patted his shoulder as she made her way to the door. "I read people very well, most of the time anyway. You're a good man; you just don't believe it, not yet."

"I guess I need to be more careful around you." His statement tangled between sarcasm and truth as he carefully crossed the hardwood and perched on the edge of his bed.

"Don't worry about me, young man. I like you, even if you are stubborn."

His lips quirked. "Glad to hear it. I get the notion you'd be a bad enemy."

"Damn right." She chuckled as she slid the tray of dishes toward her and picked it up. Balancing it on her hip, she turned to face him again. "I'll be leaving you now so you can rest. You need to get well as soon as possible. We could use some more capable hands around here."

Bret shrugged. "Yeah. Apparently I'll be spending most of my time with the cattle."

She frowned, clearly concerned. "Have you done ranch work before? I hate to see inexperienced boys doing that job."

"Yeah." One corner of his mouth ticked up at her reference to 'boys.' He was a little old for that reference. "I grew up on a ranch. I know the work and, from what Angel tells me, sounds like she needs someone with a lot of experience."

"Yes, we certainly do," Esther replied. "I hope you have better luck discovering the reasons for the losses Angel's been worried about."

"We'll know soon enough," he said, swinging his legs up onto the mattress and wincing, the quick movement making the wounds on his back ache.

"I sure hope so. We'll all be counting on you. 'Cause, you know, if this place goes, we all do."

Wow, no pressure there, he thought, feeling harassed, though he kept his expression pleasant. He leaned back against the pillows and tried not to wince again. "I'll do my best not to let anyone down."

"I'm glad to hear it, but I think Angel would be far more disappointed than anyone else. She's worked hard to build this place and even harder to keep it. Don't let *her* down."

14

Thrashing beneath the blanket he'd thrown over himself earlier, Bret woke with a start. Covered with sweat, propped on his elbows, he peered around the dim, empty room. The shadows told him several hours had passed since Esther's last visit. Another glance showed him nothing had changed since he had fallen asleep. He sighed as his racing heart slowed and he carefully pushed himself up. He kicked off the lone coverlet and swung his legs over the side. Sitting on the edge of the bed, he rested his elbows on his knees and laced his fingers together behind his neck.

Thanks to his uncle, he'd suffered horrible nightmares as a kid. They'd become less frequent as he got older and almost nonexistent once he got away from the man who'd terrorized him. After that, the only dreams he remembered were those of the sexual variety. As an adult, his nightmares about Vince hadn't troubled him in years, at least, not like they once did, and erotic dreams hadn't been on the menu for a long time. But apparently, his time at the Auction Hall revived those old feelings of helplessness and fear, and with them, his terrifying nightmares. He wasn't a kid anymore, but in those dreams, he was just as powerless as he'd been when he was twelve. And they felt so frighteningly *real*.

One hand brushed roughly over the back of his head and then he dropped both onto his thighs. Unbuttoning his sticky shirt and letting it fall to the floor as he stood, he hobbled to the closet to borrow another of Jake's. As he grabbed a blue shirt from a hanger, someone knocked on the inside door.

"Come in," he barked as he tried to slip the sleeve up one arm without causing himself pain.

The door opened and when he looked, Angel stood in the entryway with the box of medical supplies in her hands, staring at him. Annoyance narrowed his eyes and he looked away. Though he ignored her and went back to dressing himself, he didn't miss her long pause in the doorway or the way her eyes followed his every move. Ordinarily, he wouldn't acknowledge her gawking—he didn't like it, even if he'd gotten used to women staring at him—but the odd feelings she stirred in him made her gaze far more unnerving than normal. He sat on the edge of the bed once again and looked over at her.

"Are you going to come in or stand there and stare at me all night?"

She dropped her eyes and her cheeks pinkened prettily.

He grinned. He couldn't help it.

"Yeah...sorry," she muttered before she straightened her shoulders with confidence. "I brought a change of bandages."

He smirked. "Are you sure you can control yourself if I take my shirt off again?"

Her face reddened and Bret chuckled, thoroughly enjoying himself. He fixed her with a roguish grin and was pleased to see her spine stiffen and her chin come up, meeting his challenge.

"I just wasn't expecting to see you on your feet so soon. You really shouldn't be, you know. It must be very painful."

"Yeah, *very*. You didn't happen to bring anything for that, did you?"

"I might have something in here." She set the box on the

bed next to him and began to rummage through it. "You're still using the antibiotic drops in your ear, right?"

He glanced at the small bottle on his nightstand that she'd given him a few days before. "Yep."

"Is it helping?"

"It's feeling better, so yeah, I suppose it is."

"Good," she said as she grabbed a small bottle from the box and opened it. "Here," she shook two white pills from the bottle into his hand, "they should take the edge off the pain."

"Thanks, Doc," he said, grinning at her again. He grabbed a glass of water from his nightstand and downed the meds before turning to her again. "So, what else did you bring?"

"Just stuff for changing your bandages. If you'll remove your shirt and sit in the chair, I'll see if they need it."

Dropping his clean shirt onto the bed, he hobbled to the chair, straddled the seat, and rested his forearms on the ladder-back with no further teasing.

"Well, the ones you tore open last night are still bleeding a bit," she said after carefully removing the soiled dressings. "I'll have to change those, but the others look okay."

He nodded.

"Most of the lacerations seem to be healing well," she said as her fingers lightly probed his upper back. "No infection. That's a good thing." She patted his shoulder and, for some reason, the contact made him shiver.

She went into the small bathroom and Bret heard water running. She returned a few minutes later with a bowl of warm water and a wet cloth.

He winced and grunted a few times as she cleaned his wounds but he was thankful for the minor pain. At least it kept him from thinking about her hands on him.

After reapplying the bandages, she asked him to move to the bed, and followed the same procedure on his feet.

He watched her efficient work. "You're good at caring for these types of injuries."

"A lot of the men and women who ended up here had similar wounds," she said without stopping or looking up from wrapping his foot in gauze. "I got used to treating them after a while, though I never enjoyed seeing them."

"How long has that been?"

"Too long," she mumbled, releasing his foot and standing. "I try not to think about how long everything's been this way. It's too depressing."

"Yeah, it is," he murmured, swinging his legs over the side and sitting on the edge of the bed again.

Hands clasped behind her back, she bent toward him.

He recoiled. "What are you doing?"

"Just checking your face. You're looking much better this evening. The inflammation is nearly gone. You know," she straightened up and her eyes twinkled at him mischievously, "I think you might be somewhat attractive once the bruises go away. Of course, it wouldn't hurt if you shaved."

He scratched self-consciously at his stubbled jaw and gave her a ha-ha-very-funny look. To his surprise she giggled, and the sound made his skin tingle.

She glanced at him as she finished putting her supplies away and another small laugh burst from her. "You might even look good with a goatee like Jake's."

He smiled, wondering why her teasing didn't irritate him.

"I'm not the goatee type, but I could go for a shave. If I had something to shave *with*." He let the statement hang like a question.

"I'm sure Jake wouldn't mind if you used his straight razor...it's in the bathroom."

He started to get up, but Angel stopped him and pressed him back onto the bed. The contact of her small hand on his bare skin sent a blast of heat down his arm and into his chest. Alarmed by his body's reactions, he glanced at her hand and then up into her face, struggling to keep his expression mildly curious.

"Wait until your feet are healed, or at least until Jake gets back to help you. Unless…"

"What?" Irritated by the unwanted effect of her touch on his body, the simple question came out like an angry demand.

She tilted her head and gave him a challenging look. "Unless you'd let me do it for you."

"I don't think so." He glared at her from his seat on the bed, defensive again.

"Why? You think I'll use the razor for more than a shave?"

"I'd rather do it myself," he said, uncomfortable with the notion of her performing such a personal task, and for a far more damning reason than the blade's sharpness.

Until now, he'd avoided recalling how good her body had felt beneath his last night, or how much he'd wanted to kiss her. But the idea of her cool fingers on his face and neck revived the memory with intimate detail, making his body tighten.

"Don't be silly, I won't do anything you don't like." She crossed into the bathroom and he heard her collect the items, and a few minutes later, she returned with some towels, a washbasin filled with steaming water, a razor, and a shaving mug complete with brush. She set the items down on the small nightstand and turned to him. "I am actually pretty good at using a straight razor." She smiled and he had to chuckle.

"I can do it myself."

"Yes, I'm sure you can, but having a mirror would help." She had him there.

"Come on, Bret, I won't bite and I promise to be careful."

The sincerity on her face did him in. That and the itchy discomfort of his too long beard. "All right."

Resigned to the act, he sighed as she dragged the desk chair closer to the bed for him to sit in.

Smiling again, but avoiding his eyes, Angel draped a bath towel around his shoulders. He tried not to inhale, already too aware of her lilac fragrance for his own good, and he didn't want the thoughts it roused in his head.

She soaked one of the smaller towels in the warm water and rung it out. Then she carefully applied it to his beard. The act surprised him a little and he looked up at her. He caught her eyes, and her lips quirked slight, but she seemed almost as nervous as he felt.

"Do you do this often?" he asked, his voice muffled by the towel.

"Do what?"

"Groom strange men. It's a little personal, don't you think?"

A flush crept up her cheeks and he felt her hands tremble against the cloth on his face.

"I suppose it might seem that way," she said as she removed the towel and tossed it onto the sweaty shirt Bret had discarded earlier. She didn't comment further and Bret found himself wondering who else she'd performed this act on.

She picked up the shaving mug and, using the bush, stirred the frothy mix before applying it to his face and neck. Thankfully the minty smell of the shaving foam helped mask her tantalizing scent. Now, if he could just ignore her touch as easily.

He couldn't help the trepidation that stiffened his shoulders when she approached him with the razor. Sitting a little taller, his eyes darted between the blade in her hand and her face. He didn't really think she'd hurt him, not really, but then again, he didn't know her that well either. She was a slave owner, after all. If she could pay money to own people, who knew what else she'd do.

Positioning his head, she carefully placed the blade against his cheek and Bret closed his eyes. Tense and uneasy, he tried to breath evenly and hold very still, but he needn't have worried. The razor slid smoothly over his cheek, taking the foam and whiskers with it.

His eyes popped open as she wiped the blade on a clean towel and reached toward his face again. She caught his stunned expression and frowned, tilting her head. "What's wrong?"

"Nothing," he said with a shrug. "I guess I just wasn't expecting you to be so good at shaving a man."

Good grief, his inner voice groaned. *Are you fishing? I thought you didn't care what she did or didn't do.*

It was her turn to shrug. "It's not that hard when you sit so still."

Okay, not exactly the answer he'd hoped for, but then he hadn't realized he was hoping for anything.

She went back to her task and Bret did his best to ignore the feeling of her soft hands as she pulled his skin taut for the next slide of the blade or the whisper of her breath against his temple. As she worked, her long hair trailed along his arm and chest making his skin tighten and tingle, and he had to fight the urge to run his fingers through the silky strands. By the time she'd finished and handed him a towel to wipe his face, he felt as if he'd been fighting a war rather than getting a shave. Then again, battling his body's reactions to her closeness and the strange feelings that swirled around inside him were as much of a conflict as any physical skirmish.

Angel took the shaving utensils to the bathroom and he heard her clean them in the sink as he slowly moved back to his bed. Tugging at his now too tight jeans, he set the hand towel he'd grabbed aside to pluck the clean shirt he'd discarded earlier off the mattress and slowly work it up his arms.

"I can help you with that," Angel said as she reentered the room.

"I can do it myself." He knew he sounded irritable, but he couldn't help it. His body ached and other parts of him were too aware of her for his comfort.

"I'm sorry," she said softly and he clenched his jaw. He hadn't meant to be ungrateful either.

"I didn't mean to snap at you. I'm just...sore and tired, and not used to anyone doing things for me."

"We all do things for each other here," she said as she tossed the remaining supplies into the wooden box. "It's not meant as an insult."

He gritted his teeth and his back twinged as he shrugged into the shirt. Pulling the ends together to cover the evidence of his arousal—though it was fading—he fastened a couple of buttons to keep it there as he faced her.

"I know," he said, lowering himself onto the bed and picking up the hand towel again. "I'm sorry. I am grateful for your help and for everything else too. But..."

Her brows drew down. "But what?"

Inhaling through his nose, he grinned. "There's one thing I've discovered about our little room here."

"And what's that?"

"The fact that being close to the kitchen isn't always a perk."

She tilted her head in confusion, but her eyes widened when his belly grumbled, and she seemed to understand. "Oh. Okay."

As he wiped the traces of shaving foam from his face and neck with the towel, she picked up the box of medical supplies she'd brought. "I'm going to take this stuff upstairs and then I'll grab you something to eat, so don't get up. I'll take the dirty clothes out when I come back."

"Yes, ma'am," he said as he carefully piled the pillows behind him in preparation for his meal.

Twenty minutes later, Angel had returned with dinner for the both of them, but aside from a positive comment about his newly shaven appearance, they ate in relative silence, which suited him just fine.

"Who's Amy?" Her question cut the long quiet and set off a bundle of wariness inside him.

Alarmed, he glanced at her, his fork full of gravy-soaked mashed potatoes paused halfway to his lips. "How do you know that name?"

She shrugged and shook her head, as if regretting the

question. "You mumbled it in your sleep last night." When she finally met his gaze, there was no hint of a lie in her expression. In fact, he was struck again by how innocent she looked.

"No one important. Why do you care?" he answered after staring at her a little too long. Annoyed with himself, he turned back to his meal and popped the spuds into his mouth.

"Do you dislike her as much as you seem to hate me sometimes?"

"More," his unintended reply was sharp. "She tried to kill me once and failed at what you succeeded in doing."

"And what's that?"

"You made me a slave, an extremely unwilling one, but a slave none-the-less. Amy tried to take my freedom too."

She frowned at him but didn't argue.

"How did you meet her?"

"Why all the questions?" He dropped the fork onto his half-full plate and glared at her. He knew he shouldn't be so angry over such basic questions, but he felt like she was digging into a place he wanted to keep hidden.

"I'm only trying to make conversation... I didn't mean to intrude."

He hated the way her shoulders sagged in defeat. It didn't seem to mesh with the woman he'd come to know. Plus, it made him feel like a bully again.

"I'm sorry." He lowered his gaze to his plate. "I don't like to talk about her and, no offense, but you're not the person I'd choose to have that conversation with. But..." He glanced at her and then shrugged his broad shoulders. She wasn't asking him to bare his soul and she already knew Amy's name. A little more wouldn't make any difference. "I met her a few years after the wars," he said, taking another bite. "She wandered into our group one day and stayed."

"Was she pretty?"

"Yes, very pretty. She was also an exceptional liar. I'll

never be so stupid again."

Angel looked down at her plate, pushing the food around with her fork. "So, she's the reason Jake ended up with Darla."

"Apparently, but I thought you already knew that much."

"Jake didn't want to talk about his time living with Darla Cain and I never pushed him." She lifted her head and met his gaze. "The same as why he never told me how you two actually met."

"Neither one of us is especially proud of our past," he said quietly, staring down at his plate and shrugged. "Myself, I mostly don't think about it. I suppose Jake's the same."

"Sometimes it helps to talk about it," she said, but when he turned a glare on her, she put up her hands and rushed through her next words. "I'm not pushing, Bret. I don't expect you to tell me anything."

Looking into her azure eyes, he wondered what she hoped to learn with all her questions. He searched, but only found concern staring back at him. Her pretty face and that damn guileless expression once again reminded him of Amy.

"You know," he said, setting his now empty plate aside, "there was another woman who told me the same thing once, and I believed her. Until she turned on me, tried to kill me, and then stole my best friend." He scowled at her, remembering Amy's betrayal as if it were yesterday.

Angel shifted in her seat but didn't look away.

His frown darkened. "Do you really expect me to believe that you're as sweet and innocent as you act?"

She stared silently for several heartbeats and then shook her head. "You're right. It's too soon."

She sounded disappointed, and that feeling of being a tyrant returned to churn in his belly.

"No one is really ever that innocent, but you can believe what you like." She stood, her movements quick and jerky as she briskly gathered up the remaining dishes. Then she paused to contemplate him with narrowed eyes.

"Don't do anything stupid," she said succinctly. Snatching his plate off the bed and placing it with the others, she hefted the tray and crossed to the exit.

"And what's your definition of stupid?"

She rested her hand on the doorknob and frowned at him. "Anything that would force me to hurt you or someone else because of your actions."

He returned her glare, daring her to speak more plainly.

"Please don't try to run," she finally said. "If someone else finds you, they'll hurt you and there'd be nothing I could do about it."

"You think I can just accept this life?" he asked as his muscles tightened with fury over his situation—and her implication that he *should* accept it.

"I don't know you, but I think it's safe to say, that you would've never given up your freedom, not for anyone or anything. That's what scares me about you. I've seen more than enough death, Bret; I don't want to see yours."

Stunned by her response, he stared as she closed the door behind her. Once again, she'd caught him off-guard and said precisely what he hadn't expected. She was either exceptionally good at the games she played or she was telling the truth—and he wasn't sure which one he wanted to believe.

15

BRET LEANING AGAINST THE RAILING on Angel's wide
front porch, taking in the sunny winter morning and smiling
down at Grayling. The shorthaired gray cat purred contentedly
as he leisurely rubbed his small body—and his scent—all over
Bret's ankle.

"You trying to make sure all the other cats know I'm *your*
human?" he jokingly asked the cat. There weren't more than
three felines on the ranch and the other two had families of
their own. Grayling paused to blink up at him with his
changing amber eyes and then went right back to scenting
Bret's jeans. "Silly cat," Bret said, but a part of him was glad
for the animal's company. Grayling had been his companion
for a great deal of his lengthy recuperation, and now the feline
seemed like an old friend.

Chuckling, Bret closed his eyes, lifted his face to the sky,
and inhaled the crisp, cool air. He exhaled a sigh of
contentment, already eager for Jake's long-promised tour of the
homestead.

During his tedious weeks of recovery, his strength slowly
returned, but after a month of rest and as much food as he
wanted, he was nearly back to his old self again. His feet still

bothered him a little in the new cowboy boots Angel had acquired from a boot maker in town, but not enough to keep him off his feet.

Along with the boots, Angel had also purchased him a new wardrobe with everything he'd need to work in the weather— hot or cold—including two new cowboy hats—black felt for winter and a plain white straw for summer. The clothes fit surprisingly well considering he hadn't given anyone his measurements. He was better equipped now than he had been in years.

He had swallowed his pride and thanked Angel for her generosity, though it had irked him to do so. He'd felt a little like a beggar bowing for his queen, though Angel hadn't been anything but gracious. Still, he didn't like feeling indebted to her.

Being near her rattled him, stirring up sensations he didn't want. When Jake returned from inspecting the cattle several weeks ago, Bret had been relieved but he'd also felt a bit disappointed that Angel would no longer visit him as often as she had. Since then, a part of him had missed her smile and that lilac fragrance that followed her, but whenever his mind went down that path, he reminded himself not to be fooled again. Unreasonably attracted to her for some crazy reason, that didn't mean he should act on it. He didn't need to think on it either.

The front door opened behind him and he glanced over his shoulder to find a grinning Jake.

"Surprised to find you out here already," Jake said as he waited for Grayling to dart inside, and then pulled the door closed behind him.

"Are you kidding? I've been dying to get out of that room for weeks."

Jake chuckled. "Yeah, I know." His friend's tone reminded Bret that he'd been a bit of a grouch for at least the last two weeks.

"So, you ready for the tour, then?" Jake started down the

porch steps and Bret fell in with him, grinning and looking forward to getting the lay of the land.

"Absolutely."

Jake led him round the back of the house to the dormant orchard and the kitchen gardens, where long rows of raised vegetable gardens lined the area just beyond the deck off the dining hall. They were setup to keep the plants warm and growing, even during the harsh winter cold. With his shoulders back and a clear sense of pride in his voice, Jake explained their planting and harvesting strategies for the gardens. Bret took it all in, impressed with all they'd accomplished.

"You remember a lot more than you let on to them," he told Jake as he looked over the gardens.

"Nah," Jake said, "this was mostly Esther's doing. At least, the idea of putting in the garden and the fruit trees. I've done what I can with the cattle and crops, but I never knew all the ins and outs like you do."

"Still," Bret said with a nod, "this is a great setup and I'm sure you've done well too. You always were too humble, Jake."

Jake tucked his hands into his pockets and kicked at the snow, and Bret had to smile to himself. Jake always was uncomfortable with praise.

"So, what kind of fruit trees we got?" he asked to change the subject and ease his friend's discomfort.

An open area of lawn stretched between the last garden row and the start of the fruit orchard, which ran all the way up to the homestead's surrounding wall.

They strolled into the orchard while Jake explained their growing and picking timetable for the orchard and how they swapped apples for pears, peaches, and other fruits at the market or with nearby homes. Bret heard the words and stored them away, but the majority of his attention had been drawn elsewhere.

A huge weeping willow stood like a sentry atop a lone hill

several yards beyond the homestead's protective wall. Its snow-crusted limbs extended at least twenty-five-feet in every direction. Seeming to graze the bright morning clouds, it stretched out over the whole hilltop. Naked of its tiny, sea green leaves, the long boughs stirred in the light wind, the tips scraping intricate patterns in the drifts of snow.

The scene gripped Bret's tattered heart, churning up old disappointments, making his chest ache for all he'd suffered, but why he had that reaction, he couldn't say.

"It's an impressive sight, isn't it?" Jake said, breaking the strange hold the willow had on Bret.

Head swiveling between his friend and the tree, Bret was unable to fully shake the odd feeling. "Yeah."

"Kind of sad too," Jake said softly, as entranced by the odd melancholy as Bret.

Bret nodded, still staring at the tree.

Shaking himself, Jake headed into the orchard and continued his tour. Bret took one last hard look at the willow before he followed his friend.

Next came the barns near the wall-gates on the opposite side of the dooryard. Long pastures stretched out behind them where horses nickered a greeting as he and Jake approached the fence.

"She's got some good stock," Bret said, eyeing a big black stallion in the far paddock.

"Yes, she does," Jake answered with a smile on his bearded face. "Took some time getting it built up, but we've been doing okay."

"Where's the cattle? Did you bring in the herd?"

"The majority are in low fields over those hills, and another smaller group over that way," Jake said waving his hand in a southeasterly direction. "We feed them a couple times a day through the winter, but in the spring and summer they have good grazing farther out and the river's current is strong enough that it runs year-round. The mamas and calves are in the far corral with the lean-to shelter. Over there," he indicated a spot where some construction was nearly complete, "we're planning to finish the new calving barn this year, along with the new bunkhouse you saw earlier."

Bret nodded. "Good idea. Get 'em out of the weather."

"Yeah. That's what I was thinking. Good for us too."

Bret chuckled, agreeing wholeheartedly.

"So, what do you think?"

"Looks good," Bret said, taking in the surrounding hills and the mountains in the distance. Everything about the place reminded him of home. He frowned at that thought and, refusing to think of his Mistress' ranch as home, he refocused on his dreams of freedom. "So, when do I get to see the rest of the spread?"

Jake glanced at him as they both leaned on the top fence rail. "You feeling up to a ride?"

Bret shrugged. "Sure, it'll be nice to get back in the saddle again."

"I need to check on the herd," Jake said pushing away from the fence. "You can ride out with me, if you'd like."

Bret pushed his gloved hands into the pockets of his farm jacket and hunched his shoulder against the cold. "Got to start somewhere," he said, following his friend as they ambled down the muddy path to the barn. "Sooner seems better than later to me. I'm getting restless siting around the house all the time."

Jake laughed. "I noticed."

Bret smiled at his friend's gentle reminder of his grumpiness. His mood was already improving but getting on a horse again would go a long way to making him happy. Getting a look at the landscape and forming a plan for his escape almost made him giddy. But he still needed to regain some of his strength. The ride today would probably exhaust him, but it would be a start.

*　　*　　*

Two weeks later, Bret was sitting in the dining hall with some of the other cowhands having dinner, talking and joking, when Angel suddenly joined them.

"How's everything going?" she asked the table in general.

A chorus of 'goods' and 'fines' met that, and Angel grinned at their cheerfulness.

"How about the cattle?"

Seeing the other hands' eyes turn toward him, Bret's neck prickled. He hadn't spoken to her much in the last few weeks. In fact, he'd made a point to avoid her. But he'd been tasked with running this place, and that required some conversation, at least. Sitting up a little taller, he cleared his throat and jumped right in. "Everything's going well at the moment."

"Any sign of more missing stock?" Angel asked with a worried frown.

"No, we've been watching the fences and trails, but still no sign of anything."

Bret crushed the hot rush of irritation that burned through his gut when she glanced at Jake for verification.

She turned back to Bret. "I assume you have some kind of plan or schedule set up?"

Bret nodded and unclenched his jaw. "Jake did a good job taking care of that, I only expanded it a little. We'll have to adjust a bit when the weather improves, but that shouldn't be a problem. I'm going to need more people working the cattle though."

"More people?"

"Yeah." He glanced around the wide room at the ranch populous. "There are, what, a couple hundred people here? Maybe more?"

She nodded.

"Less than a quarter of them actually work with the cattle and the harvests, aside from gathering the crops. We should train more people for those jobs. We're going to need them if you want this ranch to grow."

Inhaling, Angel slanted back from the table where her arms had been resting. Her gaze swept over the room and her brow wrinkled before meeting Bret's eyes once more. "Many of that number are children."

Bret shrugged. "I started helping my dad around our ranch when I was five. I don't see why the kids can't help around here too. Nothing too serious now, they'll grow into the more difficult work."

Still frowning, Angel glanced at Jake again. Bret took a deep breath and held it as the fingers of one hand balled up in his lap. *Does she want me to do this job or not?*

Meeting Bret's gaze again, she tilted her head as if studying him before she spoke. "I won't disagree as long as they're safe. The younger children will need chaperones and the older ones, someone to supervise, at least for those who haven't already been out there. Most of them know nothing about working with the animals."

"Shouldn't be hard to train them. Kids are versatile and you might be surprised at how much they'll enjoy helping out."

Beside Bret, Jake nodded. "That's true. Think about the kids at Monica's place. A lot of them help with the cattle and horses and they love it."

"I know," Angel said with a sigh, "but this place is a lot bigger and the gap between the number of people who know what they're doing to those who don't is a lot wider. I've been hesitant to involve them."

"The only way they're going to learn is to get them out there," Bret said.

Angel gave him a look he couldn't decipher, but then her lips turned up slightly. "All right then, where do we begin?"

While the men finished their meal, they discussed and agreed upon a training plan for the spring. When the conversation wound down, Angel said goodnight and headed off to bed. Bret watched her go, curious about the paleness of her complexion and the defeated sag to her shoulders, but he pushed it aside. He was there to work with the animals, not wonder about the woman who had paid to own him like one.

* * *

A few days later, Bret and Jake entered their apartment having completed their nightly after-dinner trip to check on the animals in the barns. On previous nights, each man would sit in his bed and Jake would answer anything Bret wanted to know about the ranch and its history. He was less forthcoming about his own past.

"I wasn't lucky enough to end up with a woman like Angel when they sold me at the Auction Hall," Jake had said a few nights ago. When Bret questioned him further, the only other thing he would say was that Darla had made no qualms about forcing him to her will.

Bret hadn't wanted to push his friend, and he didn't. Knowing Jake as well as he did, Bret could see the anguish his friend tried to hide. It made him wonder what had happened to the strong, thoughtful man he remembered. What other horrors did Jake face to make him seem so willing to live as a slave? Bret still wondered about that, but he never asked.

Tonight, they'd just removed their coats, discussing when to start the spring breeding, when Angel paid them an unexpected visit.

When she didn't show up for dinner that evening, Jake had mumbled a curious remark about her not eating again. But he'd refused to repeat it when Bret asked. Now, seeing her at their apartment door, Bret immediately noted her pale face and tired, puffy-eyed appearance.

"How are you two doing?" she asked with a smile that was clearly forced.

"Fine," Jake answered from the desk chair where he sat removing his boots. "How about you? We heard you weren't feeling well at dinner."

"I'm okay."

"You look tired," Bret said from his place on the end of Jake's bed where he'd just pulled off his last boot. He tossed it toward the outside door where it landed beside his first with a thud. "Why don't you sit down?"

"Thanks." The corners of her mouth curled softly as she took his offer and perched on the end of his bed.

Bret could feel Jake studying him with narrowed eyes and purposely avoided looking his way.

"Are you sure you're okay?" Jake asked, turning his attention back to Angel. "You're a little pale."

"I think I'm coming down with something," Angel said with a dismissive wave of her hand. "I'll be all right. I just stopped by to see how things are going with the cattle."

"Everything's fine," Jake said, tossing his boot to land beside Bret's with a hollow clatter.

"The good news is that no more cattle have disappeared yet," Bret said drawing Angel's gaze.

"That's great news." Her face brightening slightly. "Hopefully, we won't lose any more." She smiled at them both, but the dark circles under her unusually dull eyes made it less dazzling than normal. She asked about Theo and the other hands, exchanged a few other pleasantries, and then Angel excused herself to go to bed.

"Get better," Bret said, and he could feel Jake's surprise and disbelief like a slap to the side of his head.

"Yeah," Jake muttered, sending another curious glare Bret's way.

"Thanks," she replied as a flush spread over her cheeks. She glanced from him to Jake and back. Then her fingers fiddled with her sleeve as she stammered another hasty goodbye and left the room.

A smug smile tugged at Bret's lips. Angel appeared as affected by his charm as every other woman he'd ever flirted with and, judging by the way Jake's jaw clenched in irritation, he had noticed it too.

This wasn't the first time they'd been in this situation—a woman seemingly forgetting Jake's existence as she spoke with Bret—but it was the first time Bret actually had to work to hold a woman's interest. With his good looks being the only power he had in this new society, he'd learned to use it to his advantage. And, just like with Sara at the Auction Hall, he would do what he had to do to aid his escape.

After Angel's departure, Jake peered at Bret with transparent suspicion.

Feigning ignorance, Bret frowned at his friend. "What's that look for?"

"What are you doing?"

"What do you mean?"

"Don't play innocent with me, Bret. I know you too well. You're up to something."

"And why do you say that?"

"Before I went to check on the cattle a couple of months ago, you were bound and determined to be a regular pain in the ass for Angel. For the last few weeks, you've been acting as if you can't please her enough. What while I was gone?"

"Nothing," Bret said, getting up from the bed and going to gaze out the window before he turned back to his friend. "I'm trying not to cause problems."

"Trying to bamboozle Angel, you mean." Jake's tone sharpened. "What're you up to? Are you planning to run?"

Bret stared silently at his friend, but Jake clearly read his face like an open book.

"Never mind," Jake said as he sat back in the desk chair and crossed his arms over his chest. "Don't tell me. I don't want to know. I don't want anything to do with it."

"Why not?" Bret asked and, seeing an opportunity for them both to regain their freedom, he scooted a little closer to his friend. "Why don't you come with me? It could be like it used to be. We could make it. You and me, brother. What do you say?"

Jake started shaking his head before Bret even finished. "No. I'm not going to live like that again. It's better here."

Bret straightened his spine and his cutting tone returned. "Safer you mean."

"Yeah, it's safer and warmer, with consistent food, and a soft bed every night. And here, unlike out there, I know what to expect. If we leave, there's a high probability we'd both be dead by the end of the week. The Section Guard patrols are diligent in pursuing escaped slaves and hard on them when they're captured, which they usually are. I don't want to take that kind of risk. I have a place here now, and people I care about."

Why Jake's words angered him so much, Bret couldn't say. Maybe it was his own disinclination to leave his friend behind. Or maybe it was the suspicion that there was more behind why Jake didn't want to leave. He was hiding something, of that Bret was sure. It had been five years after all...maybe Jake didn't feel he could trust his best friend anymore. Maybe he was protecting someone else, someone important to him, at least until he was certain Bret's loyalties hadn't changed.

The tightness in Bret's chest abated. *That would be just like Jake,* he thought, then it occurred to him that Jake's special someone may be closer than Bret realized. Maybe that 'something more' lay between Jake and Angel. Could she have more interest in Bret's best friend than either of them let on?

Heat flashed over Bret's skin and he gritted his teeth. "What *people* exactly?"

Jake opened his mouth to reply, but hesitated. His expression shifted and he sighed, apparently reading the suspicion in Bret's eyes. "It isn't what you think." He sounded defensive and...weary.

Bret shook his head in disgust. "You're brainwashed, Jake."

"I am *not* brainwashed. You're just being stubborn and stupid."

"And you're afraid to take any chances, afraid to think on

your own. What happened to you?" Bret bellowed, springing up from the bed. "You're not the man I used to know. You're not even a man!"

"You have no idea what I've been through," Jake roared, lunging to his feet, his chair skidding into the desk with a wooden thud. "What I am and what I do now are important."

"You're a slave, Jake. How can you live knowing that?"

"Yes, I am, but I've never felt like one since I moved here." Jake lowered his voice, but his eyes looked resolute. "I like running this place and Angel's been good to me."

Bret's eyes narrowed and a cold stone settled in his belly while the rest of his body burned as he angled one black brow upward. "Exactly how good *has* she been to you, Jake? Do you sing her praises because you're lucky enough to be the only man she sleeps with at night? Or is it because you really are brainwashed, but too blinded by her beauty and phony innocence to realize it?" Irony laced Bret's statement—his last words almost exactly the same as those Jake had used on him when they argued about Amy years ago.

Why are you pushing this? Bret wondered again and his muscles vibrated with tension. Why did Jake's decision bother him so much, and why did Bret's suspicions hurt in ways he didn't understand?

"You son of a bitch," Jake said between clenched teeth, his body stiff while anger flared in his hazel eyes. "You have *no right* to say things like that to me. After all you've been through, I thought you would've grown, but you're still a selfish child. When will you realize that until you get rid of whatever's eating at you, you'll never be free, no matter where you run?"

Bret's fingers curled into fists at his side and his jaw clenched tight around the angry words he wanted to hurl at his friend. He resented Jake's assessment, but he didn't want to alienate him either. He had no idea what Jake had really been through.

And who's fault is that? his uncle's voice asked, spurring Bret's anger and deepening the hurt squeezing his heart.

"There are things about me you know nothing about and still others I don't wish to share," Jake said, justifying the questions in Bret's mind. Shaking his head, Jake broke eye contact and calmly put some distance between them before he faced Bret again. "It hurts me to say that, but it's true. You're my brother, Bret, and I love you like one, but no matter what we used to be or what we've become, you have no right to judge me."

Bret stiffened at Jake's words, but in his mind, he heard Vince berate him.

You're not good enough for him anymore.

He's outgrown your friendship.

He doesn't want to listen to any more of your whining.

"Living as a slave is no better than living like an animal," Bret growled, his voice dangerously soft, sharp and quivering with barely suppressed fury, though he was no longer precisely sure who he was angry with—Jake or himself. "Only animals are chained in cold, dark cells, beaten by their Mistresses, and then come back for more. Only animals are dumb enough to stay where they exist only to serve and are never truly free. I am not an animal, Jake. I'm not like you."

"There's so much you don't understand," Jake said in a shaky voice while rubbing at his chest and shaking his head.

Bret wanted to stop. He wanted to defuse the rage Jake's ostensible rejection and his insecurities had unleashed, but it seemed to have a life of its own—wanting to lash out at the nearest target, just as it did when he was a kid. He'd been alone too long, and now the pain he felt at metaphorically—and maybe truly—losing his best friend all over again wouldn't let him go. "I understand this much, Jake...you're weak. You used to be the best and strongest man I ever knew. We have a chance to be free, but you'd rather run like a whimpering dog back to his Mistress because she's a good fuck!"

Shock flashed across Jake's face, only to be replaced by a cold, suppressed fury, and in that instant, Bret knew he'd pushed too far. He opened his mouth to apologize, to take back everything he'd said, but he never got the chance.

One minute, Bret stood toe to toe with his best friend and then the next he was sailing over the end of Jake's bed, crashing to the hardwood. He shook the dizziness from his head and tried to come to terms with the fact that Jake had hit him, hard. Blood oozed from his split lip as he glared up at a stunned looking Jake. Regret painted his friend's features, but Bret was having none of it— furious all over again.

"I see there isn't much left of our friendship after five years," he sneered while tentatively testing the damage to his mouth with his fingers before getting up off the floor. "You can tell Angel she wasted her money trying to resurrect it."

"Bret, wait. I—" Jake grabbed Bret's shoulder as he started for the outside door. Bret spun around and landed a right cross that knocked Jake into the desk.

"Now we're even," Bret said in a cold, raspy voice as he turned, picked up his boots, and left the room, slamming the door behind him.

* * *

Walking down the upstairs hallway, Angel heard muffled shouts and paused. She listened, unsure of what she was hearing. Another angry exchange reached her ears and she turned around to investigate. A loud thud stopped her as she stepped onto the foyer floor. In a heartbeat, she rushed down the hall toward the back of the house.

"…money trying to resurrect it."

"Bret, wait. I—" Jake's words were cut off and another thump echoed in the hallway as something heavy crashed into the wall.

"Now, we're even," she heard Bret say and then the door to the deck slammed shut a moment later.

Concern for both men made her knock on the inside door. When no one answered, she slowly opened it and went inside. Jake was rubbing his jaw and had just slid off the desktop as she entered. She glanced around the room, but there was no sign of Bret.

Frowning, she turned to Jake. "Is the yelling match over?"

He sighed and sat down on the edge of his bed. "Yeah."

"Who won the brawl?" she asked, pointing at the bruise forming along his cheekbone.

He huffed out a humorless chuckle. "It was a tie."

Her chest tight with worry, she pulled the desk chair over and sat down facing him. "What happened?"

"Nothing," he muttered rubbing his jaw again.

"Nothing?" Both her eyebrows climbed toward her hairline. "Jake, I could hear you both yelling from the other side of the house."

"Then you should know what was said," he snapped. She recoiled, but immediately saw regret in his eyes.

"I only understood the last couple sentences. That doesn't tell me what happened."

He shook his head and stared blankly at the floor. "I don't want to talk about it."

"O-kay." She wouldn't push him, but she couldn't just walk away either. "Are you all right, Jake?"

"Yeah," he said as he released a long breath and then met her gaze, "I'll be fine. Did you need something?"

"Well, I was going to ask about Bret earlier," she said, glad for the change in subject, "but now doesn't seem like such a great time."

"If you mean about him taking over the job, he's doing fine," Jake said, getting up from his bed and straightening the covers Bret must have dislodged. "He's getting the details down and he seems to be enjoying the work."

Angel nodded, but knew he was holding something back, and she wanted to ask, but didn't. It wasn't hard to figure out that Bret was up to something and Jake felt torn as to which one of them—Bret or Angel—he should remain loyal to. She sensed he wanted to talk, but he couldn't make himself betray his friend—even though protecting Bret meant betraying Angel's trust. But there was something else too, something Jake had been hiding for a long time, and she was terribly afraid that whatever it was would affect everyone she cared about.

"If you want to talk," she said as she reached for his hand, "I'm always here for you, Jake."

He smiled, then winced, his jaw plainly sore. Patting her hand affectionately, he nodded. "I know, but I think this is something Bret and I need to work out on our own."

"Is Bret all right?"

"Yeah, he'll be fine too. We just know how to push each other's buttons a little too well. He was alone a long time and I forgot about the things that set him off." He shrugged and met her gaze. "He's a lot better than he used to be, but I think something I said made him feel rejected."

"Why?"

"Remember when I told you he had a bad past?"

She nodded, her eyes glued to Jake's.

"It has to do with that and the fact that he feels guilty that I was captured and he couldn't help me."

"He couldn't."

"I know, but Bret's...well, Bret." He smiled at her and squeezed her hand. "Don't worry about it, Angel. He'll stew for a while and then he'll stew some more with guilt. We'll eventually get past this. You'll see."

Angel hoped he was right. She suspected that if their friendship broke, there would be nothing left to keep Bret here. Nothing to keep him from running away, and not one thing that would save him if the Section Guards caught up to him.

16

ON A BRIGHT April morning, Angel and Peggy stood side by side on the wide porch of her sprawling, country-style farmhouse. Angel idly stroked the gray cat standing on the railing, demanding her attention, as she watched a group of men and women prepare for a multi-day ride moving the herd to the spring feeding pastures. There were several families in the dooryard saying their goodbyes with children darting around the U-shaped area, some headed toward the barns with dogs barking at their heels while the others milled around. Angel saw friends joking with each other as they checked their supplies while partners and lovers said their farewells with kisses and longing looks. The scene made the ache of Angel's loneliness swell uncomfortably inside her. Her eyes inadvertently sought out Bret Masters and her heart fluttered in the vast emptiness of her chest.

He looked good after fully recovering from his injuries and having time to gain back his strength. His gauntness was gone and, in its place, stood a tall, broad-shouldered, muscular man with a face too handsome not to draw attention and confidence that was hard to miss. By March he had started making the agreed upon changes on the ranch. He oversaw everything from the cattle, to irrigation, to preparing for the first harvest, and all repairs or improvements were organized and ordered by Bret.

With Bret now in charge of the cattle, Jake's current responsibilities around the homestead increased. He still worked with Bret and the animals, but he also took over several of Angel's more tedious tasks. This allowed her time to concentrate fully on the difficult and time-consuming job of keeping the homestead running and alive. In her opinion, both men were irreplaceable.

Every aspect of the ranch ran smoothly and, from what Angel could tell, both seemed happy with the change. Bret, in particular, seemed to relish the job. He buried himself so completely in the work that he rarely had time for anything else. She knew the ranch would profit from his leadership, but she also detected an air of coolness between him and Jake. After a week of cold looks and angry silence, they were speaking again, but Angel sensed it would take more than time to repair their bond, and that thought broke her heart.

"Two days seems like such a long time," Peggy mumbled, and Angel glanced at her friend.

"Everything will be all right," Angel said for the second time that morning as her hand slid over Grayling's soft fur. "You'll see."

Her friend turned rueful eyes from the riders to regard Angel with an odd mix of trepidation and hope. Peggy was five weeks pregnant as she had learned during her most recent visit with Dr. Hillman at Monica's place a few days before. So far, the pregnancy was normal, but Peggy still worried about miscarrying yet again. Her fear was especially intense when Theo was absent for more than a few hours. That made this excursion a major trial for her.

"I hope so," Peggy replied and gave Angel a grateful smile as she left to say goodbye to Theo. The tall, blond man turned as Peggy approached and a huge grin split his rugged, Nordicfeatured face. Angel's heart warmed at his show of obvious affection, but a little pang struck her too, as a lump settled in her throat and her ribs squeezed a little tighter.

Averting her gaze, she took a deep, steading breath. The scent of lilacs filled the air from the plethora of flowering bushes nearby. The scent always filled her with hope of better things to come, which prompted her to plant so many bordering the surrounding wall years ago.

A sure way to ruin a beautiful day, she shied from the memories of her life before she found Monica. Luckily, Jake approaching the house distracted her.

"Looks like we're ready to go," Jake said, resting his booted foot on the porch's first step.

"How long do you think you'll be gone," she inquired as Bret came up behind Jake, and Grayling took the opportunity to jump down and go to his new friend.

The seamstress did a fantastic job, she thought as she admired how Bret's clothing molded to his broad shoulders and corded muscles of his body.

He peered up at her, his green eyes seeming to shine like crystal beneath the brim of his straw hat. His direct look sent an unexpected flush over her skin and her belly tightened. She tried to banish the feeling but it stayed, and she had the undignified urge to stamp her foot. *Oh! Why does he have to be so damn attractive?*

"A couple of days, no more than three, unless we have some trouble. It'll be sooner the faster we get out of here," Bret said in response to her question as he bent over to give the cat an affectionate pat. She loved Grayling, but the extent of Bret's friendship with the little feline had surprised her. Now, she found it enormously endearing.

"Then you'd better head out," she said, forcing herself to meet his disturbing gaze. *Get a grip!* "I want to sell some cattle at an auction next week."

Bret's lips visibly thinned as he straightened, and his eyes, already squinting from the sun, narrowed further. "I didn't know about an auction."

Grayling glanced up at the tall man and meowed loudly, once, twice. When he didn't get even a flicker of a response, he wandered off to find some affection elsewhere.

"I didn't either," she replied, "until last night. Then I decided to sell a few early to make up for some debt." She lifted a pointed eyebrow and, by the darkening frown on his face, Bret understood she meant obtaining him at the auction. "Some other homes northeast of here lost some cattle, but quite a few more than we did. They're hoping to buy now and catch-up before fall. It won't help much, I know, but at least they'll have a start."

"I thought we agreed; no interference with the livestock," Bret said in a low voice, wary but blunt.

"With taking care of them, Bret, not with their sale. You've done a great job and we haven't lost any more head, but this is *my* ranch and they're *my* animals. When I say they're going to be sold, they're going to be sold."

She didn't mean to be snippy, but her annoyance with him had reached its limit. He'd been making Jake miserable and now he was questioning her decisions. Then there was that peculiar thrill she couldn't shake when in his presence.

The last almost annoyed her more than the other two.

"Selling them is part of caring for them," he argued. "You didn't even discuss it with me."

"I don't have to," she said simply, unsure why she couldn't stop herself from putting him in his place. "It's my decision."

Oh... If looks could kill. She returned Bret's annoyed glare with one of her own. From the corner of her eye, she saw Jake anxiously pull his straw hat low and avert his gaze. She felt bad for his discomfort, but Bret's constant arrogance, plus his inability to empathize with anyone else's misfortunes, made Angel irritable. *Maybe I'm expecting too much from him.*

"Whatever you say," Bret finally answered through

clenched teeth, then spun on his heel and returned to his mount.

BRET SAT ON HIS HORSE and seethed. Why did he let Angel ruin his good mood so easily? She's the one who'd agreed to his terms, now she was changing the deal and doing her best to embarrass him too. His mind worked over the exchange, thinking of things he could've said, should've said, all the while knowing the result would've been the same.

After her advice to get a move on, she made him wait, sweating in the unexpectedly hot morning sun, while she and Jake exchanged a few words. Just before he opened his mouth to make some goofy cowboy comment like 'we're wasting daylight,' she descended the three porch steps and wrapped Jake in what looked to be a less-than-brotherly hug.

A burning sensation sprang up in the pit of Bret's stomach. A powerful surge of...something—he would *not* call it jealousy—hit him hard. His hands tightened on the reins, and he realized with another jolt of astonishment that he resented Jake standing there. Resented Jake embracing her. Resented everything about it.

A sudden frost seemed to settle in his belly while every other part of him steamed.

What the hell is wrong with me? He was never envious of Jake, but this was definitely an uncontrollable rush of pure...

Okay, yes, jealousy. He shook his head and looked away.

Being taunted, teased, and unwanted by a woman was as unfamiliar to Bret as flying through the troposphere would be for a fish. He didn't like it. The familiar lonely hollowness in his chest throbbed, growing larger and heavier, and he didn't like that either. What he didn't understand was why. He would be gone soon and he would *be* alone then, but he would also be free. Free from the humiliation of slavery, from his now-strained relationship with Jake, and from the troubling feelings roused by a Mistress he didn't want.

17

LATE ON THE SECOND NIGHT since Theo and the others left, Peggy sat at one end of her cushioned sofa sipping hot chocolate, while Angel occupied the opposite end doing the same. For the last hour, Angel has surreptitiously studied her friend, and more than once Peggy's gaze drifted to the pale-yellow curtains billowing in the slight evening breeze. They fluttered softly and Peggy watched them expectantly, her head tilted as if listening.

"I wonder what happened to them," Peggy murmured for the third time, her hot chocolate forgotten in her hands. It was getting late and daylight was fading.

A little nervous herself after Peggy had asked that question the second time, Angel had gone to the kitchen to heat the milk for their chocolate drinks. She had hoped the riders would've shown up by the time she was done, but she'd returned to the front room almost an hour ago, and there hadn't been a peep.

"I'm sure they'll be back any minute," Angel said and then set her empty mug aside. She didn't know any such thing, but she didn't want to increase Peggy's distress by adding her own.

Another ten minutes past by and Angel was beginning to think she may have to organize a search party, but a long heartbeat later, she finally breathed a sigh of relief when they heard the unmistakable sounds of horses' hooves and tired voices as the riders filed toward the barn. She glanced at her increasingly hormonal friend, and Peggy, looking shy and a little guilty, grinned in return as she hurried over to the small front window and peered outside.

"I told you everything would be fine," Angel said playfully as she joined her friend. "Now, sit down and finish your cocoa. You don't want Theo thinking you worried whole time. I'll lose one my best cowboys if he does, and I won't forgive you for it either."

Peggy's grin returned and she blushed. "You'll stay? Until he gets here, I mean?"

Angel tilted her head and smiled. "Of course."

Her eyelids feeling heavy, Angel once again sat curled up on Peggy's living room sofa, listening to her friend's hopes for her future family, when Theo entered the apartment well past ten.

"Evenin', ladies." His baby blue eyes lit up when they landed on Peggy. He tugged his cowboy hat from his matted blond head and, with it still in hand, he spread his strong arms wide and cocked his head. "Did you miss me, baby?" he asked in a low, sexy voice.

Peggy giggled and immediately jumped up to run into his arms, kissing and hugging him as if he'd been gone a month.

"It's good to see you, Theo," Angel said with a tired smile as she made her way to the door. "I'll leave you two alone."

Peggy pulled away long enough to glance at her friend and thank her for coming by.

"Yes, thanks for keeping an eye on my girl," Theo said, a happy grin splitting the planes of his rugged face as he gazed down at the tiny woman in his arms.

"Not a problem," Angel replied, quickly exiting the house and heading for home, intending to check in with Jake and Bret before turning in.

A curt, "Come in," greeted her knock and when she entered, she found a shirtless Bret sitting on the edge of his bed trying to pull off his boot. Behind him, a napping Grayling lay curled up in the middle of Bret's bed—where he seemed to spend most of his time now. The scene made her smile.

Her eyes swept over the flexing muscles in Bret's arms and chest, unable not to be impressed with his physique, but also pleased to see his injuries had healed well—if any scars remained, they were invisible from across the room.

Acute awareness of him as a man struck her, causing her skin to heat and her mouth to go dry. An eternity seemed to pass before she dragged her eyes from his work-sculpted muscles to his suntanned face. The change wasn't much better for her peace of mind—he was too good-looking.

"Where's Jake?" The question came out throatier than she would have liked.

Bret looked up and then back at his boot, going from wide-eyed to thin-lipped in the few seconds it took to glance at her.

Angel frowned at his reaction.

"He's out in the barn with the horses," Bret grumbled, still heaving futilely on his footwear. His sun-bronzed arms flexed as he tugged, his chest and belly tightened with his effort, and she gawked at the play of muscle under skin. Her breath halted, her eyes lingering on his splendid pectorals and the light dusting of black hair that adorned his chest. Naturally, her gaze was drawn downward to his flat abdomen. She smiled at the bit of swirling hair gathered around his belly button and followed the thin line until it disappeared into his jeans.

Eyes going wide, her smile slipped in alarm as something hot and needy tightened to an almost painful ache and then burst to life deep in the center of her body.

"Is something wrong?" His quiet question broke her trance and her eyes snapped up to his. Embarrassment burned down to her toes, but thankfully, he seemed too exhausted to care about her staring.

"No," she answered in a hasty rush and then, feeling her cheeks heat, she turned to fumble with the door she'd left open at the sudden loss of her mind.

Damn it! Remember why he's here! she sternly reminded herself while willing the unwanted sensations away. She just hoped he was too preoccupied with his boots to notice her lack of composure. "I was...wondering how everything went?"

"Fine," he said, his attention once again on his struggle.

Angel breathed a little easier. "Did you get a count?"

"North of eighteen hundred," he told her as his boot finally came off and nearly flew out of his hands.

"Good." Her fingers fiddled with the edge of the green T-shirt she wore.

He dropped the boot beside the bed and started in on the other.

Taking pity on him she asked, "Would you like some help with that?"

"Please," he said dropping his hands to the bed, sitting back, and holding out his booted foot.

She crossed to the desk and pulled out the chair, then stood waiting for him to get a clue. When he frowned at her, she glanced at the wooden seat with a small grin then gazed up at him and lifted her eyebrows in silent question.

He got the hint and moved to the chair, then held out his leg again. Arching a taunting eyebrow in her direction this time, he gave her a heart-stopping little-boy grin that started the heat burning inside her once more. She cleared her throat and attempted to play along with a forced chuckle as she turned her back, straddled his leg, and swiftly pulled the boot from his foot. His leg dropped and she hurriedly stepped away before she started to think about other parts of him between her legs.

A pleasant thrill tickled her spine as the night he pulled her into his bed popped into her mind. How his long, heavy body had felt pinning her to the mattress, not to mention the equally hard shaft of his desire prodding her thigh.

Her belly tightened and her heart sped up. *Why does he have to be so...?* She mentally cursed herself for thinking about his looks again.

Setting his footwear next to its mate, she concentrated on ridding herself of the searing hunger that now coursed through her veins. *You're only doing this for Jake,* she thought. *So, stop fantasizing about him and think about cold things—ice and snow, river water and...*

"Thanks," Bret mumbled as he crossed his ankle over his knee and began to rub his toes.

Glad for the distraction she asked, "How are your feet?" Struggling with what to do with her hands, Angel tucked then into her back pockets and silently swore again.

"Sore." His mouth quirked up as he eyed her jerky movements. "My feet are healed, but they're still a little tender."

"Is there anything else wrong?"

Bret hesitated and quickly glanced at the door. "No, just sore and tired."

"I see," she murmured, disappointed and angered by Bret's selfishness. *Hasn't he noticed how unhappy Jake's been?* Maybe he doesn't care as much as she'd thought he would.

She shuffled to the window and peeked outside. From that angle, she could almost see light leaking out through the barn doors.

"What's taking Jake so long?" she asked, pleased to have control of herself again, but still annoyed with the man behind her.

Bret's frown, when she turned, surprised her, but it lasted only a moment.

"He did my horse first," he replied as he pressed his fists against his lower back, closed his eyes, rolled his head back over his shoulders, and arched his spine.

Angel's core temperature turned to molten lava. Completely captivated by the handsome glory that was Bret Masters, her brain shutdown while her eyes got their fill.

What was it about him that always got her heart racing and her knees knocking simultaneously? *Dumb question*, she thought and then cussed him, his good looks, and herself for her inability not to stare.

Eyes still closed, Bret moved his head back and forth, stretching.

As if drawn by an invisible magnet, she traversed the short distance between them. Without thought, she placed her hands on his strong, warm shoulders and began to work the tense muscles.

Surprisingly, he didn't pull away.

"That feels good," he groaned, dropping his chin to his chest. "My mom used to do that after my uncle would—" His body stiffened.

"Would what?" She carefully worked her fingers into his knotted muscles.

"Nothing," he said, his words clipped. "We just...didn't get along."

"I see." His caginess irritated her, but she didn't stop massaging his shoulders. Instead, she marveled at the undeniable strength of his muscular frame, at the heat and resiliency of his flesh. His skin was so smooth, so hot, the temptation to slide her palms over his lightly furred chest was almost overpowering.

What is wrong with you? her responsible side screamed. *He's here for Jake and the ranch, nothing else.* She took a breath and reminded herself she was annoyed with him.

Her bad-tempered comments the morning they'd left popped into her head. The sidelong glance he'd thrown her way and his tight expression as he sat in the saddle caused guilt to thicken her throat.

"Bret?"

"Hmm?"

"I want to apologize for what I said the other morning. I

didn't mean for you to take it as seriously as you did." She paused, her small hands resting on his bronzed shoulders. She stared at them, riveted by the contrast. "It was wrong of me and I'm sorry."

She saw his lids lift but couldn't see his eyes as he stared across the room. He didn't immediately reply, and she waited, wondering what he was thinking.

"Thank you," he finally said several seconds later.

"You say that like you don't believe me," she accused, her hands kneading his muscles again.

"I'm not sure I do," he told her without any heat, though she felt a little pang of disappointment in her heart anyway.

"I mean it. I've just been...annoyed with you."

"For what?" he asked, turning his head to glance up at her with a confused frown.

She met his gaze and hesitated. *This is what you came here for,* she told herself. *You were hoping to catch him alone.* She cleared her throat. "For the way you've been treating Jake."

He turned away with nothing but a quiet groan.

"He feels bad about your fight and you'll hardly speak to him."

"And he told you this?" Bret's shoulders straightened as he pulled away and moved to his bed where he sat down again, disturbing the cat briefly before Grayling resumed his nap.

You should've pulled away from him!

"Not entirely," she said as she followed him, as if drawn forward, and settled in next to him. The nearness and warmth of his big body were distracting and did strange things to her insides, but irritated by the unwanted sensations, she ignored them. "He told me he's upset he can't talk to you anymore, which doesn't surprise me much."

He glanced at her with a wrinkled brow. "Why do you say that?"

"You're not the easiest person to talk to, Bret." She gave him a half-smile. "I know Jake. He's worried you hate him."

Bret averted his gaze and leaned away from her. "Jake and I have always been able to talk."

"You've both changed."

He sighed and nodded, his body relaxing slightly.

She marveled at his agreement.

"Did he tell you what the fight was about?"

"No," she replied, "and I don't want to know."

"Then why bring it up? What do you want from me?"

"He's your best friend, Bret, and you're his," she said, trying another approach. "Why do you think he's still out there," she pointed toward the barn, "and you're in here?" She stared into his green gaze, letting her statement sink in. She was surprised when his eyes didn't turn silvery and narrow into dangerous slits. "You'll never know how happy he was to see you again. He so obviously missed you—anyone could see that by the way he talked about you all the time. Now, you're avoiding him and your friendship. After five years, I'd think that would be the last thing you'd want to do. Don't you miss him?"

"Yeah." He sighed again, then lowered his chin and leaned forward, resting his elbows on his knees as he stared at the floor.

"He misses his brother," she said, placing her hand on his arm.

Bret nodded again, head still down.

"Was your argument more important than your friendship? Than your brother?"

"No." His response was just above a whisper.

"Then talk to him, Bret."

Before she could say another word, Jake entered through the outside door. Angel got up from the bed to greet him—a quick transition she knew appeared suspicious—leaving Bret to his thoughts.

Jake stood a little taller and eyed them both. Angel smiled and he appeared to relax.

She exchanged a few words with Jake as he removed his coat and then called to Bret as she headed for the door.

He looked up and she had to swallow before she could speak.

"Tomorrow I'd like you to cut out two hundred head for sale and bring them in. Not the best, just ones that'll bring a reasonable price and be helpful to those buyers at the auction. Do we have somewhere to hold them until then?"

"The best place would be in the holding corral on the far side of the barns, but we'll have to finish it first," he said. "We're only about halfway through the enlargement upgrade." He tilted his head as if mentally calculating. "It'll take most of the day to finish that and several hours to find decent animals. In all, I reckon it'll take a few days."

"Can you do it all in two with more help?"

He shook his head. "I told the crew to take tomorrow off. They've been working hard. They need a break."

"There are a lot of people here," she replied, "and you said we need to train more of them. I'll help dig holes and hammer nails myself if needed."

Her offer garnered a strange, almost pained look from him.

"I'm sure the others won't mind helping," Jake joined in. "We only need to finish the remaining posts. We could string line along the unfinished sections to keep the cattle in for two or three days."

Bret nodded and glanced at Angel. "Do we have enough rope, cable, or wire to close in that much acreage?"

Angel grinned. "If we don't have it, I'll get it."

"No problem then," he said, glancing at Jake, "though the enclosure will be temporary for now."

Jake nodded his agreement.

"Great," Angel said cheerfully, though the uncomfortable tension she'd sensed between the two men remained. "Just let me know what you need and I'll make sure you get it."

He nodded and dropped his gaze. Angel wondered if he was

thinking about Jake and what she'd said.

"Well, I guess I'll say goodnight, then." Feeling awkward and strangely nervous, she smiled as she left.

Bret studied his friend as Jake sat on his bed and attempted to pull off his second boot. Jake didn't appear to have a care in the world, but Angel's earlier comments and his own insight told Bret otherwise.

Jake tossed his footwear next to his other one by the outside door and started to unbutton his shirt. Bret hesitated, unsure what to say. He would do anything for Jake, and being at odds with him for the last few weeks had been torture. He wanted his friend back, but he owed Jake a lot more than a change in attitude. That debt he could never repay.

"You have anything special going on tomorrow?" he blurted out.

Jake glanced at him, a frown wrinkling his brow. "No. Why?"

"You want to help with cutting out the cattle Angel wants?" Bret asked meeting Jake's gaze squarely. "It'll go faster with someone else who knows what they're doing."

Jake's face went blank and he didn't immediately speak. Bret understood his hesitation—after all this time, his sudden attempt at making peace must seem odd.

A smile lit Jake's bearded face. "Sure. When're we leaving?"

His enthusiastic reply made Bret grin in return. "Sunup," he said and stood to slip out of his jeans. "If we have enough help, we should be back for dinner."

"Sounds good," Jake replied still smiling.

Bret nodded and started toward the bathroom but stopped in the doorway. He looked back at his friend and leaned a shoulder against the frame.

"Jake, I... I'm...I'm an ass," he said in a rush.

"Yeah, you are."

Bret frowned, taken aback by Jake's quick agreement. Jake smirked and his hazel eyes twinkled with mischief. "But that never stopped us from being family before. Don't see why it should now."

A slow grin curved Bret's mouth and the tension in his body eased. The weight that had been weighing him down for weeks suddenly lifted from his shoulders and he could breathe easily. "I'm sorry, Jake."

"Me too, man," Jake said without hesitation. "No worries."

"Thanks." Bret pushed away from the doorframe. "Doesn't mean we'll never argue again."

"I'd never think that," Jake joked right along with him. "You're an ass, remember?"

"Yeah, yeah." Bret chuckled as he closed the bathroom door, glad to have the bridge between them rebuilt. He was looking forward to a hot shower and his warm bed, knowing—even with the prospect of hard work in the morning—he would sleep more soundly and more readily tonight than he had in weeks.

THE DRIVE

1

JAKE WOKE BRET after seven the next morning.

"What part of wake me up at five-thirty did you not understand?" Bret grumbled as he rolled onto his back and threw off the covers. His ailments had zapped his strength for months, but Bret thought it was past time he get back to his normal, early-morning-wake-up schedule, especially with the amount of work he had planned.

Apparently, his body—and Jake—felt otherwise.

"It's not that much later than you had planned, Bret. Besides, the doc said just last week that you still need all the rest you can get. You've only been healed-up for a short time."

"Yeah, yeah," Bret mumbled as he crawled out of bed to get dressed. "I don't need a mother, Jake, especially not one as ugly as you."

Jake laughed and slapped Bret's shoulder.

"Someone's got to watch out for your dumb ass," he said. "I'll meet you in the dining hall. Get a move on."

Bret tossed his friend a dirty look which only broadened Jake's smile, then, with a shake of his head, Jake left for the morning meal.

After a quick breakfast, they went out to the barns where Theo and the others had already started setting the posts. Bret could tell by their progress they'd been at it for at least an hour.

He frowned and sent a questioning look at Jake.

"I talked to Theo and told him the plan for today," Jake said.

"When?"

"Last night while you were in the shower." He grinned. "He insisted on having everyone help."

Bret knew they needed the time off, but he was grateful for their assistance. It would've taken him and Jake most of the day to finish the posts on their own. And that didn't count running the lines to enclose the corral or herding in the cattle.

"I'm glad he did," Bret said looking up at the vividly blue morning sky. "It's going to be a hot one."

*   *   *

Tilting his hat back, Bret squinted up at the bright sky and swiped his forearm across his sweaty brow as he estimated the time. By the set of the sun, it was close to noon, and their work on the corral was almost done. Pride swelled inside him and pulled at the corners of his mouth as he scrutinized all they'd accomplished in so few hours.

Angel will be impressed. He frowned. *Why would I care about that?*

"Looks like we have company." Jake interrupted Bret's thoughts, tilting his head toward an approaching group. Bret followed his friend's gaze only to wince at what he saw.

Angel ambled up to where they stood, a heavy-looking canvas bag in each hand and greeted them with a cheery smile. "Are you guys hungry?"

"Yeah," both men replied in unison.

"Esther said you would be. She's made a feast and…I offered to bring it out."

Bret frowned at her brief pause and wanted to laugh at her discomfort. He'd seen the way her eyes had dropped to his bare chest as her words faded, then, how quickly they snapped back up to his face before going on as if she hadn't just been ogling him.

The sound of a motor drew his attention and Angel pointed toward a gas-powered truck coming their way. "Michelle and one of the guys picked up the cable you requested this morning," she said as the old four-by-four crawled over the uneven ground.

Bret hadn't even known they had a motor vehicle. Owning a combustion engine truck, not to mention the fuel to keep it running, made him wonder about Angel's wealth and influence. A thousand questions popped into Bret's mind, but he didn't get to ask any.

"We're almost done," Jake said, shrugging into his previously discarded cotton shirt. "I guess we meant to finish before lunch."

Still staring at the truck, Bret felt an elbow jab at his ribs. "Ow," he said, rubbing his side. He flashed a glare at his friend, but nodded in agreement. "Yeah."

"Well, it'll have to wait," Angel said, hefting the bags she carried and heading over to where the blankets had already been laid out. More boxes filled with tempting smells and lemonade sat in the truck bed not far away. Bret's stomach rumbled. If he wasn't so ravenous, he would've objected to her taking over, but hunger easily won that battle.

He turned to Jake, who lifted his eyebrows and shrugged his shoulders. Bret grinned and returned the gesture. Then, grabbing the work shirt he'd removed earlier from a nearby post, Bret followed the others to wash up before he hurriedly joined the picnic.

The meal's conversation was wide and varied, but when the discussion strayed to life before the wars and the changes in women, Bret got up and strolled to a small hill near the swiftly flowing channel that fed the reservoir. Crouching down, he rinsed his hands and dried them on his jeans while he surveyed his surroundings.

From where he stood, Bret could just see the wide valley beyond the homestead's protective wall. The rolling landscape led into the foothills and into the mountains beyond. Following the contours of the jagged peaks, he closed his eyes, took a deep breath, and visualized standing beneath the tall conifers. He could almost smell the evergreens and feel the loam beneath his boots. His skin prickled at the cool tinge of remembered mountain air.

"They don't seem so far away, do they," Angel said beside him, startling Bret out of his musings. He glanced at her and she nodded toward the serrated horizon.

"No, they don't," he answered, staring at the distant skyline. "How far are they? Fifty, seventy-five miles?"

"Too far, Bret."

"Maybe..."

Silence stretched between them, the rushing water channel near their feet muting the soft murmur of their friends several yards away. Bret's mind drifted, picturing a herd of elk in an open valley as an eagle soared overhead.

"Are you all right?" Angel's voice brought him back again.

Her gaze—as vibrant as the sky above and filled with concern—captured his mind and tugged at his heart. The sun, glinting off her silky, black hair brought out dark auburn highlights, and the way she tilted her lightly tanned face made her appear pretty enough to kiss.

His stomach tightened. "Yeah," he replied, and turned away. "Just thinking."

"About the past?"

He faced her again and shrugged.

"Me too." This time she averted her gaze.

"Bad memories?"

Neither looked at the other.

"Yeah." She sighed and, from the corner of his eye, he saw her mouth quirk. "Looks like we have something in common after all."

Annoyed by the comparison, he opened his mouth to challenge it, but stopped short. A deep, abiding sadness seemed to emanate from her as she gazed into the distance. Like a thick, dark cloud, that feeling seemed to dim even the sun. Bret shuffled his feet, troubled by the sensation, wondering what had upset her. Then he frowned again. Was it even real or just another way to manipulate his emotions?

The dark blue of the mountains always reminds me of his eyes, Angel thought, and the long-lost glow of happiness radiated through her. In her mind, she saw the strong, free-spirited man she had loved and wished he could be with her now, holding her, loving her. *I can still hear his voice...*

"Angel? Are you all right?"

The ache in her chest intensified.

"Angel?"

That doesn't sound like him. Brows drawn down, she turned her head, expecting to see *him.* Instead, she found Bret Masters frowning back at her.

Her jaw clenched. Thoughts of self-reproach burned inside, even as her chest squeezed tight and her throat choked up. Bret was not the man she had conjured in her mind, but he was real and standing right beside her. She met his concern-filled gaze and, for the span of a heartbeat or three, she longed to be wrapped in the safety of his arms.

Her breath caught and her body trembled at the sudden shock of need that slammed through her body. *Why would I think his arms would be safe?*

"Are you all right?" he asked again, his hand curling around her arm and concern filling his jade-colored eyes.

"Yes, I'm fine," she said as she looked down at his hand. The heat of his long fingers seared through the thin material of her shirt, setting her skin on fire. Hot tingles ran up and down her arm before they struck straight into her core. Her lips parted and she trembled again.

Gentle yet insistent, his fingers lifted her chin until she faced him again. His calloused palm slid over her cheek, holding her in place. "You don't look fine," he whispered, wiping away a tear with his thumb.

She hadn't realized any of what she was feeling had spilled onto her cheeks.

He stood so close, staring down at her, and it seemed as if he looked directly into her soul. The heat of his body washed over her, and her skin tightened...everywhere. A slow, almost tender smile adorned his lips and she felt oddly comforted, safer than she'd felt in many years. For some reason, that made her simultaneously want to weep harder and shout with joy.

Something electric passed between them, zipping back and forth over every point of contact, messing with her thoughts and churning up her emotions. She should pull away, put distance between them, but instead, she found herself leaning in, captivated by the concern and something more, something deeper, needier, in the depths of his eyes. They seemed to darken as she watched. Fascinated, she couldn't look away. His gaze had captured her and, along with the gentle, promising curve of his mouth, kept her enthralled. All of a sudden, she wanted to fall against him, coil her arms around his neck, and pull herself close to his long, hard body. She wanted his arms around her, wanted the comfort he could give, and strangely, she sensed he would welcome it if she took the first step.

But his intense green eyes were not the expressive blue ones she had known so well. Bret was not the man she longed for.

Still, knowing that didn't lessen her almost overwhelming desire to touch him. That realization frightened her and sent a cold chill to her bones.

Who was this man whose moods shifted as swiftly as the sands on the ocean floor?

"You know," he said softly, the deep murmur sending a little shiver up her spine, "you have the prettiest blue eyes I think I've ever seen. You look almost…innocent."

"Stop it, Bret." She pushed his hands away and backed up, the spell broken.

"What?" he asked, sounding both annoyed and confused.

"I didn't intend to cry, so please don't make fun of me."

"I didn't mean it that way."

Her eyes narrowed. "Of course not." She turned away, dismissing the conversation and the magnetic attraction that had sprung up between them. *Why did he have to be so damn handsome?*

"Hey," he growled as his hand curled around her arm to stop her retreat and then dropped to his side. "I wasn't part of whatever happened to upset you, so, don't treat me like it's my fault."

"Aren't you being a bit defensive?" Hurt and anger sharpened her voice as she lifted her chin to glower at him. "But who am I to judge, right? After all, it's good advice, so why don't you apply it to yourself, as well?" She spun on her heel, and without a backward glance, marched back to the others who were finishing their meal. A part of her wanted to go back, to recapture that supercharged feeling that had passed between them. But that was impossible and dangerous for the both of them…and everyone else too.

2

LONG SHADOWS STRETCHED across the barnyard from the rising sun as the population of Angel's ranch made their final preparations to drive the cattle northward to auction. In the midst of the hubbub, Angel led her stallion, Ebony, out of the barn and over to the fenced-in section of the corral. She looped the reins over the top rail and checked the saddle girth once more. That done, she pulled her riding gloves from her pocket and glanced around the crowded yard.

Grinning as she watched everyone say their goodbyes, her eyes stopped on the tall form of Bret Masters. He stood with Theo and a dark-haired cowhand named Dean beside the cook's wagon several yards away. They all looked every bit the cowboys they were—each handsome in their own way—but Bret, in his brown boots, blue jeans, and black leather chaps, held her attention. Like an addiction, her eyes drank him in. Her heartbeat increased, her mouth watered, and the now-familiar craving to be wrapped in his arms once again assailed her. The unwelcomed sensations that had started by the reservoir a few days ago still surprised her.

They also annoyed her.

Keeping her distance hadn't been hard. Not only had Bret

spent most of his time working outside, he also spoke to her only when he had to, and that was as briefly as possible.

"How are things going?" she'd asked him in the dining hall the day after their interlude at the picnic. He'd been out all day checking the fences for tampering and doing repairs and had just returned for dinner. She'd hoped to put the discomfort of the previous day behind them, but the tightness of his jaw and the guarded look in his eyes said he was unhappy to see her.

"Fine," he'd replied as he pierced a wedge of rosemary potato and popped it into his mouth. When he didn't offer anything more, she pressed on.

"Have any more cattle gone missing?"

He shook his head without meeting her eyes. "I'm beginning to think the tallying errors don't have anything to do with our counting."

Tugging on her last glove, preparing to mount up for the drive, Angel pressed her lips together thinking about the condescending way he'd stated that observation. Still, Bret knew his job and did it well, which was what induced her to put him in charge of the seventy-mile trip north.

"I'd like you to lead the drive to the auction," she'd said a few days ago. He hadn't needed much convincing, but his attitude grew less accommodating when he found out Angel planned to ride with them.

"Why?" he asked, folding his arms across his chest.

"Because, I am," she said in her best don't-mess-with-me tone. He'd been doing a great job, but she didn't trust his need for freedom. Their trail would pass through a spur of the densest forest of the region and she wanted to keep an eye on him. Though she wasn't about to tell him any of that.

He hadn't been pleased, but he didn't argue further; instead, he simply grunted his grudging acceptance and walked away.

Shaking her head and patting Ebony's neck—to soothe both the stallion and herself—Angel berated her fluttering heart and dragged her eyes away from Bret's broad-shouldered form. His cold shoulder attitude was getting old. In fact, it was starting to annoy her. If she was really being honest with herself, it hurt. There was no reason for him to be so bad tempered. Nothing had happened between them. She hadn't *demanded* anything of him. At least, nothing of the sexual variety he'd been so concerned with when he arrived. So, why was he acting so aloof?

"Maybe I should be thanking him," she muttered to the stallion. "What do you think, Ebby?" She murmured a few more words to the big horse, rubbed beneath his jaw, and then went in search of Jake and her head guard, Michelle. Despite having already discussed the tasks and possible threats to the ranch during her absence, Angel wanted to go over it all with them one last time.

A tall, leanly muscular, strawberry-blonde, Michelle Smithmore always reminded Angel of the mythical stories of Amazonian warriors, and today was no different. A strong, confident woman, Michelle would, as always, deal with any problems that Jake couldn't with her regular reliable efficiency. And Jake would keep everything else on track. Angel wouldn't go on this trip if she didn't have faith in both of them.

"Angel," Jake laughed, "we've done this dozens of times before."

"I know," she said, glancing between her two friends with a troubled frown.

"We'll be fine," Michelle added with a grin. "Don't worry. We won't let anything bad happen."

"I know you won't," Angel replied and returned her smile. But she couldn't help worrying anyway, her mind turning to all the awful things that could happen without her there. She particularly worried about the Section Guard's dropping in for an unscheduled inspection, or worse…Carrie Simpson. That woman's annual visit was like clockwork and wasn't due to happen for a few months yet; besides, Michelle knew how to deal with the Section Guards. Then there were the rumors about the rebels and the raids, which seemed to occur more frequency and with improved accuracy every month. And what if someone on the ranch got injured and she wasn't there to take care of them?

Monica would send the doctor to tend to them, she told herself. Shaking her head in self-reproach and reminding herself that they could handle whatever came up, Angel said her goodbyes while hugging them both and returned to her horse.

"Bret?" Jake called as he emerged from the barn.

"Mornin', Jake," Bret said with an amused grin that slipped slightly as Jake pulled him aside. "I'm surprised to see you up so early. Where were you last night?" Jake had left their apartment in the early morning hours. Bret wondered where his friend had gone, but not enough to follow him...not until the thought that Jake might be spending the night with Angel eventually crossed his mind. Then a part of him wished he had. Sleep had been hard to come by after that and Bret had wasted half the night trying not to picture them together.

"I had some things to do," Jake replied in a rush. "I wanted to talk to you about something before you go."

Bret eyed his friend with wary curiosity. "Sure. What's on your mind?"

"I'm worried about Angel."

"Why? She can take care of herself. What's to worry about?"

Jake shuffled his feet, glanced over his shoulder, and lowered his voice. "I'm not concerned about the drive."

"What then?"

"She's not...well." Jake sounded uncomfortable.

Bret tilted his head and raised his eyebrows.

Jake rubbed at the back of his neck and sighed. "I know her, Bret. She's been like this for a while. I've always been around to help her through it, but for this, I won't be and that concerns me."

"You think she'll need you during the trip?" Bret asked with a sly smile that left no doubt about his meaning, though incredulity imbued his tone.

"That's not what I meant," Jake said, more serious than before. "I'm worried that if she does need help, no one will be there for her. She won't ask for any and very few are aware of her…difficulties, which is what I wanted to talk to you about."

He frowned at Jake's vague description. "And what's that?" Bret crossed his arms over his chest, positive he wouldn't like where this was going.

"I'm asking you, as a friend, to give me your word that you'll look after her."

Bret grimaced and shook his head, but Jake didn't let him speak.

"And not just on the drive," he said hurriedly, "but anytime I'm not around."

"What?" Bret nearly shouted. Leaning forward, his hands clenched tightly at his sides, he took a quick glance around and his voice dropped to a dangerous whisper. "Why the hell would I want to do that? I don't owe her anything."

Jake's lips thinned. "Don't think of it as doing something for her. Think of it as a favor to me."

His words didn't fool Bret; Jake was peeved by his attitude. Though he didn't say it aloud, Bret still heard the silent, "Yes, you do owe her something, and you owe *me* too."

Or maybe that was just his guilty conscience talking.

"Don't you think that's a lot to ask, Jake? I don't even like the woman."

Jake crossed his arms and a muscle ticked in his jaw. "No, I don't think it is."

Bret sighed and struggled not to roll his eyes but didn't reply.

"She's not as strong as she seems, Bret."

Shaking his head, Bret tried to think of a way he could

possibly say no. Then something occurred to him, and he pinned his friend with a pointed glare. "Why me, Jake? There are lots of others who've been here longer, who know her better. Why me?"

"Because I trust you, brother. And I care about her. That's why I'm asking—as one friend to another—will you do this for me?"

Bret stared disbelievingly, reluctant to answer. The last thing he wanted was another argument with Jake and, if he didn't agree, that's what would happen.

On the other hand, what would it hurt? Angel was a strong woman, and he had every confidence she wouldn't need assistance from him. Keeping her out of trouble *in the middle of nowhere shouldn't be too hard.* And, if he agreed, at least Jake's mind would be at ease.

Still, Bret wondered why Jake worried about her so much. Then he wondered why the idea bothered him.

Mentally shrugging off the possessive sensation knotting up his belly, Bret quickly dismissed Jake's concern as his overprotective nature and disregarded the rest.

"Okay," he said, wishing there was some way he could back out. "I'll keep an eye on her for you."

3

THE HOT SUN HAD SUNK beneath the distant mountains and the low canyon—with its two short cottonwood trees, multitudes of scrub brush, and the occasional thistle—where they'd made camp was growing dimmer by the moment. The campfire caused shadows to dance over the dry, flaxen soil and shadows crept closer as the cowhands rode in on the second evening of their drive north.

"Hey, Cookie?" one of them called to the teenager by the fire. "What's for dinner?" The others chuckled as they all dismounted and began to unsaddle their horses.

Angel glanced at the young man as he stirred something in a pot over the fire, worried the cowboys' teasing might cause him to crawl back into his protective shell.

But Carl merely grinned and replied, "Beef, beans, and rice, same as yesterday."

Angel smiled, glad to see the new confidence in the young man.

Earlier, they had settled the cattle about half a mile away between the rolling, umber-colored hills amongst pale-gold grasses and a small stream. The soft lowing of the animals drifted on the slight breeze, sounding sad and lonely in the vast openness as darkness fell. The riders not on duty, their horses taken care of for the night, gathered near the campfire, waiting to dish up their evening meal.

Despite the bland fare, they ate hungrily, and after dinner, as he would every evening, Bret discussed with Carl and his driver, Karen—as the Section Guard patrols would cause trouble if they came across the young man alone—where they should setup the next campsite.

From her conversations with Bret before they left, Angel knew they would be following the ruins of the old highway north for several days. Then, about halfway through an outlying spur of the old national forest, they would cut northeast, traveling through several switchback canyons, heading east for two days. Then they would switch northeast again toward the river and their destination.

"It's about twelve miles from here," Bret said, pointing to a spot on the map spread open on the cook-wagon's tailgate. They all hovered over it as Bret marked the camp location with a small rock and their target with another while he continued to explain their trail like he'd traveled it many times over.

Angel sighed and lay back on the sandy soil. Using her saddle as a pillow, she turned toward the fire, ignoring the little group gathered around the cook's wagon. Bret's failure to consult her opinion about their trek annoyed her, but she wouldn't intervene. He knew what he was doing better than she did, and he was doing a fine job. Instead of having to make more decisions, she embraced the opportunity to leave the general running of the drive to Bret. Relaxing, breathing in the fresh scents of leather, wood smoke, and the crisp night air, she listened to the deep timbre of his voice as she drifted off to sleep.

*   *   *

Misery began on the third day of their journey over the uneven, rock-strewn terrain. A chill had settled in while they slept, and they woke to an overcast sky. As they rode out of camp and down their designated trail, Angel scented rain in the air. Less than an hour later, she shivered in the saddle as mist descended to hang about them until almost noon when the downpour began in earnest, drenching them and slowing their pace to a crawl. By the time they set up camp that evening, Angel's clothes were more than damp beneath the rain slicker she wore and water cascaded over the end of her cowboy hat from the torrent pouring out of the sky.

"We're going to make some shelters from our ground cloths," Bret said as he pulled the tarpaulin roll from the back of his saddle.

"How?" someone called as they unsaddle their horses. "There's nothing out here."

After pulling her saddle from Ebony's back, Angel glanced around. The speaker was right—she didn't see any shelter either. Only a few small, wind-twisted trees and a couple of half-buried boulders were visible. Definitely not enough coverage for all of them.

"We'll hang them like tarps, using rocks for grommets, then we'll weigh the ends down," Bret replied. "As long as it doesn't get too windy, we should stay dry enough huddled under them."

They did as he instructed and soon, they had a small shelter of sorts. Unfortunately, heavy winds blew in after nightfall. Regardless of the weights they used, the tempest blew sheets of raindrops through the openings, drenching their blankets.

A minuscule fire using the deadfall Bret had encouraged them to collect earlier burned near the center of their shelter, keeping them somewhat warm, but they still had to crowd together to conserve heat.

"How long will this last?" someone asked from under their sodden blanket. Angel recognized the soft Texan drawl belonging to Dean Williams. Quiet and a little jumpy, Dean was not one she or Jake had pegged as overly knowledgeable on a ranch. But once Bret took over and pushed the Texan, they quickly discovered a well-seasoned cowboy beneath Dean's insecurities; one who proved himself to be both smart and tough, and who knew his way around livestock of all kinds. Why Dean had kept his talents hidden for so long was a mystery, and he apparently hadn't fully adjusted to this cooler climate either.

"The rain could last several days," Bret said, glancing through the overhang as if hoping he was wrong.

"Or it could be over in five minutes," Angel added with a shiver.

Bret shrugged. "Hard to tell."

She got up from her spot with the others and moved next to Bret, who sat off on his own, as usual.

"Will the cattle be all right in this?" she asked as she took a seat beside him.

"They should be," he said, continuing with his standoffish manner while staring out at the puddles in the mud, watching each fat raindrop make a tiny splash. "They'll bunch together and find some sort of shelter from the storm. As long as it continues to only rain and blow, they should be fine."

"What do you mean, 'only rain and blow?'" She didn't like the sound of that.

"Thunder and lightning can spook them, send them stampeding," Bret looked at her and said slowly, "which would be a problem." He looked at the sky again.

She ignored his sarcasm and tried to read his expression in the dim light of the low, flickering campfire. Despite his calm demeanor, the weather clearly worried him.

"If they do stampede," she asked gazing through the darkness, "what do we do?"

Turning his head to peer down at her, he paused to shrug before he answered with a simple, "We stop them." Then he turned and considered the soggy conditions once more.

Angel didn't bother to question him further, but she didn't

look away either. Despite his unfriendly behavior, he fascinated her. Intrigued her in a way that made her brain shutdown and her body heat up. That alone should terrify her back into her protective shell. Still, even knowing she shouldn't, she couldn't stop herself from studying him, couldn't look away. Everything about him was so utterly masculine, so magnetic, and coupled with his chiseled good looks, he was impossible to ignore.

His attitude was another story...

Thanks to Jake and his storytelling, Angel knew there was more to Bret Masters than the cold anger he wore like a second skin. Despite her better judgment, she had wasted a lot of time over the last few days trying to draw him out, to build a bridge of friendship between them. But unless her observations or inquiries had to do with the welfare of the cattle, he'd met her efforts with silent disregard. She hadn't meant to engage him, but for some reason, she'd wanted to learn what lay beneath the barrier he'd built to protect himself, to meet the real man she'd heard so much about. After several failures, however, she'd given up, admonishing herself for trying and reminding that needy part of her that she'd only bought him to help Jake, not to make friends. Still, she hated to admit—even to herself— how much his silence and guarded looks made her heart squeeze tight. She shouldn't let him affect her, tried not to, but it hurt nonetheless.

Now, sitting this close to him—the warmth of his body heating her side, dredging up a hunger she hadn't experienced in years—her mind wandered into a fantasy she'd deemed taboo ever since Bret dropped into her life. Only the man she envisioned was no longer a vague depiction, but a perfect rendition of the man who was sitting silently beside her. She abruptly straightened her spine and pushed the image away.

You cannot do that, she scolded herself. *Not with him, not anymore.*

Too tired to move back to her original spot, she stayed and

rested against the tree behind them again. Bret's big body not only warmed her, but he also blocked the icy breath of wind wafting its way through their makeshift shelter.

It's just warmer here, she reasoned when the practical part of her demanded to know why she didn't move away from him. There was no reason she should freeze all night or be wary of him either. Yes, he disliked her, seeing her actions at the auction as a way to own and abuse him. Neither was true but convincing him of that seemed impossible. Still, she wished he could get past the animosity and lower the walls he always seemed to throw up in defense against her.

Listening to the repetitive sounds of the storm, she sighed, letting it lull her into relaxation. Exhaustion pulled her heavy eyelids closed and in the darkness of her mind, with no inhibitions to stop it, she drifted into dreams of a green-eyed hero with jet-black hair and a wickedly attractive smile.

BRET YAWNED, WATCHING as tiny rivers made their way through the mud, creating small lakes in every depression. Doing his utmost to ignore the pleasant heat at his side, he kept watch on the raging storm. Not that he didn't welcome the extra warmth, but he would have preferred any other woman to the one who personified his slavery. She *owned* him, and the insufferable thought never ceased to burn. But with her sitting beside him, her heat and the subtle hint of that damn lilac scent bridging the few inches between them, he couldn't seem to think of anything but her soft little body.

He could just move. Cross their shelter to another spot or scoot around the tree behind them, but that would let her—and anyone else who payed attention—know that she affected him, and he couldn't have that. Tucking his hands beneath his crossed arms, he tried to get comfortable without getting any closer to her. Not that it did much good. She was still too close. Sighing with frustration, he sternly tamped down the awareness that pulsed through his body. *It's been a long day. Get some sleep.*

Yeah, good luck with that, his caustic side replied. *With her right there, it's going to be a long, wakeful night.* But in spite of his uncomfortable thoughts and her closeness, his weariness tugged at him as the chilly air stiffened his joints.

He pulled his jacket closer around him.

It would be so nice to be home in bed. That thought made him sit up a little straighter. Wait... What? When did I start thinking of Angel's place as home?

He frowned as he mulled that over, amazed to realize he'd actually meant it. He missed the wide lawns, the gardens, the huge willow on the hill with its new buds of spring-green glory, and even Angel's big, white house. He longed to see the flowering trees that lined the protective wall, the orchard behind the house covered with blossoms, and hear the children laugh while they played in the yard. A part of him almost wished he was there now, but he hadn't been able to resist the temptation of freedom. In two days—maybe three if the weather stayed bad—he would take his chance to run for the hills and he would never return to the home he'd yearned for just now.

Banishing the unwanted emotion, he closed his eyes, but they immediately sprung open again when something heavy fell against his shoulder. Glancing down, he found Angel fast asleep. She sighed as she shifted closer, cuddling against his side. She looked peaceful, contented with her inky-black lashes brushing her cheekbones, her small straight nose, and those beautiful full lips slightly parted. They looked so soft and kissable... He pulled his mind back from that train of thought, even as memories of the evening he'd almost kissed her filled his head.

A part of him wished he hadn't so abruptly ended that encounter, but his pragmatic side knew he'd have been a fool not to. Getting involved with his Mistress was a bad idea. He'd learned his lesson, even though that softer side of him still longed for someone to share his life with.

But not her, not Angel. He couldn't trust her, no matter what anyone said. Still, after calling a halt to whatever—call it desire, call it lust—had passed between them that night, he'd been touched the next morning when he woke to find that she'd stayed all night watching over him. Touched and a little unnerved. He'd wanted to believe she'd had nefarious motives, but she obviously hadn't. Still, though he'd been grateful for her help and kindness, it hadn't been enough for him to trust her. He still didn't, but he couldn't seem to rustle up the desire to push her off his shoulder either.

She looked serene snuggled against him, and he liked the feel of her soft warmth nestled along his side. Trust had nothing to do with this—this was all about survival. At least, that's what he told himself as he finally drifted off to sleep.

*　*　*

The next morning, Bret woke before Angel to find her still curled up against him. In his sleep, he'd wrapped his arm around her shoulder and now her face lay against his chest with the crown of her head just below his chin. Her bent knees were propped against his thigh and one hand rested on his belly. His body had noticed her too, which was a bad thing, considering how he couldn't take his eyes off her. Even asleep, she had a lovely glow that tugged at him, heating him from the inside out.

She shifted, and he quickly removed his arm, easing her backward until she rested against the tree behind them. He'd just leaned back himself and crossed his arms over his chest when her eyes blinked open.

"Good morning," she said, smiling and blinking sleepily.

"Mornin'," he grunted, trying to banish the awareness she'd awakened in his body before she could take note of it. He wanted to be angry about that, but it's not as if she'd done it on purpose, and he *had* pulled her close, even if he'd done it unconsciously.

Something about her seemed off as she gazed out at the dim morning, but Bret had his own problems to worry about. Dragging his eyes from her and somehow winning the battle inside him, he examined the morning sky. The sun's rays had turned last night's black clouds to gray and somewhere in the distance, birds chirped merrily. Though a light mist still hung in the chilly morning air, the rain had stopped.

Bret sensed Angel's gaze on him. He turned back to her, and his gut twisted. She looked…unhappy. His heart clenched at the sight, and he had the ridiculous desire to do something to make her smile again. Thankfully, she picked that moment to grab her things and go before he did something stupid.

With a sinking sensation in his stomach and an iron-like vise still squeezing his chest, Bret stared at Angel's departing back. A mixture of anger at her departure and curiosity about her mood welled up inside him, and the opposing forces of the two feelings made his head pound.

Two more days, he reminded himself, trying to push away the crush of unexpected emotion. *Two more days—three at the most—to freedom.*

4

BRET SWAYED IN THE SADDLE, keeping the dappled gray
gelding he rode between the herd on the trail and the dark
green of the one-time national forest looming to the west. Fir
trees bracketed the old, dilapidated highway they followed, but
occasionally, an opening would reveal the rolling foothills and,
far off, the jagged peaks of snow-tipped mountains beyond.

They'd been slowly climbing in elevation since yesterday
afternoon, skirting the edge of a ridge cover with a dense stand
of trees. The Stuart Range lay somewhere north and west, but
closer and due west was the Teanaway Ridge. Once he crossed
over that crest, the valleys and canyons of the Cascade
Mountain Range would swallow him whole and leave no trace.
No one would find him in that vast wilderness, he was as sure
of that as he was confident in his ability to navigate it. He'd
spent close to ten years traveling along those mountains.
Disappearing into them would be almost like going home
again.

He grinned, a thrill of giddiness bubbling up inside him—
his liberation day had finally arrived. Too excited, he'd barely
been able to eat breakfast this morning for the fluttering in his
belly. The band of nerves that had tightened around his chest

made breathing a little difficult and the sensation had only intensified as the hours counted down.

Bret's gelding easily picked his way over the weed-infested terrain, sidestepping rocks and other debris spread through the overgrown foliage that sprung up between the cracks. He'd chosen the animal for his surefootedness and swift speed. Only Angel's stallion could challenge Smoke—as the gray was named—for speed and endurance, but Bret doubted she would follow him. And Ebony rarely allowed anyone but Angel on his back. Which meant that if she didn't give chase, the *Section Guards—who would undoubtedly learn of his escape and try to capture him*—would never catch sight of him because he'd be long gone before they picked up his trail.

Focusing on the trail ahead, Bret sobered as a pang of regret struck his heart. He'd finally found Jake again, and now he was leaving his best friend behind once more. That fact soured this opportunity and—despite his determination—plagued him with second thoughts.

At least they'd each made their own choices this time. This time it hadn't been forced on them. Still, he wished things were different.

Bret shook his head as he directed Smoke around a fallen log. *Wishing is for fools, you know that. This is your chance, your decision. Jake already made his, and it didn't include you. The thought made his chest tighten with the familiar ache of loss. Heaviness settled in his belly and over his whole body. He didn't want to go out there alone again. The loneliness had hollowed him out last time, left him feeling old and tired, despite being free. Meeting up with Jake had sparked his need for companionship and it tugged at him now. But he wouldn't let it stop him...not when he was this close. He couldn't.*

Coming to a break in the trees, Bret slowed his horse to study a bank of dark clouds hovering along the northwestern horizon. The high winds were blowing them southeast, which meant he and the other riders were in for more inclement weather. A slow grin turned up the corners of his mouth. Bad weather would only aid his escape.

By the time they stopped for the night, it had cooled considerably and a stiff wind blew out of the west. They'd made camp beside a row of trees, but as a safety precaution, they left the animals in a box-canyon half a mile farther up. With only one arched entrance to guard, sentries were posted outside in shifts to safeguard the animals while the others rested.

Dinner was nothing special—the same as every other night on this trip—but Bret ate heartily, saving a good portion of jerky in his coat pocket to stow with his other pilfered provisions once he'd made his escape. Then, as the sky darkened, he stared pensively into the fire. The other riders' voices faded, and Bret got lost in memories of camping with Jake and his dad.

"You're always welcome to join us, Bret," Jake's father, Jim, had said to him after their first trip. They were unpacking the truck and Bret was dreading going home when Jim slapped a big hand on twelve-year-old Bret's shoulder and gave him a gentle squeeze. "You know that, don't you?"

Bret had stared up into Jim's kind hazel eyes and wasn't sure what to say. He'd known Jake for some time, but they'd only been friends for a few months. Still, that had been long enough to know Jake's family was different from the torment he'd become used to.

"Yes, sir," he said, choking up and self-consciously lowering his eyes.

"Good," Jim said, patting Bret's back and smiling genially. "Next time you'll have to bring your guitar. The way Jake's been bragging, you must be quite good."

"Jake exaggerates."

"I do not," Jake said from behind him, returning from the garage where he'd just unpacked some camping equipment. "You are good, Bret."

He'd been more than a little unnerved by the praise and all the positive attention. He'd not had anything like that since his father died. Jake and Jim had been the best thing to happen to him in what had felt like years. But Bret doubted whether either of them knew how important those trips were to him back then, that they may have saved his life. They certainly helped him hold on to parts of the man he wanted to be. Otherwise, things would've been far different now, if he had survived at all.

Bret sucked in a deep breath, trying to stretch the vice that had suddenly constricted around his chest. He didn't want to leave Jake, but he couldn't stay; he couldn't live as a slave. He only hoped Jake would understand why he didn't say goodbye.

After everyone had settled down for the night, Bret also took to his blankets. But, in spite of his exhaustion, he felt too amped up to sleep. He kept envisioning himself riding out of camp under the cover of night, into the freedom of the foothills, and then the mountains beyond. It wasn't until sometime later that the music of the wind rustling the tall grass finally lulled him to sleep.

*   *   *

Someone was shaking him.

"Bret?" they called as if from far away. Groggy, he pulled out of their grasp, but the cool wind crept beneath the blanket and he shivered.

With the chill came awareness.

He rubbed at his gritty eyes. "Is it my shift already?"

"No," Angel's hushed words feathered his ears. The hint of anxiety in her voice alarmed him and, anticipating danger, his senses snapped to high alert.

"What's wrong?" he asked, propping himself up on his elbows and, letting his blanket fall away, he peered at her through the gloom.

"Nothing, exactly," she said as she knelt next to him, her

nervous gaze sweeping around the camp before focusing on him. "Something feels wrong."

"Something *feels* wrong?" he asked in a you-woke-me-for-*that* tone.

"Yes." In the fading campfire light, he saw her shrug. "I'm not sure what it is, but I sense something. I can't go to sleep." She looked around again as if expecting some hidden danger to appear.

Bret glanced at the inky blackness surrounding them. Everything appeared normal, but somewhere in the distance, thunder rolled. He automatically lifted his eyes skyward. As he did, the moon peeked in and out of its hiding place as ominous clouds scuttled past, and a small smile tugged at the corners of his mouth.

Looks like my luck will *turn good again tonight.*

Bret inhaled deeply and sat up. "Smells like rain and sounds like a storm coming in."

Angel nodded in agreement but said nothing as they both stood.

"Maybe I better check on the herd," he said, pulling on his long coat, anxiety beginning to trouble him as well.

"I'll go with you."

"No." He put a little too much emphasis in his reply and she tilted her head questioningly, or accusingly, he couldn't tell which in the dark.

"You can't go by yourself. You know the rules. The guards won't let you past them without a female escort. Besides, I'm awake, and I'm going."

He couldn't argue with her logic—there was no reason to wake anyone else and she would either make sure the guards stopped him if he tried to force her to stay or would simply follow him anyway.

"All right." He picked up the compound bow—taken from the wall in his and Jake's apartment—from under an oiled tarp next to his bedroll. "Do you know how to use one of these?"

"Yes, but it's been awhile. I'm out of practice."

"Can you hit what you're aiming at?"

She angled her head as if considering her answer. "Probably."

"Good." He quickly collected his things. "There's another one in the cook's wagon. Go get it," he said and, though she eyed him for giving her what amounted to an order, she did as he bid without argument. She returned and, at his insistence, tested the bow while he observed. When he was satisfied, they mounted and headed for the canyon.

Bret glanced up at the wrathful sky as they rode, uneasiness building inside him. If everything worked out right, he could still slip away without notice, but if not... He pushed all thought of failure aside. This would be his best chance to escape, and he needed to ensure Angel would be too distracted to wonder what he was doing until it was too late. The darkness and approaching storm should keep them from searching for him at least until morning—about six or seven hours away— and by then, he would be long gone.

WHEN THEY CAME upon the sentries guarding the herd, Angel slumped in her saddle when Bret sent them back to camp, saying he and Angel would finish their watch.

As the two guards rode away, he met her disgruntled look with innocence and one ached brow. "What?"

She huffed out a breath. "You didn't have to send them back."

She barely saw his shrug. "This was your idea."

Shaking her head, she heeled her stallion forward. "I came to check on them, not spend the night," she muttered, but let her protests go.

They entered the box-canyon with caution, but the hair on the back of Angel's neck stood on end. Her horse's feet shuffled and his ears twitched nervously.

"Something's wrong," she said, shivering from a sudden

chill and rubbing at Ebony's powerful neck to calm him.

Bret glanced at her but didn't respond. Instead, he rode ahead, and she followed. He pulled out his bow and motioned for her to go around one side of the range while he checked the other and they'd meet on the opposite end. She nodded, took up her weapon, and moved off to her right then stopped.

She looked over her shoulder. "Be careful, Bret."

His head swung around and he stared back for a moment. She could only make out the general outline of his handsome face in the cloud-filtered moonlight, though his eyes glittered in the mottled glow.

"You too," he whispered, and then disappeared into the blackness.

Warmth filled her chest at his response, surprised by it.

She watched him ride off, wondering if this was such a good idea. She shivered, the fine hairs on her nape rising up again. She couldn't pinpoint the cause of her unease, but she didn't think it had anything to do with Bret.

The moon winked in and out of the clouds, painting the landscape in eerie shades of gray and black. The wind whistled as it swirled through the valley and the combination gave the night an ethereal quality. Angel half-expected ghosts to appear or wolves to howl. She shook off the impression of impending doom and rode east along the far side of the vale.

Ebony's head jerked up and he sidestepped apprehensively, sending her heart into her throat, but she calmed him with soft words and a reassuring pat on his strong neck. "What are you sensing, boy?"

She glanced over at the cattle all bunched up some distance to her left. The rough contours of their heads and legs and backbones as their black shapes shifted in the gloom were not quite visible in the muted light. They seemed as uneasy as she was restless, and their nervous lowing came to her over the keen breeze whipping around her.

They sense it too.

The wind had tugged several stray curls from her hair-tie and she absently tucked them behind her ears as she studied the surrounding area. Nothing seemed out of the ordinary until a loud crack snapped through the canyon and the cattle suddenly erupted in a wild chorus of frightened lowing as they stampeded. The unexpected cacophony of mooing and rumbling hooves as the animals took off toward the opposite side of the canyon made her jump in the saddle. Staring after them, she wondered what had happened, and then her throat constricted.

Was Bret in trouble? He had ridden in that direction. Was he in the path of the stampede? Something worse? A dozen possible scenarios raced through her mind in the short few seconds she watched the swiftly departing cattle.

Angel gripped the reins, trying to decide if she should go after him when something nearer at hand caught her eye.

A brief flash of moonlight revealed smooth, sleek movement in the grass. Her skin prickled and her stomach dropped. Instinctively, she focused on the darker object stirring the long stocks, but the clouds overhead continued to drift and she lost the entity in the shadows.

Her heart thundered in her chest and all her senses cranked up to high, reaching into the darkness for the danger she could feel but not see. She pulled her stallion to a jittery halt and scanned the meadow. Spotting movement out of the corner of her eye, she fixed on the location. The wind blew tendrils of her hair across her face, but she didn't move. She recognized the slow ambling figure. Her breath halted and her blood froze in her veins as she stared at the huge, yet graceful feline form. The cougar took one deliberate step at a time; his sleek, beige-colored body appeared grayish in the dim light, his eyes intent on the retreating herd as he lurked among the tall grasses. Upwind from her location, the perilous creature was unaware of Angel's presence, or perhaps he simply ignored her for a more preferable prey. Either way, the danger he presented was too real to ignore.

An icy finger slid down her spine. *Damn*, she thought. *I hate being right sometimes.* She sucked in a calming breath and forced herself into action.

Pulling an arrow out of her quiver, she nocked the end on the bowstring and urged Ebony forward. Regrettably, she knew she wouldn't be able to frighten the predator away, not with an easy meal so close, and Ebony was as likely to run, which meant she had no other choice but to kill the prowling creature. She hated to do it but attempting anything else on her own would be far too dangerous.

When she was ten yards away, she stopped her horse, never taking her eyes from the hunter as he slowly advanced. She brought up the bow, drew in a deep breath, and pulled the string back to her cheek. Taking careful aim, she prayed she could stop the animal with a single shot.

In the split-second of her targeting, his tail twitched first one way and then the other as her breath released, followed by her arrow. The shaft flew straight for its mark, but too late.

"Damn!" Angel muttered the curse as the cougar sprang forward in pursuit of its withdrawing prey with the arrow buried deep in the animal's rear flank. If she had taken half a breath longer, the bolt would have missed altogether; sooner and the wildcat would be dead. "Damn." She scrambled for another arrow.

Even as she cursed, the animal let out a blood-curdling cry and then disappeared into the tall grass. She waited for a sign to indicate its position, but there was none. She once again urged her uneasy mount forward while her eyes surveyed her surroundings and her finger nocked another arrow. She heeled the stallion into a faster pace, wholly intent on finding the now injured, far more dangerous and unpredictable animal, unwilling to let it suffer unduly because of her ill-timed shot.

She wondered if Bret had heard the cat's cry and if he was, even now, on his way to help. If he was still anywhere within the cliff's confines, he couldn't have missed the scream, but a nagging doubt prickled her brain.

Her horse's anxiety increased with each step, the muscles of his huge body tensing beneath her. When he halted completely, she was forced to hold the reins and encourage him to carry on.

"I'm nervous too, Eb," she murmured to him after leaning over to pat his neck again. She took another deep breath to calm her rattled nerves, knowing her agitation only added to Ebony's. When the stallion settled down, she heeled him forward once more, alert for unusual activity.

The moonlight illuminated the shadowy valley through the thickening veil as she searched for the danger lurking in the grass, but he was nowhere in sight.

Ebony stutter-stepped several times, tossing his head nervously. Angel attempted to soothe him as best she could, but he only seemed to grow more agitated. Suddenly, the stallion sidled to the right then swung around and reared up. Angel dropped her weapon and grabbed for the saddle horn. Her blood turned to ice as the wounded cougar materialized behind them. Her mount reared again. This time she slipped in the leather seat and slid from Ebony's back. She hit the ground hard and rolled away from her frightened mount. Ebony continued to rear up to ward off the angry mountain lion as Angel got to her feet. She searched the long grass for her bow but couldn't locate it. Giving up on the weapon, she looked to her panicked horse. She watched, as if in slow motion, as a huge paw swiped at her stallion's forelegs. That was enough for him. Ebony bolted for the gateway, leaving the predator between Angel and her only chance for escape.

She stared longingly after the disappearing stallion, knowing a call or whistle wouldn't bring him back. Heart heavy in her chest, Angel's attention shifted to the injured animal, not more than ten yards away. A deep-throated growl emanated from him as he limped slowly toward her and her heart seized. She broke out in a cold sweat and forgot to breathe for several beats. She didn't think. She couldn't think. She ran. It didn't occur to her that running was the worst thing she could do or that the direction in which she fled would not lead to escape. None of it registered until she reached the weather-beaten wall. Her gaze followed the high barrier upward and her shoulders slumped with sudden understanding. She spun around, pressed her back against the rough, uneven stone and sought for her pursuer with wildly desperate eyes.

The wind picked up again and swirled around the encircling walls. It gave voice to a howl of its own, drowning out every other sound. The loud rustle of the trees and grasses added to the clamor of the impending storm as she searched for the injured animal. Heavy drops of rain struck the top of her head and, with a disheartening sob, she glanced up at the churning clouds.

The herd, still stampeding across the canyon, caught her attention, and she wondered if something other than the cougar had set them off.

"Bret!" she called, hoping he would hear her cry over the howling wind. "Bret, can you hear me?" There was no reply. Her shoulders slumped further as the nagging feeling from earlier seemed a certainty now.

Bret Masters was gone.

She was alone, unarmed, and in trouble.

She sensed more than saw as the cat stalked her as he once stalked the cattle and her horse. Her heart pounded with fear as she fought to squelch the ensuing panic rising inside her. She stopped her frantic hunt, took a slow, deep breath, and told herself to calm down and think.

As the moonlight filtered through the clouds again, she turned to look up at the craggy cliff wall, frantically searching from some way to save herself. Determination straightened her shoulders when she saw a small outcropping about twenty feet above her. Without looking back, she began to climb as thick, wet drops showered the valley in earnest.

Quick and agile, she made her way up the rain-slicked cliff, her fingers and toes searching for holds to take her upward. The downpour pelted her face whenever she looked upward, but she kept moving.

The heavy drops turned into sheets and fell harder as she climbed. The accumulated clouds blocked the moon entirely and the persistent deluge made the rocks slippery. Her arms and legs shook with cold and unfamiliar use as she struggled to keep her hold. She squinted into the murky heights, now unable to locate the ledge above her. Breathing heavily, she chanced a look downward but could not see the ground. Hazarding a quick glance behind her, she could just make out the shining eyes of her lithe stalker making its way toward the cliff base. The trembling assault in her limbs increased, but she continued her ascent with renewed intent.

The shadow of the ledge appeared above her and, terrified, she made a desperate lunge for its safety. When her hand seized only air, she slipped on the wet rocks and, losing her balance, she fell, sliding painfully down the rough surface. She landed hard, slamming her head against the stone wall, seeing stars and almost losing consciousness. Trailing rubble clattered down around her as she struggled to focus.

Mindful of the hungry predator tracking her, she pushed herself into a sitting position and tried to stand. Sharp blades of agony shot through her left leg. She looked down at her foot, wedged in a fissure at the base of the rocky cliff. Her fall had brought down a mass of debris, which was now crammed into the gap over her foot and ankle. She tried to pull herself free and a scream ripped from her throat. Her leg didn't budge. Panting, she lay back and closed her eyes, waiting for the pain to ebb before sitting up again. She brushed the dirt and pebbles off, ignoring the ache in her throbbing appendage as she examined her situation.

Then the cat's irate growl stabbed her with fear.

Her head whipped around, frantically searching the

darkness. The rain having slowed to a drizzle and the moon once again peeping timidly through the clouds made finding her stalker easy. He lurked less than twenty feet away. Panic jumpstarted her heart once more and a chill ran its icy fingers down her spine, kicking her survival instincts into high gear. She grabbed at a nearby rock for defense but refrained from throwing it at the last minute. Even if she hit the cougar, all her actions would do is anger it further and possibly make it move more quickly.

She dropped the stone like a hot coal and began to dig at the rocks jammed around her leg. Clearing some of the debris with trembling fingers, she hastily jerked upward to free her foot and sobbed as another shot of pain sliced through her ankle. She tried again, frantic to get loose, digging and pulling and whimpering.

She had longed for death many times before, but she never would have guessed her sorry existence would end this way. She shook her head as a pang of regret tightened her chest for all those she would leave behind, but she couldn't help them now. She only hoped the precautions she put in place would keep them safe.

Finally able to wiggle her foot within its confines, she pushed up onto her feet and tried to ease it out of the hole, but pain brought another cry to her lips. Frustrated, she leaned back against the jagged rock wall. Closing her eyes against the inevitability of her demise, she concentrated on welcoming the freedom from heartache death would bring. Still, her human desire to live wouldn't allow her the peace she sought. Instead, the thought of being torn apart by the animal's claws and teeth made her moan.

She shivered, her hands and feet like ice, as the pain in her injured leg throbbed in time with her galloping heart.

Will anything be left of me?

She opened her eyes, morbidly seeking the creature. She stared at the animal's moon-glinted yellow-gold eyes and the sheer terror of being trapped washed over her. The icy sweat coating her skin felt more frigid than the rain on her face. Her respiration tripled and her lids closed once more. She muttered an old childhood prayer as she heard the rumbling growl of the angry cougar come closer. She risked a fast peek to see the cougar coil and spring, surprisingly agile with its injury. She flinched, turning her face away and squeezing her eyes tight. Her fists clenched and her shoulders pressed so snugly against the cliff wall she became part of the rough surface. Her breath halted, anticipating the coming pain. One rapid heartbeat later, something seized her shoulder and she jumped. Eyes still closed, face averted, a terrified scream bubbled to the surface and echoed wildly through the canyon.

5

"Angel, are you all right?"

Her knees sagged with relief as the sound of his deep voice reached her over the wind and her eyes flew open to gape into his concerned countenance. He stood so close that the heat of his body enveloped her frozen one and his broad shoulders blocked out the rest of the night, but she could make out his face in the murky light. He'd lost his hat somewhere and his long jacket was unfastened, revealing the white button-up shirt he wore. His hand on her shoulder—big, strong, and capable, just like the rest of him—calmed her terrified sense.

Bret.

Mesmerized, trembling from fear and overloaded adrenaline, she stared mutely, unable to form sentences.

Hell, she wasn't able to think.

She stared into his dark green eyes, glinting in the intermittent moonlight, afraid to blink for fear that he might disappear.

Brows drawn down, a mixture of anger and alarm painted his expression, and she wondered about his reaction.

Then she remembered the mountain lion. Her shuddering breath stopped and her eyes widened.

His frown deepened and his hand tightened on her shoulder. "Angel, what's wrong? Are you hurt?"

She wanted to reply, but she still couldn't speak. All she could muster was a brief shake of her head as she dragged her gaze from his intent stare and peered around him. She winced as a red blade of agony shot through her leg again, but she needed to know the proximity of the predator hunting her. She searched, but except for the tall grass swaying with the storm, she saw no movement.

Her pursuer lay lifeless with an arrow through his chest no more than ten feet away. Regret mixed with relief turned her trembling muscles to jelly. She grabbed the lapels of Bret's jacket and, letting out a soft sob, she buried her face in the warm folds of his damp shirt. His sheer masculine presence and the intoxicating scent that was all Bret soothed her terror-stricken senses. Her knees sagged, and one of his long arms snaked around her waist to haul her up against him.

She snuggled closer and sighed. She felt...safe.

BRET CRADLED HER QUAKING BODY against his chest in a protective embrace. He stroked her soaked hair and murmured words of comfort, waiting for her to tell him what had happened. Not wanting to unnerve her further, he reined in the hot torrent of angry fear he wanted to unleash on her and pulled her closer.

What the hell was she thinking? She could've been killed standing there like that.

When her breathing slowed and she relaxed against him, he held her at arm's length and asked her to explain.

Slowly, and still a little shaken, she told him.

"Are you all right?" he asked again when her quavering voice faded.

"I bumped my head and got a few scratches," she touched her temple and stared down at her battered hands, "but I think I'm all right."

"Why didn't you move after you fell?" He ran his fingers over her abraded palms and felt her shiver. "Or start climbing again?"

"To where? There was nowhere to run. Besides, my foot is caught. I can't move."

He could see his frustration annoyed her, which was better than tears—not that she'd shed any yet.

"Yank it out. You should be strong enough now."

"You think I didn't try?" she snapped. "The way it's twisted, I can't get at it myself and it hurts too much to move."

"Poor baby," he teased as he knelt to examine the damage more closely. He shifted her ankle one way then the other and upon hearing her sharply indrawn breath, he peered up at her. Her face had turned ghostly white, her eyelids pressed closed, but she appeared calm. He admired her for that, for not sobbing or screaming. Her leg might be broken, but he doubted it. She more likely had a bad sprain or a bruised bone, both of which were painful and would keep her off her feet for a while. Again, her courage and refusal to dissolve into a blubbering mess impressed him. A lot of shaking and panting and obvious terror, but no tears.

"It's going to hurt a lot more when I really try to extract it," he warned, gazing up at her.

"Just do it," she said without opening her eyes.

Feeling strangely proud of her resolve, Bret dug at the rocks and dirt that trapped her, being careful not to cause her more discomfort, but the debris was too tightly wedged. He needed a lever, something to widen the gap. He reached into his boot and pulled out the hunting knife he had tucked inside before leaving the ranch. Officially, slaves owned nothing, not even the clothes they wore, and definitely not something like the knife, but Jake got it from somewhere and had lent it to Bret before he left. A good thing too as its long, thick blade was the best tool in his possession to chisel away the opening—though he'd have to spend some time sharpening it again after this.

It only took him a few minutes to widen the gap to where her foot might squeeze through. Tucking the knife back into his boot, he lifted his head and found her watching him.

"I'm going to try to pull you free now."

She didn't speak for several seconds, and though her eyes were masked, a thoughtful expression suffused her pale face. "Where did you get the knife?"

"A friend lent it to me."

"Jake…"

Bret didn't reply. The last thing he wanted was to drop Jake into hot water with Angel, so he pretended the blade was of no concern. "I'm going to try to pull your foot out now. Are you ready?"

She rested her head against the stone wall, still watching him. "Yes."

Clouds swirled over them and the moon's eerie radiance glimmered in her eyes. Something in her gaze tugged at him. His love-scarred heart thudded in his chest and his body tightened as an overwhelming, innate need to protect her erupted deep inside.

Stop it, the hard part of him shouted. The tender side of him—the one so devastated by her expression—instantly receded, but the desire to help her, to keep her from harm, remained.

Cursing silently, he turned back to his chore.

Grasping her calf with both hands, he gently shifted her limb. Pleased with the result, he prepared to ease her booted appendage from its trap as delicately as possible.

"Oh, God," she muttered in a frightened whisper. He froze, and when he glanced up, her eyes were once again wide, only not from pain. They were filled with fear and fastened on something in the grass. Instinctively, he reached for the weapon he'd set down beside him. Shoulders tightening, he brought the bow up as he rotated to target whatever menace stood behind him. His breath stopped when he discovered a second mountain lion, a female, sniffing the dead body of the first.

"Where did she come from?" Angel wondered in a soft voice.

"Probably his mate," Bret said. "They're solitary animals, except when mating." He watched the second cougar, following its every move, but hesitant to end her life too. He might be reluctant to kill her, but he didn't want to be her evening meal either. She would undoubtedly turn on them when she finished with her mate and realized their original prey had run off.

That had been Bret's doing. He'd thought sending the cattle on a route opposite to where Angel rode would draw her farther away from the canyon's gateway. But when she didn't appear, and after hearing the piercing cry of the first cat, he went looking for her.

Now, because he couldn't leave her behind, he would lose not only his freedom—*again*—but he might also lose his life. The last thing he wanted was to be ripped apart by another hungry cougar. He kept the predator in his crosshairs while furiously considering their options.

He knew they might scare her off if they made a show of force, but the old rules about dealing with wildlife, especially hungry wildlife, didn't always work as they once did. Yet, if they tried, and the animal didn't run, he would have to kill her.

The pressure of Angel's small hands against his back reminded him of her presence and added an additional burden to his current situation. Angry with himself moments before for returning to help her, the protective instincts her slight touch engendered in him was both unnerving and unexpected. Still, he wanted to protect her, to be her hero, and finally, win her affections—a jarring reaction he hadn't experienced in a very long time.

Why would I want that?

Quit thinking, he admonished himself, his arms beginning to shake from the strain of holding the drawn bowstring.

The cougar lifted her head. Her yellow-gold eyes turned in their direction. Bret straightened his back and tightened his hold on the bowstring, preparing for release.

"Bret?" Angel urgently whispering his name shattered his concentration.

"What?" he barked in a low voice.

"Don't kill her unless you have to."

"*What?*" Forgetting himself, he almost lowered the bow to turn around and gape at her. Refocusing on the threat, he settled for a hasty glare over his shoulder. "What do you want me to do? Let her have us for dinner?"

"Please, Bret. We might be able to scare her off. I'd rather not kill her...she may be carrying kittens."

Yes, he knew that. But this was not the time to argue about animal conservation.

"Yeah," he relented, still watching the wildcat. "All right, we can try to frighten her, but we may not have a choice if she doesn't leave."

"I understand."

"Okay then. We'll need to look big and bad so she won't want to deal with us. So, hold open your coat, wave your arms, and shout, but stay close to me."

"I don't have a choice there," she said dryly, and he remembered her trapped leg.

"This isn't going to work," he said, glancing over his shoulder. "We can't let her get close enough to be intimidated and I can't leave you here alone."

"We can try, can't we?"

He didn't think it was worth the risk, and he was about to tell her so when he remembered something. "Yeah, we can try something. Reach into my pockets and pull out the bags inside."

Angel did as he asked.

"Okay," he said when she held the packages in her hands,

"open them and toss each toward the cougar, but away from the entrance."

Angel opened one package to reveal a small but healthy portion of beef jerky. Lifting her head, she could almost make out his profile as she stared up at him with questions in her eyes and an accusation on her lips.

She kept silent. He was here. He saved her life. Now this meat was about to save them both. Without another thought, she threw the open bag. It landed no more than ten feet from the predator. The second fell a little closer to the cougar and, its curiosity roused by the savory scent of the flying containers, immediately tracked them, seemingly forgetting the humans for the time being.

Waiting long enough to be sure of the animal interest, Bret lowered his weapon, handed it to Angel, and crouched to wrench her leg free. She muffled a tortured cry behind her hand and he stood. Looking into her face, he swore softly and brushed his fingers lightly over her cheek.

"I'm sorry I couldn't be more gentle," he murmured before he reached for his bow. "Can you put any weight on your foot?"

He tossed a wary glance back at the cougar and she automatically followed his example. She felt almost giddy to see the sleek creature sniff the air and prowl toward the meat.

Turning her attention to her injury, she tentatively shifted her weight to her other foot, but then gasped and tumbled forward. Bret caught her with an arm around her middle and she clutched his shoulder for support.

"I don't think I can walk," she rasped as she met his eyes.

"Then I'll carry you." Making true his words, he leaned over, wrapped one powerful arm around her thighs, and lifted her easily over his broad shoulder.

"What are you doing?" she whispered breathlessly. She felt both foolish and useless with her head and arms hanging down his back.

"We have to leave, and this is the easiest way for me to carry you *and* run."

"What about me?" she mumbled as she bounced on his shoulder.

He either didn't hear or ignored her comment as he gradually skirted the predator. Then he turned and rushed toward the mouth of the canyon, eating up the distance with long, sure strides.

"Keep an eye out for the cougar," he hissed over his shoulder. "Tell me if she starts to follow."

"You know a cat's instinct is to chase, right?" Angel asked, suddenly remembering her own mistake.

"Yes, I know that," he panted but kept running. "We don't have much choice at the moment." He sounded annoyed as he tightened his grip on her and picked up the pace.

Twice, as they crossed the canyon, he asked if the cougar followed and each time Angel answered in the negative. She craned her neck to keep their stalker in view until they were far enough away that the cat disappeared into the blackness. Even then, Angel kept checking as they jogged toward safety. When they reached the archway, Bret set her on the ground where she collapsed onto her rear.

"How're you doing?" he asked, out of breath and hovering over her. "Any other injuries?"

"No," she said with a narrow-eyed glare for his rough handling. "Unless you count the shoulder-shaped wedge in my stomach."

He gave her a quick grin and stood to survey their surroundings. "Stay here."

"Why? Where are you going?" Though she tried to hide it, fear crept into her voice.

"I'll be back," he assured her as he hurried away; then he spun on his heel and took a few backward steps as he supplied more details. "I'm going to find my horse. Hopefully, he's still where I left him and didn't run off like yours."

Panic rose within her as his dark silhouette disappeared into the night and she tamped it down.

She was safe, for now, but as she sat in the darkness, her previous concerns about Bret returned. The conviction that he would run as he'd clearly intended grew stronger as the minutes ticked by. Her certainty brought up a whole new kind of fear that seized her by the throat. Would he really leave her here all alone, unarmed and unable to walk?

Yes, she thought dismally and slumped a little farther down on the rocky outcrop behind her. He didn't have the same feelings for her that she inadvertently held for him. Why would he? He hadn't bothered to get to know her and made no qualms about his opinion of her either. And she knew how much he yearned for freedom. The storm tonight must've seemed like providence to Bret, arriving just in time to aid his escape. This opportunity would be too good for him to pass up.

She wanted to be angry with him, but all she felt was grief and an urgent longing to be in his arms once more.

She sighed with frustration. Why can't I stop imagining that?

Because you've longed for it for years. Sometimes she hated that little voice in her head. Tears welled in her eyes and she began to tremble, oddly desperate at the thought that she would never see him again.

6

ANGEL STARED UP at the night sky, watching the clouds swirl past the moon. A much bigger storm brewed in the low, brooding sky. The wind picked up another notch and in her soggy clothes, it felt far chillier than normal for June.

Angel hoped Bret would return soon, that he hadn't abandoned her permanently this time.

She hoped the rain held off until they got to camp.

"God," she groaned, "I hope he finds his horse." She still reeled from their hectic trip across the canyon and not only from being hefted like a sack of grain. The back of her thighs tingled from the weight of his arm wrapped around them and the shape of his shoulder seemed imprinted on her middle.

Something moved in the darkness and prickles of fear lifted the hair on her neck and arms. Then Bret materialized out of the darkness and relief flooded her veins. Then she stifled another groan upon seeing he'd returned without his mount

"What now?" she asked, watching him examine the churning black sky. His hat was back on his head and it shadowed his face when he lowered his eyes toward her.

"Well, with your leg, it's too far to walk to camp and, from what I can see, there's no real shelter around here, which we're going to need with the sky about to open up again. This archway is the only cover I know of." He swore and kicked at the dirt. "I wish I knew this area better."

"There's a small cave not far from here." She pointed over her shoulder to the west. "Less than...maybe a quarter mile that way."

"There is? How do you know?"

"I...I lived near here," she stumbled over the lie, but she refused to give him the whole truth. "We...used to drive out here to explore when I was younger."

"Did you?" he asked, suspicion lacing his tone. Apparently, he didn't miss the hesitation in her explanation. "How far is it again?"

She ignored his first question and answered the second, repeating the distance through chattering teeth as the cold wind blew hair into her face.

Bret glanced at the billowing sky once more.

"Let's get going then," he offered his hand and helped her to her feet, "before the rain hits again or the cougar decides to pay us another visit."

As much as they both hated the thought of getting further drenched, a decent cloudburst should keep the cat from following their trail. Luckily, the way the night sky roiled, the prospect of more rain appeared inevitable.

Once standing, Bret lifted Angel in both arms and cradled her against his chest.

Yay, no more bouncing over his shoulder!

Grateful but unnerved, she shifted uncomfortably. This new position put her into disturbing proximity of his face, and her arms—with no conscious directive from her—automatically wrapped around his neck. Though she tried not to let it, her head rested in the hollow just below his stubbled jaw. The heat of his skin warmed a spot on her forehead and worked its way down in a way having nothing to do with warding off the cold. The iron bulge of his biceps ground against her back and thighs and the fingers of one hand brushed the underside of her breast—an unintentional side effect of the way he held her, but the innocent contact caused tingles in places she didn't want to notice. She tried to keep her mind on their situation, which was to survive the night, but her brain had other ideas.

Combined with being borne tight against his hard body and his manly scent filling her senses, she felt an unnerving need to taste his damp skin.

Would it be salty?

Nibbling on his neck, her tongue rasping slightly over his nearly weeks' worth of whiskers, came to mind and her body ached. She wanted to kiss him so badly, to pull his mouth to hers and see what it would be like. This man was not a faceless stranger, he was real and far more than she'd ever imagined. Smart and kind, and despite his dislike of her, he'd forgone his escape to save her life. With all of that, and the fallout from their battle with the cougars, it's no wonder she felt such a strong attraction to him and his too-handsome-for-his-own-good face.

Struggling, she finally got her rapid breathing and thudding heartbeat down to normal levels, but then floundered for something to say. When she did speak, she blurted out the first inane thing that came to mind.

"Why are you carrying me like this now?" A silly question, but it seemed the safest topic of conversation.

He shrugged. "It'll be easier for you to direct me this way and I don't want to retrace my tracks while lugging you around."

She nodded but said nothing more.

They only stopped once to rest and get their bearings before they reached the nondescript cavern she remembered from years ago. Unfortunately—or fortunately, depending on how one regarded the situation—before they located the shelter, the floodgates opened up and inundated them with heavy, stinging drops as the howling wind whipped the torrent into their faces and soaked them both in varying degrees.

When they reached their destination, Bret hurried in and set Angel down inside the mouth of the cave as a burst of lightning split the night sky. Thunder sounded almost a minute later, and she jumped at its rumbling roar. He stretched his arms as he went to stand near the entrance with his back to her. The rain outside was heavier than before, the wind so strong it fell in thick, sideways-slanting sheets. But all Angel saw was his tall, broad-shouldered silhouette, impressed and startled by how large and menacing he looked against the brilliant flashes of lightning.

"We need to get warm," she said through chattering teeth.

He turned. "Yeah, we do." His voice was as sure as ever as he moved toward her and pulled off his slicker. "But first, we get out of these wet clothes." He laid his garment down on the dirt floor and then stripped off his coat to gain access to his damp shirt.

"Shouldn't we build a fire first?" she asked as she stared into the gloom that enveloped him while he undressed. "We're warmer with our clothes on for now."

"Not with what I have in mind," he said with a wink. She only caught his playful display because another flash of light lit his features as he knelt next to her, his clammy flannel forgotten and only half-unbuttoned. Before she knew what was happening, he'd tugged her slicker over her head, pulled open her coat, and had begun to unbutton her top.

But she hardly noticed as her mind raced.

Was he really suggesting what she thought he was suggesting?

What else could he mean?

Anger bubbled inside as she realized she had left herself open to this by trusting him, providing him with an opportunity to take revenge for all the wrongs he believed she had done him.

"Stop it," she said in a raised voice and grabbed at his

hands. "You can't do this."

"Do what?"

The lightning illuminated the craggy interior for an instant and in the intense rush of light, she saw his wicked grin. Her face grew hot, realizing he was teasing her, or so that mischievous smile said. A wave of humiliation swept through her, and she dropped her eyes not wanting to see his expression in the next flare of brightness.

When will I learn when he's being serious and when he just wants to make me look foolish?

"May I have my hands back?" Humor bubbled in his voice.

Her fingers sprung open and he pulled his hands out of her defensive grasp. He stood and the shadow he cast over her made her foolishness seem far greater than before.

"Maybe I should start a fire first," he said with a chuckle.

"There might be some wood over there," she mumbled and, jumping at the opportunity to put her embarrassment behind her, she pointed toward the back of the cavity for added incentive. She felt idiotic again when she realized he couldn't see her. "In the back of the cave."

Thankfully, she heard him saunter to the rear of the cave, leaving her alone. They might be stuck there, but she needed a minute to catch her breath without him around to muddle her mind.

Shaken by the range and weight of the emotions running through her, Angel pulled her sodden jacket closed and hunched forward.

What's wrong with me? she wondered and a second later, another flush suffused her body when she admitted the shameful truth—she had *wanted* him standing close, removing her clothes!

Memories of his warm, strong body crushing hers into his mattress all those months ago flooded her brain. How cozy and safe she'd felt being held there. She wondered if he intended to hold her tonight. And if he did, would it be the same? Would it be more? The idea warmed her, even as guilt thickened her throat.

She'd forgotten how marvelous those intimacies felt, but she hadn't missed them until Bret awakened something in her that night—something hot and needy and undeniable. Her thoughts wandered, fantasizing as she used to about his hard body and what it might feel like to kiss him, to have his long, tanned fingers trail across her skin...

"Angel?" His deep voice brought her sharply back to reality.

Her face heated again, and she abruptly shoved her imaginings aside.

Backlit by the flickering nimbus, Bret appeared much larger and more formidable than normal. His raven-colored hair laid slicked back from his forehead while curling slightly at his collar. One cheekbone and his strong jaw were highlighted in the fire's wavering light, but nothing else was visible. Not until the lightning flashed and she could once again see his too handsome face.

Damn! Even wet and freezing, he looks too damn good!

"I've got a fire started," he said, his face tilted toward her. "Would you like to sit by it?"

He was teasing her again, she was sure of it this time.

Some of her previous annoyance returned. He knew she wanted...no, needed the warmth of the fire, but her irritation at his raillery didn't show through in the response he barely gave her time to give. "Yes, thanks."

Before she'd even started to speak, he had leaned over to gather her up, setting her to tingling again wherever their bodies touched. She held her breath and tried not to think. She specifically didn't think about how his body heat seeped through her clothes to thaw her side or how hard his arms were wrapped around her as he transferred her to the rear of their rock hollow.

He set her down on the slickers he'd laid out overlapping each other near the back wall, a barrier against the chill of the ground.

"Now, get out of those clothes," he ordered as he reached out to pick up his flannel from the ground where he'd left it before coming for her.

"No," she said in defiance and shied away from the narrow-eyed glare he turned on her. But then she straightened her shoulders and lifted her chin. "I don't have anything else to put on."

"I've seen women before," he said with a disparaging smirk and went back to arranging his shirt over a rock outcropping near the fire. "Don't worry, you won't shock me." He crossed to the other side of the fire, crouched down, and stretched his hands out to it for warmth.

She stared down at her clenched fists in uncertain silence.

When she didn't move, she felt his eyes on her again.

"Oh, all right," he muttered, followed by a muffled curse. He stood and pulled the top of his long underwear over his head. "Wear this." He threw it at her and returned to stoking the small blaze.

She held the garment in her lap and stared at him. His skin turned an orangey-red in the firelight glow and the glimmer played games along the masculine lines of his face. The muscles in his arm and chest shifted intriguingly while he poked the fire with a stick and she couldn't help but gawk at the marvelous display.

Dragging her gaze away from him, she stared down at the cloth in her hands. Though a little damp around the collar and shoulders, the garment appeared to be dry. His gesture was too personal, too intimate, and his selflessness surprised her, though she didn't know why it should. She'd seen him show kindness before, it was just never directed toward her.

The idea of wearing his undershirt, with his scent all over it and the warmth of his body still lingering in its layers, was enticing and brought with it other, far more explicit thoughts. She glanced at his naked torso and her belly tightened. She dropped her eyes, trying to still the images dancing a mad romp through her head.

It abruptly occurred to her that without his shirt he would be just as cold as she would in her waterlogged attire. She didn't know what else to say, but to mumble an appreciative thank you.

He lifted his head and his eyes locked with hers. He seemed angry, but the expression on his face was inscrutable.

"Just put it on before I change my mind," he growled, his scowl never wavering. She waited for him to turn away so she could do as he said, but as he kept staring back at her, a supercilious smirk transformed his face.

Her back stiffened and, feeling nervous and shy, and more than a little annoyed, she frowned. "Are you just going to sit there and watch?"

"Would you rather I put on it for you?" His eyes stayed on her and she opened her mouth to tell him off, but nothing came out.

When the moment stretched and she made no comment, his smile turned nasty and knowing as he leered at her, his eyes raking over her body.

She shifted under his examination, and, again, she wanted to call him out for his rude behavior. Instead, she closed her mouth, looked away, and began to undress.

She wasn't afraid of him, but his sneering smirk and lengthy perusal heated her skin in the most alarming way. Her body's previous reaction to his touch and her lack of control over it made her realize his nearness was the last thing she wanted right now.

She scanned her surroundings, rapidly searching for a method of changing without his eyes on her, but no option presented itself. She was too unsteady on her feet to attempt either standing or walking, and her head ached as well—unsurprising, after smacking her skull on the canyon wall, being carried off upside down by a caveman, and then having to deal with the same man across the fire from her. No wonder she had a headache. She couldn't move away, and he was not turning his back. So, what other choice did she have?

None, I guess.

Shivering, she shrugged and started to undress.

Bret watched her pull off her jacket and flannel, but she hesitated at her undershirt. She glanced at him once and, when he still showed no sign of leaving or averting his gaze, she untucked her garment, determined not to let him get the better of her. Steadying her nerves and making sure not to meet his green stare, she pulled the shirt over her head.

She heard him growl a curse but couldn't fathom why. Then her undershirt was snatched from her hands and tossed aside. Bret grabbed her by the upper arms, his long-fingered grip strong but not hurtful, and hauled her off the floor.

"What the hell are you doing?" he shouted. "What kind of game are you playing at? Are you trying to tease me, or do you just enjoy making the fact that I want you clear?"

He glared down at her, waiting for her response, but she was too aware of her near-naked body as they inadvertently surged together to speak. Her hands rested on his bare chest and she couldn't help but marvel at the smooth heat of his skin. His heartbeat thudded rapidly beneath her palm and hers felt like it might explode in her chest. Her mouth watered and the desire to taste his flesh struck her again. The tension in the air sparked and stretched between them but neither moved.

Angel stared up at him, stunned and annoyed by his unreasonable reaction to a situation he created. "What are you talking about?"

"Do you always put on a show undressing in front of a man? Or am I a special occasion?" He cursed, released her, and turned away as if he could no longer stand the sight of her.

She swayed at the abrupt removal of his support but managed to remain standing.

"You didn't even make an attempt at modesty," he

grumbled shaking his head, once again on the other side of the fire.

"Where would I go?" she demanded, her temper bubbling to the surface, while she rubbed her chilled arms. "I can't walk and you wouldn't move. What did you expect?"

He wouldn't look at her. "I didn't expect you to play games."

"Who's playing games, Bret? You're the one who threatened to undress me, whether I wanted you to or not and—" She was ready to go on about his disappearance earlier in the evening when his loud curse interrupted her.

He glowered at her with silver-green eyes that frightened her in a way his leering could not, and the look on his face suddenly made her wish she could run.

7

BRET SILENTLY RAGED at himself. Angel was right. He had created this problem and made an utter fool of himself in the process. What made it worse? The overwhelming urge he still felt to pull her close and kiss her soundly. The only thing she did tonight was force him to see this situation was entirely his fault. And that, maybe, he had done it on purpose.

Her quiet, "Thank you," a few moments ago had startled him out of his racing thoughts and when his gaze locked with the startling blue of hers, his gut had twisted and his heart sped up. She was so damn beautiful in the firelight, with her glossy black curls a slick curtain around her shoulders and her big azure eyes staring at him with what looked like a mixture of fear and desire.

Was that really what she was feeling?

He still didn't understand why she affected him so easily or so much. It's not as if he was an untried adolescent. He'd been around enough to resist a pretty face. Yet, though he'd tried to keep his distance, something about her always drew him back, just like she had tonight.

His grip on the stick he used to prod the fire tightened in annoyance. Not only were his plans ruined, but she kept throwing him off balance and his spiteful side wanted her to feel just as uncomfortable.

Then why did you give up your shirt?

Logic told him he did it because he could tolerate the cold better than she could. A deeper part of him—a part he steadfastly ignored—knew it was because he couldn't stand the thought of her discomfort.

Now, with the yellow-orange light from the fire warming her lustrous flesh and her eyes spitting blue sparks, he let his gaze roam over her, admiring the effects of the cold on her skin. The hard nubs beneath her lacy bra held particular interest. He imagined what she would look like without the thin garment...or the rest of her clothes for that matter. His face softened, and a smile brightened his granite features. She trembled as she averted her eyes and crossed her arms over her breasts, hiding them from his open admiration.

"Are you cold?" he asked, his voice low and alluring as he ambled toward her.

"No," she snapped, her eyes locking with his once more. He stepped closer, and her eyes dropped to his naked chest and then lower still to the proof of the effect she had on him. A little shiver ran through her and he wondered if it was the cold or the obvious bulge in his wet jeans. She licked her lips nervously and hurriedly met his gaze again.

Heat set his skin on fire, burning him from the inside out, and the rhythmic throb between his thighs increased. He smiled. She's feeling it too.

Every reason not to get involved with her disappeared as he gazed into the fathomless blue pools of her regard.

"You're very beautiful," he murmured as he brushed a wayward curl from her cheek.

Trembling, she shook her head and gave him a disbelieving glare, but she didn't move away.

He put his hands on her shoulders and reveled in the supple warmth of her bare skin. She tensed as he slid his calloused palms to her back, drawing her closer.

"Put your arms around me, Angel. Let me warm you up."

SHAKING HER HEAD, she tried to look away from the hunger in his eyes. His hands slid up to her neck, the heat of his long fingers leaving a burning path in their wake. Her skin prickled and felt too tight, too aware of his touch. His thumbs tilted her chin up and then he imprisoned her face between his palms.

"Hold me, Angel," he purred in a husky voice as his head lowered but stopped inches from hers. Her arms, still crossed over her bosom, pressed against his naked chest. The crisp swirls of hair adorning it tickled the upper slopes of her breasts. She wanted to rake her nails over it, to curl her fingers in the silky strands, to test their resiliency. Instead, she tightened her folded arms.

His hands trembled against her cheeks and growing expectation quivered in her belly. His bronzed face hovered over hers as if waiting for something, and his gaze bored into hers. Transfixed, she stared as a warm, inviting smile softened his expression and lit his green eyes with mirth…and desire.

"Thank you," he spoke in a smooth, silky timbre but the two words echoed in Angel's head as if bouncing through a vast, sprawling canyon.

Her hands had moved of their own accord to rest on his ribs and had slowly slipped to his back. His skin felt hot and velvety over the hard muscle beneath. The thin material of her bra was the only thing left between their upper halves. Molded along every inch of his tall, masculine body, a titillating thrill shivered along her every nerve ending. She wanted to give in. She wanted to do everything, anything he asked, but she knew, despite how much it hurt to refuse, she couldn't. No matter how intensely attracted to him she felt, she could not allow him to seduce her. With that thought in mind, she pulled away.

But he would not let her go.

"Bret…" She meant to convince him of the erroneousness of

his actions, but her voice made his name sound like a plea rather than a warning. She opened her mouth to fix her mistake, but her attempt came too late. His lips converged on hers, immediately weakening her resolve and waking the secret passion she held only for him. His lips felt soft and firm as they met hers, so warm and enticing that she got lost in how *good* it felt. Gently, his tongue slid along the seam of her mouth and before she knew what she was doing, she'd opened her lips and invited him in.

He slanted his mouth across hers, deepening the kiss, sliding his tongue into her mouth, invading the moist cavern like a conqueror, stroking her, teasing her, coaxing her to do the same. He laid his claim to her and demanded her response, lingering until she gave it.

She moaned softly as he left a trail of hot, wet kisses along her jaw and down her neck. Her fingers dug into the hard planes of his back. Wanting him closer, she pressed against him, longing to have the heat of his flesh warm the perpetual chill of hers. She wanted to feel the pounding of his heart against her breasts and the rise and fall of his chest with each rapid inhalation.

His scorching mouth returned to tantalize hers, driving her insane with her greediness for it, for *him*. Unable to stop herself, she leaned into him. Not caring about anything but Bret, her arms slid upward to wrap around his neck. Letting everything go, she kissed him back with a fervor she hadn't realized she could still muster and clung to him as he ravished her willing lips.

Even when he released his hold on her to unfasten her jeans, she held him, kissed him, demanded his full attention. The button undone and her zipper lowered, he pulled her against him, taking control once again. Sliding his hands down her back to her hips, he pushed the denim down her legs. He slipped his fingers inside the confines of her long underwear, caressing the silky curve of her hip before they slipped down to cup her buttocks, forcing her body to arc into him. Carefully disentangling her injured leg from her jeans, she wound it around the strong pillar of his thigh, careful not to jar it. It hurt anyway, but her need to be close was so much stronger. She wanted the contact, wanted him, and she wanted to let him know it in every way possible. His other hand joined the first and together, they pulled her more firmly against him. She could feel his hardened shaft prod her stomach and longed to pull it free.

While his mouth remained lock on hers, he ground that swollen heat against her, inching her long johns downward, exposing the warm, sensitive skin of her belly. The rough material of his damp jeans and the metal buckle of his belt were a cold exhilaration along the full expanse of her belly. The contrast made the throbbing heat between her thighs explode.

This is Bret.

This was her fantasy—this man holding her, kissing her, touching her, heating her blood, thawing the frozen winter living within her. She had dreamed of him, wanted him, needed him, for so long…for *years*.

She strained to get closer. His hands roamed over her, one still cupping her rear, lifting her onto her toes, the other sliding across her back. She moaned against his lips as he bent her over his encircling arm. His mouth devoured her, traveled down the delicate column of her neck to the soft valley between her breasts. Mindless with wanting him, she pressed her hips against his, grinding the most intimate and demanding part of her against his hard, hot shaft and his body trembled as he released a groan.

His reaction struck white-hot sparks inside her like the lightning that flickered beyond the confines of their small rocky haven. Her fingers skimmed down his back, one hand slipping between their bodies. She cupped his maleness in her palm, gently squeezing, and he trembled again. He pressed his face against her neck and moaned, the sound so low in his throat it was almost a growl.

Knowing how much her simple touch affected this big, gorgeous man turned her on, turned her wild. And she wanted more.

His arms tightened around her. Wrapping her arms around his neck again, she wiggled wantonly against him. Her heart pounded in her chest. He kissed the tender valley between her breasts and she tangled her fingers in his raven-black hair, holding him against her. His long fingers fumbled with the back of her bra, even as his mouth teased first one taut nipple and then the other through the thin, lacy fabric.

Resisting was useless.

She wanted this.

She needed it. She needed him.

She'd deprived herself of a man's affection for too many years and this frustrating, infuriating, astonishingly beautiful man awakened what no one else could—the passion she had locked away, presumably forever.

He was her weakness. She was ready to give in to him, to do anything to encourage him to take her higher until she forgot everything, especially the blue eyes that haunted her nightmares. She wanted to forget, and, for a moment, she did. The chill of the night no longer bothered her, only the strong beat of Bret's pounding heart against her chest, the heat of his body all around her, and his fevered kisses scorching her flesh were real.

"You're so beautiful," he said, his lips tickling her neck as his unsteady fingers continued to fight with her bra clasp. "You feel so good." His tongue flicked out to lap against her throat. "And you taste so sweet, so heavenly, my little Angel."

"Oh, no," she groaned and cold prickles of dread raced over her skin.

"My Angel..." he crooned, unaware of her distress.

She stiffened. Was that in her head or did Bret actually

mumble those lost words?

Hot tears scalded her cheeks as all the merciless misery crashed in. Wracking sobs wrenched up from her core as she relived the horrible pain she could never escape. Her chest ached, her eyes burned, but she could not stop the deluge any more than the torrent of memories flooding her tired mind.

"Oh, no. No, no, no," she cried, heartbroken and ashamed.

"What's wrong?" Bret pulled back to frown down at her, concern etching his features.

"I'm sorry," she muttered. Unable to stand his worried scrutiny, she shook her head and averted her face. Her knees buckled and if not for his hold on her, she would have fallen. "I'm so sorry..." Her voice nothing more than a hoarse whisper. "So...s-sorry..."

8

BRET DIDN'T KNOW what had caused her unexpected breakdown and was uncertain how to feel about it. At first, inadequacy and outrage straightened his spine, but seeing the heart-wrenching pain on her face instantly dowsed his initial reaction. His chest tightened upon seeing her utter devastation and the reddish hue of shame tinging her cheeks triggered a rush of protectiveness he couldn't ignore.

"Shhh," he murmured as he pulled her shuddering body against him, and, cradling her in his embrace, he rocked her gently. "It's okay. You're okay. You're safe." He didn't know what else to say, so he continued to whisper reassurances while she quaked and sobbed in his arms.

For Bret, there had been no escape. So caught up in his need for her, he'd forgotten everything else. He had wanted her to respond to his kisses and with that unexpected desire, discovered he'd also wanted to please her. To give her himself, all the tenderness he had been so willing to provide. And she *had* responded, encouraging him, lighting him up, pushing him further with every touch, every kiss, until she suddenly shattered in his arms.

He wondered if he'd frightened her, if the sexual act itself frightened her. She had reacted as if she wanted his hands on her, kissed him as if she was starving for him, and clung to him as if she needed his strength. She gave no indication she disliked what he had done, but he might've been too lost in the touch, smell, and taste of her to notice.

Or did she suffer an attack of conscience, suddenly remembering someone waited for her at home?

That thought knotted his stomach.

He had no proof that she and Jake's relationship was anything more than platonic—only his dark suspicions—but what else could've caused her reaction? Whatever the reason, her inexplicable breakdown rattled him and, with more questions than answers, he tried to discover what brought on her emotional meltdown.

"Hey," he said, trying to pry her away from his chest so he could look into her face. The pain in her eyes struck him like a gut punch, and he wondered if he'd done something worse than kiss her. "Hey, hey, honey, what's wrong? Are you hurt? Did I hurt you?"

Her dazed yet anguished expression crumbled again as she squeezed her eyelids closed and shook her head. "N-No, n-not you... I'm s-s-sorry," she sobbed as tears spilled down her cheeks.

"Come on, darlin', talk to me. What happened?" But no matter how often he asked, she would only cry harder and apologize. After a while, he stopped asking and simply held her against his chest, giving her all the comfort he could, until she finally rested, hiccupping and sniffling, in his arms.

When her sobs subsided, he helped her sit on the bed of rain slickers he had laid out earlier. She didn't stop him when he pulled his undershirt—after retrieving from the floor near the fire—over her head. Then he helped her remove her leggings, leaving only his shirt to cover her damp bra and panties, which, he noted with an uncomfortably erotic twinge, were white and lacy just like her bra. She sat stony-faced through it all, her eyes down, sniffling and trembling as if freezing, until he finished. Then he went to stoke the dwindling coals and added more fuel to the fire as she curled up alone on their improvised bed, using his long jacket for a blanket.

When the flames were rocking again, he tugged off his boots and slipped out of his wet jeans. He organized their clothing so they would dry by the blaze, then he went to lay down next to her. He reached out and she slowly cuddled up to him. Wrapping his arm around her chilled body, he drew her closer to his side, and she nestled her head on his shoulder, tucking her hands against his side. He arranged their makeshift blanket over them both and then smoothed her hair away from her face.

The only sound beyond her post-weeping breathing was the soft ticking of the fire as the flames slowly devoured the fuel. The air around them felt heavy with disappointment and embarrassment. The hot, mind-blowing sparks that had zinged between them were dowsed in the oppressive atmosphere. Silence reigned and weighed on Bret like the world had settled on his shoulders.

The whole scene had disturbed him and left him feeling confused. His chest throbbed with fear for her and the return of his perplexing need to care for her, to keep her safe, swelled inside him. Those emotions tangled up with anger—for what, precisely, he didn't know—weighed him down further, crushing him like the tremendous pressure of the deep ocean trenches. Worse, the inexplicable feeling of inadequacy, as if he would never be enough for her, never be able to ease her hurt, wouldn't leave him.

Wondering why he felt any of that left him more off balance than before.

He shifted and tucked his free hand beneath his head. He needed to let it go, push the memory of her body, her mouth, her taste, her scent from his mind. He was too tired to figure it out anyway. *Hell, exhaustion is probably the reason I lost control in the first place.*

Her hand came to rest on his left peck and all his recent hard-won emotional poise shattered. Strangely, the weight of her small hand comforted him, and he hugged her to let her know everything was all right. She remained silent, quaking, sniffling, physically pressed against him, but emotionally apart from him. He wanted answers and missed the heat they'd built up earlier, but he was not going to push her again.

He stared at the ceiling of the cave as shadows made by the fire danced over its uneven surface. He waited for weariness to take him, but sleep was a long time coming. His mind kept turning over what might've happened between them, twisting around inside him like a windmill in a storm.

Part of him knew he couldn't trust her, but another part wanted nothing more than to do just that. Their kiss tonight had been as astonishing as his unexpected desire to please her, to experience her passions burning only for him, driving him on to the bliss awaiting them both. All the mistakes of the past had dwindled away along with the painful memories warning him against her. Then something splintered inside her, and his heart broke right along with hers. Now he was left with no idea how to fix any of it, or even if he should try.

When they let everything go and the world narrowed to just the two of them, he felt like nothing else mattered, that she wanted him for him and not for all the shallow reasons he'd heard so many times before. He knew women found him attractive, but he didn't want to be wanted for his looks or for what he could do for them physically. He wanted someone to care about the man inside, to accept him, to work with him to build a life together. A woman who would share her life with him, do for him the way he would for her, but he also knew what he wanted was no longer possible. Women didn't share anymore—they took what they wanted from a man, demanded he comply without complaint, or suffer. How could he still harbor such stupid illusions?

Besides, his uncle had been right about him all those years ago.

"You're nothing but a little pretty-boy," Vince had told him the first day a young, brokenhearted Bret had arrived on his doorstep.

Despite the terror shooting through his veins, the twelve-year-old version of Bret had stood taller and stubbornly lifted his chin. "I'm way more than that!"

Vince had answered that small show of defiance with the back of his hand.

Too many times, Vince had found fault with his nephew and took the opportunity to explain just how powerless and meaningless Bret really was.

"You aren't special, boy. No one wants you. Even your mama was more interested in getting lost in a bottle than dealing with you or saving that pathetic ranch after my baby brother had his accident."

Bret had only glared at his uncle, unable to deny the bitter truth of those insults, and feeling the pain of them ripping the already gaping hole in his heart wider still. But just like every other time, Vince's taunts and torments never ceased.

"Get used to it, pretty-boy. No gal's ever going to want you for anything more than your pretty face."

The women Bret had known seemed to verify that prophecy, and he had the battered heart to prove it. Still, despite his uncertainty about Angel, he had to admit, if only to himself, something about her was different. He just couldn't decide what. And he couldn't stop thinking about her. Even now, he envisioned her eyes and how she looked at him. The way she had given him aid when he first arrived, the concern on her face, and the gentleness of her touch. All the little kindnesses she performed for no other fathomable reason than to be helpful. Maybe the difference was her kindness, but the mercy she showed him didn't mean she wouldn't turn around and have him punished.

His jaw clenched. Not wanting to follow that train of thought, he banished it to the far reaches of his mind. Then he took a deep breath and felt calmer.

Angel stirred beside him, and he tightened his hold protectively.

"Bret?" she called, her voice so soft he almost didn't hear her.

"Yeah, I'm right here."

"I'm sorry," she whispered, sounding so small and miserable it tugged at his heart.

"It's okay, honey. It's probably better this way."

She wiggled again and then lay quiet. Soon, her regular breathing told Bret she'd fallen asleep.

It was not that easy for him. Still too immersed in her amorous response to relax and, with her body cuddled next to him, sleep wouldn't be easy.

But, he reminded himself as he stared at the firelight dancing on the stone ceiling, *it* is *better this way.*

Isn't it...?

After tonight, part of him wasn't so sure.

9

SITTING ON THE TAILGATE of the cook's wagon, Angel sighed and glared her displeasure up at Bret. He stood beside her, giving her his best stony stare to let her know this was one argument she wasn't going to win.

"I *can* ride, Bret," Angel insisted again.

Bret had awoken that morning with Angel still cuddled in his arms. But once they woke and started to interact, something was different—something had changed between them during their little adventure in the cave. He had wanted to explore it a little more deeply at the time, but the others had come looking for them and, for some reason, neither of them had wanted to be discovered in their hideaway. They had dressed quickly and since she couldn't walk, he carried her back to camp, where they were now preparing to hit the trail again.

Still meeting her frustrated glare, he shook his head. "No, Angel, you can't. You can't even get your boot on. You may not have broken any bones, but a severe sprain is still serious. Besides, I'm already going to catch hell from Jake for not taking better care of you." He grinned at her narrow-eyed look and lowered his voice for her ears only. "Not something I relished doing until last night." He winked and his smile broadened.

Her eyes widened and she quickly glanced around before meeting his playful gaze once more. She lifted her chin, crossed her arms over her chest, and Bret braced for a battle.

"All right, fine," she said, keeping her voice down. "I'll ride in the wagon, but I can take care of myself. You *and* Jake had better remember that."

Surprised by her acquiescence, but not her reminder, he wasn't sure if she agreed because he was right or because she didn't want anyone overhearing about their night alone together. Either way, he chuckled, glad to get his way so easily.

Later that day, Bret located a small creek and, knowing Angel needed to soak her swollen leg, he rode toward it with her seated across his lap while the rest of the crew halted for lunch.

"The water's nice and cold, which should help with the swelling,"
he said as he sat her down near the creek's edge.

While she rolled up her pant leg, Bret quickly unpacked the sandwiches and cold beans he'd asked Carl to prepare for their lunch.

Angel's groan of complaint snapped his head up. She had one foot tucked under her and the other hanging, dripping wet over the gurgling creek.

"It's not going to do you any good there," he joked and grinned when she turned a withering look his way.

"No kidding," she said dryly and lifted a sarcastic brow.

He chuckled. "Twenty minutes. You need to soak it for at least that long or…I won't bring your lunch to you." He could tell by the way she rolled her eyes that she knew he wasn't serious about not feeding her. Still, she slowly lowered her swollen appendage back into the icy water and he smiled as he brought over the food.

They ate quietly, but Bret kept mulling over what had

happened the night before and one of his many questions spilled from his lips before he could stop himself. "How did you know about that cave again?"

She glanced at him—guiltily, he thought—and then finished chewing the piece of chicken sandwich before she answered.

"I lived not too far from here when I was...younger. We used to come out here to explore sometimes."

"We?"

She flicked another quick glance at him and then down at the creek. Keeping her eyes averted, she shrugged. "Family. Friends. We."

He nodded but didn't believe her. She was always hiding something, always so secretive about her past—not that he could blame her overly much. There were things in his past he didn't want her to know either. Yet, knowing she wasn't telling him the truth not only made him wary, but, for some reason, it hurt too. Unnerved by that reaction, he didn't push for more. They finished their meal in mutual silence and went back to join the others.

They followed the waterway for almost two days and utilized it as often as they could to ease the inflammation in her foot and ankle and by the end of the second day, the swelling had decreased but was still pronounced.

"You were right, Bret," Angel finally admitted, "riding would've been impossible with my leg like this."

Bret cocked his head and smiled, obligingly accepting her admission without comment. He respected her for admitting that she'd been wrong, and it pleased him that she'd willingly confessed it to him too. Why he felt that way, he didn't know exactly, because—besides that kiss in the cave and everything it had engendered—nothing else about their relationship had changed. She still argued with him, still *owned* him, but Bret felt less anger toward her and a lot more...admiration. Even though his wariness remained, he realized with some shock that he *wanted* to care for her, to protect her from harm.

Every time he gathered her in his arms to transport her from one place to another, his body came alive, all too aware of her soft curves snuggled against him, and not only when they were together either. Throughout the day, he found himself thinking about her and not the job at hand because her damn lilac perfume lingered on his clothes. He'd done more chasing of wayward bovine in the last two days than he remembered doing in six months back before the wars. Of course, back then there hadn't been any one woman who instantly attracted his attention the way Angel had when he first laid eyes on her.

During the long hours between halts, Bret often directed his mount to the back of the cook's wagon for a visit, not only to alleviate Angel's bored restlessness but also to grudgingly appease his new impulse to get to know her. She was a puzzle his mind couldn't quite figure out, and he found himself wanting to do just that. He took her to the creek twice a day to ice her leg and share a meal. At night, he would sit beside her by the campfire to listen to the other riders' stories. He'd also took her riding with him. At least once a day, he'd helped her from the wagon and onto his lap to ease her lonely convalescence. With her feet dangling over one side of his horse and her back against his chest, he'd wrap one arm protectively around her and hold the reins with the other. Then he'd make a tour around the herd, explaining their progress and discussing the possible profits from the sale.

"Where did you learn so much about ranching?" Angel asked on the third day since the cave.

Bret shifted in the saddle and hesitated, but the answer wasn't much more than she already knew.

"I grew up with a tough rancher for a father," he said with a fond smile. "He taught me all about ranching and to work hard from a very young age. I started mucking out stalls and milking cows when I was five years old. Though I learned to ride before that. My mom always joked about me being born in the saddle and she wasn't far off. As I got older, I did everything my father did or...at least, I tried. All of it helped me later when I got my other ranching job before the wars."

"How old were you then? When you started at the other ranch?"

He tilted his head. "About eighteen."

"And you ran it at *eighteen*?"

He laughed. "No, I didn't start training for that for three months. That's when Mace, he was the foreman, approached me about a promotion. Mace was an *old* cowboy," Bret said fondly. "He was just as hardy as my old man before he died, maybe more so. Leathery skin and a face full of wrinkles, but his mind was sharp."

"What did he say?"

"He wanted to know if I was interested in taking over for him when he retired. He'd already talked to the owner, and it was a done deal if I agreed."

"Did you?"

"Of course." He laughed again. "Running my own place was what I wanted. Even if the land wasn't mine on paper, ranching's in my blood, it's what I love to do, and I was happy to have the opportunity."

"How long did you wait to take over?"

"Not long. Mace died almost two years later. Cancer."

"I'm sorry." The compassion in her voice and the memory of the old man he'd thought of as a second father brought a sad smile to Bret's lips.

Many of their conversations went much the same, Angel asking questions and Bret talking while they shadowed the herd. Several times, after turning in at night, he berated himself for being so chatty with her. Hadn't he learned his lesson about trust? Sharing his stories was akin to sharing parts of his inner self and doing so gave her too much power. But he found he couldn't help himself. He liked to hear her laugh, see her smile, and he hated the dejected look in her eyes after being stuck in the wagon for hours. Every time he pulled her from that confinement, he felt as if he rescued her somehow. Maybe he did. Maybe his visits kept her from brooding over whatever horror she kept hidden. He still sometimes saw the misery of that mystery in the depths of her gaze and wondered if it hadn't been there all along.

Either way, the brilliant grin she awarded him whenever he arrived at the wagon was the best reward he could receive. Somehow, that smile wormed into his heart and lured him back to her several times a day, hopeful to witness the same beaming beauty again. He tried not to think about why, because sultry images of her half-naked, warm, and exquisite in his arms would permeate his brain. He didn't want to go there. Still, he found himself asking her questions about her life, hoping to break through her barrier, telling himself that learning about her might aid him in the future.

"Do you still have family here?" he asked one afternoon near the end of their trip. She didn't speak for some time and avoided his eyes—not difficult considering she sat across his lap—but he couldn't miss the stiffening of her body and the cold turn of her attitude. Jake had told him she never talked about her past, but after sharing that she'd grown up in the area, he thought she might've changed her mind. After several long seconds of silence, he decided he'd been wrong about that.

"No," she said suddenly. "They all died a long time ago."

He quickly recovered from his surprise and tried another question. "Were you ever married?"

"No."

"Have anyone special?"

She glanced at him, an odd, slanting look over her shoulder, but said nothing and presented her back to him once more. Then, her soft reply barely reached his ears. "Yes."

The sadness in her voice made his chest ache. And while he couldn't see her expression, he sensed the turmoil that shimmered below the surface of her calm.

Before he could speak, she glanced over her shoulder again. "I don't want to talk about the past. Okay?"

"Sure," he agreed, but his body tightened as she turned away. An intense bolt of jealousy, so strong it shocked him, ricocheted inside his constricted chest. He took a deep breath and found it painful. Shrugging to loosen the tightness in his shoulders, he tried breathing again.

He didn't care if she cried over an old flame.

Did he?

But why else would he feel such an overwhelming need to crush her in his arms and kiss her until he was all she thought of, while simultaneously wanting to shove her off the saddle and ride away? He didn't like to see her cry, but he also didn't like the conflicting emotions he kept experiencing around her. It was more than just her tears, and the lead weight now settled in his chest made ignoring those sensations impossible.

She had loved another man. That man may be gone now, but her regard for him remained. The insight burrowed inside Bret and set his teeth on edge. Reflexively, he considered his last and devastatingly ill-fated affair. He wondered if the man in Angel's past had returned her affections or if he'd betrayed her, the same way Amy Hensford had done to Bret.

Strangely, he found both scenarios unsettling.

ANGEL LOOKED AWAY. Too wrapped up in the pain his innocent questions caused, she didn't note the subtle alteration in his mood, the tensing of Bret's arms around her, or the taut shifting of his body. She only wanted to ride under the sun with this man—whom she was beginning to think of as a friend— and enjoy the cozy warmth of his embrace.

They rode in silence.

Bret shifted his seat in the saddle and the pressure of his hand on her hip increased as he also automatically adjusted her weight. No more than that, but in her mind, their night in the cave bloomed to life—his long, firm body pressed against hers, his beautifully chiseled mouth enticing hers, his lips firm and warm against her skin. In an instant, awareness of her position nestled between his spread thighs accosted her. His solid muscles flexed beneath her as he used his legs to guide his mount and another jolt of longing shot through her. The steely clamp of his arm clasping her to his chest seemed too tight. The bulge of his biceps brushing against the edge of her breast sent tingles along her nerve endings and tightened her nipples into sensitive nubs that chafed inside her bra.

Damn it! she thought in frustration. *Why can't I forget about the cave?* A part of her was appalled by her actions that night and thankful for the return of her sanity. And the other half? That side regretted not letting go completely, not giving Bret everything, all of herself. He stirred up emotions she didn't know she could still feel, and she didn't have a clue what to do about the storm swirling inside her. She couldn't act on them. Yet, she couldn't get him out of her head either. Listening to him talk about his life before the wars only warmed her already intense longing for him and failed in lessening her fantasies about this man she barely knew.

She reminded herself of what she had lost, everything that led her to the life she lived now. Bret Masters was her employee—not a slave, never that—maybe a friend, but nothing more.

Still, she wondered if he was as mindful of her soft curves as she was of his hard planes. Tilting her head to watch him from the corner of her eye, he appeared more intent on steering them back to the cook's wagon than on the woman snuggled so intimately against him.

She averted her face and frowned.

Could this change between them be because he seemed friendlier since their passionate night in the cave? Bret had been unbelievably kind, holding her and comforting her when she'd erupted into inconsolable weeping. But *she* had been mortified. She never broke down like that. Not like that. Never.

And especially not in the company of others. No one but Monica and, in the last few years, Jake.

She shifted uncomfortably.

"Everything okay?" Bret asked.

"Yeah, fine," she lied and forced a smile. "Just needed to move a little."

His arm tightened briefly as he returned her grin and then she went back to brooding.

The crying episode particularly embarrassed her because her collapse happened while he was kissing her, setting her on fire, and awakening things she'd expected to never experience again. Her cheeks heated as memories of his hands and mouth on her body filled her mind.

"I think we need to get you out of the sun," he said, startling her with the suddenness of his statement. She could feel her face glowing pink, but thankfully, he'd attributed her heightened color to the warmth of the afternoon sun.

"I am feeling a little warm," she lied again.

"Here," he said after grabbing his canteen and pulling off the lid. "Take a drink. We're almost back to the wagon. You can have some more when we get there. Then you can get some rest."

"Thanks," she mumbled and took a drink. Replacing the lid, she hung the canteen's leather strap over the saddle horn and attempted to sit straighter, to not *feel* so much of him pressed against her, but it didn't make any difference. He was all around her, his warm breath tickled the back of her neck, and she couldn't breathe without inhaling his leathery masculine scent.

Why did I have to make a fool of myself in front of him? She again lamented her breakdown in the cave. *He must think I'm crazy...* Her brain played games with her when she least expected it, which made life very difficult at times. But Bret never said a word about that night, and he had earned her gratitude with his silence.

Allowing herself to enjoy a man holding her again had sent a rush of passion crashing through her too potent to ignore, and she still felt the after-effects days later. But Bret was different, so vastly different from her previous, albeit long ago, experience. She and the young man she had once loved were so inexperienced, so naive. Bret was far more certain of his abilities, too much so to think of him as anything but an experienced, complex man. A self-confident, extremely attractive and arrogant with it, man. Being with Bret was devastatingly more intense than she had remembered. He was so big, so utterly male, and so...so... She didn't know what. Perhaps her years of loneliness coupled with her fantasies about him made Bret unique. Or could it be the taboo holding him carried with it? Or something else altogether? She couldn't say, yet she knew that none of that mattered. Any kind of personal relationship with Bret was too dangerous, especially for him. He'd been hurt enough, and so had she. Bret Masters was off limits for anything more than running her ranch. That's how this new world worked and how things must be between them.

There was no other choice.

*　*　*

They arrived at their destination only twenty-four hours late. The morning after, Bret sent Theo and Mary Danby, a guard who'd accompanied them on the trip, back with a message that they would be a few days longer than originally planned. The next afternoon they received approval from the resident doctor for Angel to leave the small clinic Bret had insisted she go to as soon as they reached the settlement. They set out for home early the following morning and Angel expected Bret to disappear during their return trip, but he didn't. Instead, he hurried them along at such a rapid pace that they made their way home in less than a week.

Preparing for the reaction Bret had predicted, she grinned

when Jake greeted them at the barn. Jake took in her state with narrowed eyes as she exited the cook's wagon, obviously favoring one leg, and immediately confronted Bret as he helped her sit on a nearby hay bale.

"Damn it, Masters, what the hell happened?" Jake demanded, though he took care no one else overheard. "You said you'd take care of her."

"I did," Bret replied and relayed the events leading up to Angel's injury. "It was a fluke accident."

"And you just happened to be on the other side of the valley." Jake said, obviously suspicious about what Bret was really doing.

Bret shrugged, but didn't argue.

Jake remained unconvinced, exchanging accusatory words with his friend until Angel raised her voice to interrupt.

"He's telling the truth, Jake. It's not his fault," she said and noted the astonished glint in Bret's eyes, there one second and gone the next. "The outcome would've been worse if not for him."

She reassured Jake several times while he glared at Bret as he unsaddled his mount before finally relenting.

"I'm glad you finally believe us," Angel said with a mocking smile, annoyed by his overprotectiveness, but touched by it too. "Remind me the next time you have a strange excuse to give *you* a bad time."

"It's not that I don't believe you," he replied, "but Bret knew he'd catch hell if anything happened to you. And I wouldn't put it past him to lie to save himself." Jake tossed his friend a sideways glance and the other man laughed.

"I don't lie."

"Okay, stretch the truth, then."

"I didn't need to," Bret said, feigning hurt. "It's all true."

Angel watched their exchange with amusement, thinking what odd friends these two men made. One powerful and forbidding, the other, while strong in his own right, still one of the most sensitive men she'd ever met. His compassion was one of the things she most admired about Jake Nichols.

While the others finished with their animals and left the barn in twos and threes, Jake helped his friend finish brushing down his horse while they tossed playful insults over the animal's back. She smiled, enjoying their banter and the feeling of family that washed over her. Jake was dear to her heart and Bret seemed to have wormed his way right in there beside his friend. They were both decent, hard-working men, and seeing how much they loved each other made her absurdly happy.

When they finished grooming Bret's mount, they tossed their brushes onto the shelf, exited the stall, and closed the door behind them. Bret glanced at Angel sitting on the hay bale and turned to Jake.

"I guess we'll have to carry her up to the house," he said as if disgruntled. She could see the glimmer of humor in his green eyes and in the crooked smile he tossed at Jake.

"Yeah, I guess you're right," Jake said, commiserating. "Man, I hope she's not as heavy as she looks." He spoiled the remark by winking at her with a silly grin on his bearded face.

She laughed, appreciating the easy atmosphere, wholeheartedly thankful to be home again, and feeling happier than she'd been in a long, long time.

THE COUNCIL

1

ANGEL SAT ON HER BACK DECK staring beyond the walls of the homestead recovering from her injury. An abundant array of trees grew in the hills surrounding her home, but the huge weeping willow was striking in its distinction. Clothed in its simmering summer-green glory, it stood atop the tallest hill to the west like a stalwart king upon his throne. The tree was extraordinary and not only because of its size.

Special, she thought as her mind drifted. *Yes, but only because of the secret hidden at its feet.* She shivered in the warm sunlight, tucking her suddenly icy fingers between her knees. Memories she would sooner have forgotten filtered through her defenses and goosebumps painted her flesh. She steadied herself as she gazed at the willow, knowing the recollections would consume her if she let them.

Not this year, she promised herself. This time, on the anniversary of that awful day, she would not succumb to the overwhelming sadness that had overtaken her every autumn for the last six years.

Turning away from the darkness of her past, she remembered her visit from Peggy that morning. Her friend's excitement over the new life that was growing inside her made Angel smile.

"It's so good to see you," Angel had said as she hugged her friend.

"You too," Peggy replied and moved to sit in the second deck chair. "How are you doing?" She dug through the bag she'd carried up with her and pulled out her sewing tools as she spoke.

Angel shrugged. "Bored, but fine. The doctor stopped by yesterday and said I'll be up and around in no time. How about you?"

"Dr. Hillman says we're doing fine too." Peggy glanced down at her rounded belly, affectionately running her hand over the small mound with a smile.

"Well, judging by your size," Angel teased, "you'll have twins or even triplets!"

"That would be wonderful," Peggy said radiating happiness. She beamed at Angel again, then threaded the needle in her hand, and picked up her work on her child's ever-increasing wardrobe, intent on keeping Angel company all through the morning.

Angel was grateful for the distraction. She'd spent several days in convalescence, periodically entertaining assorted visitors, but almost never the one she really wanted.

She didn't see much of Bret since their return. His attention was focused not only on the cattle but also on the soon-to-be harvested crops. He did visit when he had time to brief her on what was happening, but he mostly worked long days checking on everything from a sickly steer to irrigation problems in the fields. He rarely came home early, and if late for dinner, he didn't come back until well after dark. After spending so much time with him on the drive and getting better acquainted with the kind man beneath the anger, Angel missed his constant presence. She had grown to like him and value his insight.

During their few interactions since their return, neither of them had mentioned the cave, yet echoes of that night seemed to spark whenever he was near. A part of Angel missed that sensation, while another was wary of it and glad to have some time away from him.

When Bret, Jake, or any of the others were unavailable, she'd spend her time alone, going over the books, paying bills, and planning meals with Esther, anything to keep busy and avoid dwelling on her past—or on recent events that left her more lonely and confused.

By the time first harvest rolled around, just over two weeks later, she was healed up and ready to help the others in the fields. Dressed in soft, well-worn blue jeans and a white, short-sleeved cotton T-shirt, she joined the majority of the ranch's population at the horse barn.

"You should change into something with long sleeves if you don't want to get sunburned," Bret advised upon seeing her.

"I'm only going to be out a short while. I have other duties at the house."

He shrugged his athletic shoulders as he turned to leave. "It doesn't take that long."

She watched him walk away, feeling strangely forlorn as her eyes unconsciously traced the pleasing V-shape of his back.

Annoyed by the surety of his tone—not to mention her over-attentive gaze—she floundered to come up with an imaginative reply. One that would keep him from leaving so fast.

Closing her mouth without a word, she reminded herself, *It doesn't matter if he doesn't hang around to chat. You can't risk getting closer to him, and you shouldn't want to either.* But every time she repeated the admonishment, a niggling doubt tickled the back of her mind.

A half hour later, a team of men, women, several teens, children with their toys, and an assortment of family dogs rode out the front gate on their way to the fields.

In the north valley, the alfalfa grew thick and green, dotted with pale purple and yellow flowers in long, wide rows. A cooling breeze stirred the bushy plants that appeared to spread endlessly across the dale, a vast sea of shifting color.

"This is more than we'll use in a year," Angel said, astonished by the amount to be harvested. "What are we going to do with it all?"

"We'll store ours and sell the rest as needed," Bret replied as they unloaded the equipment from the wagon. "There's sure to be someone who's short this winter. It'll help out other ranchers and we can make a profit if we do it right, but it's up to you to spread the word."

Angel smiled. She had wanted to attempt something just like this for years, but other things always got in the way. It would take a small army—which she supposed they had now—to cut and harvest the alfalfa growing in this one area, and there were four more and multiple fields of hay too.

"You've done amazing work, Bret," she told him appreciatively, impressed with his planning.

"Just part of the job," he said with a shrug and abruptly walked away.

ONCE THEY UNPACKED the tools, Bret allocated people to tasks and they all got to work. After several hours, he was pleased with their progress and surprised by how hard everyone labored at their jobs, especially Angel. She worked harder than some and with more eagerness than others. He caught himself watching her, his mind drifting to their night in the cave. He couldn't get the softness of her body or her passionate response to his kisses out of his head. He kept picturing how she looked that night—black hair hanging in wet ringlets around her pale shoulder, nipples poking up under her lacy white bra, hardened with cold and desire, fathomless sapphire eyes gazing at him with need...

Damn, just the thought of it stirred him! Longing urged him to take her in his arms again, but he'd purposely kept his distance since their return home. Still, whenever she was around, his heart beat faster and memories assailed him. He did his job, kept her informed, but he also kept the visits to her bedroom short, because being close to her and not touching her was one of the hardest things he'd ever done.

Now, no more than ten yards away, Angel stood helping some of the teens rake the cut alfalfa into rows. Unexpectedly, she turned her head Bret's way and their eyes collided. His brain deserted him and a more devastating heat than the sun scorched and tightened his skin. Her eyes twitched one way then the next as if she wanted to break the contact but couldn't, and a flush slowly darkened her already pink cheeks. Her shaky smile made his heart jump, but he returned it and then forced himself back to work.

Bret lost count of the number of times throughout the morning that he had dragged his gaze away from the woman who occupied his thoughts. Thankfully, she didn't catch him staring again. He cursed himself and grumbled admonishments for his weakness, but it didn't seem to make any difference.

Hours later, with the sun still shining brightly, they had cut through a good portion of the bushy alfalfa field and were working their way to the end of the long row when Bret abruptly realized he was standing still. The others were swinging their scythes, but he stood like a statue, once again gawking at Angel.

He mumbled another self-deprecating curse and got back to work.

"Enjoying the view while the rest of us work, huh?" Theo accused a moment later from Bret's side, one arm propped casually on the wooden handle of his scythe as he wiped at his brow.

Bret glanced at the other man, a defensive comment on his lips, but Theo's grin and the mischievous glint in his blue eyes stopped him.

"Not that I blame you any," Theo said with a wink as he

picked up the cutting tool and prepared to swing it again. "An exceptionally nice view, if you ask me."

Bret flashed him a shameless grin, his green eyes sparkling in agreement, then focused on swinging his scythe smoothly, being certain to keep his gaze away from Angel and, as much as he could, his mind on the work.

2

LUNCH WAS QUICK and late that afternoon, and the evening meal was even later when the second batch of workers stumbled into the dining hall to eat. They were all sweaty, tired, and hungry after completing everything scheduled for the day. There was more work to come in the following days, but for now, they were all eager for a tasty dinner as they shuffled around the hall to find their seats.

Esther did not let them down.

"You've managed a miracle once again, Esther," Angel said, and Bret had nodded in agreement. The whole kitchen staff had prepared well for this new two-shift working arrangement. The food was hot and ready, and smelled heavenly, right on time for every meal. "Give the crew my compliments too."

"Ah, you are kind, Angel, dear." Esther beamed as she wiped her hands on her too-clean apron and gave Bret, who stood a couple feet away, a conspiratorial wink. "It isn't so hard when there's good planning. Bret here," she nodded toward him, "let us know months ago what he intended to do, which made it easy for us to organize feeding the lot of you. Not that it isn't a lot of work, mind you." She gave Angel another sly wink and went back to the kitchen.

Angel gave him a grateful smile which did strange things to his insides, and then went to join her head guard, Michelle, for the meal.

Most everyone was too tired to linger or chat after eating and, individually or in groups, they all retired to their rooms for the evening. Bret, the last to arrive, was also one of the last to leave. Though just as exhausted as everyone else, he decided, for reasons he was too tired to work out, to check with Angel before he turned in himself. Except for that brief moment in the dining hall earlier, he hadn't seen her since mid-afternoon when she finally returned to the house. She hadn't taken his advice about covering her skin and he wondered how she was doing.

He trudged wearily up the stairs and down the hall, thinking about the work ahead of him in the morning. When he reached her bedroom door, he knocked and entered after she called for him to come in.

The scent of lilacs struck him as he crossed the threshold, not strong but definitely there. A little surprised by the enormity of her neat yet not overtly feminine space, Bret pushed away the sensations dredged up by the flowery perfume and took in the rest of the room. A tall, antique grandfather clock stood beside the door and lavender rugs surrounded a huge, four-poster bed situated between two French doors across the room. The doors led out onto a deck, which, by Bret's estimation, was built over the dining hall downstairs. On the threshold of one of these doorways Angel stood, waiting for him. Her thick hair and the ankle-length white robe she wore stirred in a waft of wind.

"Hello, Bret," she said pleasantly. "Come in."

He closed the bedroom door and followed her onto the balcony but stopped just beyond with his white straw hat in his hands. Now that he was here, his tired mind couldn't quite remember why he'd come in the first place. He admired her slim back, the pleasant way it bowed into her hips, and the luscious roundness of her backside where the thin fabric of her robe pulled snug, accentuating her curves. More than a year had passed since he'd last been with a woman and, ogling her pleasing shape, his body reminded him sharply of the lack as his mouth went dry and his groin tightened uncomfortably.

The cool evening breeze rustled her black hair and the ends of her robe fluttered around her knees, giving him a fleeting vision of bare feet and tanned calves before she pulled the garment back into place.

"To what do I owe this visit?" she asked, glancing over her shoulder at him, her soft voice bringing him back to earth.

"How are you doing?" he inquired, feeling awkward and somewhat distracted by her and the scent of lilacs that floated out of the room behind him.

"I'm okay," she answered. "A little tired, but fine. You?" She turned to face him, the rosy hue of sunburn on her nose and cheeks evident.

"The same," he said stepping toward her. "I see you got a bit burnt." Without thinking, he reached out and brushed her cheek with the back of his fingers. Tingles shot through his arm and he didn't miss the strange look that passed through her eyes as she stared up at him. Her head tilted ever so slightly toward his hand and he instantly knew touching her was a mistake. The slight contact set the unwanted sensations in his body to burning and he couldn't pull his gaze from hers. Something about the innocence of her eyes always affected him in ways he didn't want to contemplate.

"I should've taken your advice sooner," she said breathily, moving away from him and breaking their connection. She leaned her hips back against the deck railing, one hand holding her silky robe against her legs as the wind blew again, tugging the material ever so slightly apart. "My arms are burnt too."

He forced his eyes to focus on her face. "I tried to warn

you." He smiled.

"Yes, you did." She ducked her head but returned his grin. "I hadn't planned to stay out so long, but once I got into the job, it was kind of fun."

"It's hard work," he said, turning to lean against the same railing she used. He crossed his arms over his chest and told himself it wasn't to keep his hands from roaming, it was just more comfortable.

"Yeah, but isn't that just another way of saying nothing worthwhile is easy?"

He shrugged. "I never thought of it that way."

"I don't suppose many people do." She turned back to the view of the hills. "Anyway, it was good to be outside working again."

"There's still more to do tomorrow if you feel up to it." A twinge of hopeful anticipation swirled in his chest, but then he berated himself for the reaction. He didn't want to spend more time with her than necessary.

Then what are you doing here? a little voice chided him. He thrust the voice into a box in his mind, effectively silencing it.

"I'd like to." She smiled over at him. "But I can't."

"No?" Thankfully, he didn't sound disappointed.

"Unfortunately, no. I have a council meeting tomorrow. Getting there and back will take hours and the meeting itself will eat up the rest of the day. I don't expect to be home until late." She looked up at him and blinked as if startled.

Bret had known about her participation in this section's governing body—Jake mentioned it months ago—but until this moment, he hadn't cared. Now, he was unexpectedly furious that she was tangled in politics. A part of him had grown to like her and wanted her safe. Politics was anything but and the combination made him angrier still.

This reminder of her ambition was like a cold shower. Here he was, yet again panting after another woman who wanted to enslave men, who sat through meetings discussing the best ways to punish them for the smallest infraction. *How often has she gone out with slaving parties to round up men for auction?* The thought intensified his fury. Then he realized he now equated Angel with Amy Hensford.

"I see," he growled in reply to Angel's explanation. Tight-lipped, he dropped his arms to his sides and lunged off the railing. He took several steps, trying to get his sudden rage under control, before whirling to face her.

"Making more laws to enslave mankind?" he asked with a saccharin edge as cruel as his heated gaze.

"It isn't always like that, Bret," she said, wrapping her arms around herself and lifting her chin. "There are some of us who are trying to make things better."

"You've done a great job so far," Bret grumbled, crossing his arms over his chest again.

"I didn't say we've accomplished very much. There's a lot of resistance, but we're trying."

"Give it up," Bret advised, angrier than before. "The only way to make our lives better is to let us go, but I don't suppose that notion ever occurred to you."

"Yes," Angel murmured, her eyes drifting back to the tall weeping willow on the hill, "it did occur to me and some others as well, but too many women want men exactly where they are."

Sadness percolated in her voice and made him hesitate before making his next remark. Something in her changed, melted somehow, and he thought she seemed more vulnerable in that moment than the one before. But he ignored his irksome need to discover the reason for her altered mood and plowed forward, wanting to upset her as much as she had him.

"There are other ways for a man to gain his freedom," he said, letting the insinuation hang in the air between them.

She caught his meaning and her wide, alarmed gaze swung back to him.

He'd intended to shock her, and her eyes said that he had.

But what he hadn't expected was the pain he saw or the magnetic attraction that tugged at his soul. Some secret concealed in the deep expanse of her azure gaze drew him to her again. He almost gave in to it. Almost asked what frightened her so much—what happened that night in the cave? But at the last second, he pressed his lips together and resisted.

"Trying to escape gets men like you killed," she said, locking his gaze, blue dueling with silver-green.

"At least I would be free."

"Would you?"

"Yes!"

She stared at him quietly for several seconds then stunned him with her next question. "Do you see freedom in death?"

"Sometimes," he said at length, intending to shock her again, but she merely nodded in agreement. Her swift mood change struck Bret as odd, nothing like what he would've expected when faced with his sudden anger. Her peculiarities pulled at him, luring him in further, until, unable to stop, he allowed himself to go.

"Do you?" he asked, referring to her last question.

"Yes." The single word made a whole statement.

"Why?"

"I have my reasons, Bret, and they're not anything you need to know."

"At least my reasons have cause," he said, deliberately trying to bait her. The fact that she met what should've angered her with calm surety, confused and annoyed him.

"I used to have a cause too, a reason to live, but it died long ago, as did my will to fight for it."

"What does that mean?"

"Why are you so interested?" she asked, turning on him, chin lifted stubbornly, angry at last. "Why do you want to know my reasons? You don't like me or what I stand for, and I don't like you or your arrogance. So, explain to me, why should I tell you anything?" She pushed away from the deck rail, not waiting for an answer, and, head held high, she strode purposefully by him into her bedroom.

"Please leave," she said from inside, her voice cold and controlled.

When he reentered, he caught her wiping her eyes as she perched on the edge of her bed, one palm pressed to her knee holding the ends of her robe together. When she saw him, she instantly dropped her hand and straightened her back.

"You know where the door is," she said dismissively. He would've thought her cool and composed, if not for the movement of her hand and the slight quiver she'd been unable to hide in her voice.

He stopped a few feet away to consider her and his anger over what she might do at council seemed to seep away through his pores. He sensed sorrow flowing out of her like cold sleet from a gray sky and the chill doused the heat of his resentment. The fury of his earlier thoughts sizzled into meaningless steam and blew away with the breeze. He cocked his head. "You're a weird one."

"Please leave," she repeated, glaring at him, looking as if she would burst into tears at any moment, but concealed it admirably.

"What're you hiding, Angel?" he asked, his tone gentle. "Is it really that bad?"

"Get the hell out of here!" She jumped to her feet. Her silky robe slipped open, affording Bret a tantalizing image of creamy cleavage. His eyes dropped to her heaving chest and a burgeoning fire sparked below his belt. He clenched his jaw and lifted his eyes to her just as she let out a frustrated gasp and pulled the recalcitrant edges of her gaping garment back together.

"Get out!" she screamed again, this time grabbing the nearest available object to throw at him, which happened to be one of her pillows.

He stepped aside as the pillow, with a soft rustle of cloth, fell to the floor where he once stood. His eyes trailed from the harmless cushion back to her face and grinned. "Is that the best you can do?"

Angel, clearly exasperated, growled and immediately searched for something else to throw.

He chuckled softly and decided to leave before she found another more substantial item to pitch at him, like the oil lamp that sat on the bedside table. Beating a hasty though fearless retreat, Bret spun on his heel and headed for the exit.

"All right, I'm going," he tossed over his shoulder and then chuckled again as he pulled the door closed behind him.

3

AS SOON AS THE DOOR CLOSED and she heard Bret's footsteps carry him down the stairs, Angel crumpled onto the bed, buried her face in a pillow, and, unable to stop them, let the tears come.

Why, of all things, did he ask her those questions? Why did she answer even one? And why did she get so angry?

What did he care, anyway? As he kept reminding her, he hated her for making him a slave. He didn't seem to realize his life would be much worse if she had let Darla have him. She understood his pride, but not his blind anger.

Unbidden, gentle dark-blue eyes full of love filled her mind and she wept harder for a past she couldn't change.

I have to let him go! I must let them all go!

Everything she did now, all the people she'd helped in the last six years, she did in memory of those she had failed in the hopes her deeds might keep someone else from experiencing this hollow agony she couldn't shake. But only one thing would liberate her from the constant anguish and sometimes the allure of leaving everything behind almost overpowered her. At those times, she asked herself two questions—if she gave up, what would happen to all those she had gathered under the measly protection she provided? And what if the safeguards she had put in place didn't hold?

Either way, the answer was the same, and always made her pause.

Jake and Theo would be given into the less than tender care of Darla Cain. The new man from Texas, Dean Williams, would return to Carrie Simpson—the most fervent of Darla's cronies—for more humiliation. Many of the others, including Bret Masters, would be forced to return to the Auction Hall to be resold. And the children would suffer as much if not more than she did at her worst moments.

Could she do that? To any of them?

No, not now. But she dreaded the day when she became so lost and desolate that their fate no longer mattered.

She rolled onto her back and, flinging her arms wide, stared at the ceiling. Her breath came in halting gasps, but she was slowly regaining control. At least she was until Bret's face popped into her head again.

Why does he make everything so damn hard?

Her bouts with depression had grown easier with Jake around. He anchored her and kept her rooted in the present. But before long, Monica Avery would repay her for the aid she'd given and Jake would leave. Angel considered herself lucky that Monica had trusted her so much, especially in these times, and she was more than grateful for the both of them. Yet, their constant friendship was not enough to stop Angel's heartache.

Then there was Bret Masters...

To say he was good-looking would be a gross understatement, but there was more to him than that. Something about *him*, the man beneath the handsome surface. Maybe it was the kindness he seemed to reveal only to the animals or workers under his care. She'd also seen him interact with the children and had marveled at his patience and compassion for them.

"Our daddy doesn't live with us anymore," one little boy

had said in the barn only a couple of days before while Bret instructed him on how to curry a horse. "He's dead."

At the boy's heart-wrenching revelation, Bret's hands had ceased their movement and his head tilted downward. She'd only been able to see the side of his face from the central aisle where she stood, but what she read there—and after hearing the little boy's tragic words—broke her heart a little more.

"I'm sorry, Gavin," Bret had said as he hunkered down beside the tense-shouldered youngster. "Do you want to talk about it?"

The boy dropped the currycomb and with a quiet sob, threw his arms around Bret's neck. "What's g-going to ha-happen to us? M-me and my brother... When we g-get big. What's g-going to happen to us?"

Bret seemed to hold his breath for a long second before he hugged the boy close. "Nothing's going to happen to you or your bother, Gavin. You're safe here. You know Miss Aldridge won't let anyone hurt you."

That statement surprised Angel... and warmed her a little too.

"The older b-boys said they'll take us away from our m-mom...take us away and ma-make us do things we d-don't wa-want."

Bret's jaw had hardened upon hearing Gavin's mumbled words. "No, Gavin, that won't happen."

The boy pulled back and looked up at the man with teary eyes. "How d-do you know?"

"Because," Bret had said, gently wiping the boy's tears away, "I won't let it happen. I promise. Okay?"

Just like every time she'd noticed him chatting with Grayling the cat or one of the horses, she'd been moved by his tender treatment of the small child who was obviously still in pain over the loss of his father and terrified of a future beyond his control. But she'd sensed something else in Bret, something more than just sympathy for Gavin's loss and anger for his fear. Then she remembered Bret's father had died when Bret was young, and she knew what she'd sensed in him—empathy. He still carried a similar pain and something else, a somber, deep burning anger for wrongs done to him in the past—long ago and more recently too. Things she wasn't privy too. That scene in the barn with Gavin had made her wonder again, what—besides his father's premature death—had happened to make Bret so untrusting of people in general and her in particular.

She still didn't know, but now she had other questions on her mind. Such as, why she was so attracted to him? There were dozens of handsome men living on her ranch, but not one of them ever made her heart beat faster, or tied her tongue into knots, or made her body come alive with a single touch. Something about Bret beckoned to her like a dark, inescapable seduction, yet she resisted, and for good reason.

"Am I really unwilling?" she asked the empty room. Her eyes burned a little and she shivered as she reached out to extinguish the lantern on the bedside table, then pulled the blanket around her.

In the darkness, she relived Bret's long fingers sliding over her skin, giving her chills. His mouth weakening her limbs as he traced fiery kisses along the slim column of her neck. The way his eyes darkened as he gazed down into hers. She kept seeing those images in her dreams. They bewildered her and made her heart ache.

It was Bret's kiss in the cave that had turned her world totally inside out. She hadn't felt her body clench with anticipation or respond with so much passion in years. She'd almost surrendered to him, teetered on the brink of betraying everything...just for his kiss.

She inhaled sharply, remembering the hard heat of him, how he tasted faintly of coffee...

God, she groaned and rolled onto her back. If he'd teased her lips a little longer, if he hadn't spoken those remembered words, she wouldn't have stopped.

She realized that she'd wanted the comfort of Bret's strong arms around her and, in her weakness, had given in to the temptation.

She let out another frustrated moan and turned onto her side. The robe she wore twisted around her body and tugged at her shoulders. Irritated with the garment, as well as herself, she sat up, yanked the clothing from her body, and tossed it onto the floor. She flopped back onto her pillow and curled up beneath her comforter as her mind returned to that stormy night on the drive.

Bret had intended to escape that night—it was obvious—but she didn't understand why he didn't follow through.

Would she ever know why he came back to help her?

After listening to Jake talk about the man for almost three years, she felt like she knew Bret. But meeting him in person was far different than she'd expected. The man she first met was not the sweet, sensitive man Jake always spoke of in his tales. This Bret was angry and arrogant, but she'd still been drawn to him. Now that she'd witnessed the kinder side of Bret, her attraction to him intensified.

She didn't blame him for disliking her or being angry about his situation. After everything he'd been through, she would've been astounded if he'd shown anything more than wary acceptance. Yet, she had still been a tad disappointed.

"It's not my story to tell," Jake had replied over the years whenever she'd asked for details about Bret's past. Bret had filled in a few of those gaps during her conversations with him but added a few more questions too. She gathered something had happened with his mother when he was younger, but she didn't know what. She also sensed he hid something else, something dark and threatening. Was his pain similar to hers, and could that be what created the irresistible connection between herself and the angry, brokenhearted man?

Jake's easy friendship was the closest she'd allowed herself to be with a man for many, many years, but the way she responded to Bret's simple touch on the deck tonight clearly evidenced her growing attraction. She'd barely managed not to look away and blush like a silly young girl. She was a mature woman, damn it! Why couldn't she control herself around him?

She gripped her pillow in both hands, pressed her face into it, and shouted her frustration. She would not let her ridiculous infatuation with an outlandishly attractive man undo all she had accomplished. Nor would she risk his well-being by giving her adversaries a target to aim for while attempting to harm her. Bret Masters was already a neon sign for them to flock to, and she didn't want to make the situation worse by getting involved with him. Her enemies were many. Powerful and sleazy enough to wrestle him out from under her protection—though meager as it was, it was better than being with them. He was just stubborn enough to do something rash that would give her adversaries the opportunity they have been waiting for. She could not risk his life.

She groaned again. "I never thought I'd have this problem," she muttered into the darkness. "Why did I let myself have this problem? There can be no one else…ever."

Tears welled in her eyes and she vainly brushed them away. The thought of what her enemies would do to Bret if their reach extended inside her home made her shiver. She choked on a sob as dread bubbled to the surface, not just for Bret but for all of them. She had a duty to protect everyone she'd brought here; to all those other women she'd convinced to join her against Darla and to treat their slaves like human beings. That weight of responsibility always felt heavy, but for some reason, it seemed heavier now.

She pulled the blanket tighter around her shoulders, huddling into the safety of its warmth. She pulled a pillow to her chest and, wrapping her arms around it, she buried her face in its soft folds and wept bitterly for the past and the unknown future, for the love she lost, the life she lost, and the man she wanted but could never have.

4

EARLY THE NEXT MORNING, Angel rode east toward for the Section Council meeting. She wasn't in a hurry and kept Ebony at a sedate pace while she admired the scenery and listened to the wind whistle over the landscape. She left the tall evergreens surrounding her home behind and crossed the wide, swift current of the Yakima River, rode through the rolling hillsides and down into the green valley to her destination. The sun peeked over the horizon shortly after she left home, but now shone brightly in the cloud-dappled sky as she directed Ebony toward the gates of the Auction Hall.

Monica awaited her at the stables adjoining the compound. After she handed Ebony over to the groom—one of Darla's many slaves—with instructions for the stallion's care, Monica joined her and they headed for the exit doors.

Angel stopped her friend with a hand on her arm before they exited the barn and then hauled her into an empty stall. Angel glanced around before pulling a letter from her pocket. She smiled at Monica's expression when she presented the thick envelope with her name scrawled across the white surface in blocky, masculine letters. Monica's face lit up like the little girl who found everything she wanted under the tree on Christmas morning.

Seeing Angel's grin, Monica reddened prettily—being blonde and fair, the color change was spectacular. Not usually so easily embarrassed, and plainly uncomfortable with the sensation, Monica snagged the message from Angel's fingers and whipped out a second sizable missive of her own. One word was written on the front in Monica's bold, scrolling hand—*Jake*.

"I had hoped you wouldn't mind delivering the mail," Monica said, her blush still bright on her cheeks, but she recovered rapidly when she wound her arm around Angel's as they exited the stable.

"Of course not," Angel replied. "You've both done so much for me. I'd do anything for either of you. Delivering a letter is the least I can do."

"What you did for Jake and me meant the world to us. You don't owe us anything. We. Owe. You."

"You don't *owe* me either. I didn't do anything special, just helped out my friends."

"Still, we're more than grateful."

"And so am I."

They exchanged meaningful grins and pushed through the doors.

"I hope I'll be able to come by in person soon," Monica told her, tucking Jake's note into her pocket as Angel did the same with Monica's. "The ranch has been so busy lately. I haven't been over to visit in forever."

"You're welcome anytime. You know that."

"Yes, I do," Monica swung her arm over Angel's shoulders and gave her a quick squeeze as they walked across the courtyard, "but I feel a little guilty...because I want to see more of you, of course." She grinned.

"Of course." Angel went along with her friend's teasing. "But I'm sure you miss Jake more." Her mood altered, became earnest. "I'm not jealous, you know. I'm happy for you both."

"I know," Monica answered as she pulled open the door to enter the building. "I meant I miss you both, but," she winked at Angel with a wide grin, "I do miss Jake *a teensy bit more.*" She held her thumb and forefinger to indicate the amount. If her tone hadn't conveyed her meaning, her lusty smile would have.

"Oh, brother." Angel rolled her eyes and chuckled at the unabashed look Monica threw at her. "You know, you don't have to share *all* your thoughts with me. Some things are better left unsaid."

Monica giggled. "But then how will you live vicariously through me?"

Angel laughed again at her friend's brazen sexual insinuation. "I don't know what came over me," Angel said with exaggerated distress. "Please, please do continue."

It was Monica's turn for a lively chortle as she followed her friend inside the Auction Hall and through the vestibule to the meeting chamber. The conference room was big enough to hold two hundred people, but a twenty-five-foot table with forty chairs circling the antique oak and several other cushioned seats for audience members filled the room. She eyed the women who occupied those chairs and recognized most as Darla Cain's cohorts. One in particular, a new landowner and one-time guard in Darla's home, a woman named Hailey Tate, returned her gaze with steely regard. Something about the woman put Angel on edge, but Monica's next lighthearted comment distracted her from the stern-looking woman.

"Don't tempt me," Monica said in reply to Angel's sarcasm, and then gave her another wink as they joined the other women of the council.

Unsurprisingly, once the minutes of the last assembly were read, Darla Cain opened the meeting with a call for a vote on the new controversial bill of law they had been debating for months.

Angel stifled a groan. She and Monica had argued against this obvious attempt to legalize theft, but too many others agreed the statute had merit. Outnumbered as they were, she suspected she already knew the outcome of the vote but was here to make her dissatisfaction with this legal code quite clear once again.

"So, Angel," Darla began, singling her out, "would you like to provide your opinion on the new bill we're voting on today? I wouldn't want you to say we didn't give you an opportunity to be heard on the subject."

"I don't like it," Angel said, her voice clear and hard.

"I didn't think your opinion had changed," Darla muttered.

"But it's a good bill," Carrie Simpson, Darla Cain's protégé, said. Angel looked over at the woman and tried to hide her disdain.

Carrie, like Angel, was a petite woman, but their height was where the similarity ended. Carrie's blonde hair hung in sculpted waves to her shoulders and her brown eyes currently stared back at Angel with phony, wide-eyed innocence. Though pretty, her thin figure didn't have the allure Angel's voluptuous curves did, something the other woman often openly envied.

"Passing this into law is important, Angel," Carrie said, playing her role as a caring friend.

Angel disliked Carrie for her devious and cruel ways almost as much as she detested Darla, but she tried to keep her distaste in check. As the head of the Section Guards, Carrie could make life very difficult, particularly when it came to Angel protecting the people on her ranch. The Section Guards claimed to maintain a scheduled pattern in their rounds, when in reality, they spent far more time patrolling the outskirts of Angel's property—and those of others who followed her example—than they did any other homestead.

"I know why you like it, Carrie," Angel said. "If this bill is voted in, then when you arrive, *uninvited*, at my home to harass me about *borrowing* my breeders, you could just goad one or more into attacking you or breaking some other rule instead. All so you can demand whatever punishment you wish and steal him away, after I, as always, deny your requests."

"That's not the intention of the statute," Carrie protested, completely ignoring the unpleasant tone of Angel's comment.

"Right." Angel didn't care if the single word sounded like an accusation. So far, Angel had successfully kept Carrie and the Section Guards in check, but Carrie's yearly visits were a problem, as was the woman's increasingly aggressive tactics.

As Carrie gave her a phony hurt look, Monica's sharp elbow in her side reminded Angel she *should* care.

Allowed to enter anyone's property if the situation appeared suspicious, the Section Guards investigated slave misconduct and searched for hidden runaways. Though required to show cause for entry, the guards often overlooked this stipulation— most notably when the owner didn't possess enough authority or advocates with influence to stop the investigation. As the leader of the Section Guards and Angel's supposed friend, Carrie controlled a vast array of options to accomplish the exact scenario Angel had just outlined. Antagonizing her would only make things worse, especially considering Carrie's often-irrational behavior.

"The whole idea behind this legislation is so there'll be fewer attacks on Mistresses, guards, and guests within our homes," Darla butted in.

Angel silently seethed. If Carrie Simpson was cruelly demented, Darla Cain was mercilessly brutal, and Carrie took orders from her. Darla also wanted to destroy Angel and take her slaves. If the rumors were true, the woman coveted one man in particular—Bret Masters.

Rumors whispered around the market in town and other places where her guards had overheard that Darla was still angry over how Angel had won the bidding war for him. Apparently, Darla had ranted to a number of her lackeys that she would get him back. The word *obsessed* came up more than once when the stories were relayed to Angel. Darla's fixation worried her. The woman could be formidable, but Angel could do little else to protect Bret and the others than she'd already done.

"If your slaves knew I would be in control of their punishment for a certain length of time," Darla said, clarifying the virtues of her legislative offering, "then they'd be less apt to assault me while in your home."

"And yours would be more prone to try if I came to visit yours."

"I'd have them beaten for daring to lay their hands on a woman without permission, especially a council member," Darla said, paying no attention to Angel's obvious mockery.

"Your concern for my well-being is touching," Angel responded caustically, "but I'm no more welcome in your home than you are in mine."

A hushed murmur followed her cutting remark and Angel smiled as Darla's eyes narrowed with indignant fury.

She can't ignore that!

"I agree with Angel," Monica blurted out before Darla could respond, hoping to avoid the ensuing argument between the two stubborn women. "There's too many things that could go wrong. Too many possibilities we have no regulations to cover."

"Like what?" Darla snapped.

"Like what if one of my men dies in your care? What then?" A few heads nodded and raised voices heralded another argument at the far end of the table.

"The guilty party would be required to reimburse you with gold or another slave," Darla shouted above the others.

"I'm amazed at how little you think of human life," Angel said after the giggles and gasps died away. "Do you really think you can simply *replace* one for another and everything will be fine?"

"Men are little better than animals," Darla said, dismissing the rest of Angel's comment. "They proved that long ago. We saved this world from their barbarism, saved ourselves too, by stripping them of their power. Does anyone here really doubt they'd be any different than they used to be if we let them go free?"

Several variations of, "No they'd be the same," rang out around the table, but many didn't speak at all as Darla continued.

"I have good reason for hating and mistrusting them. We all do, or at least, we *should*. Just look at what they did to their female captives during the war."

Angel didn't bother to dispute that those male renegades had reasons for their anger too.

"I'll never allow a man to have more power than me again, and I won't let another woman fall prey to their cruelty and lust either. We defeated them. Now, we let them live to please us and do our bidding. The only reason we shunned their annihilation is because we needed them for physical labor and, of course, children."

"At the rate men die in your home, Darla, it's a wonder they're not extinct," Angel said with loathing, furious that anyone could be so asinine as to suggest men were something less than human.

"That's inaccurate," Darla said, though the remark came out a little too defensive.

"More men die in your home than in any other home in this section!" Angel yelled, leaning forward and slamming her small fist on the table; incensed by their callousness. "And Carrie is a close second. Don't expect me to believe you treat your slaves the way you do because of the past. You do it because you like it!"

A multitude of gasps followed that statement and Darla, her face read with fury, opened her mouth to retaliate, but she didn't get the chance.

"That's enough," Jewel, an older woman who was sitting at the head of the table, said, interrupting before a bigger argument could break out. "We've heard from the both of you. Now, let the others talk."

Fair and not partial to the brutality of Darla's high-handed ways, Jewel Stewart was a strong authority figure on the board. Even though her olive skin had wrinkled around her eyes and mouth and her dark hair was streaked with white, her amber eyes demanded respect from everyone—and she typically got it. With no real power to influence, the head of the assembly merely mediated the meetings and arbitrated disputes. However, Jewel carried herself with quiet dignity that encouraged admiration. No member would question Jewel's authority, Angel least of all. But rumor had it that Darla plotted to one day replace Jewel as head of the council.

Angel and Darla fell silent but continued to glower at each other while others voiced their opinions. They debated for several hours, discussing the merits and downfalls of the new proposal and a few others too. Angel and a number of other women brought up the possibility of abolishing some of the more corporeal punishment laws, claiming them to be cruel and inhumane. The rest loudly disagreed, stating those laws had discouraged slaves from getting out of line and kept them from banding together against their mistresses. Fear of retribution and encouragement of division among the slave ranks kept them unbalanced and more easily controlled.

"They have to get their perverse pleasure somehow," Angel whispered to Monica when the outcome of the discussion became obvious.

"I know," Monica mouthed the words and then hushed her friend to keep any others from overhearing and to avoid further argument at the table.

When the ballots were tallied after the silent vote, Darla's proposed legislation became law. Angel was not surprised. Too many of the women not in favor of keeping men as slaves feared to speak out or vote their conscience. A lot of those at the table—and some sitting on the sidelines as well—owed their position to members like Darla or Carrie, and they didn't want to lose their monetary sponsorship—at least not yet.

Ratification of the bill outraged those who didn't have to fear retribution and had voted against the new law. Even Jewel, who kept few men in her home and rarely voiced her views on slavery, appeared annoyed by the ridiculous new code. But there was nothing they could do now except continue to oppose this law as they did the others that abused the power women wielded over the enslaved men and women in their care.

Once the furor had settled, one further order of business remained on the agenda, which, after hearing it, Angel thought should have been first.

Three other neighboring sections reported coordinated rebel raids on homes containing large populations of slaves. They suspected the attacks were an attempt to gain additional troops. The news was concerning, but most of the committee, still confident in the current power structure, held firm in their belief that the rebels were a thing of the past. Their record for failed attempts at overthrowing the ruling authority was well known and, thus, the majority of the council members perceived the danger as minimal.

Angel's opinion varied greatly.

In the twelve years they had been active, the rebels won a few skirmishes but failed to become a major threat. Their success in these new activities was what startled Angel. The rebels had never been organized or unified enough to attack fortified homes before, and the few times they had tried were disastrous for them. This show of a united, organized assault was a definite shift in their previous lack of faction cooperation, and their continued success would only uplift their *esprit du corps*. If they kept on with their raids and continued to have such efficacious results, they could have an army in a very short period—an army that could possibly have vengeance as one of its primary goals. Angel feared for the safety of her friends and everyone on her ranch if that happened. She doubted the rebels would stop to differentiate between the women who'd tried to help and those who had kept them enslaved.

5

WITH EVERY PLODDING STEP Ebony took through the moonless night, Angel swayed like a pendulum, the saddle creaking softly beneath her, the sound of the stallion's rhythmic hooves lulling her senses. Since she'd said goodbye to Monica at the crossroads, Angel had been lost in thought as she traveled the dirt track leading to her homestead. Worried about the men living on her ranch, she kept going over how many of them she'd acquired by out-bidding Darla Cain or one of her friends. She wore an anxious path through the names and faces in her mind, spiraling through the list until it led to Bret Masters. She wondered how far Darla would go and whom she might use to get at him, because, of those she'd saved from the unpleasant woman, Bret was the only one Darla lost her temper over.

Was her uncharacteristic loss of control due to jealousy or simple frustration? Did she only want to prove to Angel that she wouldn't roll over again? Or was Darla as obsessed with Bret as the rumors had implied? She had no way to know. All she knew was that none of the others were beaten the way Bret had been after the auction. Maybe it just had to do with ethical beliefs.

In Darla's opinion, Angel gave her slaves far too much freedom. She also craved power and despised Angel's politics for interfering with her plans to dominate the region. The balance of power teetered between them over the last few years, and Darla constantly searched for ways to throw the scales in her favor. The new law they'd passed today would only aid her struggle. Far too aware of this, Angel understood that if she made a single mistake, she could lose everything she'd built. Everyone knew she didn't lend out her slaves, but this law—Darla's baby—was a method to force Angel and those who followed her example to bend to Darla's will. To give Darla the means to have whatever she wanted despite the wishes or morals of others.

Angel had no doubt acquiring Bret Masters was topmost in Darla's mind. She understood the attraction—physically, he *was* gorgeous—but once Darla procured a breeder—or any slave—she considered him her personal toy to use and abuse at her whim. At least, until she tired of him. When she did, she locked him away and forgot about him, until someone else showed interest in her castoff. Then her leash would tighten again so no man, once under her control, would ever be free of her. He became a pawn to exert her wishes over the woman who wanted him. That's what happened to Jake, but the proposal Angel made his release far exceeded what Darla expected to receive for a slave she deemed past his usefulness, and she couldn't turn the offer down.

Angel didn't want anything like that to happen to Bret or the others. But it was only a matter of time before Darla came after him, and Angel feared she wouldn't be able to protect him. How could she? How could she protect any of the men in her care when her enemies had the freedom to antagonize or goad them into responding? The offended woman now had the right to demand the slave be punished as she saw fit and could then take him to live with her for further punishment.

How am I supposed to stop that?

The dark and quiet matched her brooding disposition as she rode through the night. The gray, billowy clouds hovered overhead as if irritated by the silvery light of the moon. In the stillness, the occasional hoot of an owl, the screech of a bat nearby, and once the baying of coyotes in the distance reached her ears, but not much else beyond the soft wind blowing over the hills and Ebony's hooves in the dirt. With home not far off, the stallion picked up his pace, eager for his feed bin.

"Damn it," Angel said as she passed through the gates of her home, frustrated by the day's irritations. Her stallion's head snapped up and tossed nervously as he sidled, looking for a threat. Skillfully, she controlled her mount, pulling one rein back and angled down, forcing him to circle to keep him from bolting.

"Good boy," she crooned calmly once Ebony had settled. Reaching down to pat his neck, she glanced around them. She couldn't see anything that would've spooked the horse, but that didn't mean much since it was late and very dark. The porch light from the bunkhouse barely illuminated the dooryard and this far away, everything beyond the walls was pitch-black. She relaxed her hold on the reins and they continued along the familiar trail as her mind returned to her troubles once more.

Bret Masters... She sighed. His importance to her had increased daily since his arrival and not only because of his skillful attention to her ranch. Everything about him relentlessly preyed on her mind and being unable to control her attraction annoyed her. She couldn't let herself trust him—his stubborn desire to regain his freedom assured her of that—but she didn't have much choice as far as the ranch operation was concerned. For him to perform his duties to the best of his ability, trusting him was necessary, but anything beyond that she could not allow—no matter how handsome or dazzling his smile was. Besides, letting him turn her head could lead to more heartache than her own.

Bret's opinion did not waver when it came to trusting her.

He simply didn't. He had made that clear. He didn't seem to have the same apprehension toward physical pleasures as she did; however, he'd made that just as clear. The problem was she looked forward to seeing him each day and the possibility of finding herself alone with him secretly thrilled her.

A dark and empty building met them when she and Ebony entered the stables. All the other ranch members were, undoubtedly, fast asleep by now. Exhausted by the tension of the day, Angel intended to take care of her horse and then head in herself. Shunning the too-bright overhead lights in favor of a single lantern, now hanging from a nail on the wall, she brushed the stallion down. Her mind still pondered over the outcome of the meeting's vote, Bret, and her feelings when she heard something near the front of the building. A twinge of fear shivered through her; no one should be wandering around at this time of night. As thoughts of a rebel raid danced through her head, adrenaline flooded her system and her body tensed, ready to fight.

"When you say 'all day,' you mean it," Bret's deep voice floated through the shadows to calm her strung-out nerves.

She sighed and her muscles relaxed.

"I told you not to expect me back early," she said, glad for the dim lighting to help hide her relief at hearing his voice. She went back to brushing her horse.

"I know." He entered the stall and reached out to slide his hand over Ebony's neck and scratch behind his ears. Not always so amiable with strangers, the stallion's tolerance of Bret's familiar attention amazed Angel. Ebony normally took his sweet time accepting new people, but he took to this man straight away. Angel tilted her head to hide her smile, finding his fondness for her beloved Ebony endearing and sweet.

Bret took another brush from the shelf on the wall and helped her with the chore.

"So, how did it go?" he asked as his hands worked over Ebony's black coat. "Did you improve man's lot in life?"

She glanced at him, a little surprised by his interest, but then thought better of it. She wouldn't put it past him to want to pick up their earlier argument, and she was in no mood to discuss—more like quarrel—the ridiculous law and its ramifications with this man.

"Not today," she said before she changed the subject. "What are you doing out here so late?"

"I was up and saw you come in," he said, sliding the brush over the stallion's flank. "Thought I'd come out to bother you." He leaned around Ebony's rump, winked at her playfully, and then awarded her a stunning grin. The weight of his disarming smile struck her like a blow. Her breath caught, her mouth went dry, and her stomach fluttered. Flustered, she dropped her gaze and continued to brush the stallion, again thankful for the dimness to hide the sudden heating of her cheeks.

"How nice," she replied, moving around the horse to place her brush back on the shelf behind Bret and pull the lamp off the wall. "Well, you're not going to have much time to bother me. I'm going to bed."

"Is that an invitation?" He tossed his brush onto the shelf next to hers and followed her into the hallway. She glared at him for a moment, startled by his sudden alteration of topic, unable to keep her eyes from gliding over his tall form. She bit her lip and then, realizing she was staring, she barked an unamused chuckle.

"No." Her tone was flat as she moved to close the stall door. "Look, Bret," she started, prepared to put him in his place, "you ca—"

Her admonishment that he stop flirting with her died when she turned and found him only inches away. Her eyes caught his dusty boots first then slid up the long length of him, taking in the contrast of lean waist and wide, muscular shoulders, the tan of the skin on his neck, and the masculine beauty of his face. She had to tilt her head all the way back to meet his steady stare and regretted doing so immediately. The look in his captivating green eyes unsettled her. They looked like smoky emeralds in the lantern-light. A smile twisted the corners of his sexy mouth and dimples formed in his stubble-shadowed cheeks.

Her breath halted as he moved closer and she retreated only to come up short against the wall. The metal case of the lamp in her hand clanged as it bumped into the wooden barrier behind her, but she didn't notice the rattling noise. Words were beyond her. She was trying to remember how to breathe. The heat of his tall frame, an inch or two from her own, burned through her clothes. The scent of the soap he showered with invaded her nose and a tremor shot through her as images of his long, lean form, shimmering and wet, bloomed in full vivid detail in her head.

She sucked in a lungful of air and almost moaned.

Don't go there! her rational mind shrieked, but her visceral self would not give up the vision of a naked Bret Masters standing under steamy cascading water. She had no idea she'd catalogued his body so minutely that day in the Auction Hall's sale yard. But in her head, she saw him showering in exquisite detail. His blue-black hair laid slicked back from his face, head back, eyes closed. His wet skin shimmering as the water rained on those wide shoulders and thick biceps, rolled over his well-defined pecks, down the center of his flat abs, around his innie bellybutton, into the triangle of wiry black hair that surrounded his splendid manhood, and down the long length of his powerful legs.

The image stopped her breath.

He was so big, so wonderfully male, and a part of her body—ignoring her mind's pleas to get away—responded eagerly to the potency of his presence.

His gaze devoured her, stroked her like a physical caress. Transfixed, her world seemed to slow and narrow to just the two of them. The desire to kiss him and drag him into an empty stall was almost overwhelming.

Unexpectedly, his fingers brushed her cheek and she jumped like a hunted rabbit.

"You're not interested?" he asked with a crooked curve to his perfectly chiseled lips.

"N-No," she said and could've kicked herself in frustration. Not just for the unsteadiness of the single word, but because her voice had been a low, sultry rasp. Her breaths were coming too fast and she couldn't stop staring up at him.

A startled look flashed in his eyes and broke the spell his nearness had cast over her. She laughed. "What's wrong? Not used to that response?"

"No, but you'll change your mind." His grin never faltered.

She pushed against his chest. "No, I won't."

"You will."

She froze, feeling trapped, knowing he was right. He had that kind of effect on her and she didn't know how to break free—didn't know if she wanted to. Her heart drummed a ferocious tempo. She wouldn't be surprised if he could hear the rapid beats as close as he stood. His other hand crept up her arm, over her shoulder, then up her neck to her face. Her head tilted into the warmth of his palm. Her legs shook and a shiver shimmied up her spine.

"No," she said again, but there was no force behind it. She was lost in his eyes, in the way her skin burned wherever he touched her, and how the rest of her tingled in anticipation of his next caress.

"Your mouth says no, but that's not what your body's telling me." The warmth of his breath tickled her face.

"My body's not in charge," she said almost breathless. She felt ridiculous and so damn *needy*.

"You're very beautiful." His voice was a husky murmur.

She stared for a moment, then her head dropped back and she laughed again. A bitter, broken sound.

"Sure," she said, pushing against the solid wall of his chest once more, conveying what she thought of his compliment and its intent in her caustic tone. "There are a lot of beautiful women in the world."

"Yes, and many live here. Would you rather I found them more interesting than you?"

"Yes!" Almost frantic, she pushed his arm with the hand holding the lantern. The flickering flame threw odd moving shadows over the walls, making the darkness seem ominous, but still less dangerous to her in that moment than Bret Masters.

He was too close; she could feel his hot breath on her cheek. She had to get away from him before her body overrode her better judgment.

"All right," he said as his magnificent mouth descended the last couple of inches and took hers in a possessive kiss that halted her movements and rocked her to her toes. The lantern tumbled to the floor, miraculously landing upright as she lifted both hands to push at his chest in an abortive attempt to shove him away. But he wouldn't budge nor would her arms obey her commands. She wasn't frightened or angry exactly, so no luck with increased strength to help move him, but her problem didn't involve her lack of strength. Instead of pushing at his shoulders, fighting to be free of him, her fingers curled over them and drew him closer. Her arms coiled around his neck, her fingers tangled in the short, silky hair at his nape, and, as much as she should, she didn't want to pull away.

His warm, velvety tongue skimmed over her lips and to her disbelief, they opened at his gentle insistence. He slid inside to stroke her, tease her, drive her mad with a flare of desire so intense it seared through her skin. He tasted vaguely of coffee and his natural cologne of outside, soap, and Bret assaulted her senses. Everything about him surrounded her and she liked it, pulling her body closer as she went onto her toes to return his kiss.

Trembling slightly, Bret leaned into her, trapping her between the wall and the broad power of his body as his hands skimmed down her sides. He found her waist and kept going, reaching lower to cup each side of her bottom, and lifted her off her feet. His lips never ceased tantalizing hers, drowning her in the twin raptures of heat and need. He pulled her thighs apart only to press them tight against his hips and she eagerly wrapped her legs around his waist. He groaned against her mouth, but held her against the wooden panels, prolonging her pleasure, showing her precisely how much she really did crave him. The rough planks scraped her shoulder blades, tailbone, and the back of her head, but she didn't care. She strained to draw him closer, wanting every part of him touching every part of her.

He traced slow kisses across her cheek and down her neck as her fingers crept into his hair, clutching him to her. She wasn't thinking anymore about anything but his large body pressed firmly against hers. Heat poured off him like an oven. She was lost in the sensations of the hard bulge grinding between her spread thighs and the raw masculine power of the arms holding her. Disoriented by the emotions he awoke within her, she moaned as his fingers unfastened her shirt. Her back arched in silent offering. His mouth rained hot, wet kisses over the curve of her breast as he cupped the quivering mound surging against his palm, her nipple hardening on contact. He flicked his thumb over the sensitive tip and she moaned, pushing harder into his palm. The fiery brand of his hand seared through the thin layer of her bra, scorching her, making her squirm. An overpowering urge to have his hand on her without the barrier of her clothes swept over her and she moaned a third time in supplication.

How much she wanted this man struck her like a lightning bolt but realizing that her walls were crumbling didn't bring the sobering effect it should have. Instead of feeling shame for enjoying the self-imposed taboo of his touch, shivers of excited anticipation danced through her. She wanted his hands on her skin, his mouth on her breast, his solid body heavy on top of her. She wanted *him*. To the point of desperation, she wanted him. Every cell of her being was in tune to him—his hand on her bottom holding her in place, his muscular form tight against her, and his mouth kissing, his tongue stroking lower, slowly lower.

She lost her mind under his sensual assault.

Her breasts swelled into his palm and her hardened nipples quaked in anticipation of the scorching heat of his mouth. She clung to him, marveling at the strength in his arms as he held her, reveling in their hard contours as her hands slid over them, too far gone to pay any attention to the fact that these muscular arms belonged to a different man—and not the one she remembered so well. It didn't matter. Her body was in control. It had been so long.

She. Wanted. *Him.*

She pulled at his shirt to expose his chest, wanting the steely strength of him against her softness. Her hands flattened against the satiny firmness of his pecks and traveled upward, her back arching. The skin-on-hot-skin sensation fed the yearning ache deep within her, heating and tightening the almost painful coiling sensation that was building between her thighs. She surrendered; her head thrown back in abandon, ready to give him anything, take everything he would give, when he suddenly stopped.

Confused, her body screaming with need, she met his dark, hungry gaze, and was a little startled to see his eyes were green. His wonder-causing, lust-inducing lips curved into the nasty smile she had learned to dislike and an icicle of fear slide down her spine.

"Are you sure you want me to go elsewhere for this?" he asked in a nearly breathless whisper.

6

SHE SWALLOWED AS SHE STARED at him, her tongue flicking out to wet her dry lips and Bret grappled for every ounce of self-control he could muster to keep from diving in again. He only meant to prove her wrong about her interest in him, but somewhere in the middle, she'd wrapped him up in the power of her response.

He hadn't intended to kiss her when he followed her into the barn, but something came to life inside him when he spotted her reflexive assessment if his body, the telling blush that rouged her cheeks, and how she bit her lip during the process. She looked so innocent and alluring, and combined with his sudden heated desire, Bret's original intentions change from a teasing, flirtatious distraction to a more serious proposition.

Ignoring the warnings in his head, he had tested the softness of her skin, to see if it was as silky smooth as he recalled and then revealed in the accuracy of his recollection. She started like a trapped animal when he touched her, her pulse beating wildly against his palm, but she didn't move away as he pressed closer.

She was everything he remembered. Her response as hot and seductive as it was in the cave. He wanted her, was so hungry for her, his need was almost painful, but he would not be a purchased stud. She must admit that she wanted *him*. He didn't want her picturing someone else or completing the act because she needed sexual relief, only to hate him for it later. He didn't know why the thought of her hatred bothered him, but it did, and he wouldn't risk her resentment, no matter how much his body screamed for release.

Her pretty azure eyes narrowed. She had come back down to earth.

His shoulders sagged with regret at the anger he read in her expression. Part of him wished he'd kept his mouth shut. They could've been enjoying the bliss of each other's bodies by now and he wouldn't feel this ache in his chest or the hungry throb below his belt.

"Put me down," she commanded, pushing at his shoulders with far more force than she'd used before.

"Are you sure?"

"Yes," she hissed, her eyes blazing blue flame.

He released her and stepped out of range. He didn't want to be within reach if she struck out at him. With her ire up, her adrenaline was running on high, which meant her strength was too. He could handle her, but she would be a handful. Keeping a fair distance between them, he watched while she refastened the buttons of her shirt, concealing the luscious curve of her breasts. He admired the blush adorning her silky skin from the top of her bosom all the way to her forehead. Whether from his kisses or her embarrassment, he couldn't tell.

Once finished—and without even sparing him a glance—she turned and headed for the door. He chuckled and couldn't resist teasing her the smallest bit more.

"You seemed to be enjoying yourself," he said as she passed the wall adorned with tools used for various chores around the ranch. "Are you sure you don't want to pick this up again at the house?"

She stopped cold. Her back stiffened and she turned to glare at him.

"No," she said through clenched teeth, her hands fisted at her sides while her eyes shot blue sparks, "I don't want to pick it up again *anywhere*. In fact, I don't want you to touch me ever again! Do you understand?"

He smiled, crossed his arms, and leaned against the opposite wall. "You'll change your mind. You always do."

His grin broadened as her cheeks darkened further and her eyes blazed blue lightning. A furious groan hissed from her clenched teeth and without looking, she reached toward the wall of tools, yanked a machete off its peg, and threw it at him.

The instant the tool left her hand, he saw her face change from furious to dread-filled shock, and for a split-second, he was distracted by her obvious distress. Then, just in time to avoid injury, he ducked, and the sharp blade bounced harmlessly off the wooden planks behind him. He turned, wide-eyed and leery, unsure what to expect next and worried about a follow-up attack with some other sharpened object. Instead, he caught a glimpse of her slipping through the door. The small flicker of hope he'd harbored that her sudden terrified expression had been fear that her reckless act might harm him instantly died and his ire ignited. Grabbing the forgotten lamp off the floor, he followed her, intending to have a word about throwing sharp objects, especially in his vicinity, but she was already lost in the darkness. Certain of her path, he headed for the house.

He was almost parallel with the side of the closest set of bunkhouses when he glimpsed her only a few yards ahead. She tripped and fell to her knees. A sob broke from her lips as she dropped, and he stopped in his tracks. His body tensed; he wanted to run to her, but he hesitated. He called out her name as concern filled his mind, dowsing his anger. She flinched at the sound of his voice and glanced over her shoulder. The wet glint of tears reflected in his lantern's light. She shook her head, her eyes looked terrified—of *him*?—and she stumbled to her feet to run for the house.

He jogged to where she fell and stopped again. The porch lights on the bunkhouse and apartment housing illuminated her way, allowing her to move with far more speed than before. The house's porch light was not lit, but it should've been burning in anticipation of Angel's late return. He'd noticed the darkened entry earlier, but not wanting to tip anyone to his presence outside, he'd left the light off. He tucked the knowledge away for now and concentrated on his immediate issue.

Angel had already mounted the steps and pushed the front door open. She closed it behind her with nothing more than the soft snick of the handle latching into the jam. For an instant, he considered going after her, but he pushed the ridiculous idea aside. Dropping his head, he sighed, feeling like the biggest ass on the planet. He'd made her cry, though he didn't understand why. Again. Which made him the last person she'd want to see right now.

Turning away from the house, he walked toward the wall's gateway. He had seen Angel ride in, that part of his story was true, but he'd left out the real reason he'd been outside.

The light in the barn had drawn him in, yes, but only after first being lured into the night to follow a shadow creeping around the side of the barracks. Angel's sudden appearance separated him from his quarry and by the time he'd made his way back to where he had last seen the shade, it was gone.

Deciding to check the area in the morning when he didn't have to slink through the darkness for fear of being caught, he had started back to his room. Instead, of going to the main house, however, he found himself at the stables chatting with Angel.

Now he needed something to do while he cooled off. Checking the area where he'd last seen the shadowed intruder with the barn-lamp he still carried seemed like the best option.

His mind only half on investigating as he strolled to the

gateway, he had to admit that kissing Angel again had been a bad idea. At the time, he'd told himself he could teach her a lesson and walk away without a backward glance.

Can you? That thought annoyed him.

Yes, of course, a separate voice carelessly answered. There was absolutely no reason he couldn't or shouldn't.

He shook his head. That was a lie. He wanted his freedom, yes, very much so, but now, he wanted Angel almost as much.

There were other women after Amy had tried to kill him. Two separate women a few times each, but neither of them held his attention the way Angel did. There had been no others for the last year—no, a year and a half now.

That long? He groaned and swung the lamp near the ground by the gate. No wonder he was so damned horny.

To him, Angel was a beauty, though he suspected she didn't know or believe it. He got the impression she thought he was lying whenever he told her so. Maybe she thought he only complimented her to get in her pants—well, that may be partially true, but his desire for her didn't make his compliment a lie. Hers was the softest skin he'd ever felt, and her big cerulean eyes were oceans enough for a man to drown in if he wasn't careful. And she seemed to have a tender heart. She cared about the people who lived there, even arranged to acquire a doctor for her want-to-be-a-mama guard.

"Are you okay?" Bret remembered Angel asking in the display yard before the auction. At the time, he'd thought her concern a ploy, but now he wasn't so sure.

Jake was right. Angel differed from the women they'd come to fear. She cared. But Bret also believed in the old adage, 'If something seemed too good to be true, it probably was.'

He kicked at a rock on the side of the road and lifted the lantern to peer into the long grass. Nothing new turned up in the dirt near the gate, only an indication of footprints leading away, but they disappeared in the darkness beyond the road. Whoever had been creeping around the homestead earlier was long gone now. Staying out here searching in the dark was pointless. No longer needing the lantern's light, he doused it and headed back to the apartment he shared with Jake, planning to talk with his friend about the intruder and check on the tracks again in the morning.

As Bret entered the dooryard, his mind swirling with thoughts of Angel once more, he glanced up and saw someone sneaking around the corner of her house. The person, cloaked in darkness, went straight to the unlit front entry. Bret froze. His stomach turned as he thought of Angel first. The shadow-draped form on the deck seemed to stretch an arm up to the lamp beside the front entry, did something there, then reached to turn the handle. The door cracked open and the shade dashed through the breach. The outside light came on a moment later and everything went still once more.

Bret ran across the yard, hurdled the front steps in a single leap, and slid to a halt at the entry. He let himself in through the same door only about thirty seconds after the unknown individual. He quickly combed through the lower level and the back porch. Not finding anything, he checked the upper floor, but discovered nothing there either. With nowhere else to search and exhaustion from a long, hard day working the ranch weighing on him, he headed back down the upstairs hall.

The person who'd snuck inside must live here—it was the only thing that made sense. Why they were rambling around in the middle of the night was a question for another time. Besides, he had been wandering around in the middle of the night too, and he didn't intend to tell anyone either. Well, he would talk to Jake, but no one else. He didn't want anyone to start pondering on his activities, day or night.

As he crossed the floor, he paused outside Angel's door; he thought he heard the soft murmur of quiet sobs coming from the other side. His stomach clenched and his jaw tightened. He hated to think of her hiding inside, crying because of him. He wanted to knock, to go in and kiss her tears away, but that was a stupid idea. Kissing her caused this mess in the first place; going in there now would only make everything worse.

He sighed and went back downstairs.

Bret was too tired to care about much of anything else, and he had a woman to get off his mind, though sleep wouldn't help with that. Dreams about their erotic interlude in the barn were sure to trouble him. Angel's damn lilac scent still lingered on his skin and clothes, his flesh still tingled everywhere they had touched, and his groin pinched uncomfortably in his jeans. His brain buzzed with everything Angel. He'd been trying to ignore all the aggravating reminders of her, but now her perfume was driving him crazy and amping up his desire all over again.

When he entered the room he shared with Jake, he found his friend asleep in the bed that had been empty when Bret went out after the intruder. Jake's absence was the reason for him peeking out the window in the first place.

Suspicion lanced through Bret's mind. *Maybe it was Jake sneaking around outside.* No, that didn't make sense. Bret couldn't picture his friend spying on Angel, but then he sometimes wondered how well he knew his best friend. For all he knew, Jake's bed may have been empty because he was plotting his own escape. *Or maybe he just got up to grab a late-night snack.*

Bret shrugged, stripped off his clothes, and crawled into bed.

Tomorrow, he thought. Tomorrow he'd talk to Jake, feel him out, and then decide whether to share his story or not.

THE SHADE CROUCHED behind the broad, leafy bush and held his breath as the Tall Man who'd followed him stood in the gateway examining the ground by moonlight.

As many times as he'd traveled here to meet with the informant who lived on this ranch, he had never been detected in any way. This time, however, the Tall Man had seen him and followed him. If the woman on the big black horse hadn't ridden in when she did, the Tall Man may have caught up to him and ruined everything.

No one knew or suspected the presence of the spy who supplied the Shade and his comrades with golden nuggets of information, which partly accounted for the spy's success. They were all so happy to live in their slavery, so happy to serve. But the Shade couldn't complain. Their complacency allowed the spy's work here to be successful. If not for their mole, the Shade and all the others would have starved last winter. This year, however, could be leaner because of the Tall Man he observed now.

Before his conversation with their spy tonight, the Shade hadn't known the Tall Man existed. The Shade still didn't know who he was, but their mole said his knowledge about the cattle and the wilds exceeded that of anyone else living there. His presence could jeopardize their operation and they needed to lay-off for a while. The Shade had refused to believe any of that until the Tall Man caught sight of him and had nearly captured him while trying to exit the grounds. The Shade prayed the other man would give up his search. He didn't want to kill him. The man's death would cause too many questions and might endanger the mole they prized, and their other operations too.

The Tall Man crouched in the dirt near the gateway entrance.

Damn it! A rush of adrenaline shot through the Shade's veins. *He found something.*

The Shade wanted to run, but he didn't dare move.

This man was savvy and, the Shade reminded himself, he wouldn't be fooled as easily as others in the past. Their spy's information was proving accurate once again. They would need to be far more careful performing their operations in this area. This small evidence of the Tall Man's perceptive manner and skillset convinced the Shade of that. He must get a warning back to the others. Their spy would let them know when it was safe and where to go.

Crouching for so long, unable to move, a cramp seized the Shade's calf. To ease his discomfort, he shifted on the balls of his feet, but his movement made a grinding noise beneath his boots like rocks clacking together. In the stillness of the black night, the sound cracked too loud in his ears.

The Shade stifled an angry curse.

The Tall Man's head came up and he straightened to his full, intimidating height.

The Shade froze. He barely breathed. He counted the heartbeats slamming against his chest and felt sweat trickle over his temple.

The man took several steps in the Shade's direction. The Shade held his breath. He watched the Tall Man stop in the middle of the road and listen for several minutes, saw him shift and look toward the barns where the woman had disappeared a short time ago.

How long?

Five minutes?

Ten?

The Tall Man glanced at the ground, then out at the landscape where the Shade hid as silent as the night. The man paused and shook his head. With another quick glance at the ground where the Shade had passed, the Tall Man turned and made his way to the barn.

The Shade didn't move until the other man disappeared from sight. He waited until he heard the barn door open and close. He waited a couple minutes more to make certain the Tall Man was gone and then the Shade ran. He wanted to put as much distance between himself and his would-be tracker as possible, knowing that, by his persistence in tailing the Shade tonight, the Tall Man would be back in the morning to examine the ground in better light. From his tenacity in the darkness, the Shade was positive the Tall Man would trail him as far as he could if he found anything useful. He hoped the footprints he left in his haste to flee wouldn't be enough to encourage the Tall Man to track him further. Either way, the Shade intended to be long gone before first light, and, from this point on, he would leave far less for the other man to find. If the Tall Man managed to follow the Shade beyond the road, he would have to stop at the boundary of his Mistress' land and the Shade could breathe easier.

Good thing he had a horse tied a couple of miles away. He would never make it off her property by morning without it.

8

ANGEL DIDN'T STOP until she reached the confines of her bedroom. Luckily, no one else had been wandering the house as she dashed down the familiar halls. Once inside her room, she leaned back against the door. Relief washed through her, but the shame remained. She dropped her chin and sobbed as her shaking legs gave way, depositing her rear on the floor. Knees bent, head down, hands resting palm up on the hardwood, she squeezed her eyes closed, vainly trying to banish the image of Bret as she'd last seen him in the barn.

She'd lost her temper, but as she glared at him, fully prepared to negate his arrogant assurance that she'd change her mind about his kisses, everything transformed.

A bleak image superimposed itself over the scene and, to her eyes, they were no longer in the barn. The palest glimpse of long, thin branches swayed around them, mud and grass were beneath their feet, and a remembered autumn breeze rose goosebumps along her arms. In the dim light of the lantern, Bret's face had gone unnaturally pale. Blood had tainted his lips and one side of his beautiful face, and his eyes had turned glassy. The image had stopped her breath, sending cold chills over her skin.

Instinctively, she'd known it wasn't real, that her mind was playing more tricks on her, but she couldn't shake the terror that trembled her limbs. Just like the other times when these kinds of visions assaulted her, it had felt all too real. Worse was that no other man had ever entered those nightmares, not until Bret.

It seemed like days had passed while she stood there staring at him before she ran for the door—running from him, her memories, her past. She hadn't wanted to see him die again. So, like the coward she'd become, she ran.

Now she couldn't stop the tears any more than she could banish that horrific image. Nor could she reason away the guilt she felt for her mind confusing two very different men. As she slouched against her bedroom door, she let go, and the floodgates of guilt and shame engulfed her.

Bret kept interfering with the vow she'd made and confusing her emotions until she didn't know which way to turn. She knew she shouldn't trust him, shouldn't get involved with him, shouldn't encourage his advances, but anytime he came close, her senses went crazy and her brain shut down.

What's wrong with me?

Getting control of herself, she pushed away the remorse and tried to think. Minutes seeming like hours slipped by as she sat unmoving except for the slight trembling of her body and she struggled to remember the man she'd made those promises to so many years ago. To picture his face, his cobalt eyes, his teasing smile, but a different visage with smoky green eyes and a devilish grin kept intruding her treasured memories.

Her throat thickened and grew tight with regret.

Yet, she had wanted Bret to kiss her. She wanted his caresses, his hands and mouth on her flesh, and her selfish weakness mortified her.

So much for not encouraging him.

Why didn't she stop him? She could have if she'd wanted to, if she had dredged up the anger she should've felt coursing through her veins. Instead, she clung to him like a sex-starved floozy.

No encouragement there.

And why did she always lose her mind whenever he touched her? She didn't need a man, at least not enough to risk what their involvement would mean for him. Yet, every time Bret's warm flesh connected with hers, her self-control flew out the window and she melted from the heat of his simplest caress.

No wonder he keeps kissing me.

Then she acted like a spoiled child in the fit of tantrum and threw something at him. She wasn't even sure what she'd hurled at his head—though she suspected the tool to be something sharp. She felt a little bad about that. She didn't want to hurt him; she had only wanted him to stay away from her. At least, her rational side wanted him to stay away. But somewhere deep down, she craved his touch, his kiss, and yearned for *him*; not for the memories of a lost love or for the fantasy-man who'd aided her through long, lonely years. Her heart and body burned for the living, breathing, stubborn, irritating, outlandishly good-looking man who was Bret Masters.

Dropping her head on her bent knees, she squeezed her legs together at the memory of the heat Bret had stirred between her thighs.

God, I'd been ready to let him take me in the barn!

She moaned and new tears slid down her cheek onto her denim-clad knees.

If only Bret would leave her alone and find another woman to flirt with, then she might get herself under control. Go back to her sad, pathetic existence. She had to admit she didn't really want that, but she shouldn't want him either.

She must remember the danger.

If I can remember anything when he's around!

The whole situation was impossible. If she let him go, she might as well sign his death warrant. At the very least, when the section patrols caught him, and they would, they'd torture him, and she would be powerless to stop them. The harsh punishment for escape attempts—and several other acts considered criminal—typically entailed a long public flogging, an event which would kill the recipient. If the whip stripping away his flesh didn't do the job, infection would. Unless she got the council to turn Bret over to her after they finished with him, his chances for survival would be bleak.

The image made her cringe. She shivered, wrapped her arms around her bent legs, and wept harder.

She could not give Bret what he wanted, neither his freedom nor the physical relationship that would lead nowhere. Whether a lie or not, she should have conveyed her disinterest in no uncertain terms. Why didn't she find something better to say to make him stop pursuing her? She'd told him to never touch her again, but that was useless, no matter how furious the delivery. She gave him no reason to believe she wouldn't respond to him again, that she didn't want him, and she must. She had to quit melting like an ice cube in August every time he was near— hell, anytime she set eyes on him.

You're only suffering from a ridiculous attraction to an outrageously handsome man, she told herself. Maybe if she kept away from him, resisting wouldn't seem so futile and her mind wouldn't show her any more awful images of him dying.

Slowly, her tears abated once more, but her problems with Bret remained. Her arms dropped to her sides and her head fell back against the door.

"What the hell am I going to do?" she whispered into the dark, empty room.

You know what you must *do*, a strong, loving voice murmured inside her head.

"Yes, I do…" she responded to her father, whose voice she always heard when she needed strength.

She must get up, wash her face, stop thinking about Bret or anything else, and go to bed.

A ton of work remained with the harvest and she'd already committed herself to a great deal of it. Now she wished she hadn't. Bret went out every day, monitoring their progress and checking on the cattle, which meant there was no chance she wouldn't see him for at least a few hours each day. But that she could handle. Other people would be around and his attitude toward her usually bordered on distant with an audience. The tension in her body, the magnetic attraction pulling her toward Bret...that's what worried her.

She pushed herself up off the floor and got ready for bed. Then, crawling under the sheets, she snuggled into her pillow and tried to think of anything other than the feel of Bret's hard body and the hungry look in his smoky green eyes.

THE RIVER

1

BRET SAT AT A CORNER TABLE in the long dining hall, attempting to force himself to concentrate on the day's work ahead. Most of the ranch's population surrounded him, enjoying their hearty breakfast and chatting amiably while he picked at his food and brooded.

Toiling through long days keeping busy in the fields, he'd been doing his best to stay away from the homestead. There was plenty to do, but his devotion to duty had little to do with the crops or cattle.

His chat with Jake the morning after he'd tracked the intruder turned up nothing but suspicion. Jake had claimed to be in the kitchen when Bret woke to find him gone the night before. When he'd told Jake about the intruder, his surprise seemed genuine, but Bret was certain Jake had lied, which unsettled him. Jake had never lied to him before. But no matter how often Bret reminded himself of that fact, the nagging doubt wouldn't leave him.

Angel was the cherry on top of that disconcerting feeling. As she had every day since their kiss in the barn almost two weeks ago, Angel made sure to sit as far from him as possible.

She'd barely eaten this morning as she laughed and talked with Peggy and Theo, so obviously avoiding Bret's gaze that he had to chuckle. He'd considered approaching her several times to discuss what had happened that night in the barn—he still wanted a word with her about throwing things at him...sharp things in particular—but he decided against it, just as he had before. Despite the palpable sexual attraction between them, there was little reason to discuss it. She owned him. She could do what she wanted.

Bret shook his head and put down his fork. Pushing away his half-eaten breakfast, he cupped his coffee mug in both hands and stared over the rim as his thoughts returned to that night in the barn.

He had no doubt that Angel was as attracted to him as he was to her—perhaps more. Each time he'd kissed her, she'd wanted to be there, wanted him. Then, inexplicably, a change would come over her, and she'd pull back as if surprised to be in his arms. At first, he'd assumed she was ashamed to be so enamored with a slave. Now, he was not so sure.

Whatever her reasons, they didn't matter. Bret Masters was not chattel, nor did he want to be involved with a woman who thought it acceptable to own humans as property.

Frustrated with his thoughts and the desire Angel stirred within him, Bret finished his lukewarm coffee in one quick gulp and pushed the empty mug toward the teen who was busing the tables. He smiled his thanks and then headed for the barn where he saddled Smoke and rode to the fields alone. Angel wouldn't be working in the fields today, which was good, considering Jake had witnessed enough of her less-than-friendly behavior. Over the last several days, his friend had eyed Bret more than once, his brows drawn together in confusion. Bret was grateful not to have received another lecture about not provoking her.

Even if Jake asked, he wouldn't explain, and he couldn't blame Angel for being upset with him. He had frightened her and did something to make her cry, though aside from kissing her—and being kissed in return—he didn't know exactly what he'd done to bring on her tears. Or if it had anything to do with him at all.

The women he had kissed in the past seemed to like his advances. Angel did too—most of the time—and he was happy to oblige. The fact that she had purchased his skills, his body, his *life,* should've cooled his interest, but it didn't...not even the tiniest degree. He still wanted her. He wanted her with a red-hot, incessant need he could not shake. Especially at night, when the memories of their kiss in the barn kept him awake.

When it had become clear she was avoiding him, he saw it as a challenge, and decided to prove two could play at that game. Which was why he spent so much time away from the homestead.

Now, riding the gray over the hilltops to the grazing fields, Bret sighed as he paused to gaze over the muted colors of the meadow. Then the lavender-blue of the mountains serrating the horizon drew his attention. The wind in his face and the beauty of the scene reminded him his frustration would not last forever. He sat a little taller in the saddle. Thoughts of Angel may plague him, but he hadn't given up on his dream for freedom. His opportunity would come again. And when it did, he would take it and never look back.

* * *

As July slipped into August, the ranch buzzed with secretive whispers about a surprise party to celebrate Angel's upcoming birthday. Jake and Esther took it upon themselves to organize the whole thing. Soon, everyone was assigned a task, sworn to secrecy. Bret was the only adult not roped into participating—thanks to the dark glower he turned on anyone who had asked—but Jake eventually changed that.

"Why do I have to be the one to distract her?" Bret asked in a louder than necessary voice.

"Because you're the only one who doesn't have something to do, and because it won't seem strange since you have a relationship with her already."

Bret's eyes narrowed. "We do *not* have a relationship."

"That's not what I meant and you know it," Jake shot him a look. "It wouldn't sound strange for you to ask her to ride out with you to check on the herd or whatever excuse you come up with. If anyone else tried that, it would seem weird. Besides," Jake continued with a teasing smile, "if you would've helped out sooner, there might've been someone else available."

Bret let his glare tell his friend what he thought of that, but after making Jake promise to escort her to the party, he finally agreed.

Spending time with Angel was not high on Bret's wish list. He still had unsettling dreams about their last encounter, which disturbed him more than a little and, judging by her behavior lately, she wouldn't be thrilled about the prospect either. Still, Jake expected him to distract Angel and keep her away from the homestead for several hours. But how? Sick cattle? An injured animal? He shook his head, the unwanted weight of this assignment settling in his stomach like a boulder. Whatever story he gave her, it needed to interest her, not cause her to worry.

How the hell am I going to do that?

* * *

The day of the party dawned, and everyone waited for Bret to ride off with Angel so they could get to work on setting up. Angel, however, had slept in and by late morning, she was still in bed. Jake, growing impatient, finally sent Bret to get her up and out of the house.

The faint scent of lilacs filled her room. Bret had forgotten about that. At first, the fragrance assaulted him and his body stiffened at the resurgence of remembered passion. He closed his eyes, took a deep breath, and forced himself to relax. His body's awkward response confused him, but the sensual anticipation did not, especially since it had been haunting him for days.

Calm down, cowboy, he mentally ordered as he tried to slow his breathing.

Then he saw Angel—her hair mussed, eyes sleepy, sitting up in her huge bed. The blanket pulled across her chest did little to hide the luscious swell of her breasts, nor did it keep his eyes from soaking in the image. The display hit him like a shot of adrenaline and, in that moment, there was nowhere else he wanted to be.

He stared. Hell, he probably drooled. Seeing her all soft and tousled as if just roused from sleep made him hard with longing. *You're here to distract her, nothing else*, he told himself. *Get a grip!*

Somehow, in the space of a few heartbeats, he reined in his stampeding lust and pressed forward with his planned story.

NOT EVEN A LITTLE EXCITED to get up or about Bret visiting her in her room, Angel blinked when he asked her to go riding with him. He said he wanted her help, something to do with the cattle, but she was too tired to fully comprehend his request. Unable to sleep, she'd been up late the night before, tossing and turning for hours. Exhausted was not a strong enough word to describe her current condition, and the man before her was the cause of her plight. The sight of him only brought back all the feelings she'd been trying to deny for days and every one of the old fantasies she'd spent the better part of the night trying not to recall.

"Why is it so important that I get up and go out now?" she asked sleepily, eyeing him in his white T-shirt and jeans. The soft cotton shirt clung to his broad shoulders and brawny chest, contrasting with the bronze skin of his face and arms. The blue jeans hugged his hips and the long muscles of his thighs, all of which made her even more uncomfortable. His masculine perfection struck every feminine chord inside her like a symphony, and her utter dishabille under his eagle-eyed scrutiny left her feeling embarrassed. Heat bubbled up inside her, spreading over her skin and up her neck; it was all she could do just to meet his gaze. Here he was, looking gorgeous and gazing at her with her sleep-matted hair and rest-deprived eyes, making her heart beat faster and her ears feel impossibly hot.

Talk about beauty and the beast, she thought caustically considering herself the latter.

"You said you like to ride, and you haven't been out since we came back from up north," he interrupted her internal bemoaning. "You've spent most of your free time up here."

"Yeah, yeah, yeah," she mumbled, stretching her stiff muscles. The move was innocent, natural, but Bret's eyes slid over her small form, making her feel anything but innocent. She dropped her arms and tried not to blush. "You've been talking to Jake."

That sounded like an accusation.

Maybe it was.

"Does it matter? It's a nice day for a ride and we need to make a head count. There's also a spot in the fences I'd like to inspect while we're out. I thought you might want to ride along, but if you're not interested…" He let the statement hang and waited for her response.

"It isn't that I don't want to go," she said. "I'm just a little tired."

"You'll feel better once you're outside." Bret gave her a dazzling smile. "Come on, Angel, ride with me."

She stared at him and tried to think of all the reasons she'd been avoiding him, but nothing came to her in the wake of his glorious grin. Apparently, her growing melancholy was more obvious than she'd thought if Bret was attempting to coax her outside. But she shouldn't go anywhere with Bret unaccompanied. Should she? It was only a ride, and his request concerned the ranch. What could possibly happen on horseback?

She had planned to stay in bed for most of the day, feeling tired, rundown, and unhappy, but she loved to ride. And despite her internal protestations, the fact that Bret would be riding with her made going more enticing, though she didn't admit that to herself.

"All right," she gave in. "I'll meet you at the barn in half an hour. I need to clean up first."

"Okay," Bret replied with another bright smile as he moved away from the edge of the bed where he'd been standing. "I'll have the horses ready."

She stared at the door after he left, trying to recover from that flash of his devilish grin. Their kiss in the barn popped into her head, followed by an image of the night they spent together in the cave. The combination swiftly swept her into the passion she'd experienced in both of those scenes. She caught herself beaming as memories cascaded over each other and warmth suffused her body. Her skin tingled and her limbs quivered as if in anticipation of his caress.

She shook her head and wiped her mental slate clean, banishing the wayward thoughts to the dark mental vault from which they had escaped.

Thirty minutes later, dressed in jeans and brown boots, her black curly hair pulled back into a braid and covered by a cowboy hat, she headed downstairs. When she stepped outside, she found Bret sitting on the porch steps waiting for her. Ebony and Smoke—who'd quickly becomes Bret's favorite horse on the ranch—were saddled and standing in the shade at the side of the house snacking on the thick green lawn.

Bret's mouth curled upward as he stood, dusting off his black jeans, and she looked away, pretending to admire the bright sunny morning. But her brief glimpse of him was enough to brand his image in her mind. He must've shaved since talking to her earlier as his shadowed cheeks were now clean, the strong line of his jaw clear, and his dimples prominent. His white straw cowboy hat and dark green work shirt set off his eyes and the bronze of his skin. He appeared every bit the cowboy and completely comfortable with it too.

She could still see him out of the corner of her eye, but she did her best to ignore the image he made. She smiled despite her sudden unease.

"I told you, you would feel better once you got out here," Bret said.

"It's beautiful," she said, beaming at him.

"Shall we get going? Maybe then I'll see more of that smile."

She tilted her head and narrowed her eyes. *That's an odd thing for him to say.*

The flash of his devilish grin only made her more suspicious. Still, her body lit up at the sight of him and, enthralled once more, she couldn't help but return his smile.

"Yes, let's go," she said as she headed for their tethered horses, anxious to see where the day would lead.

2

THEY RODE FAR LONGER than Angel had anticipated. Thankfully, aside from the occasional comment, they rode in silence to the farthest reaches of her property, checking on fences and cattle as they went. When their tasks were complete and Angel told her grumbling tummy to expect another long ride home, Bret surprised her again.

"Well, I don't know about you," he said, leaning a forearm on his saddle horn, "but I'm glad Esther packed us a picnic lunch. I'm hungry." His chiseled lips curled up charmingly and dimples winked in his cheeks when he looked at her.

The comment and that smile struck Angel like lightning. "A picnic?" A part of her wanted to refuse, to demand they head back immediately, but the bigger part that yearned to see more of that flirty grin held her tongue.

"Yeah," Bret said, sounding eager as he sat back and lifted the reins in his gloved hands. "All we need to do is find the perfect spot."

Angel swallowed hard. Conflicting emotions knotted her stomach as she stared at the enticing V-shape of his departing back. But instead of arguing that they should return home—as she should—she simply followed as Bret headed north.

Half an hour later, they pushed through a thick screen of undergrowth into a small clearing on the banks of the meandering river.

"Here we are," Bret declared as he dismounted and started to remove his saddlebags while his horse dunked his nose into the river for a drink. "There's not much here for the horses. So, pull your bags and I'll lead them to that meadow we passed where they can graze while we eat."

A good idea for the horses, but it was Bret's motives that concerned her. If he took the horses and headed for the mountains, it would be hours before she could walk home on foot. The prospect of him leaving saddened her, but she could do little if he decided to run.

Maybe if he got a head start, he could outrun the Section Guards. She shook her head. They'd never stop chasing him though...

"You'll find a blanket in your bags," he said, pausing in the act of unknotting the straps holding his saddlebags. He tipped his head toward the clearing behind him. "Spread it out wherever you like." Not waiting for a reply, he returned his attention to the knots.

The long ride had stiffened her back and legs, and she took a moment to stretch the stiffness from her body before opening her saddlebags. On one side, she found wrapped packages which she held up to show Bret. "What's this?"

He glanced at her as he pulled his bags from the saddle. "I believe that's part of lunch," he said, dropping the heavy leather packs beside her and then vaulting onto Smoke's back.

She set the packets aside and opened the other bag. Inside, she found a thin, red wool blanket. After she pulled it free, she shook it out as she turned to look around the small glade. Compared to the pine-needle-covered areas under the trees, the small patch of green within the clearing was a lush paradise.

"I'll be right back," he said, and with a flick of the reins and a tap of his heels, he headed through the trees with Ebony trailing behind but trying to take the lead. She smiled fondly at the stallion's antics and at how easily Bret handled him. Then it slipped away as the foliage finally hid them all from view. A pang of loss and regret made the area around her heart hurt and she rubbed at it absently.

Sighing, she went to their picnic area and set out the food. She wondered if he would really take off with nothing to eat. *Unless he has it in his pockets,* she thought with another brief grin, remembering the night in the canyon with the cougars, but, again, worry replaced it.

When Bret came strolling back through the trees a short time later, the knot of tension around her chest loosened considerably. She greeted him with a timid smile as he approached, but, though she would never admit it, she was thrilled to see him again.

"Sorry it took so long," he said as he dropped to the ground across from her. "I unsaddled them too."

She had been sitting cross-legged, gazing out at the rolling water while she waited for him. "No worries," she replied with a casual shrug to hide the rush of relief she felt.

"Mmm... What did Esther make us? I'm starving."

Birds and the gurgling melody of the river rushing over rocks serenaded them while they ate. As usual, they discussed the work still to do that summer and when that wound down, Angel told him about moving into her home on the ranch. Unwilling to discuss anything beyond that time, Angel smiled and laughed while Bret told her wild stories about his and Jake's raucous exploits as teenage boys. When he wound down, they listened to the river and soaked up the warmth of the sun.

In the quiet tranquility, Angel relaxed with a contented sigh. Bret had chatted with her as if they were old friends and she'd soaked up his attention like a dry sponge, the trepidation that troubled her earlier strangely absent.

She studied Bret from the corner of her eye as he finished

the last of his meal. The more she learned about him, the more the enormity and strength of her inexplicable attraction to this man she hardly knew intensified. Happiness inflected his voice, caused the cheerful glimmer in his eyes, and infused his easy smile as he entertained her with stories. The more he talked, the more she could see that Bret's affection for Jake was as strong as Jake's for him. That realization warmed her heart and made her smile.

Unsure what exactly set off the flash of insight and not really caring, she discovered she liked this man's company very much. She liked the way his eyes lit up when he spoke about things he enjoyed and how they crinkled at the edges when he grinned. She liked the sound of his voice, his laugh, his smile, and, to her surprise, she liked *him*. Not due to his too-handsome face, but because of the man inside, the one who prized his friendship with Jake, who had saved her life, who cared about animals, and who had spent the last hour or so doing his best to make her smile—though she didn't understand why.

An icy tingle of fear tickled the back of her neck and slid down her stiffened spine as comprehension sent terror through her like a lightning bolt.

She could not get mixed up with anyone again. The pain involved was too harsh and the loss intolerable.

Vivid images of blood assailed her mind, of a time and another man to whom she'd also been drawn to in much the same way. A man with a quick smile and easygoing personality, who'd loved her unconditionally and died a horrible death because of it.

She started to shake.

Sweat broke out along her spine and her heartbeat sped up.

Cold penetrated her soul.

She tried to swallow the giant lump stuck in her throat, but she couldn't. She tried to keep her breathing normal, but she couldn't do that either.

Don't do this, she admonished herself. *Not now. Not with him!*

"Ah," Bret said, patting his belly as he twisted and lay back across the blanket.

Angel jumped at his contented utterance.

He stretched out his long legs and crossed them at the ankles, then pulled off his hat as he lowered his head to the ground. "I need a nap after all that."

She returned the smile he gave her, though it felt more like a grimace, as he dropped his white hat over his eyes and his hands to his chest with another satisfied sigh. She focused on his strong fingers, how lean they looked, the slightly distended veins that roped through them and over the backs of his hands, remembering how they had felt against her skin.

Her breath turned ragged with alarm as her mind conjured the bloody images again, only more vividly. Pulse racing, body trembling, she stared at him as the horrible picture flashed on and off like a bad movie playing in her brain. One moment, Bret lay there healthy and snoozing; the next, scarlet stains overlay his hard body. Her mouth went dry and everything inside her seemed to quiver.

Only the lower half of his face peeked out from beneath his hat, his skin a dark contrast to the bleached straw. Her eyes drifted over him again as she fought the images in her head, taking in his strong arms, his flat belly, his long, powerful-looking legs. Heat rushed through her as she recalled how he'd trapped her against his chest, how those long fingers had caressed her body, how his hips pressed intimately against her own. The memory made her shiver. Then her breath came in short, frightened gasps when the gory scene superimposed itself over Bret once again. She blinked and the blood disappeared. He looked as safe and content as ever. His green shirt against the red wool coupled with the white hat made her tumultuously floundering mind think of Christmas.

A splendidly handsome gift just waiting to be opened... I

wonder if his skin tastes as good as his mouth...?

A massive surge of desire exploded to life deep inside her.

A wave of hysteria bubbled up in her chest.

She turned away as the inevitable rush of icy panic crashed to the surface.

Oh, no! No! No-no-no-no-no, her mind shouted. *Don't go there!*

She stared at the river and let herself think about the past and the man she had once loved and lost. She tried to recall his face, his happy blue gaze, but an image of a black-haired man with striking green eyes was all she could bring to mind.

Her regard drifted to Bret again, thankful to see him still sprawled on the blanket, completely unaware of her mounting distress. She wanted to giggle with unrestrained relief as she stared at him, disproportionately overjoyed by the rise and fall of his chest as he breathed. He looked alive, big and strong, and so tremendously handsome...

Damn, I can't do this!

She needed to forget about his kisses and the sensations his hard body awoke inside hers. Having these feelings for him was wrong for so many reasons and she tried to invoke them all while she drank in every chiseled line and muscle.

As her eyes hungrily devoured him, her mind once again conjured an ugly image all its own. A vision of Bret in the same reclining position, but not at rest. She saw him covered in blood. A hideous wound yawned wide in his belly while his long-fingered hands attempted to hold the contents inside. His face was bone-white, and he was having trouble breathing. Blood stained his lips and his green eyes were wide with fear and pain.

Her breath caught and she turned away. She fought to banish the vision, but it coalesced into a blurred concoction of past, present, and possible future. The picture so vivid, so real, she could almost detect the nauseating tang of blood and suddenly...

She was under the old tree again. In her mind, she envisioned everything the way it had been—the tiny yellow-brown leaves covering the ground, the thin dead-looking limbs swaying in the cool autumn breeze, and the slate-gray sky. She sat in the cold mud next to the enormous trunk, leaning her shoulder against the gnarled bark. In her lap, lay a man's head. Not the one she usually saw though. In this waking nightmare, Bret stared up at her from his too-white face and tried to smile.

She knew this wasn't real, wasn't right. As the familiar ache banded her chest and more tears burned the backs of her eyes, she struggled with the inevitable, but she couldn't keep the tragedy from playing out inside the mental minefield.

I tried to save him, she cried for what must have been the ten thousandth time. *I tried, but I was already too late.*

"Don't cry, my angel," she heard him say and, for the briefest of moments, the man she remembered gazed up at her. His eyes were incredibly blue, like a deep tropical pool off a white sandy beach.

She plastered a shaky smile on her face.

"Don't talk," she whispered, mopping the sweat from his brow and brushing back his dirty-blond curls with an unsteady hand, stained crimson with his blood. "Save your strength."

"Don't cry, angel eyes," he told her, ignoring her gentle admonishment and trying to smile. "I love...you. I al-ways will."

She hadn't realized she was crying. Using her filthy sleeve, she brushed her tears away. When she focused once more on the man in her mind's eye, his face had changed again. His black hair, limp and dirty, slicked back from his forehead, his green eyes dull and shining with pain.

This is Bret, she thought.

She wanted to shout, *This is wrong!*

She said nothing.

She struggled against the spell that had her trapped, squeezed her lids closed, trying to banish the images in her head.

The thick, achy lump in her throat strangled the scream that wanted to come out.

She shook violently. A cold sweat broke out over her flesh. Her heart tried to beat its way out of her chest, and she couldn't seem to get enough air. She sucked in huge gasps through her mouth, but her lungs still felt deprived. This was a whole new level panic; an entirely new grip of terror she was utterly unprepared to handle.

No, no, no! Not him!

Head down, eyes clamped shut, hands fisted in her lap, she was suddenly terrified that if she looked at Bret again, either in her mind or under the warm summer sun lying on the red blanket a few feet away, she would see him dying.

3

SHE DIDN'T HEAR him speak, didn't hear him move, but suddenly, Bret was there in front of her. Her frozen hands engulfed in the calloused heat of his as he called her name in earnest.

"Angel?" His soft voice held an edge, which indicated he had called to her more than once. Her lids popped open and she stared at him wide-eyed, part of her stunned to find him kneeling before her, alive and well, healthy and whole. His dark head bare and his hair mussed, a frown marred his handsome face as he looked down at her with concern in his crystalline jade-colored eyes.

She couldn't breathe. Her heart pounded painfully in her chest. Frantic, she visually searched for injury.

Ten long seconds later, she sighed with relief.

He's fine. Of course, he's fine.

The horrific images unfolding in her head were only her mind playing tricks on her again.

I'm an idiot, she berated herself. *A foolish idiot. They're not real, not anymore.* But no amount of harangue could stop the terror still crashing through her, couldn't keep her eyes from gazing up at him in fear.

"What's wrong?" he demanded, looking more than a little worried.

"Nothing," she hedged. "Nothing, I'm fine."

"The hell you are," he countered, unconvinced. "You're shaking like a leaf in a storm and your hands are freezing. What *is wrong*?"

"It's nothing!" She stared down at their joined hands and tried to tug hers free without success. The warmth of his work-roughened palms sent tingles up her arms. The sensation freaked her out on a whole different level, but he wouldn't let go.

She couldn't meet his gaze.

"It's something," he said with certainty. "What?"

She stopped tugging her hands.

"It. Is. Nothing," she said again, giving up on making him release her. She forced herself to inhale and release the breath in one long, slow exhale. When she spoke again, she concentrated on not sounding as totally out of control as she felt. "Just talk to me, Bret. It'll go away if you talk. Please..." She lifted her panicked eyes to his face. "Please, tell me another story."

A disbelieving frown creased his brow and he held her fearful stare for longer than she thought she could stand. Afraid he would argue further, she tried again. "Please, talk to me." She sounded pathetic, even to her own ears, and silently cursed herself again.

"What do you want me to say?" His self-assured tone slipped.

"Anything," she whispered.

He glanced away then back to her eyes, seemingly at a loss for words. She realized he needed a detailed request, something to direct him.

"Tell me about..." Her frantic brain searched for a topic. "Tell me about the ranch you worked on before the wars."

"The Double H?"

"Is that what it was called?" She tried to smile, but her lips trembled and tears pooled in her eyes.

He regarded her for a moment longer. "Are you sure you're all right?"

"Yes," she said, her voice a little shaky. "I'm fine. Please, tell me about the Double H. Was that its name?"

"Yeah," he muttered, still frowning at her.

"Why H? Double H, I mean."

"Herman Hendricks."

"What?"

"He owned the place," Bret told her, his eyes roaming her face. "Herman Hendricks. The Double H was his ranch."

She nodded, comprehending the significance. "Was he a good boss?"

"He was hardly ever there," Bret told her and then explained how the man only visited the ranch four or five times a year. How Herman had no interest in being a rancher and used the place as a vacation home.

"Why did he own cattle if he didn't want to be a rancher?"

"They came with the property."

"But he wasn't a rancher?"

"No, he worked in Seattle as a banker of some sort," Bret told her and laughed. "He said if he owned that much property, then it should at least turn a profit. Luckily, I made the business lucrative enough to keep him interested. That's why he paid us. I didn't care what he did as long as his checks cleared and he let me run the place my way."

"What did you do there?" She needed him to keep talking. He must have understood because he obliged, pausing only long enough to release one of her hands and move to sit next to her. He wrapped his free arm around her waist and tugged her closer, sheltering her against his side. She didn't resist. Instead, she rested her head against his shoulder and slowly relaxed against him. She still shivered, but the warmth of the sun and the heat from his body began to melt the ice that engulfed her.

Bret was confessing tender sentiments for a half-wild barn cat he'd once befriended when she interrupted him, "You really do like cats."

"Yeah, I do." His wary tone told her he had been teased about his affection for the feline. "What's wrong with that?"

"Nothing," she replied, a small smile curving her lips. "I know you like animals, but I thought you might just be tolerating Grayling."

"Nah, he's my buddy. It's kind of hard not to enjoy the animals when you work with them all the time."

"I guess so," Angel agreed. "What was she like, the cat?"

"She was a smart little thing," he said with a fond chuckle, "and kind of a stinker too." He smiled. "The other guys would try to pet her, but she wouldn't have any of that. Some of them tried too hard and ended up injured."

"Did she have a name?"

"Bossy," he said and laughed again. "She talked. A lot." A simple explanation, but Angel understood. "She didn't have a problem letting you know what she wanted either."

"What happened to her?"

He quieted and his body tensed.

I shouldn't have asked…

"Don't know," he stated in a far-off voice and she sensed a wealth of emotion hidden behind his straight face. "When everything fell apart… I searched, I would've taken her with us, but I never saw her again."

"Oh, Bret, I'm sorry."

He shrugged, but he couldn't fool her. She'd heard the regret in his voice.

They sat without speaking. Angel could still feel the tension in his body and wished she had not reminded him of the unhappy memory. She shivered and his arm tightened around her.

"Do you have any other stories?" she asked, looking up at his somber face, hoping to distract him. "Something funny, with a happy ending?"

His eyes flicked to hers and then he turned to peer at the river rushing by, his dark brows pulled into a V. He took a deep breath, considering her question. Then he smiled, and she thought once more how attractive he looked. He peered at her and the warmth of his gaze reached down to her toes.

"Well," he said in a drawn-out tone, "there's one, but I don't tell it very often."

"Why?"

"'Cause the story makes me look ridiculous."

"*You?*"

The oh-you-are-so-funny face he gave her made her giggle.

"Tell me," she said.

He glared at her, wary, but his lips curled upward ever so slightly. He searched her eyes for a moment as he measured his response.

"If I do," he said with a cautious chuckle, "you can't bring it up later, *especially* around Jake."

"Why?" She pushed away to better read his expression.

"Because, like I said, it makes me look ridiculous and if Jake's reminded, he'll tell the others and I'll never hear the end of it."

She smiled and leaned back against his shoulder. "Okay. No teasing and no reminding Jake." She met his eyes. "I promise."

He took a moment, clearly reluctant to reveal something that would paint him in an unflattering light.

His voice was soft as he started his story. "It had been raining a lot that spring, and with the thaw of heavy snows, everything was very wet. We had trouble every year with cattle getting stuck in one muddy bog or another, so we rode the property to check for trapped animals as the water drained off.

"Unfortunately, Jake wasn't working there yet. So, being the new guy and the odd man out, I ended up going on rounds alone. It didn't worry me. I knew what I was doing." He laughed. "Famous last words, right?" He flashed a quick grin she couldn't help but return as he shrugged and continued, "Anyway, I came across a cow stuck in a wide, deep, grimy hole. She'd gotten herself buried to her hips with a lot of standing water mixed in, worn-out from trying to free herself. I figured I would use the horse to drag her out and maybe make a couple of points with Mace, the ranch foreman I told you about."

"You didn't try that on your own?" Angel understood the dangers of attempting to free a full-grown bovine alone. Just last year, one of the cowboys on her ranch attempted the same act Bret described and had nearly been crushed when the frightened ungainly cow slid in the mud and fell into him. He'd been lucky just to break his leg.

"No way would I do it now…not unless I had no other choice," he admitted, "but I was young and cocky back then."

"*You? Cocky?*" Her loaded look earned her another shrug.

"It was a long time ago," he said softly, a wry turn to his mouth. "Besides, it isn't impossible, just reckless… Plus, as I said, I was the new guy, and I did know more about ranching than most of the others, though it had been a while." He didn't have to explain; he'd told her about living with his uncle for several years after his father died.

"I went into the mud thinking I would dig around her a bit then see if my horse and I could haul her out." He scoffed in self-reproach, "I should've secured the rope to my saddle first, a grievous lack of forethought on my part. I ended up as stuck in the muck as the cow."

Angel couldn't stop the giggle from escaping.

"I was frustrated and irritated at first," he confided, "trying to heave myself out without success, getting wetter and dirtier by the minute. I got a little scared when I couldn't drag myself out and no one came looking, not until the next day. I ended up spending the night out there and, let me tell you, it was not pleasant. But nearly freezing was nothing compared to the humiliation when they finally found me. They had to pull me *and* the cow out of the mud. I was as bad off as she was by then—stiff, freezing, and exhausted. But as you can see, I recovered just fine." He peered down at her and she giggled again at his purposely self-satisfied expression.

"Hey," he barked, feigning annoyance. "It isn't *that* funny."

"I never said I wouldn't laugh," Angel answered, pinching her fingers together and grinning up at him to take the sting out of her words, "and it *is* a *little* funny."

"Yeah," he chuckled, "maybe a little. Now…"

"Yeah," she continued to snigger. "I have a hard time picturing you covered in mud though."

"I was," he said, an exaggerated look of honesty on his face. "Completely filthy from head to foot. My boots were so full of muck that they didn't make it out of the hole. I had to ride back to the house without them."

This time Angel laughed unfettered at the image he described, almost disbelieving he could've done anything as ridiculous and irresponsible. "You made that up," she accused through a sprinkling of effervescent chortles. "You wouldn't have messed up *that* bad."

"It's all true," he said, returning her smile. "I really was covered in mud," he waved an arm along his length indicating his whole body, "even my hat." He snorted. "I was so dirty that when they got me back, they wouldn't let me inside the barn. Mace made me stand, shivering in the yard, while the boys hosed me off."

Angel snickered again. When she peered up at him with an apologetic air, he smiled. He seemed more relaxed now since she'd finally calmed down.

They sat—her head on his shoulder, nestled against his side, with his arm wrapped protectively around her—listening to the rush of the waterway.

"Thanks," she murmured, peeking up at him.

He tightened his hold on her as he looked down and grinned. "No problem."

Then he turned his face up to the sky, squinting in the sunlight. Angel followed his gaze as she judged the time of day. It was getting late, but a part of her didn't want to move.

She snuggled more cozily into the warm, solid comfort of his body. The closeness and his hard strength soothed her, gave her a sense of safety. She sighed, content with his arm encircling her, her head on his shoulder, and his heart thumping a slow steady rhythm in her ear.

He'd been a perfect gentleman during this whole trip, and for that, she was grateful. Yet, deep inside something besides the ever-present attraction tugged at her. Something that felt like…disappointment.

"What time do you think it is?" she asked to avoid thinking about that odd sensation.

"About three I'd guess, maybe a little later."

"That late?" She straightened away from his side, immediately regretting the separation. "We've been out most of the day!"

"Well," he drawled, "we did start a little late. *Someone* stayed in bed until almost ten."

"I was tired." She gave him a dirty look, but there was no heat in it. "Besides, I didn't know you had this planned for today."

"I didn't really plan it. It just sort of happened."

She beamed at him. "Well, I'm glad it did. This was a nice change."

4

BRET DIDN'T MISS the double meaning in her comment but keeping their interactions purely amiable was not easy. He still wanted to take her in his arms and pick up where they'd left off that night in the barn. He had no doubt she would respond, but Jake would be furious if he did anything to ruin the surprise they had planned for so long. And, strangely, a part of him would regret it too. They should head back before the temptation became too much for him, but he lingered, reluctant to leave, to allow this afternoon to end.

She'd surprised him by somehow getting him to chat. He was not the chatty type, and he especially never casually discussed Bossy. A comfort when Jake hadn't been around, that little cat had given him something to care for during a time when he'd believed he would never care about anything again. Losing Bossy had been a blow, but one he couldn't have avoided and not something he like dredging up. Yet, that's exactly what he did, and he knew why—Angel.

It was good to see her cheerful again. So much better than the terror he'd seen shinning in her eyes. He had disliked that and, somehow, seeing it made sharing his affection for Bossy feel like the right thing to do.

He had wanted to press Angel about her alarming episode but demanding an answer would ruin the camaraderie they'd nurtured over the afternoon. So, instead, he gave her a little piece of himself. Then, to see her smile again and to distance himself from the emotions his memories had dredged up, he embellished the tale about the cow and the mud hole. Not much, but enough to make it amusing for her. He wouldn't disclose it now, but back then, he had been mortified by his lack of prudence.

"Shouldn't we be getting back soon?" Angel asked.

Bret glanced at her and inwardly cheered to find that the color had returned to her face. She'd looked pale as death earlier and her pallor had frightened him more than he wanted to admit.

"Yeah," he replied and stood to offer her help up. "We probably should."

Bret grabbed his well-worn hat off the blanket and fit it on his head. He scanned their picnic area and then peered down at her. "You mind packing this up while I get the horses?"

Glancing down at what remained of their lunch, she shrugged. "Sure," she said, a dull glimmer in her eyes and a leery tone in her voice.

"Is something wrong?"

She blinked and her apprehensive face went blank. "No."

Not believing her, he tilted his head to one side. "What are you worried about now?"

She shot him an irritated yet anxious glance. "You *will* be back, right?"

"Don't worry," he said with a lopsided grin, "I wouldn't leave you out here alone." She nodded, but palpable relief shone in her eyes as he turned to go.

ANGEL WATCHED HIM WALK away, admiring his taut backside while still fretting about whether she would really see him again or not.

You have no reason to think he lied, she thought and then shrugged.

Except for his very real desire to go almost anywhere else, her cynicism replied.

She shrugged again and, pushing her fear and doubt aside, she began to pack up the evidence of their pleasant afternoon. Once everything had been tucked away in the saddlebags, Angel picked up the canteens and took them to the river. She stepped down from the grassy knoll onto a sandy, pebble-strewn shoulder and crouched down to reach the water. Uncapping the first canteen, she held it under the cold flow as she squinted at the sun's reflection off the shiny surface. The twinkling light and the loud swirling torrent of the water as it rushed over rocks hypnotized her.

Movement mirrored in the water caught her attention right before clacking stones tumbled down the riverbank behind her. She glanced over her shoulder, expecting Bret with the horses. Instead, she gasped, and barely had time to register the tall, unkempt stranger before he reached for her.

Ducking but too late to avoid him, his big hand knotted in her navy work shirt. She heaved in a breath and opened her mouth to scream as he jerked her backward. The sudden lurch cut her cry short and then she felt herself flying. She landed on her back, the air knocked from her lungs, and her head struck something hard. She blinked, her grasp on awareness slipping as her lanky attacker and another shorter, stockier man entered her field of vision. She sucked in air and tried to scream again, but with the knot of fear in her throat, it was pitifully soft.

The adrenaline pumping down her arms and legs made her shake, and for once, she didn't detest the sensation. She'd counted the seconds until its full effect took hold. Yet, even as her body reacted to save itself, her new assailant reached down to grab the front of her shirt. A ripping sound rent the air as he yanked her off the ground and buttons flew off in very direction, but she didn't care. Anger and alarm pulsed through her as adrenaline rushed to the rescue. The fight would be more even now, but if she didn't act quickly, the two of them would overpower her.

She wrapped her small hands around his fingers and pulled back as she released an ear-splitting scream. He grunted when her knee connected with his groin and she used her other leg to trip him as she pushed him to the ground. The second man approached. A stiff kick to his knee and a heel-hand-strike to his nose dropped him too, and he grunted as he rolled away.

Mouth dry, pulse pounding, Angel spun to the stocky man rising onto his knees. She kicked him in the ribs, hard, causing him to tumble over onto his back, his arms flung out to either side. Angel stomped her sturdy boot into the man's exposed forearm. He howled in pain and tried to roll into her. She kicked him again and brought her foot down on his arm once more. A sickening crunch cracked beneath her heel and he screamed again.

Sensing movement, she dismissed him and spun around, but too late. The lanky attacker launched himself from directly behind her. He crashed into her midsection and they tumbled together into the water. She landed on her side. The weight of his body collided with hers and crushed her against the rocks. Her forehead hit a sharp edge that cut into her hairline while he groped at the front of her light blue undershirt. The fabric stretched to its limit then split completely as she strained to wiggle out from under him.

Her stomach felt as if it had turned to stone. Whether her arms and legs trembled more from fear or adrenaline, she could no longer tell. All she knew was she had to fight. She struck blindly upward and her fist connected with his teeth, slicing open her knuckles. She swung again, not caring about the pain. He avoided her second blow and used her momentum to flip her onto her stomach. She gasped at the dunking of her head into the icy water, then closed her mouth and concentrated on escape.

She tried to turn, to wiggle out of his grasp as he held her under the cold river. Holding her breath, she struggled to push herself up, her heartbeat racing so hard she thought it might explode. But the rocks were slippery, and he'd knotted his fist firmly in her hair. No matter what she tried, she couldn't gain leverage or loosen his hold. Fear amped her strength, but she couldn't force herself above water. Her head spun and panic tightened her chest as a dire need to breathe assaulted her. She fought the compulsion to inhale as strongly as she fought his hold, but his lean fingers were strong and tangled so tightly in her hair that she couldn't move her head.

Just as her body's need for air overcame her will to hold her breath, he jerked her upright, coughing and wheezing. Swiftly, her arms were tugged behind her back and something wound tightly around her wrists. She had only a moment to revel in the sweet breath of life before her attacker grabbed her hair once more. With her hands bound and no way to stop it, her head hurtled toward another rock and the world went completely black.

5

SMOKE'S SADDLE AND BLANKET were on the chestnut gelding's back with the girth almost tied when Bret heard the first scream split the air. He knew the cry came from Angel the minute the sound broke the silence. He froze in place, fear wrapping around his chest like a clenched fist, gripping him, rooting him in place. Then, with his heart suddenly jackhammering in his chest, Bret tightened the girth with one hard tug, hauled himself into the saddle, and, sensing his rider's urgency, the gelding jumped into a gallop.

Closing in on the glade, Bret pulled Smoke up short of breaking through the trees, not knowing what might lie beyond and not wanting to lose the element of surprise. He heard muted sounds of a struggle come from the other side as he dismounted. Quieting his horse with soft words and a hand on his nose, Bret inched forward to peer through the thick branches.

"Yeah!" a man screeched encouragement from just beyond the natural barrier. "Teach that bitch who's boss."

Two dirty, travel-worn strangers stood in the clearing where he and Angel had eaten lunch. One man stood with his back to Bret, holding the reins of their lone scrawny horse, cradling what appeared to be a broken arm. The other was in the river, forcing Angel's face into the water with one hand and gingerly probing his broken nose and bloodied lips with the other.

Anger tightened Bret's muscles and an urgent need to protect her goaded him to act, however prudence made him pause. He had no idea if the two men were alone.

The tall brute in the river grabbed a handful of Angel's hair and hauled her to her knees. She coughed, gasping for air as water ran off her in sheets and jerking at the bonds that secured her wrists behind her. The man spoke and Angel shook her head. With a wicked yet eager smile on his face, he jerked her to her feet and slammed his fist into her belly. She splashed to her knees again, bent over and wheezing as the river rushed by.

Arms and legs quaking with the burst of rage that suddenly surged through him, Bret swung up onto his horse and set his heels to the animal's sides.

Wild laughter assaulted his ears once again.

"Yeah," the closer man screamed, "let's see how she likes being a naked slave."

Bret's, mount broke through the screen of undergrowth as Angel screamed again. Her high-pitched cry stabbed straight through Bret's chest, leaving him almost breathless with fear, but did not halt his attack.

The stocky man's raucous laughter died abruptly when Bret's booted foot connected with his head.

The corpse crumpled into a heap

A heartbeat later, Bret launched himself at the man tearing at Angel's clothes. Too late, the lanky fellow looked over his shoulder. Bret's flying tackle knocked them both into the dirt and away from Angel. They wrestled, each vying for the upper hand, while Angel curled into a ball and struggled with her bonds.

The two men pulled apart and circled, sizing each other up.

Bret hurled himself forward and they exchanged punches. It seemed an even battle; and while Bret was more muscular, his opponent was taller and stronger than he looked. Various blows connected, bloodying them both. But the stranger had already fought with a terrified, angry woman—who, by the looks of the man's face, knew how to defend herself. In Bret's opinion, the stranger had been lucky and a part of him was ridiculously proud of her for that.

Now, the lanky man struggled against someone who'd spent an ample portion of his life fighting with his fists. Bret pushed the advantage, landing several punches and a right cross to the man's jaw. The stranger stumbled and Bret jabbed repeatedly until a punishing uppercut finally took the stranger off his feet. He rolled away and reached for his boot. When the stranger jumped up, a long-bladed knife was clamped in his fist, flashing in the afternoon sunlight.

Bret's muscles tightened, preparing to meet this new threat, and his eyes swiftly searched for a shield. Locating a ratty old coat on the ground, he faked a move in the opposite direction and then reached for the wad of cloth. His opponent lunged at him. Bret turned to avoid the blade and used the stranger's momentum to throw him onto his back. Then Bret dove into a roll, grabbed the coat, and wrapped it around his forearm.

A sharp pain unexpectedly burned up the back of his arm. He ducked and jerked sideways, putting distance between him and the blade. He could feel the long gash oozing blood, soaking his shirtsleeve. The laceration hurt like the devil, but he ignored it as he once again faced his adversary, studying the lean man with his ruthlessly cut brown hair and coal-black eyes. The sinister smirk that pulled at his thin lips made the hair on the back of Bret's neck stand on end. He got the message loud and clear—this was a battle to the death.

The man lunged and Bret parried his attack with his cloth-draped arm and landed a punch under his adversary's ribs with the other. The stranger stumbled away, wheezing and rubbing his side, but managed a backward blow that sliced a bloody line along Bret's thigh. He winced, knocking the blade away before it could do more damage, but kept his eyes on his opponent. A slow, peculiar smile bloomed on the thin man's lips. "You're very good at this," he said through wheezing breaths. "Where did you come from?"

Bret narrowed his eyes. "I live here. Where did you come from?"

They continued to circle each other, both sweating, both breathing hard, but Bret was in better condition.

"Where I'm from isn't important," the man said. Then he leaned forward and lowered his voice as if revealing a dark secret. "It's where I'm going that matters."

"Yeah, to an early grave," Bret taunted.

The other man grinned wider. "Nah, to the rebel camp."

Bret's heart seized in his chest. *Did I hear him correctly?*

"We could use a man like you," the stranger said. "Why don't you come with me?"

A gentle breeze swept through the clearing as the meaning of the stranger's words settled into Bret's brain. His heart started beating again, only with eager anticipation rather than fear or anger. Freedom stood a word away and the temptation to take it burned the back of his throat.

A muffled whimper reached his ears and Bret glanced at Angel shivering in a ball a few yards away. Seeing her nearly naked and bound form ignited his fiery rage once more. He shook his head as he stared at the woman in need of his help. *I'll find the rebels one day, but this guy won't be the one to lead me there.*

"Forget about the bitch," the thin man said. "You don't owe her anything. Do you?" It was more of a statement than a question but Bret didn't answer. "We could leave her here... Or better yet, bring her along. Turn the tables, so-to-speak."

"What's that supposed to mean?" Bret demanded, turning narrowed silver-green eyes on his foe.

"Aren't you tired of being her slave? Doing what she wants, giving in to her demands, *protecting* her?" The thin man's tone said volumes beyond his words. "Don't you want to be free?"

"I am *no one's slave*," Bret growled.

"Whatever you say, man. But I'll share her with you anyway."

As they'd circled each other, Bret waited for his opponent to drop his guard. At the end of his last statement, the man cast a lustful look at Angel and Bret got his chance.

He lunged forward, grabbed the hand holding the weapon, and twisted it. He heard the crack, and the thug cried out as the blade fell from his grasp. Bret kicked the stranger's feet out from under him and at the same time, reached for the knife. The man lay on his belly, his elbows braced against the ground as he held his broken wrist. Bret dug his knee into his opponent's spine and wrapped his arm around his jaw. Bret jerked his head back so far, he could look into the man's black eyes while his other hand pressed the blade against the stranger's exposed throat.

"Wait," his enemy said, all the fight suddenly gone out of him, "it was a good offer. Don't kill me."

Bret stared down at the thin man like the barrel of a loaded gun and menace filled his voice. "I don't need your offer."

"Please," the man pleaded as he started to shake and new beads of sweat rolled down his long face. "Let me go and I won't bother you again. I promise. I'm sorry about the...t-the woman. I didn't think... I didn't know anyone would care."

"Shut up!" Bret shouted, jerking the man's head back farther. "I won't kill you on one condition." His cold tone sent another bout of tremors through the stranger's body and his muscles stiffened like stone, expecting the worst.

"What?"

"Where's the rebel base?"

"I can't tell you that," the man replied. "You might be a spy. I can lead you to them, but no more."

"I'm not a spy and you're not leading me anywhere." He pressed the blade into his prisoner's throat, pinching the skin and drawing blood. "Tell me what I want to know or I *will* kill you."

The stranger's eyes flicked to his fallen cohort and then words stumbled over one another in his haste to get them out. "It's near the b-big mountain. An old resort that hasn't been used in years. They…They built it up and are using it as their central base."

"How far and which direction?"

"About eighty or ninety miles southwest if you follow the old roads, shorter if you hike through the hills."

"Rainier?" Bret asked after considering the geography.

"Yeah."

Bret released the man and stepped back. "Get out of here. If I see you again, I won't hesitate to finish this."

"What about my friend?" the stranger asked as his eyes drifted to his fallen comrade. "I can't…"

"Take him if you want. He's dead," Bret said, backing toward where Angel lay. "But do it quick."

The man dashed to his horse, mounted, and without a backward glance, he rode away, leaving his friend's body where it lay.

"Are you hurt?" Bret asked, going down on one knee to cut the bonds around Angel's wrists.

While she covered her nakedness with her arms and tried to sit up, he pulled off his green work shirt and wrapped it around her shoulders. A blush rode high on her cheeks and she trembled under his hands as he steadied her. He thought her reaction a sign of embarrassment, but when her eyes collided with his, the hair on the back of his neck rose up in warning.

"I'm surprised you bothered to ask," she said bitterly as she pushed his hands away. "In fact, I'm surprised you're still here."

6

"WHAT ARE YOU TALKING ABOUT?" Bret stood and tucked his white T-shirt back into his jeans while she buttoned his shirt over her nakedness.

"I'm not deaf, Bret," she said, her voice shaking as she brushed her face with the over-long sleeve of his work shirt. "I suppose you're going to run now that you know where the rebels are."

"You heard that?"

"Yes, I did."

Maddened by his carelessness, Bret's heart plummeted into his burning belly. "And I suppose the first thing you'll do when we get back is make sure someone finds their camp and raids it."

She stopped wiping at the thin trickle of blood along her scalp to frown at him as if offended. "Why would I do that?"

"I don't know," he said, disgusted—with her or himself, he couldn't tell. "Why do you do anything?"

She ignored the question and began to roll up the sleeves of his too-big shirt. She glanced at him again and her expression appeared sad, fearful, and wary all at the same time. "Are you going to leave?"

A simple question, but something in her countenance made him pause.

Were her eyes begging him to stay?

Or was it fear he read in them?

Why did he even care?

Something about the innocence in her gaze, the way she responded to his kisses, and her flares of her fury when he annoyed her enthralled him, and he felt himself wanting more. More words, more touches, more kisses.

A stab of regret cut through him for letting her attacker leave with nothing more severe than some broken bones and a fright.

But there was nothing he could do about it now.

Not that he understood why it should matter in the first place.

"Are you leaving, Bret?" Angel repeated and her lips seemed to tremble slightly before she pressed them into a tight line.

"Do you want me to stay?" he asked, all his previous irritation forgotten. When she bit her lower lip and turned away, he knelt and reached out to cradle her face, compelling her to meet his gaze. "Answer me, Angel. Do you want me to stay?"

She stared back at him, clearly debating her response.

Yes or no, he wasn't sure which answer he wanted to hear more.

He could feel the pulse in her neck rapidly tap against his fingers. Something tightened in his chest, but he ignored it to focus on her.

She inhaled shakily. "I don't want you to run."

"Why?"

"Because I'm afraid for you."

He laughed. "For me?"

"Yes, for you, you big jerk!" She tried to pull her face away from his grasp, but he held her trapped.

Fascinated, he had to know more. "Why?"

Her eyes locked on his and something strange played in their depths. She licked her lips and the small movement drew his eyes, galvanized him. He remembered exactly how soft her lips were, how warm her mouth was, how sweet she tasted...

"Because," she said interrupting the vivid recollection replaying in his mind, "you are so blinded by your need for freedom that you can't see the danger around you." Her voice cracked and her eyes glimmered with unshed tears as she leaned toward him. "I don't want you to be injured or...or killed." Her cold fingers curled around his wrists and goosebumps raced up his arms. He couldn't look away, couldn't release her. She had him trapped, the plea in her eyes stronger than her gentle grip, more potent than her words. "Please, don't run!"

He wanted to argue, to find a lie in her expression, but he found none to question. All he saw were tears spilling over her cheeks and raw desperation pouring from her eyes. She was trembling. He wanted to ease the pain he sensed in her, the one that never seemed to leave her, to wipe away whatever marred her heart. He wanted to know if she really did care...

Don't, the angry voice inside him scolded. *Don't be a fool again!*

She shuddered and more tears leaked onto her cheeks. Common sense and his cynicism said her tears had more to do with the assault than any fear for his safety. Still, the entreaty in her gaze never faltered. She looked miserable and achingly beautiful. His heartbeat raced and he tried to breathe through the heavy weight in his chest.

"Not today," he said through the tightness in his throat and then lowered his head to press his lips to hers. When she didn't struggle, he slanted his mouth to caress her with his lips, his tongue—encouraging, enticing her to respond. She leaned into him. Her arms snaked up around his neck, her lips parted, and she kissed him back. His already galloping heart sped up at the urgency of her response, and his arms crushed her against him with a desperation he'd thought never to feel again.

I'M KISSING HIM... Angel's thoughts moved sluggishly as if in a dream, a warm, pleasant blanket of comfort drugging her senses.

Then a trickle of alarm rocketed through her. *I shouldn't be kissing him!*

But just as it had been in both the cave and the barn, she couldn't make herself stop. She should remember her promises and wrench herself out of his embrace, but she was too weak, too selfish, and too greedy to do either.

He felt so good—warm, solid, and secure—while she was so cold, tired, and afraid.

He said he wouldn't go. The distant thought left a warm tingle in her heart, easing the tightness in her chest and the throbbing in her head.

She trembled with shock and horror... and relief too. She willed herself not to cry, but she had no control. She could no more stop the tears spilling onto her cheeks than the quaking of her body and her frustration at her inability to do either made everything worse.

She choked out a sob against his lips and he pulled back. He took one look into her wide, tear-filled eyes and cursed. Then he turned her and pulled her into his lap.

He held her close as he sat in the dirt with Angel situated between his spread thighs. His body surrounded her, shielded her from everything outside. She breathed deep, dragging his heat and scent inside her, where he became a part of her, swirling, consoling, and breaking down her defenses. She snuggled against his chest. Her hands fisted in his T-shirt and she nestled her forehead beneath his chin. One arm held her against him, his hand a familiar pressure on her side, and the other cradled her head, brushing her wet hair away from her face as she wept.

She felt warm and safe in his embrace, but the flood leaking from beneath her eyelids and the trembling in her body wouldn't cease.

"It's okay," he whispered into her hair. "You can cry. It's all right. Don't hold it in; it'll just get worse if you do."

His words were all the encouragement she needed. The dam burst. She clung to him in fearful desperation as sobs wracked her body, her hands grew cold, and tears flowed like the river rolling a few yards away.

"You're safe, now, Angel," he murmured and tightened his embrace, rocking her.

Her sobs slowly subsided, and she sniffled as she squirmed against him. She let out a shuddering sigh as she settled against his shoulder and stared up at him. Meeting her tear-stained gaze, he grimaced and his arms inadvertently constricted around her as if he could cure her pain with the power of his body.

He's partially correct.

Embarrassed by her complete lack of composure, Angel burrowed her forehead against his neck and cuddled against him.

"Thank you," she muttered against the warmth of his chest, "for coming back."

A slight tremor rocked him. "I wouldn't have let them hurt you, even if I had planned to run," he said, giving her a gentle squeeze to reinforce his words. "Besides," he put more cheer in his voice, "I told you I'd be back."

She tilted her head to smile up at him bleakly and then pulled away. He released her and watched as she wiped at her eyes. She turned her head, searching the grounds.

"If you'll help me find the rest of my clothes," she said avoiding his gaze, "I'll get dressed and we can head back."

"Sure," he said as he stood and dusted off his denim seat. Spotting her boots, he went to collect them. She reached to pull her half-submerged jeans from the river and winced at the sharp pain in her side. Bret's arm coiled around her waist and pulled her back against his chest, saving her from another cold dip.

"Are you all right?" Worry edged Bret's voice from beside her ear. Glancing over her shoulder, she lifted her eyes to his, surprised by the tone of his query, but her side gave another twinge as she straightened, her own questions washed away.

She pressed her hand to her hip. "My side aches a little."

"Let me see," he said as he crouched beside her and drew the shirt up to expose her skin. He mumbled a curse as he gently tested a darkening bruise on her side and a breath hissed through her teeth.

His fingers pulled back and he peered up at her. "Does anything feel broken?"

Despite the pain, his touch left small points of heat on her flesh. She pushed his hands away and, disconcerted, her reply came out sharper than she intended. "No, I'm just sore, but I'll be okay. Let's get out of here." She smoothed her shirt down, totally unnerved by the sizzling trail of outward-spiraling-sensations his fingers left on her skin.

"There could be something wrong," Bret said, his eyebrows pinching together. "We should wait for your adrenaline to go down. You might have a serious injury."

"It isn't."

"Are you sure?"

"Yes, I'm sure." When he continued to scrutinize her, she elaborated, "I haven't been feeling the effects of adrenaline for some time...long enough to know if there was a problem or not."

He didn't appear convinced.

"Look," she said tugging on her wet jeans, "if it gets worse, I'll go to a doctor. Okay?" His eyes never left her as she sat down to pull on her boots and then stood to dust herself off. She made a concerted effort not to wince at the small ache in her side when she turned to him again. "Shall we go?"

He stared at her as she tucked in his too-big shirt while she walked to where his gelding nibbled on the tender grass of the clearing. She patted Smoke's neck and waited for Bret to join her. He shook his head, his eyes on her as he followed.

He went to mount, but she stopped him with a hand on his shoulder.

"You're bleeding," she said, pointing to the trail of blood on his arm.

"Yeah, he caught me a couple of times," he said with a shrug as he glanced first at his arm then his leg.

"You need to treat those," she told him, stepping back from the horse and gazing around the clearing. "Infection could set in if it's left like that."

"It's nothing," he argued as she walked away. "Just a scratch."

"It is more than a scratch." She mimicked his grumbling tone as she picked up the remnants of her torn T-shirt from the ground. Then she took his hand and led him back to the river's edge. "I'll wash those out and bandage them for you. Then we can go. Now, drop your pants and sit down."

He complied, but his chuckle sent a shiver down her spine and the smile he gave her made her cheeks heat. She ignored his amusement—and the sudden awkwardness that tightened her belly when his jeans fell to his knees—as she inspected both wounds.

The effect of his hard limbs beneath the clinical assessment of her fingers worsened her discomfiture. He sat calmly in his white tee and dark green boxer-briefs with his jeans pooled around his boots unconcerned by it all, which unsettled her even more.

She floundered for something to distract her as she cleaned debris from his wounds and her mind settled on the two men who'd come upon her. She didn't think they had planned their attack. The comments she'd overheard implied they'd simply found her alone and decided to take out their anger and frustration on her. Who she was and how she felt about their plight didn't matter; they'd been intent on punishing her for the pain and humiliation they'd once suffered.

Her hands trembled slightly and her body quivered with remembered fear.

Things could have been so much worse, she thought, recalling another man who had hurt her and tried to violate her in the same vulgar way. Her heart rate picked up, realizing once again what she'd narrowly escaped in this clearing. *Thank God, Bret came back.*

But she wanted more than to express her gratitude. More from him. She wanted to be in his arms again, to have his hands erase the memory of her attacker's fingers on her body.

It would be easy to encourage him—she could slide her hands over him, move her body close, and stare up into his green eyes. She wouldn't have to say a word. He seemed to want the same thing most of the time; he would understand what it was she offered. But would he take her up on it? And how would her lack of restraint affect them both later?

She already knew the answer to that.

Yet, she still wanted him. She wanted to touch him. She wanted him to touch her. She wanted… She wanted so much but couldn't have any of it.

Unbidden, her mind conjured an erotic scene—his mouthwatering, naked body before her, his sultry green gaze promising her the wonders she longed for. Her body ached and pulsed, heated, and wept for him to fill the emptiness she couldn't satisfy with promises.

Her cheeks reddened again. *What is wrong with you!*

Forcing the images out of her head, she concentrated on his wound and kept her face averted.

She could do nothing about her frantic heart.

Once his wounds were clean, she used the knife left by her attacker to cut strips from her torn shirt, then folded and tied them securely in place over his wounds.

"Okay," she said as she completed the last knot. "They'll need to be examined again when we get back, but we can go now."

"This wasn't really necessary, you know," he said, grinning with a strange humor in his eyes that froze her in place.

Did he somehow know what she'd been thinking? Or how much being near him affected her?

Don't be stupid.

"Yes, it was necessary," she said and quickly turned away, the same awkwardness warming her face again. She crossed the clearing to where Smoke had stopped to graze. Bret followed her without another word. She stood aside as he mounted and then met his gaze as he looked down at her.

"Be careful," he said, the strange light still twinkling in his eyes, "or I might start to think you care for me." He winked as he reached down and pulled her up.

"Don't be ridiculous," she said as she settled in behind him. "I care about all of my people." He stiffened against her as he urged the horse into the trees. Somehow, she'd offended him and she rushed on, not wanting a fight. "I'd do the same for any of you." She tightened her arms around his waist as they broke into a canter.

"Your people, huh?" His comment sounded dry, but there was a wealth of bitterness in his voice.

"Yes, of course. I'd help everyone who lives on the ranch and any of our friends too."

"You mean everyone you *own*." There was no mistaking his angry tone. He heeled his mount into a gallop, forcing Angel to cling to his solid form to stay seated behind the saddle.

Hurt weighted her down and the first spark of anger too. The last thing she'd wanted was to upset him, especially after he'd been so kind to her. But after all he'd witnessed and all their time together, how could he still believe she thought of him or any of them as a slave? An explanation—or argument—however, would have to wait as the bouncing, the wind, and the ache in her side hindered any discussion.

"Get down," he ordered when they reached the clearing where her stallion waited. Seeing no reason not to, she took his offered arm and slid to the ground.

Bret dismounted and without a word, crossed to the log where he left her saddle. He carried it and the blanket to her stallion, then set them gently on Ebony's back. Again, Angel was reminded of his fondness for animals. Unreasonably furious about her innocent comment, he still took care not to frighten or upset her horse.

She frowned at Bret's back, feeling oddly jealous of the stallion.

Bret finished tightening the girth, grabbed Ebony's reins, and led him to Angel. He handed them to her, still without speaking or meeting her eyes, and returned to his gelding.

She pressed her lips together, debating whether to question his abrupt mood change. Annoyance for his seemingly purposeful misinterpretation of her meaning decided the debate.

"Why are you so angry?" she asked, lifting her face to frown up at him sitting stiffly in the saddle.

The look he gave her was colder than the river she'd been dunked into earlier.

7

"I AM NOT YOUR POSSESSION," he said through clenched teeth, his eyes hard and flinty with suppressed fury. "I'm not your horse, your saddle, or your boots. I'm not a *thing* you can own or sell at your leisure. And I'm not a toy you can play with until you tire of it. None of us are *your* people."

His speech—delivered in a cold, dispassionate voice—sent a shiver up her spine.

Apparently, she must overcome his misconceptions about her. Again.

She took a deep, calming breath and let it out slowly. "That's not what I meant, Bret."

"Really?" Sarcasm could be so very sharp coming from him.

"Yes, really." Heat swept over her, and she fought to keep her annoyance in check. Pressing her lips into a thin line, she winced as she mounted Ebony. Aware of the tension between the two riders, the stallion sidled nervously, but Angel controlled him with practiced ease, just as Bret did with his gelding.

"Then what *did* you mean?" he demanded while she pulled herself into the saddle, even as he turned Smoke for home without waiting for her. "Please, do enlighten me."

"Would you stop that!" she snapped, gathering up the reins.

"What?" His eyes, when he peeked over his shoulder, belied the innocence of the question.

"Stop always assuming the worst about me. I'm not a monster, you know." She finally caught up to him.

"I wonder..."

She lifted her chin and fixed him with a hard stare. "You wonder what exactly? Whether I'll change from Dr. Jekyll to Ms. Hyde? If I'll have you beaten daily? Or starved? Or both? I am what you see, Bret. Nothing more, nothing less. I'm not perfect; God knows I make mistakes, but I care about the people around me. That's all I meant. So, would you *please* give me the benefit of the doubt for once?"

He glared at her in mute irritation and urged his gelding to greater speed. Obliged to do the same if she wanted to keep up, she followed suit.

An hour later, they were almost home. She was stiff, tired, and sore from her ordeal, and sadness at his angry withdrawal had settled like a lead weight inside her. Bret's refusal to acknowledge her the whole way back irked her and the pain in her body kept her temper on a low simmer, but she would not beg him to speak. Instead, her mind returned to the incidents of the day, and something he'd said earlier stayed with her.

"Not today," she said into the thick silence and he peered over at her with a frown.

"Hmm?"

"What did you mean when you said, 'Not today'?"

He frowned outright. "What are you talking about?"

She glared at him as if he were dense. "When I asked if you were going to run, you said, 'Not today.' What did you mean?"

He sighed and looked away. "Just what I said." He sounded bored and a little annoyed, but the flexing muscle in his jaw and the stiff set of his shoulders told her he disliked the fact that she remembered.

Angel suspected what he meant and didn't like it one bit. Her anger simmered to life. "Does that mean you'll go tomorrow, or next week, or a month from now?"

He simply shrugged. "Maybe."

Something clenched in her chest and she swallowed the thickness that clogged her throat.

He eyed her as she glared at him, fighting to keep the unexpected ache inside her from breaking to the surface. Then he shook his head and turned away. "I can't live as your slave forever. I told you that a long time ago."

"Why? Why can't you just stay and be happy?"

"Because I'm not, and I won't make a promise I can't honor."

"You've been here for almost eight months," she said, knowing he would either lie or reveal what she'd already assumed to be the truth. "If you've been so unhappy, then why haven't you tried to run before?"

He turned his head, his eyes studying her. "I have," he said with a shrug and then faced the trail again, "but you were dumb enough to get trapped with a cougar stalking you and I had to come back to save you."

She sat a little taller in the saddle as fury—and hurt—burned through her like a heatwave. "I knew that was you!" Her eyes shot blue sparks at him. "You stampeded the cattle that night."

"Yep," he answered, sounding self-satisfied.

They had passed the gates of the homestead and were almost at the barn.

"Did it occur to you," she asked while fighting to keep her voice steady, "that the cougar came after me because you scared off its original prey?"

He sent a heated glare her way, but something else glimmered in his eyes. "You don't know that."

She frowned. *Maybe he did know and felt guilty...?*

They entered the barn and dismounted, Angel with a little

more caution than normal.

"Yes, I do know that, and I think you do too," she said once she'd slid from the saddle without a groan. With a hand pressed to her achy side, she led Ebony into his stall and pulled at his girth to untie it. "The cougar didn't even notice me until the herd was gone."

"You should stop riding the stallion," he said from the next stall.

"What?" Her brow furrowed, unclear as to how her mount entered this conversation.

"I said," he told her after returning from the tack room with a currycomb in his hand, "you should try riding a horse you can control. He's too much animal for you if you can't keep him from throwing you in a crisis."

Her hands tightened on the length of leather she was working on. "You bastard," she fumed, understanding precisely what he implied—she needed a babysitter, wasn't capable of taking care of herself, and was not a good enough rider to control the stallion. She was a grown and capable woman, she'd mastered horsemanship years ago, and Ebony loved her. Still, she didn't like looking foolish and, if she was honest, she didn't like him thinking of her as foolish either.

Despite his baiting, Angel clamped her teeth shut and remained silent, though she seethed with the words she wanted to fling at him.

Bret also remained quiet until she began to brush down her horse. Finished grooming Smoke, Bret leaned over her stallion's stall door as she combed Ebony's coat. She didn't say a word. If he wanted to be taciturn, she was happy to work in silence.

"Maybe a mare," Bret said with a condescending smirk. "Then I wouldn't have to come to your rescue all the time."

Angel felt her hair practically bristle around her head like an angry cat's tail as her eyes slowly turned to glare a warning at him. "Oh, yeah, *my hero,*" she said, every word dripping with sarcasm, as she went back to work on Ebony.

He winked. "It's starting to look that way." His mocking grin broadened with insinuated meaning and her blood pressure exploded along with her temper.

"You son of a bitch," she hissed, coming around Ebony to hastily brush down his other side.

"Such language," he teased. "I didn't know you had it in you."

"Shut up!" Her mind suddenly made an undesirable connection and she turn to him once more with narrowed eyes and suppressed fury in her voice.

"You were going to leave me out there that night, weren't you?" She ran the comb over the stallion's side in one final stroke then threw the grooming utensil onto the shelf. With hurt and anger brewing inside, she spun on her heel and faced Bret across the stall door. "Was your *plan* to let the thing attack me? Is that why you took so long to show up?"

Surprise and guilt flickered in his eyes but they hardened again. "That hadn't actually occurred to me," he said, tilting his head as if recollecting. "I'll have to keep it in mind for next time."

Another smug smile bloomed on his handsome face and her already boiling temper spiked. How could he joke about almost getting her killed?

Impulsively, she swung her open hand and slapped the grinning fool as hard as she could. The loud smack reverberated through the small area as his head snapped to the side.

The new noise and commotion caused Ebony's stiff ears to twitch, and he snorted a loud warning, but Angel—too focused on the man standing in the aisle—was oblivious to the animal's distress.

Bret's slow, menacing movement as he rotated toward her set alarm bells off in her head. A murderous glare glittered in his silver-green eyes as his fingers touched the red handprint staining his cheek. Her mouth went dry, and she took an unconscious step back, suddenly sorry for allowing her temper to get the better of her.

"YOU'RE GOING TO REGRET THAT," he growled as he swung open the door and stalked inside.

"Stay back," she ordered, stepping away.

Bret didn't stop.

Ebony ears twitched backward and his head jerked up. When the gate slammed against the wall and rebounded back, the huge animal gave an ear-shattering neigh and charged for the opening.

Bret was so fixated on Angel that he'd missed the stallion's warnings, but the animal's ear-wrenching cry stopped him cold. Caught off-guard, Bret stood in the stallion's immediate path with no way to avoid the charging animal. With only seconds to take in his options, Bret braced himself for the impact that would slam him into the wall, followed by the punishing weight of the frightened horse crushing him against the wooden partition.

Damn, this is going to hurt!

8

SOMETHING SNAGGED BRET'S SHIRT and yanked him sideways. The twelve-hundred-pound horse's flank brushed his shoulder hard enough to knock him further off balance as Ebony's long, wiry tail slapped his face. The tightness in Bret's chest knotted a little more when he ran into a soft form, tried to adjust his momentum but tripped over his boots. He landed hard on his knees, fell forward, and his hat went flying as he banged his head against the far wall. Propping up on his elbows a moment later to investigate what had cushioned his fall, another second or two had passed before his muddled mind grasped that the smaller, softer body wriggling beneath him belonged to Angel.

"Are you all right?" she asked, stilling her movements beneath him.

Strange, he'd been wondering the same thing about her. His breath caught when her small hand touched his abused cheek and the remorseful look on her face cooled his blood and softened his heart.

I'm still an idiot, he thought as he peered down at her, his body tightening expectantly. A moment ago, his heart rate and blood pressure had been skyrocketing with fury. Now, the slow thudding in his chest felt calm yet anticipatory.

Damn it, why were his emotions around her all over the map? He didn't like that one bit. It left him feeling edgy and on very unstable footing. He needed to get a handle on himself before she found another way under his defenses.

"Yeah, I'm fine," he breathed as he moved away from her. He pushed back onto his knees, gingerly checking the top of his head for any blood. "I just bumped my head." He grimaced when his fingers found the small lump a few inches above his temple.

Slow to sit up, groaning and wincing as she did, he refrained from asking Angel about her health. She leaned against the wall and turned to him, her own hat forgotten on the straw-covered floor. When he saw her watching him, he sighed, dropped his arm to his side, and sat next to her.

"You pulled me out of the way, didn't you?" He hadn't meant to, but he sounded accusatory. After all, he might not have suffered any serious harm if Ebony had collided with him. He winced inwardly. He would've been crushed or trampled, and either would've left him injured, possibly grievously.

"Yes."

He turned his head to frown at her. "Why?"

"Why not?" she asked with a blank stare. "Was I supposed to let you get hurt?"

"You could've solved a problem and repaid me for taunting you too."

"It would've caused all new ones or..." she paused not meeting his gaze and a blush slowly stained her cheeks, "or worse ones."

"But then you'd be free of me."

She turned her earnest cerulean eyes on him. "I don't want that. I don't want you hurt or dead. Don't you know that?"

He nodded and looked away. He knew next to nothing about what she wanted, but he didn't want to argue the point.

Angel's horse had dashed up and down the barn's

passageway while they talked, looking for a place to hide from what had spooked him. He finally settled into another open stall. They could hear him munch on hay found in the bin.

"Why did you do it?" Angel asked quietly after the silence stretched into minutes.

Bret met her probing gaze, raising his eyebrows in silent inquiry.

"Why did you come back for me? That night with the cougar... Why didn't you just ride off?"

He sighed and reached for his hat. "I wanted to be away from you, not see you dead."

He stood, set his straw hat on his head, and held out a hand. She took his offered assistance and he pulled her to her feet.

"Afterward," he continued as they left the stall, "you were hurt and frightened. I couldn't leave you out there alone."

"Because you thought you could seduce me," she said.

He heard the accusation in her voice as he followed her down the hall and shook his head. "No, that wasn't the reason."

"Like hell it wasn't," she said heatedly and halted at the barn doors where she swung around to face him. "You're an incredibly selfish man, Bret. You see what you want and try to take it, never caring who you hurt along the way. Did you ever stop to think who you'd hurt if you ran? Sure, you'd damage my reputation, but more importantly, you'd ruin the lives of everyone here. And what about Jake?"

"What about him?"

Her eyes narrowed at his calm reply. "How do you think he'd feel when they caught you and killed you? Do you even care about that?"

"They won't catch me," he told her with a confidence he only partially feigned.

She scoffed and her tone turned unpleasant, "Arrogant, too. Don't be so sure of yourself, Bret." With her chin held high, she turned to the door. "I know where you're going."

Rage unexpectedly erupted within him and before he knew

what he was doing, he grabbed her and spun her around.

"Don't threaten me," he growled as his strong hands curled around her throat. "I could kill you now and ride out of here without having to justify myself to anyone. Nothing will stand in my way. Not you. Not Jake. No one. Do you understand?"

ANGEL HEARD THE FURY In his voice, but none of what he said could match what she read in his silver-green glare.

Had she truly been certain he wouldn't harm her?

Had she actually felt safe in his arms?

Was this the man Jake claimed as his best friend? Or had he changed so much that the humble, gracious man she'd come to know never really existed? This scowling, snarling beast certainly wasn't the man Jake had told her so much about. Nor was he the man who comforted her by the river after risking his life to save her. Hate burned in this man's eyes, directed at *her*.

She had only wanted to take down his certainty about escape a notch or two. She'd expected him to be angry, but not violent.

Cold fingers of fear crept up her spine, and she held very still as he glared down at her.

"I asked you a question," he said, the taut muscles of his forearms flexing as she gripped them.

Something like self-disgust flickered in his eyes but disappeared so fast she wondered if she'd imagined it.

He knew exactly what he was doing—scaring the pants off her, for one—and, despite the surge of adrenaline strengthening her body, he was capable of following through with ease. Yet, the hold on her neck, though solid, was not constricting. He wasn't trying to harm her, he was trying to scare her—and was doing a great job of it too.

Realizing that settled the fear that had kept her immobile and she nodded her understanding.

He released her. "Good," he said as he stormed past her. "Don't forget it."

Hurt and anger for his callousness and her wounded pride swelled up inside her. She kept trying with him, but now she understood that even if he wouldn't harm her outright, everything he did, everything he said, was designed to lead him to his ultimate goal—his freedom. It didn't matter who or what got in his way, he would brush them aside, consequences be damned. He infuriated her past reason, past caring about what he thought or did.

"I hate you, you selfish bastard." She regretted the words as soon as they left her lips.

Pausing mid-step, his back stiffened and he glared over his shoulder. He reached up and pulled the makeshift bandage from his arm and tossed the material to the ground, then raked cruel eyes over her and gave her his nastiest smile.

She lifted her chin and refused to back down.

"That makes the feeling mutual," he said before he exited the barn.

Angel stared after him, suddenly wanting to cry. She shook her head. Why couldn't she control herself around him? If she wasn't arguing and shouting at him, she was kissing him and longing for more.

She lifted her head and squared her shoulders. She would not sit out here and feel sorry for herself, not about this. She had other things to do, other concerns that deserved her attention and would value it more than the frustrating man who'd just broken her heart without looking back.

Straightening her spine, she began what seemed an endless, aching walk back to her house, unsurprised that the cause of her dismay was nowhere in sight.

As she crossed the dooryard and wearily climbed the stairs of her deck, she considered what to do about Bret. His need for freedom could endanger everyone on the ranch and she simply could not allow that to happen. Head down and deep in thought, she turned the knob of her front door and crossed the threshold to an elated chorus of 'Happy Birthday', which startled her out of her gloom.

After the tense happenings earlier in the afternoon and her incident with Bret only a few minutes before, her nerves were on edge and her heart gave a painful lurch at their exuberant shout, then fluttered in her throat as she gaped at the beaming faces around her. The whole foyer was jammed with people all dressed for a formal party. They spilled into the living room, up the stairs, and along the hall, everyone smiling and staring at her.

"What's this?" she asked, scanning the grinning faces, their good cheer warming the chill and lightening the heaviness in her chest.

"Your birthday party," Jake said, looking handsome in his black suit.

"But..." Tears filled her eyes as she surveyed the room. "Thank you, everyone!" She tried to smile as she leaned toward Jake. "I'm extremely underdressed," she whispered, smoothing her wildly frizzing hair down against her head.

He grinned, a glint of humor and affection in his hazel eyes. "Don't worry," he said with a wink, "we've got you covered." Then he turned and raised his voice above the chatter. "Okay, everyone! Head to the dining room and we'll start the party shortly."

As people shuffled down the hall, Angel noticed Bret, looking amazingly attractive in his dirty white T-shirt, standing in a corner of the living room leaning in close to a lovely brunette Angel only vaguely recognized. They looked cozy and a stab of jealousy struck her so hard that she took a step toward them before she realized. Stopping herself, she turned to Jake, wanting to know more about who was in her house.

"Jake?" she murmured, a hand on his arm, and he turned to peer down at her still smiling. "I don't recognize some of these guests." Angel glanced toward Bret, who had his hand on the brunette's back to guide her from the room as if they had arrived together.

Angel reminded herself to breathe and refocused on Jake.

"Yeah, I know," Jake said as he scanned the people making their way out. He met her gaze again and his smile widened. "But some of them you do."

She opened her mouth to ask what he was talking about, but her confusion disintegrated when he stepped aside to reveal Monica Avery standing behind him. Everything suddenly clicked—those strangers had arrived with Monica.

In a knee-length, scarlet dress and six-inch black stilettos that made her legs appear longer than they really were, and her long, pale-golden hair styled into an elegant French roll, Monica looked as classically beautiful as ever. The broad, happy grin adorning her face enhanced the familiar mischievous twinkle in her hazel eyes. Angel's unease for her own unsavory appearance returned, but she pushed it aside and smiled brightly.

"Monica!" Angel shouted in surprise and wrapped her arms around her old friend. "What are you doing here?"

"Jake went to a lot of trouble to get me here," Monica said with a big smile. Then she sent a sly peek at Jake over her shoulder and leaned in closer to Angel, her voice low. "Do you think he had another motive?"

Angel laughed and hugged her friend again. "Probably," she agreed, grinning at Jake.

He rolled his eyes at their teasing. "If you want to change before dinner, you should get to it," he said, looking her up and down, suspicion entering his gaze. "We can only wait so long before they start attacking the food."

The weight of his glance made Angel blush.

He reached over and plucked a piece of straw out of her hair. "What were you doing anyway?" The smile slipped from his lips as he pinched the sleeve of the green shirt she wore and tugged. "This isn't your shirt." He met her eyes, and she read the unspoken question in his.

"It's Bret's," she said, hoping she sounded more casual than it seemed to her own ears. "I had a...a little accident, and he lent me his shirt."

Jake frowned. "What happened?"

"Nothing serious," she replied, trying not to appear as nervous as she felt. She didn't want Jake insisting she take a guard every time she left the house, and he would if he knew the truth. "I tripped and took a dive into the river." She tried to laugh.

"What happened to your shirt?"

She stared at him for a moment, at a loss to explain, but then stumbled forward with what she hoped was a plausible explanation. "It got torn." She knew it was a lame explanation, but she hadn't put any thought into excuses for her appearance.

Jake reached over and fiddled with the hole in the back of the left shirtsleeve. He met her eyes and she saw the doubt in the hazel depths. "Looks like his got torn too."

Good thing he didn't see the slash in Bret's jeans, she thought. *Crap! Maybe he did.* She fumbled in her mind and finally settled on a vague resemblance of the truth.

"Yeah," she shrugged. "He must have snagged it on something. His arm too." She pointed out the blood.

"Looks like it," he agreed, but she read incredulity in his frown.

"Are you all right?" Monica asked worriedly and Angel was thankful for the interruption.

"Yes," she said, pretending not to notice the dark look on Jake's face. "I got a couple scrapes and bruises, a bump on the head, and soaking wet, but I'm fine."

"Oh, honey," Monica said, "that water is cold!"

Angel laughed. "Yeah, tell me about it."

"Where was Bret during your little swim?" Jake's voice sounded hard and his face looked like granite when she turned to him. He seemed angry and she suspected it was directed at Bret.

Angel didn't want to tell Jake the exact details, she didn't want to tell anyone—and she would have to make sure Bret didn't either—but she also didn't want Jake to accuse Bret of something he didn't do.

"He was with me. In fact, the situation would've been worse if he wasn't." The statement was not the absolute truth, but not one word was a lie.

Jake shook his head and grunted, still disbelieving.

"Really," she said as she met Jake's doubtful gaze. "I'm glad he was there."

Monica glanced between the two of them and interrupted before Jake got the chance to ask any more questions. "Do you want some help getting ready? I'll put your hair up if you like?"

"Yes, please." Angel jumped at the opportunity to leave Jake's questions behind. She patted his arm with a smile. "We'll be down in about thirty minutes. Can you hold them off that long?"

"I'll see what I can do."

Relief shot down to her toes when he grinned and winked at her.

"We'll try to hurry," Monica said as she hustled Angel away. "You just keep them busy until we get back."

JAKE NICHOLS WATCHED as the two most important women in his life disappeared down the upstairs hall, his mind a flurry of possibilities. He knew Bret wasn't happy with his situation, and he wouldn't put it past his friend to do whatever was necessary to gain his freedom. He didn't blame him, but he'd need to remind Bret of the damage he would cause if he tried to escape, what he would suffer if they recaptured him, and try to convince him of the futility of it as well.

Jake also knew Angel didn't tell him everything that had happened, and he wondered if Bret would fill in the gaps.

I doubt it, he thought with a shake of his head, but that wouldn't stop him from asking.

THE DANCE

1

THIRTY MINUTES LATER, standing in front of the full-length mirror in her room, Angel examined her appearance with a critical eye. Monica had arranged her bangs to cover the small gash and purplish bruise at her hairline and swept the rest of Angel's black tresses on top of her head, allowing them to hang in a loose cascade of curls down her back. An old strand of pearls with matching stud earrings accompanied the dress and her modest makeup accented the blue of her eyes, the dark lashes surrounding them, and the blush of her lips.

She wore a plain black dress, but the color was the only plain thing about it. The same seamstress who made their everyday clothes had designed and sewn it for a governing council party years ago; Angel had never worn it again, until now. Comprised of a body-hugging under-slip with a corset top and a shimmering overdress, the gown's fitted bodice showed off her womanly shape, while the waist flared into a skirt made up of a multitude of translucent scarves like a veil of shiny onyx-colored clouds ending just above her knees. Even with its dark coloring, the whole dress shimmered in the light like polished obsidian and clung in all the right places. Despite the scratches she acquired during her battle at the river, Angel's suntanned legs were bare, and she completed her ensemble with a pair of black heels with straps that coiled once around her ankles and fastened with a small silver buckle.

Feminine and sexy, her entire outfit was nothing less than revealing. She shook her head. *I don't have to wear this. It's a birthday party, not a beauty pageant.*

A pair of clear, jade-green eyes filled with masculine appreciation popped into her head. She straightened her spine and stood a little taller. *I did not choose this outfit to impress Bret Masters.*

That pesky voice piped up from the back of her mind again. *Liar!*

Running her finger along the dress' V-neck front, Angel glanced apprehensively at her friend through the mirror. "I think I should change into something…a little more modest."

"Why?" Monica replied as she adjusted the twist of Angel's curls then stepped back to admire her friend's reflection. "You look beautiful!"

"I feel overdressed and these scratches—"

"Those scratches hardly show and you are not overdressed," Monica admonished, checking her own makeup in the mirror. "You're dressed the same as I am, the same as every other woman here." She fixed Angel with a suspicious eye. "Or do you *want* to look dowdy?"

Angel almost groaned. She recognized that familiar glare and its meaning.

A bold, self-assured woman, Monica knew what she liked and she went after it. Her holdings were slowly growing, and she was more than an ally when dealing with the other less-than-humane slaveholders on the council. But, in Angel's opinion, Monica had one major fault—her constant hint that Angel needed to end her self-imposed celibacy. The woman was shameless when it came to men—one man, in particular, which explained the red dress and ultra-high heels—and she refused to accept Angel's decision to remain alone. Because unlike Angel, Monica never gave up on one love for herself, until she met Jake.

Three years ago, Monica sent Jake to Angel with a request to save him from Darla Cain's wrath. Angel happily did everything she could for them and would've paid a lot more to save her friends from the same heartache she had suffered. Jake quickly became an integral part of Angel's makeshift family and her reliance on him significantly grew over the years. Monica had been actively searching for Jake's replacement so he could return to her. She also repeatedly encouraged Angel to let someone into her life again.

Angel sighed. Monica's concern for her was endearing, but Angel also found it frustrating.

Recognizing the contrary glint in her friend's narrowed eyes, Angel shook her head and spoke before Monica could voice her argument once again. "I'll wear the dress."

Monica grinned in triumph and Angel gave her a resigned look. Then, eyeing herself in the mirror, Angel grimaced at the abrasions above her knee. Only a little red, but to her, the wound stuck-out like an old neon sign through the transparent black fabric of her skirt.

"You look great, Angel," Monica said. "Besides, you don't have time to change." Her smile broadened as she headed toward the door. Angel took one last glance at her reflection and then—thankful she'd downed some aspirin in the bathroom to take the edge off her aches and pains—she headed downstairs with Monica.

Jake met them at the kitchen, his eyes glowing with appreciation. "You both look beautiful."

They rewarded him with spectacular smiles that made their eyes sparkle.

He laughed and shook his head. "Wow. You ladies are almost too stunning for us mere mortals."

Bret's gift for sweet-talk is rubbing off on him, Angel

thought as her face reddened and Monica kissed his cheek, then whispered something in his ear that made him chuckle. Jake offered each woman an arm and then proudly escorted them into the dining hall.

Angel couldn't believe the decorations. They'd transformed the utilitarian dining hall into a ballroom. Small lanterns were suspended at regular intervals from several crisscrossing wires mounted on the ceiling. Assorted wildflowers in glass mason jars sat as centerpieces on the tables surrounded by small, homemade candles. Sweeping, snowy fabric with lilac-colored accents adorned the French doors opening onto the back porch that overlooked the garden, and thinner strips twined around the cables holding the lamps above. The delightful display must've taken the better part of the day to complete, and she grinned remembering Bret's overlong search for their picnic site that afternoon.

Everyone stared as the three friends crossed the wide-open space in the middle of the dining hall. Their eyes weighed on Angel, but it wasn't unpleasant. The laughter and smiles were cheerful and lifted her spirits, rather than drag her deeper into the sadness she'd felt ever since her argument with Bret.

Don't think about him now, she warned herself. *Think about Jake and Monica, and everything they had to do to set up this sweet surprise.* She looked up at Jake and he gave her a playful wink that made the smile return to her lips.

As they neared the far end of the dining hall, Angel noticed a three-tiered, lavender-colored cake that read, 'Happy Birthday, Angel' in dark purple lettering on the table to the left of where they were to sit. A lovely creation with dark-purple flowers and spring-green leaves, and Angel would bet anything Esther—who knew purple was her favorite color—made her famous chocolate cake and had decorated it herself.

Jake pulled out a chair for Angel while she still gazed around at the décor, then assisted Monica with hers before coming to stand between them and turning to the crowd.

"Hello, everyone," he said loudly, picking up a wine glass filled with a dark liquid and every adult at each table lifted one as well. "As you know, tonight we're celebrating Angel's birthday." A murmur of assent buzzed around the room. "It is also a way for us to tell her what she means to us and to say *'Thank you'* for everything she's done for us too. So, I would like to make a toast." He turned to Angel and raised the glass he held, while the rest of the room followed his example. "Angel, we wanted to show you how important you are to us and how much we appreciate all you've done to keep us happy and safe. Sadly, the best we could do is throw you a party with your own food and wine." There was a smattering of laughter and Angel returned his jovial grin.

He sobered suddenly.

"We owe you so much more than we can ever repay," he said, and Angel's chest tightened at the serious tone of his voice and the suspicious shine in his hazel eyes. "I wish we could've arranged to give you everything you deserve, but our undying gratitude will have to do. Thank you, Angel, for everything!" He took a sip of the burgundy liquid along with the rest of the crowd. Applause and a hearty cheer immediately followed.

Tears burned the backs of Angel's eyes as she stared at the man who had become her family. Jake had been talking about himself in his heartfelt toast and knowing that spread the tightness in her chest up to her throat. There'd be no clearing that out anytime soon, so she just smiled her gratitude and reached out to squeeze his hand.

He returned the gesture, leaned forward, and whispered, "I owe you everything."

Angel shook her head and kissed his cheek. "You owe me nothing."

Straightening, he gave her a crooked grin, glanced at Monica on his other side, and then turned back to his audience. Waving at them to quiet down, he waited to speak again.

"Dinner is served at the buffet." He pointed to the long tables along the wall near the kitchen. "Help yourselves," he said, and then added a good-natured, "but no pushing!"

Monica and Jake ushered Angel to the front of the line. Several minutes later, everyone, including the kitchen staff, was seated and enjoying the amazing feast.

When the assembly began to not-so-subtly hint that the time for dessert had arrived, Jake and Monica led Angel to the cake, where she was surprise to see that the three-tiered confection glowed with lit candles.

A shout rang out and her face heated for the second time that evening when the crowd broke into a rousing rendition of *Happy Birthday*. The song ended, she made the required birthday wish, took an enormous breath, and, to her amazement, blew out all the candles on her first try.

This feat was followed by another ear-shattering cheer.

Until this point, Angel had resisted the urge to look for Bret. She hadn't wanted to see him with the woman who'd been hanging on his arm—or *any* woman at all. But, as she scanned the room during the singing, she found him standing with his arm wrapped possessively around the brunette's waist. Dressed in a clean, crisp black suit similar to Jake's, Bret appeared showered and ready to charm the pants off some lucky woman. In a word, he looked gorgeous. Angel ground her teeth, annoyed—with herself or Bret, she wasn't sure. Then she went cold as she wondered whether his change of appearance had been for the party or the brunette.

She fought the irritation that welled up within her and forced a gracious smile onto her lips.

The painful truth was, when he wasn't being a world-class-ass, Bret Masters made Angel feel beautiful and desirable, and in all honesty, she liked his attention. Maybe a little too much, because, right now, Angel was quietly seething. Even more so because the dark prickly feeling in her chest was completely unlike her. The damn emotion simmered inside her like a pot of stew over a raging campfire, but as much as she disliked it, there was something worse about her situation.

Despite all he'd done to prove himself undeserving, she wanted to trust Bret. She wanted him to trust her and so much more. Something about him set butterflies to flight in her stomach every time he came near and caused her pulse to quicken at his touch. How was she supposed to stay away from something she knew she couldn't have but wanted so desperately?

Remember the cost, she told herself. She must stay away from him, only speak to him about the ranch as she'd intended—something she tried to stick to before.

Yeah, right, she thought. *Like that worked so well the last time you tried it.*

She pulled her eyes away from Bret and, being careful to keep her smile plastered on her face, allowed Monica to hustle her back to her seat while Jake followed with cake for each of them.

In the middle of her dessert, her eyes had drifted over the crowd coming to rest once again on Bret. Leaning in close as they finished their cake, he smiled and chatted amiably with the brunette. That, Angel could have dealt with, but the damn woman would not stop touching him—his arm, his hand, his shoulder, and, Angel was positive, his thigh. With every touch and laugh, Angel's skin grew hotter and it got a little harder to breathe.

"He's very handsome," Monica murmured in Angel's ear. "That *is* Bret, isn't it?"

Angel nodded and then mentally berated herself, not only for letting Monica see her staring but for gawking at Bret in the first place.

"Kristine's a lucky girl," Monica said, trying to get a reaction out of her friend.

Ah, so that's her name, Angel thought sourly, though she didn't let her irritation show. *I knew she looked familiar. What was it I didn't like about her...?*

Dismissing her thoughts with a disinterested shrug, Angel kept her voice passive. "She won't feel so lucky once she gets to know him."

"Hmm," Monica said at length and then pierced a bite of cake with her fork and popped it into her mouth.

Angel didn't bother to respond or acknowledge the knowing look in her friend's studious gaze.

As they finished dessert, Angel was chatting amiably with several other friends when a sudden, loud blast of stereo music surprised everyone in the room. Angel turned toward the corner where her head guard, Michelle, stood beside the old piano appearing as startled as everyone else. Looking exceptionally feminine in her dark-blue sheath-dress and low, matching heels, Michelle hastily turned a knob on the offending stereo equipment—another sign of Angel's wealth—on top of the piano. Michelle then faced the assemblage with a sheepish grin, but her pale blue eyes twinkled with glee. Her expression seemed almost giddy. Angel thought her guard's behavior odd, until Michelle crossed the room and Dean Williams stood as Michelle drew near. The way his blue-green eyes roamed appreciatively over Michelle's fit leggy length spoke volumes.

Taller by several inches, Dean was another extraordinarily attractive man Angel had rescued from her enemies at the Auction Hall about a year ago. He always struck Angel as pleasant and courteous—in a submissive sort of way—but distant and reserved. Given the expression on his face, however, he appeared to be coming out of his wary shell.

He gave Michelle a genuine smile as he took her hand and led her out into the center of the open floor. They made a handsome couple, swaying along to the slow two-step, and several others joined them, including Jake and Monica.

Angel sat alone watching everyone else enjoy themselves, and declined every offer to join in. With a friendly smile and a regretful voice, she claimed to be too tired and sore after the long ride and supposed accident to attempt it. The aspirin made her claims only small white lies. In reality, she didn't want to dance, not with any of them. The music and the dancers brought back bad memories and if she joined them, she feared she might embarrass herself.

And, besides, she thought, *only one man could entice me onto the floor.* Unfortunately, after their angry exchange in the barn earlier, Bret would never ask her.

Good, she told herself. *I don't want him to ask. I don't want to give him any more ammunition to use against me.* Caving into her weak longing to be in his arms again would definitely give him plenty of ammo.

When her friends returned to the table, Jake held out Monica's chair and then he turned to smile at Angel. "Would you like to dance?"

Her lips curled up, but she shook her head. "I'm sorry, Jake. I'm not feeling up to it."

"You mean the right guy hasn't asked you yet," Monica said.

Angel couldn't keep from rolling her eyes. "No, I just want to talk and enjoy the music."

"Right," Monica replied, dragging out the word meaningfully. "And there's no way to do that while dancing."

Angel ignored her.

"It's your party, Angel," Jake said. "It would be a shame if you didn't dance at least once."

Not you too, she groaned internally, but smiled at him.

"I don't think anyone could talk me into going out there. Sorry, Jake."

A knowing smirk tugged at Monica's lips. "I bet there's one man here who could convince you..."

"No, there's not," Angel said, knowing where her friend was going.

Did Monica cajole Jake into helping her play matchmaker while they two-stepped?

"I'll take that bet," Jake said with a conspiratorial wink at Monica.

Angel groaned. *Yep*, she thought, *Monica can persuade him to do anything.*

"What're you two up to?" she asked suspiciously.

"Nothing," they said in unison, appearing guilty as hell.

"We just want you to enjoy the party," Jake said as he sat beside her.

"I am," she said a little too emphatically.

"It could be better."

"And who do you think is going to change my mind?" Angel asked, knowing the answer and dreading it.

"If I can't," Jake said with a grin and waited for her to shake her head before he finished his statement, "the only man I know who could charm you out of that seat is Bret."

"Right." Angel chuckled humorlessly. "That isn't going to happen. He doesn't want anything to do with me."

"Oh, I don't know about that. He can be surprising and quite charming when he wants to be." Jake smiled and Angel wondered again when he became a matchmaker.

"He can also be a jackass!" She couldn't help the peevish response.

Monica laughed. "A-ha! Someone's gotten under your skin."

"Not in the way you're implying."

Jake's teasing expression turned troubled in the blink of an eye. "What did he do?"

She peered up at him, standing beside her chair, afraid she'd said too much. The last thing she wanted was to put a wedge between the two men, and if she told Jake about Bret's behavior at the barn earlier, that's exactly what would happen.

"I thought you said he was charming," she remarked, trying to make light of his concern.

"I said he can be when he wants to be. That doesn't mean he can't be an ass like you said."

Angel hesitated but knew Jake would not be dissuaded. "We had a disagreement, that's all."

"What kind of disagreement?"

She shrugged. "It's nothing, really."

Jake lowered his chin and gave her a look that said he wasn't buying it.

Sighing, she shrugged again. "He takes offense with almost everything I say. Especially if he assumes I'm trying to put him in his place."

"Were you?" Jake still sounded suspicious.

"No, he just misunderstood me. Sometimes I think he does that on purpose."

"He can be stubborn," Jake said. He glanced at Monica then back to Angel and changed gears again. "But that doesn't mean he won't dance with you."

She glared at the huge grin on Jake's face. "Uh-huh…"

"Come on, Angel. If he asks, will you dance with him?"

"He won't."

"He will."

She shook her head. If Jake and Monica had hatched some kind of matchmaking plot, she intended to avoid it. Yet, she was positive the chances of Bret leaving his attentive partner to dance with her were just on the other side of never. He wouldn't risk a sure-thing-with-no-strings for her.

She slumped in her chair and released a resigned sigh. "All right, Jake. If he asks, I'll dance with him. But if he doesn't, the two of you will stop playing cupid and keep your noses out of my personal life…for good."

Jake's grin said he expected to win the bet, but Monica didn't look pleased. Being forced to abandon her mission to end Angel's voluntary solitude wouldn't sit well with Monica.

Angel almost laughed at the silent exchange that passed between her friends.

Jake dropped a quick kiss on Monica's cheek and hurried off before she could say another word.

"You're just as bound by that bet as he will be," Angel said with a triumphant smile and a nod in Jake's direction.

"Yeah, yeah." Monica waved away her comment and smirked. The glint in her eyes made Angel nervous as her friend crossed her arms over her chest and sat back in her chair. "The night ain't over yet."

2

BRET SLOUCHED UNHAPPILY in his chair, pretending to enjoy the party and the woman beside him. A guard from another home who'd arrived with her employer to attend the party, Kristine had demanded his attention mere moments after he first entered the house. He'd welcomed the distraction to cool his raging temper. By the time Angel had entered, his blood had stopped throbbing in his ears and his need to lash out at something, anything, diminished with Kristine's quick, adoring smiles.

Kristine gave him another meaningful grin and he stifled a groan as her gaze returned to the dancers. When he'd first taken up with her, he'd been hoping for a distraction from the mess of emotions Angel had provoked in him. Pretty and seemingly sweet, Kristine was perfect for the task. But, despite her evident sexual craving for him, Bret discovered—to his confusion and utter dismay—that he felt disinclined to oblige her.

As he surveyed the room, he found the subject of his desire sitting at her table in deep discussion with the woman he'd been introduced to just before Kristine captured his attention. Bret had to admit Monica Avery was a gorgeous woman.

Though he'd only first meet her tonight, Bret had heard rumors around the dining hall about her connection to Jake, and Jake had mentioned her once or twice in conversation, but Jake had also been overly secretive of his relationship with her. Bret had wondered if Angel made theirs a triangle affair, and the thought burned. Still, if nothing else, it had been obvious, to Bret at least, that there was something between Jake and Monica. In that red dress and high heels, he could see why Jake would be tempted, but Bret's eyes didn't linger long on the fair-haired beauty. His interest lay in her ebony-haired conversation partner.

Angel didn't appear pleased with whatever they were discussing. Seeing that he wasn't the only one who made her lovely features scrunch-up with irritation made him feel marginally better. Still, he frowned, wondering what caused her reaction.

The guilty knot of tension in his belly twisted again and he shifted in an attempt to ease the discomfort. His behavior toward Angel in the barn had been reprehensible. He hadn't wanted to hurt her, only to scare her into thinking twice before revealing what she knew about the rebels. Thinking back on the encounter, he didn't understand why her comment infuriated him as much as it had. Now, it seemed her implied threat had only been meant as a warning.

Her profession of hate after his disgraceful conduct had also rankled and, unsurprisingly, when he'd turned his back to walk away, a bitter war had erupted inside him.

She just saved your life, the traitorous side of his mind had railed, *and this is how you say thank you?*

She threatened me first, his other side shouted down the turncoat as he stalked out of the barn. Self-preservation had pushed him to get away from her, as far and as quickly as possible. Because if he didn't, he would either strangle her or kiss her again and neither of those were an option.

"Bret?" Kristine's increasingly annoying voice interrupted

his contemplation.

He turned to the woman beside him. "Hmm?"

"Let's dance." She smiled the same suggestive smile she'd been giving him all night.

"We just sat down," he said, rubbing at the burning wound in his thigh. The pain wasn't enough to keep him off his feet, but her constant requests to dance—not to mention her wandering hands—aggravated the discomfort.

"I know," she said with a practiced pout, "but it appears I need to do something to keep your attention."

"What do you mean?" He hadn't meant to let her see his eyes wandering Angel's way.

"It's no good, you know."

He frowned, unsure what she was getting at. "What's no good?"

"Pining after Angel Aldridge."

He chuckled humorlessly. "I am not pining after anyone."

"She doesn't like men," Kristine said with a cattish undertone.

"How do you know that?" He told himself that information was the only reason for his curiosity.

"I've been here several times over the years," Kristine said, staring down at her nails as she ran her thumb over the manicured edges. "Angel's never shown anyone any favoritism. Well," she paused and tilted her head for a moment as if thinking, "except for Jake Nichols. With the amount of attention she pays him, many of us wonder how she and Monica are still friends."

Bret's jaw clenched and he fought the angry rush of heat that suddenly boiled his blood. "And why's that?"

"She and Jake are *very* friendly. We've known for years something was going on between them, but amazingly, Monica still considers her a friend."

"There's nothing going on between them," Bret told her, dismissing the idea even though a part of him seethed at the possibility.

"Have you *seen* the way they act together? The way they *look* at each other... You couldn't have missed her kiss him in front of everyone earlier. There's definitely something going on with those two."

Bret averted his gaze and didn't reply. Kristine might be right. Angel had kissed Jake's cheek after his toast and no matter the situation, Jake always seemed to take Angel's side. Bret had suspected there was something more between them than the simple friendship Jake claimed, but he'd seen little evidence of it before that kiss. Bret tried to tell himself he cared as little about a relationship between Jake and Angel as he had when he first arrived, which is not at all. But deep down he knew he cared more than he should.

She kissed me back, damn it! he thought bitterly. *What was she playing at with that?* A bolt of irritation stiffened his spine and mortification pulsed up his neck. He would not be a pawn in her game. If she wanted to share a lover with her friend, then that was her choice, but Bret would not do the same with Jake.

He quickly suppressed the angry emotions and shifted his gaze back to Kristine, a smile bowing his lips. "I don't care about any of that," he said, ignoring the knot of hurt that tightened around his heart. "You want to dance?"

"Yes," she emphasized the single word as she lifted her chin.

Bret stood and led her onto the dance floor. If he was a little stiff, he told himself it was from the pain in his leg, the long ride, and the fight by the river, not from indignation. He had no reason or right to be angry. Angel could do whatever she liked...and so could he.

As the next song began, he pulled Kristine into his arms, grinned down into her soft brown eyes, and tried to regain the lucky sensation he'd felt when she had first approached him.

"You haven't answered my question about later," she said, grinning at him like a cat after cream.

Bret's lips twitched. He'd been waiting for her inquiry since her low, purposely seductive greeting. Letting the hint of promise touch his eyes, he gave her his most charming smile and saw the glittering spark in her gaze burst into an inferno.

He leaned toward her and whispered, "Why should I go back to your room later?" He felt her shiver as he gazed into her eyes again.

"You'll enjoy it," she promised. "Believe me."

"Tell   me   more."

3

"ANGEL," MONICA SAID exasperated as Angel took a sip of wine, "you have got to get your head and your heart out of the past. Start living for the future and yourself."

Angel frowned at the floor.

Not as confident as she appeared, and terrified Jake's bet would backfire on them, Monica had jumped wholeheartedly into trying to convince Angel of the error of her ways.

"I'm fine, Monica," Angel snapped. "*You've* got to stop worrying about me."

"Somebody needs to do it."

"I don't want to talk about this tonight," Angel retorted as she took another sip from her glass.

"If I'm about to be required to never bring the subject up again," Monica complained, "then I want to talk about it now." This old debate always led in circles. Yet, the reason for Angel's sadness hung in the air between them like a heavy weight crushing them both. *I will find a way to help you,* Monica thought. *I can be just as stubborn as you.*

Angel closed her eyes and sighed. "Well, I don't."

After a couple more attempts to draw her into a conversation, Monica sat back and studied her friend as she slouched in her chair. Angel stared at the people on the dance floor, her eyes drifting over the dancers until her gaze finally locked on one couple. Monica followed the path of Angel's gaze and was both stunned and hopeful at what she discovered.

Bret Masters. His handsome face was even more appealing with the charming smile he bestowed on the woman in his arms. Their bodies were close as he spun Kristine around the dancefloor, and they looked…intimate.

"He *is* unreasonably attractive," Monica mumbled to herself and not for the first time. Then she glanced at her friend. *Could that be what it takes to draw Angel's attention?*

For years, Angel had never looked at men in any way other than friendship and denied herself any form of more intimate affection. Yet, several times in the last few hours, Monica had noticed her friend staring at Bret with naked hunger in her eyes. But unless she let go of the past, she'll never do anything about it.

The time had come to talk about the elephant in the room. Monica always avoided pushing her friend too hard, but it was far beyond time to do so.

"You know," she said, leaning her elbows on the table and glancing over her shoulder at her friend, "Michael wouldn't want this for you."

"Don't bring him into this," Angel said, her eyes snapping with cold blue fire.

"He's the main reason for your actions," Monica replied, undeterred by the fury in her friend's gaze. "And you know I'm right; he wouldn't want this for you, not the life you've been leading, this perennial sadness and self-denial. He loved you, Angel. He'd want you to be happy. Why won't you try?"

Angel gulped her wine then set the empty glass on the table. Crossing her arms, she averted her face, but not before Monica caught the injured look in her friend's eyes. Monica knew this would hurt the both of them, but she must try. For Angel's sake, she must make her see what she was doing to herself.

ANGEL SHOOK HER HEAD at the irony of her friend's comment. Michael had saved her life that day so long ago. She wondered if he still would have done it, knowing that she would be responsible for his death.

"I love you, my sweet Angel," he'd said so many times, and he'd proved it in the way he pulled her close at night to let her know she was safe and not alone. And in how he kissed her forehead every time he comforted her while wiping away her tears. She missed the way his mouth curved up on one side when he teased her or how his eyes would darken to midnight-blue when they made love. He had always look at her with such tenderness and trust. And it was her pride and anger that destroyed him.

Tears of frustration and grief burned her eyes. *Why now? Why couldn't Monica wait? Or, better yet, leave the whole damn thing alone?*

The perennial sadness—as Monica called it—had already begun. It was a living thing, growing inside her, making her weak and irritable. She just wanted to get through this year's bout with as little discomfort and disruption as possible.

Does she really think I want to feel like this?

If there was a way not to suffer this aching loneliness, Angel would've found it by now. But her reasons for happiness were long dead, and she had no intention to repeat that mistake.

And how did either of them know about Bret?

She'd never said a word to anyone about her unexpected interludes with him, nor did she ever divulge how much he confused her. So, how did they know? She was almost certain he hadn't said anything to Jake. For some reason, she couldn't picture him telling Jake, or anyone else either. Bret was arrogant, but she didn't think he would brag about his conquests, which seemed idiotic when she considered the prospect more closely.

Maybe he did say something.

Or maybe she just needed to control herself and stop visually devouring him like the eye-candy he was whenever he was within sight.

That's what did it. Monica saw her ogling him earlier and then roped Jake into helping play matchmaker. *Not going to happen,* she thought with bitter certainty.

Monica touched her arm. "Angel?"

Angel looked down at it, unable to meet her friend's eyes or speak through the thickness in her throat.

"I know you're hurting," Monica said, her voice full of compassion. "I know what you went through. You told me, remember?"

Anger shot through her like a bolt of red lightning. How dare Monica use their friendship, and Angel's trust, against her! "I told you too much." Angel would not meet her friend's gaze

Monica's hand dropped as she sat back and adjusted her seat so she faced her friend. "No, we care about *you* too much. I love you, Angel, so does Jake, and all these other people here too. They all know. They all worry about you."

Angel finally lifted her eyes as shock and fear swirled in her chest.

Monica shook her head at Angel's sudden unease. "Not about Michael or your family, nothing specific. But they know about your sadness; they sense your suffering and they want to help. And that's what I'm trying to do."

"To help?" Angel straightened in her chair as her hands balled into fists in her lap. "You think what you're doing is *helping*?" She tilted her head. "What? Are we at the tough love phase now?"

"Something like that," Monica said and sighed.

Angel slumped back in her seat, hurt and disappointment thickening the knot in her throat.

"Look," Monica said, "all I'm saying is if you put yourself out there again, maybe life wouldn't seem so bleak."

"So," Angel drew out the word, imbuing it with derision, as she reached for her wine glass. Realizing it was empty, her hand dropped to her lap and she turned indignant eyes on her friend. "You still think encouraging me to have sex with some random guy is going to make me forget everything and suddenly bring meaning to my life. Are you crazy?"

"No, that isn't what I'm saying...at least, not all of it."

Angel fisted one hand and thumped it against her thigh in frustration. "Then what do you want from me?"

"I want you to let someone in," Monica said as if the weight of the world weighed on her shoulders. "Give yourself permission to be happy. Find a reason to live other than for this place. You know as well as I do that the rebels are far more active than they used to be and more organized too. Another war is coming; it's only a matter of time.

"This place and the people in it may be gone one day. But all that aside, Jake won't be here much longer and neither of us want you to be alone. This hurts us too, you know."

Monica's last remark struck a chord that tightened around Angel's middle and drew her gaze back to her friend.

"What hurts?" she asked, her brows drawn down in confusion.

"Seeing you suffer like this. We watch you go through this every year and it's not getting better. Jake is worried sick and so am I. I don't want to lose you, Angel. We've been through too much, and you're too important to me to leave it alone anymore."

Tears filled Angel's eyes as she stared back at her friend. She hadn't thought her sadness would affect them so much, but the emotions were all there, easy to read—fear and pain and worry—in Monica's anxious gaze. Her earnest confession had touched Angel in ways that none of her previous arguments had. Angel's heart clenched painfully. She didn't want them to hurt, and she especially didn't want to be the cause.

Maybe Monica is right. Maybe I should let someone in.

She glanced at the dance floor where Bret and Kristine still moved to the music, gazing at each other, and the same surge of anger attacked her. *Not with him,* she thought. *I can't trust him.*

Who then?

Angel peered at Jake, who stood across the room with Theo and Peggy, and Monica's ranch foreman, Shawn Brohm. Shawn was waving his arms animatedly, clearly retelling a humorous tale. They all laughed when he finished, and Angel noted Peggy's smile. When she turned her eyes on Theo, Peggy radiated happiness—hell, the woman practically glowed.

A wave of jealousy washed over Angel, an all-consuming rush that shocked her. She had no interest in Theo and she certainly didn't want to bring a child into this messed-up world. Yet, she deeply envied Peggy. Why?

A sudden wave of shame heated her cheeks and realization struck her.

It's their happiness, she thought. She didn't wish the couple ill. She just didn't believe she'd ever find anything like their joy and, secretly, she craved the deep and easy intimacy they shared.

While Angel watched, a brunette she'd meet during her last trip to Monica's tucked her arm through Shawn's elbow. Just like with the other couple, they too exchanged a blissful smile and Shawn brushed a quick kiss on her lips. Seeing Shawn so content cheered Angel's heart. She'd met him at the same time she met Monica and he'd been a big part of getting Angel's ranch started. As attractive and fun as Shawn was, Angel never felt more than a familial connection with him.

Her gaze drifted to Jake.

She'd heard the rumors about her and Jake Nichols. They were only partially true—she loved Jake, but like a brother. He was handsome and kind and everything she would've wanted in a man. But aside from his relationship with Monica, which she would never mess with, Angel felt nothing more for him but affection and exasperation for the often-overprotective sibling he'd become to her.

Glancing around the dining hall, she noted the numerous unattached, attractive men who lived on her ranch and let her gaze glided over each of them. She cared about them all in one way or another, but none of them interested her in any deeply emotional way.

Her eyes settled on Bret Masters again and a wave of dread rolled through her stomach.

She glanced at Monica, who still watched her intently, and shook her head, shame and sadness making her voice rasp. "I'm sorry. I don't mean to upset you and I don't want you to hurt, but I can't help how I feel."

"I know you don't, and I do understand," Monica said, leaning forward to take both of Angel's hands in her own. "I'm not asking you to forget, I realize that isn't possible. And I'm not suggesting that taking a man to bed will change anything, but if you let yourself open up, the connections you make may help you start to heal." She smiled at Angel and gave her fingers a little squeeze.

Angel returned both gestures, thinking that maybe she would take some of that advice.

4

"Bret, do you have a minute?"

Only slightly annoyed by the interruption, Bret turned from the eager expression on Kristine's face. He leaned back in his chair and looked up at Jake standing behind him, an uneasy smile on his bearded face.

"Hello, Kristine." Jake barely glanced at her.

"Nichols," Kristine replied in an arctic tone that surprised Bret.

He glanced between them, getting the distinct impression that they didn't care for each other, but now wasn't the time for curiosity.

"What do you need, Jake?" he asked, then lowered his voice so Kristine wouldn't overhear. "I'm a little busy at the moment, can it wait?"

Jake shook his head. "It'll only take a minute." He nodded toward the set of French doors behind them and then gave Bret a significant look that screamed, *Alone,* before he headed outside.

Bret sighed and turned to Kristine. "I'll be right back."

"You better be." She smiled up at him, but her tone was acidic as she flashed a narrow-eyed glance at Jake. "Don't let him keep you too long."

Bret got the message loud and clear. She wanted to leave. With him. Soon.

No longer certain he wanted anything more to do with Kristine, he returned her smile with apprehension. She seemed to think she had a right to demand certain physical acts from him, whether he wanted to perform them or not. Her attitude also indicated obligation on his part because of his current station. Her expectation of his compliance irritated Bret, but his body's needs had kept him from walking away.

Bret let his smile fade as he stepped out into the cool August evening. The smell of herbs, vegetables, and flowers struck him as he crossed the threshold onto the narrow deck running along the back of the house. More than a dozen raised gardens split by a long pathway stretched beyond the deck. Even in the dim light from the room behind him, he could see the abundance growing in the rich soil, but he suspected Jake didn't ask him out here to talk about the gardens.

Pushing his black suit jacket behind his hips, Bret slid his hands into his pockets as he faced his friend. "So, what's up?"

Jake stood tall. "I want you to ask Angel to dance."

"What?" Bret laughed, rocking back on his heels. "That's what you wanted to talk to me about? I *have* a date, Jake"

"Yeah…" he grumbled, shuffling his feet, "and you can do better."

Bret frowned. "What do you mean by that?"

Jake glanced over his shoulder into the room, and then turned back to his friend. "Kristine's not what she seems."

Bret raised an eyebrow. "She's pretty. She's nice. She's willing. What else does she need to be?"

"More reasonable for one, less domineering for another."

Bret tilted his head, perplexed. "I don't know what you mean. She's fine."

"Shit, Bret, you can really pick 'em," Jake chided gently and smiled to take away the resentment the old phrase might dredge up.

Bret frowned again but didn't take offense. "I appreciate you're trying to tell me something here, Jake, but could you get to it already?"

"What I said. She's not what she seems."

"Look," Bret pulled his hands from his pockets, annoyed, "I realize you don't like saying anything bad about people, but could you be a little more specific?"

"She's looking for a daddy."

"She's... *What?*"

"She wants a kid, Bret, and..." He glanced into the dining hall once more. "She's not what she seems."

"Ah. I see." That changed things a bit. The knowledge also sent a chill racing down Bret's spine. "Is that all?"

"Isn't that enough?" Jake's eyes widened. "She wants to use you as a breeder and you're okay with it?"

"I didn't say that. Why does it matter to you anyway?"

"I told you before. I don't want you to suffer like I did."

"With Kristine?"

Jake's tone grew more aggressive. "With others like her, only much, much worse."

"You keep saying that. Someday you're going to have to explain it in more detail," Bret said, his brows drawn down.

"Someday, if you need to know, I might." Jake sounded offended and his fists hung tensely at his sides.

Bret sighed and rubbed his hand over the back of his neck. "What are we arguing about here?"

Jake's shoulders drooped, his hands loosened, and he let out the breath he seemed to have been holding. "We're not arguing. I'm trying to tell you that Kristine will expect you to do *exactly* as she wants...whether you want to do it or not. It's the mentality of a lot of women, but not all of them. You can do better."

Bret's head jerked back, a little surprised to hear his own thoughts echoed so clearly in Jake's words. "And you think

Angel is better?" He couldn't keep his cynicism out of the question.

"Considerably better," Jake said and then lifted his hand when Bret opened his mouth to disagree. "I'm not saying you should do more than ask her to dance."

"Why?"

"Have you seen her dancing?"

Bret shrugged. "I haven't paid attention to what she's doing."

"Well, I have, and she hasn't. It's her birthday and she should be having fun, but she's not."

"Then you ask her to dance." Bret started to go back inside, but Jake's reply turned him back.

"I did. She won't dance with me. She's turned down everyone else too."

"And you think she'll say yes to me?" Bret poked two fingers against his chest and then scoffed incredulously, "I think you're wrong there, Jake."

"I've seen you charm a nun out of her rosary and offer you more," Jake said with a silly grin. The remark was an exaggeration and they both knew it, but he was not far off. "If I couldn't get her out of her chair, I *know* you can. If you try."

Bret laughed again, with actual mirth this time. "What's in this for me?"

"I'll owe you one."

Bret folded his arms over his chest. "You already do."

"Another one then."

He narrowed his eyes and tilted his head. "I'm not fond of your favors, Jake."

"Will you do it or not?"

Bret sighed and dropped his arms. Jake wouldn't have asked him if it wasn't important to him, and Bret owed him. A lot. Jake knew that. Bret just wished there was some other way to pay Jake back without having to spend so much time with Angel.

"What're you getting out of it?" Bret inquired suspiciously, remembering Kristine's comments earlier about Jake's relationship with their Mistress.

Jake grinned. "I'll win a bet."

"What?"

"She said you wouldn't do it and then she said you couldn't convince her to dance even if you did ask her."

"Did she?" Bret sensed the challenge Jake had just laid down.

Jake's grin widened. "Yep."

"I'm going to collect on all your favors one day," Bret told him, the corner of his mouth ticking up.

Jake groaned. "I know, just try not to make repaying too painful."

Bret laughed again. "All right, Jake, just give me a few minutes and I'll see what I can do."

5

BRET STEPPED INSIDE the dining hall, leaving the doors open to the cool night air behind him. Kristine smiled as he entered and he sighed. He knew what she expected of him tonight, but he wouldn't do it. The decision had already been made, he just hadn't acknowledged it until now. He'd ignored her less-than-desirable attitude because of his need for some female attention. But after what Jake just told him, and what he'd begun to suspect himself, he'd have nothing more to do with her, despite the needs of his body.

Instead of going back to his seat—delaying the inevitable and wondering how unpleasant Kristine would make his departure—Bret searched the room for Angel. He found her across the open floor, sitting in a chair, showing off her shapely legs through the folds of her diaphanous dress, laughing with Theo and Peggy.

Angel's entrance to the party had affected Bret more than he thought possible. The fact she acted as if she'd forgotten he existed galled him further. From the moment she walked in on Jake's arm, he hadn't been able to take his eyes off her and she never turned his way once. Assailed by the familiar surge of jealousy for Jake's easy association with her, he'd been so focused on his Mistress that Kristine elbowed him in the ribs to get his attention. After that, he did his best to ignore Angel's presence.

He'd been mesmerized again as he stood in the crowd and sang *Happy Birthday*. She'd stood innocently beside the glowing purple cake, her eyes closed, and a bright smile on her face. As the others sang, his mind had been flooded with vivid images of her in his arms, kissing him with a passion that stole his breath. Something about the curve of her face, the arc of her neck, the way her dress conformed to her soft contours brought on the erotic fantasies he'd once thought were under control. And that had triggered his body. He was still struggling with the need she'd awoken in him, one that kept reminding him just how long it had been since he'd been with a woman.

The roaring cheer at the end of the song had brought him back to reality.

Even now, he was transfixed as she bent forward, supplying Bret with an appealing view of her ample bosom. His body tightened uncomfortably and suddenly, all he wanted to do was hold her in his arms. He wanted to crush her softness against him, have her thighs brush his as they moved together, the curve of her hip under his hand, and her small fingers in his palm...

Stop it! He shook his head at his overactive imagination. *It's just a dance. She's not going to invite you into her bed, you randy idiot.*

He forced his eyes away from her and turned to where Kristine sat. The look on her face said she knew what he'd just been doing and didn't like it one bit. He held back a sigh. The thought of turning her down didn't upset him overly much. Kristine was attractive and eager for him, but what she wanted, what she would demand, he was unwilling to provide. Moreover, she expected his obedience. That might not bother other men considering the circumstances, but it bothered him. He wouldn't perform on command like a trained pet or the slave without free will they considered him to be.

Kristine's expression was a study of insatiable desire whenever she looked at him. A torrent of revulsion engulfed him as her greedy gaze swept over his body, making his flesh itch. He shrugged the irritation away. She smirked at him again, a predatory gleam in her eye, and he sighed as he allowed his lips to turn up in a minimal response.

Nope, spending the night with her is not an option.

He approached her chair and widened his smile.

"Something's come up," he said, planning to let her down easy. "I won't be able to join you tonight."

The abrupt change in her eyes from avid greed to indignation caused the hair on the back of his neck to rise.

"The hell you won't," she hissed, and Bret understood precisely what Jake had been trying to tell him. "I've spent a lot of time catering to your ego tonight. You don't have a choice now."

Bret gave her a nasty grin, his silver-green eyes narrowing on her face. *So much for easy,* he thought, irritated and resigned.

He shrugged. "Sorry, but my Mistress is calling." He nodded toward where Angel sat and almost laughed when Kristine's eager expression faded and her shoulders slumped.

Then she straightened and turned burning eyes on him again. "I'll have a word with her. She wouldn't want one of her guests disappointed."

Bret didn't miss the veiled threat and his skin heated in response, both furious and wary. Some of the men had told him what happened in other women's homes when a slave dissatisfied a guest. He didn't believe Angel would have him beaten, but whether she would or not made no difference.

"Honey," Bret drawled as he placed one hand on the table and the other on the back of her chair, hovering over her menacingly, "it doesn't matter if you talk to her or not. I won't be going anywhere with you tonight or any other night."

Her shocked gasp made him smile as he straightened and walked away.

"YOU'VE BEEN HANGING AROUND with Esther too much," Angel laughed after Theo delivered the punchline to another dirty joke. Her eyes drifted across the room, instantly drawn to Bret. He had just reentered through the French doors with Jake. A shock of something warm and tingly fluttered around inside her and the smile froze on her face. She hadn't seen him go out onto the deck, but then she'd tried not to pay attention to his activities tonight. He stood in the entry, his gaze panning the room, and she turned away. She didn't want him to catch her gawking and she didn't want to see him with Kristine. She pushed away both the pleasant tingles and the sudden sharp twinge of jealously that made her frown. She couldn't deny seeing him with the other woman made every part of Angel itch with irritation. It annoyed her. So what if he was a great kisser and that she practically went up in flames when he touched her or that she couldn't get him out of her head. He kept proving she couldn't trust him, and because of that, she refused to acknowledge her body's wants. So, she was doing her best to ignore him.

For some reason, regret tightened her chest and disappointment filled the hollowness inside her. She shouldn't, but she resented his shameless flirting with Kristine, and was angry with herself for hoping to impress him. She could admit—to herself, at least—that's what she'd wanted, to impress him. Judging by how closely he danced with Kristine and all the ear whispering, it had been a waste of time and effort on Angel's part.

Angel's head began to throb and she rubbed her temple. *What's wrong with me?*

Bret didn't owe her anything. She didn't owe him anything either. Not only that, she didn't need the hassle he would bring to her life. Though incredibly attractive, Bret Masters was already more trouble than she'd wanted—in more ways than one. Getting involved with him would make everything in her life worse, and, damn it, she knew better.

Her spine straightened and her hand dropped into her lap. If Bret wanted to spend the night trying to seduce Kristine, it made no difference to her.

Right! The word echoed in the valleys of her mind and made her headache worse.

Shoulders slumping a little, she rubbed at her head again. Angel knew she may not be the strongest woman at times, but, in this, she would be strong. She must. Angel averted her gaze, telling herself she was better off, but the ache inside her didn't cease.

Her eyes searched for a distraction and found Jake. He strolled across the room to whisper something in Monica's ear. Monica's face lit up with a bright smile and she jumped to her feet to kiss him. Angel almost groaned. Her friend's reaction could only mean one thing. She glanced toward the French doors, but Bret no longer stood beside them. Kristine still sat in her chair, but now an irate glare marred her pretty face.

Angel did groan this time. No doubt, she'd be hearing about whatever made Kristine look so angry before the night was over.

Tracking the path of Kristine's gaze—having no doubt about the source of her irritation—Angel discovered Bret making his way around the back of the room. Angel hoped he would leave, but she'd never been that lucky.

She focused on Theo's latest story, intent on ignoring Bret's presence. Perhaps if she tried hard enough, she would forget he was around at all. But she felt his approach, every nerve ending acutely aware of his arrival as Theo's tale ended. She laughed with Peggy, though with her blood suddenly racing and pounding in her ears, she didn't hear the how the story ended. Every fiber of her being was too fixated on the man standing behind her. Butterflies took wing in her stomach and it took all her self-control to keep from turning to look at him.

"Hey, Bret," Theo said with a welcoming grin. "Having a good time?"

"Fantastic," Bret replied, and Angel wondered if anyone else heard the sarcasm in his tone.

"Hi, Bret." Peggy also smiled up at Bret, female appreciation for an attractive man in her expression.

"Peggy, you're looking lovely tonight."

Irritation tingled up Angel's spine. *Does he have to flirt with everyone?*

"Thank you," Peggy smiled as her cheeks reddened. The woman giggled. She giggled!

Angel battled back her groan of annoyed frustration and fought to keep from rolling her eyes. *Was no one immune to his charm?*

She sat up straighter, determination stiffening her spine, and glanced at him over her shoulder with something less than a smile on her lips. "Hello, Bret."

"Angel," he said. "Are you all enjoying the party?"

Theo and Peggy nodded, and then spent several minutes exchanging pleasantries with Bret while Angel sat quietly trying to calm the nervous anticipation fluttering in her belly.

"I wonder if you two would mind giving me a minute alone with Angel?" Bret directed the question at Peggy.

"Sure." Peggy's voice held a little too much enthusiasm. "I've been wanting to dance anyway." She stood up slowly, one hand on her slightly protruding belly. Then she took Theo's hand. "You want to dance with your pregnant woman," she teased her partner. "After all, this," she patted her belly, "is all your fault."

"My fault?" Theo laughed as they wondered off to join the others on the floor and the rest of his reply was lost in the party noise.

Confused about whether to be happy or angry at finding herself alone with the one man she couldn't stop thinking about, Angel swallowed the nervous lump in her throat and pressed her palm over her wildly fluttering stomach. She said nothing as Bret pulled out a chair and turned it to face her before sitting. Clasping his hands and resting his elbows on his knees, he sighed and then met her gaze with a smile that lit his eyes and brought out the dimples in his cheeks.

Nope, not immune to him either, Angel thought hopelessly as the butterflies in her belly multiplied exponentially.

"*Are* you having a good time?" he asked.

"Fantastic," she mimicked his earlier reply, all the way down to imbuing it with a tiny bite of sarcasm.

He laughed and the icy walls she'd erected around her heart began to melt.

"You should be enjoying yourself," he told her. "It's your party."

"I *am* enjoying myself."

"Then why aren't you dancing?"

"I don't feel like it."

"Why?"

She scoffed and, crossing her arms over her chest, she shook her head. She leaned forward as if about to reveal some big secret and said in a low voice, "Because some *jerk* kept me out on a horse all day."

He laughed again, and she stared at the twinkle of humor in his eyes. She couldn't take her eyes off the gorgeous transformation on his face. She'd seen him grin before, had even seen him laugh, but somehow, he looked...different. Better, sexier, more handsome than before.

"I see," he said.

"That's not really the reason," she said with a slight smile, shaking off the surge of attraction that had just washed over her. "I just don't feel like it. I'm enjoying watching everyone else."

"No other reason?" he asked. "You're not hurting or...?"

She frowned for a moment and then shook her head. "No.

I'm a little sore, but none the worse for my..." she glanced around, "*accident*. At least, nothing that would keep me from anything I want to do."

"I'm glad to hear it," he said with a smile as his eyes quickly slid over her, checking her visible wounds. She had an inexplicable desire to hide the more obvious ones from his view. She was fine and she didn't care for his reminder, as subtle as it was, but she didn't comment on his unsolicited concern either.

Still grinning, he looked down at his hands and rubbed them together like a mad scientist hatching an evil plot, but he didn't speak. Instead, he turned to the dance floor to study the other couples enjoying the music.

Dressed in his black suit, Angel was not at all surprised at how his broad shoulders filled out the jacket or how his white shirt almost glowed next to his bronzed skin. A grin tugged at the corners of her mouth when she saw he also wore his shined-up black cowboy boots. She eyed his brushed and styled blue-black hair, his high cheekbones, and strong jawline and felt a small prickle of irritation that there wasn't one thing about him that she didn't find attractive. Every cell in her body had come alive when he approached and continued to spark with his nearness. Her heart beat harder, her breath came a touch too fast, and her skin warmed in some kind of crazy expectation. Of what, she wouldn't speculate.

When he shifted his eyes to hers, the lamplight reflected in their crystalline green depths like moonlight on the northern ocean. Her mouth went dry, her heart jolted in her chest, but she did remember to breathe, one long, deep inhale.

It's not fair, she thought.

The butterflies turned into condors.

She thought she might vomit from the massive case of nerves twisting in her stomach.

"So," he began, "what would it take to get you outta that chair?"

"For a dance?"

"Yes."

She glanced across the room at Jake and Monica and found them watching her exchange with Bret. She suppressed the groan that bubbled to the surface.

So much for being positive about anything concerning this mercurial man.

She considered deliberately starting a fight. He would leave her alone if she annoyed him enough. Provoking him wouldn't be difficult, but she didn't want to cause a scene. She'd also told Jake she would dance if Bret asked her. Doing anything else would make her a liar.

She met his gaze and the flock of condors in her stomach abruptly settled and a cool stream of calm floated through her. Maybe it was the wine she'd been consuming that was eating away her inhibitions, but she wanted to dance with Bret. She wanted to be in his arms again. She didn't *want* to want that, but she did, and no amount of hedging would change how she felt.

What could it hurt? she asked herself, ignoring the warning voice in the back of her mind. *One dance, I can do that.* Then Monica and Jake might leave her alone for a while.

She smiled at Bret and saw something flicker in his eyes. His grin slipped off his lips and his expression became impossible to read. In the next moment, he returned her smile and turned up the wattage on the charm.

"So," he purred, "what do I have to do?"

"Well," she murmured with a sly grin, "you might try asking."

6

JAKE AND MONICA WATCHED with varied expressions as Bret led Angel onto the crowded floor. Monica's face reflected excited anticipation and Jake looked both smug and anxious.

"Told you he would do it." Jake didn't sound too pleased.

"Yes, *you* did, and *I* told you she would dance with him," Monica said merrily.

"Are you sure about this?"

"Positive." She beamed at him and patted his thigh. "Don't worry so much."

"I hope you're right," he said, shaking his head. "Cause, if you're not, the fallout will be terrible...for both of them."

"I'm not wrong about Angel," she replied. "And if Bret is anything like you've described, I'm sure about him too. He's been watching her all night."

"I don't know about that. I didn't notice anything."

Monica chuckled. "Jake, honey, you wouldn't." She touched his shoulder and grinned to take the sting out of her words. "You're a wonderful man, but not very observant when it comes to stuff like this." She gave another little laugh and tucked her arm through his. "You didn't even suspect my interest in *you* until I told you outright."

"That was different." He sounded defensive. "I was afraid of you—of women in general—when I came to you, but I was willing to listen. Bret isn't. And, for the record, I *did know* you were interested, I just didn't know what to expect. If you'd been like Darla..." he gave a humorless laugh, "I considered running for my life or killing myself."

The pain in his voice struck her like a gut punch no matter how many times she heard it, but if she was right, she'd found Angel a replacement for Jake.

"Do you think Bret is any better off than you were?"

"Bret doesn't realize how lucky he is." Jake's dark tone squirmed beneath Monica's skin, making her ache for the pain tangled in his words.

"You haven't told him what you went through?"

"No." The one-word answer spoke volumes.

"Do you think he's any less worried about his well-being than you were?"

"Probably not," Jake said. "He's never been a trusting man, and he's suffered a lot in his life, even before the wars."

"I remember," Monica replied, remembering all he'd told her over the years about Bret. Monica thought it might be time Angel learned the rest of Bret's story. Maybe knowing would help her understand him better. Monica made a mental note to mention that to Jake later.

This party was the first opportunity for Monica to see Bret Masters up close. Earlier, when he'd come through the front door like a thunderstorm, his physical appearance had stunned her. She'd briefly seen him from a distance at the auction and she'd known he was attractive, but he was far better looking than she'd expected. The word gorgeous came to mind, but something had been amiss. The man looked out of sorts and, upon seeing Angel when she first entered the house—right before the "Happy Birthday" shout that shocked her into a smile—Monica knew something had happened between them. At first, assuming they had quarreled, Monica had been concerned for her friend—after all, Bret Masters was a formidable man. Yet now, she thought their disagreement might not have been such a bad thing.

"Just the thought of being a slave used to terrify him," Jake said, interrupting Monica's thoughts. "He never said it out loud, but I knew. Now that he is one..." Jake shook his head. "The reality must be intolerable for him, but he doesn't comprehend what..." His shoulders slumped and he sighed.

Monica nodded, tightening her hold on his arm.

"Are you sure about this?" Jake asked again, his eyes glued to their friends as they swayed in time to the music.

"Yes," she answered, then peered at him with caution in her eyes. "Unless you think he'll hurt her?"

"No, not intentionally," he sighed and shook his head again. "He's the most stubborn man I've ever met. He's angry and mistrustful of women, *way* worse than I was when you met me and, considering what I'd been through, that's saying a lot. Though, after what Amy did to him, what he let her do, I don't blame him. The problem is, he can't separate her from Angel or anyone else. I'm not sure he's ready for this or if I trust him with her. She's fragile, and in his state, he *could* hurt her."

"Jake," Monica said drawing his worried eyes to hers, "you have to stop protecting him. He's not a child. He lived on his own for five years and did fine. And *she* is stronger than you think. She just doesn't realize it yet."

"Yeah, he did fine, all right..." Jake's lips twisted. "He got captured. And Angel's already acting like she's closing up again. I had to send Bret to pry her out of bed this morning." Seeing Monica's startled expression, he explained, "She didn't get up at her normal time, so I had him go talk to her. Distracting her was his job. I was busy." Defensiveness rang in his tone.

"I didn't say anything," Monica said with a little too much innocence.

"Right." Jake smiled. "I know what you were thinking."

"He is *very* good-looking." She grinned at the narrow-eyed expression he slanted her way. "Don't look at me like that. I only meant I wouldn't be surprised if he had women fighting over him everywhere he went. Kristine didn't waste any time grabbing his attention earlier."

"He did. Apparently, he still does," Jake said, nodding toward Kristine. He tilted his head, a wary glimmer in his eyes, and Monica knew his old fear of not being good enough had resurfaced. Bad experiences with past girlfriends meeting his best friend had made Jake understandably leery. "You're not going to be one of them, are you?"

An air of hurt settled over her and she frowned.

"You know better than that," she snapped and then her voice took on a sultry, possessive note. "I'm with you and only you. You'd better believe that and do the same."

He grinned at her gentle threat. After three years of only seeing each other sporadically, she'd wanted him to know how much she still loved him. From his expression, she'd done just that.

"You know it, babe," he murmured, reaching for her hand. He brought her knuckles to his lips and kissed them. The masculine twinkle in his eyes returned her enduring affection and promised intimate proof of his ardent adoration once they were alone.

UNEASY WITH BEING IN BRET'S ARMS again, Angel avoided his gaze. She could feel the intensity of his regard, the blast of heat radiating from his big body, the muscles in his arm and shoulder shifting under her hand as he led her around the floor, the gentle strength in his fingers as he held her much smaller ones, and his thighs brushing hers as they moved. The multitude of sensations almost overpowered her, causing her body to tingle with unwelcome anticipation.

She shouldn't have agreed to this, should never have taken Jake's bet. She should've kept to her earlier convictions about staying away from Bret for everything except the ranch. Now, stuck here in his arms, she felt ridiculously nervous and afraid to meet his gaze. She stared at his shirt buttons instead, or what she could see of them behind his black tie, trying to ignore how much she enjoyed having his arms around her and to be dancing again.

Out of the corner of her eye, she saw several partygoers stare at them. The more she paid attention to this, the more she realized they were the cynosure of all eyes. She almost groaned aloud. After turning down so many offers, her agreeing to dance with Bret had sent a message. But broadcasting her stupid attraction to him was precisely what she didn't want.

Why didn't I think of that?

Catching a glimpse of Kristine glaring at them, Angel grimaced slightly, knowing she would catch an earful from her later too.

Concentrating on the steps, trying not to stumble over them—it had been a long time since she danced like this—she remembered she'd wanted to talk to Bret about their misadventure earlier that afternoon.

"May I ask you a favor?" she blurted out, and realizing how impulsive she must sound, her eyes lifted hesitantly to his face.

"You can ask, but whether I do it or not depends on what the favor is," he said with a genuine smile and the flutter of butterflies in her stomach overwhelmed her again. He really did have an extremely nice smile. Her mouth went dry and she licked her lips.

His eyes dropped to her mouth and a spark of something flickered in the green depths that made her skin tighten and her brain forget everything but how close he held her.

She must've made some kind of noise because his gaze suddenly delved into hers. She tried to swallow, but her throat was so dry.

"You wanted to ask me something?" he said.

"Oh. Yeah…" Her brain stuttered for a moment, unable to

articulate intelligently, but she took a sharp hold on her swirling senses and went on with her request. "Yes, I wanted to ask you not to tell Jake what happened at the river today."

"That isn't a favor," Bret said with a laugh. "That's self-preservation."

"What do you mean?"

"I don't want to tell him any more than you do," he confessed, still smiling. "It would be another one of those things I'd never hear the end of."

"Why do you say that?"

"In case you hadn't noticed," Bret turned her in a circle under his arm, "Jake can be a little overprotective." His smile slipped slightly and a sour expression crossed his face. In a blink, his pleasant expression returned and Angel wondered what had caused that look or if she'd only imagined it. "And," Bret continued, "he's already shown that he'll react that way with you."

"Yes," Angel agreed, "he can, and he does." A moment of silence stretched between them before she probed a little more directly. "So, will our afternoon adventure be our little secret?"

7

HER PERFUME WAS MAKING BRET CRAZY! That lilac scent hovered over her like a fragrant haze, permeating his senses and making his head spin as he led her through the waltz. He fought the sensations being this close to her always kicked up. Still, he wanted her to enjoy being in his arms and he intended to make every effort to accomplish the task.

Her request for his silence about the attack took him a little off guard. Surprise brought Bret's eyes to hers. This was the first time she had asked him for anything for herself, and a part of him wanted to turn her down.

"Yeah," he said slowly, "you have my word." He almost laughed at the look of amazement that painted Angel's face. Keeping his promises was important to him, and she obviously hadn't expected such a strong vow.

She smiled. "Thank you."

Struck dumb by her smile, he stared, unexpectedly all too aware of her small hand on his shoulder, her arm resting against his, and the warmth of her body brushing against his own. Every muscle inside him tensed, and he felt a growing need troubling his lower regions. If the steps of the waltz had not been automatic for him, he would've stumbled. Staring into her eyes, he was plagued by his familiar and intense attraction to her. He wanted to kiss her, badly. His primal instincts screamed for him to claim her lips right there in the middle of the floor.

God, I want her!

"Is something wrong?" she asked as he continued to gape down at her like a lust-stricken teen.

"You look beautiful," he murmured without thinking and his face heated.

What's wrong with me?

She blushed prettily, but nothing else in her demeanor hinted at how she felt or what she thought. The rose color in her cheeks may only be the warmth of the room and their increased activity, or perhaps, some slight embarrassment at being regarded so closely. He couldn't tell.

"Thank you," she said. "You look quite handsome yourself."

"Thank *you*," he replied slowly, surprised by her return compliment. She never hinted whether she found him attractive or not, at least, not aloud. But he'd already known she found him attractive. Hearing her say it outright was more than a little enjoyable.

He smiled and, when she reciprocated, his body tightened. Something in his expression must have alerted her to his sudden arousal because anxiety flickered in her eyes just before she shifted her regard to his shirt again.

Get ahold of yourself, he thought viciously.

Once again, there was nothing to say as he guided her through the steps of the waltz. The smooth, slow music floated around them like dandelion fluff on a summer breeze as they glided across the floor. Bret didn't consider where they were going or who might be watching, and he couldn't keep from remembering how her body felt plastered against his as she had been in the cave last June and in the barn a few weeks ago. So close now, her warmth and his over-awareness of the distance between them heightened his sense of touch. The longing expectation that her soft body would make contact with his was exquisite torture. He tried to stop staring, but his eyes kept drifting back to her face and he struggled to find something to say to distract his errant musings.

"Happy birthday," he said for lack of better conversation.

Her gaze fluttered up to meet his before returning to his shirt buttons. She still appeared nervous. He wondered if he'd caused her reaction. Was her edgy manner because of him, the dancing, or something else entirely?

"It isn't my birthday yet," she said softly and lifted her eyes to his once more. She gave him a small smile. "It's tomorrow. Jake wanted to surprise me."

"Did he? Surprise you, I mean."

"Yes," she said still staring up into his face as she followed his lead. "I wasn't expecting all this." She waved her hand in a circular motion to indicate the festivities before placing it on his shoulder again. "It's been a long time since I've had a party like this. A very long time."

He watched as her eyes turned blank and distant as if she stared right through him. She gradually came back to herself and met his gaze. He smiled at her but said nothing. That vacant look had disturbed him. He'd seen it before, on his mother's face when she was lost in the past.

Fear dropped like a rock into the pit of his stomach. *What was so bad that it still haunted her this much?* he thought, realizing he wanted to help her, wanted her to heal. Then he wondered if he could be the one to help her do that, or whether—just like with his mother—he'd never be enough to pull her heart back into the present.

"I'M SURPRISED YOU ASKED me to dance," she said.

"Why do you say that?"

"You looked pretty cozy with Kristine earlier. I thought you'd spend the rest of the night with her."

"Are you jealous?" His smile was lazy and his tone was teasing as his hand slipped to the small of her back and pulled her a little closer.

"No." She frowned and attempted to put more distance between them, but he wouldn't budge.

The flock of butterflies in her belly returned in spades.

"Then why did you notice?" he prodded with a lopsided smile that made her anxious all over again. Her heart sped up at the multitude of promises that lived in his smile.

Tensing, she straightened her backbone, suddenly annoyed with him and herself. *Does he really think I'm going to fall all over him after he spent the evening letting another woman paw at him? Fat chance!*

She was so furious she forgot to be unnerved by his nearness and the butterflies in her belly, or about the heat coming from his muscular frame and that they were not alone. She wanted to prick his arrogant pride, and she knew the perfect ammunition.

"I didn't think Kristine was your type," she said with forced cheer, remembering it was Kristine's pushy attitude and sense of entitlement that she'd never liked.

"You don't think, huh?" he asked still smiling, completely misreading her body language. "Why's that?"

"Kristine likes to flaunt her new toys," she said deliberately, and triumph rushed through her when the grin dropped from his face, "and knowing how you feel about that... I just assumed."

"What do you mean, 'new toys'?" His voice dropped dangerously, and his eyes turned lightning green as he locked them on her.

"You know exactly what I mean," she said, her bright gaze darkening in turn. Uncertain why she was suddenly so angry with him, she still would not back down.

He lifted his head to survey the room and his body stiffened. She had definitely hit her mark. When his eyes collided with hers once more, they were cold.

"Maybe I should show *you* what it's like," he said with suppressed anger as he pulled her against him. Stunned by the sensation of being flattened against his hard body, she didn't detect their subtle change in direction over the open floor.

"Let go of me, Bret," she said, letting her wrath shimmer in her eyes as she glared up at him.

"Why?" he asked with a ferocious smile that should've frightened her, and would have, if she hadn't been so infuriated. "Don't you like being held by a man? Or do real men frighten you?"

"No," she said a little too loudly, drawing a few stares from those nearby. She glanced at the curious faces and caught a glimpse of Monica pulling Jake back into his chair, her face earnest as she spoke to him quietly. Jake directed his concerned stare at Angel while he listened to Monica, no doubt she was telling him to let Bret and Angel work it out.

Not wanting to upset her friends or let anyone else see how furious she was, Angel adjusted her expression. Plastering a grin on her face, she lowered her volume and lifted her chin. "Let me go, Bret."

"The song isn't over yet." He maneuvered her toward the open doors leading to the deck where he'd spoken with Jake earlier. "Besides," he said, "I think it's time someone showed you what it feels like to be played with."

"I don't care about the song," she hissed, trying to appear calm for the sake of those around them. The last thing she wanted was to make a scene.

"I do," Bret said and laughed at the glare she turned on him as he, apparently ignorant of the curious glances they garnered, practically dragged her across the floor.

Angel tried to devise a way to escape him without creating the spectacle he seemed determined to make. *Why the hell did I agree to dance with him? I should've known this would happen.*

"How do you like being toyed with?" he growled, his deep voice soft and unpleasant.

"Stop it, Bret."

"No." He swung her around, his hold on her increased with the rapid motion. "How do you like being played with, Angel? Is it fun?"

Goosebumps broke out on her bare arms as the temperature around them dropped and the lighting dimmed. She tried to take in her surroundings, but Bret spun her around several more times, the world twirling by so fast she could barely see.

"Please slow down," she breathed a moment later, her heart thumping painfully and a slight pain starting in her injured side.

"No," he said as he stopped abruptly and pulled her body tight against him, his arm an iron band around her waist and her fingers throbbing in his fist. She stared, breathless and transfixed, as his head lowered and he kissed her parted lips. Something hard and thin jabbed into her lower spine as he pushed her back a step and a cool draft washed over her heated flesh.

Are we outside? she thought vaguely as he bent her over his arm and got lost in the sensations he awoke inside her. He dropped her hand to cradle her head, slipping his long fingers into her hair, capturing her, holding her still as he slanted his demanding mouth over hers, his whole body crushing her in the most pleasing way. Her arm hung in midair where he'd left it. Too dazed by his firm lips on hers and his hot, wet tongue as it invaded her unsuspecting mouth, to do anything but respond. She melted against him, all thought lost in the onslaught of his kiss. One minute she was furious, the next, her arms were wrapped around his neck, her fingers tangled in the crisp hair at his nape. She clung to him as if he were the only solid thing in a wildly tilting world, her knees going weak as her body strained against him, offering herself wantonly to his touch.

All at once, he pulled away and stared down at her face,

breathing hard, but still crushing her against him. Angel moaned in complaint when he drew back, and when her eyes fluttered open, she returned his fiery gaze, wishing she'd had enough self-control to remain mute. He held her there in silence, his expression unreadable, and Angel realized this was what she wanted—to have him hold her, and kiss her, and never let her go.

He stared at her. She could feel his heart pounding in time with her own against her breast. His arousal was a thick, red-hot iron rod against her belly as he held her bent back over the deck rail. A thrill struck her as she realized how much she affected him. A breath later, his expression hardened and his eyes turned cold.

"How many men have you used, Angel?" he asked in a harsh, raspy voice.

She stared at him, blinking in confusion, utterly baffled by his fierceness.

"How many men have you seduced with your beautiful body, only to use and show off like a dog on a leash, leading him on and on?"

"No one," she whispered, shaken and sickened by his accusations. "I've never done that, would never do that!"

"Yes, you have," he said with a knowing smile that made her shiver for its nastiness.

She didn't want to ask, but she had to know. "Who?"

"*Me.*"

"What?" Shock made the utterance a wheeze. Then in disbelief, she questioned him further. "When?"

"The cave."

She held in her shocked gasp, but her emotions must've shown on her face because his smile widened. Tears stung the backs of her eyes and the huge lump burned in her throat. *I will not cry!*

Wrestling the hurt he'd caused into submission, she took control of her wayward emotions and fought back. "I did nothing of the sort. You're the one who started that."

"What about the night in the barn when you nearly took my head off with the machete?"

"Again, that was you."

"And by the river today?"

"That was because of the situation," she said with a dismissive shake of her head. "You had nothing to do with it. And *you* kissed *me!*" She pushed his shoulders with little success, unable to draw on adrenalin-induced strength to help escape his hold. "I have never had any intention of sleeping with you." She shoved at him again.

"Then why do you look at me as though you do?"

His reply halted her struggle. When she lifted her head, the look in his eyes pinned her in place.

"Why do you tremble when I touch you or return my kisses so passionately if you don't want me?" he asked. "Why can't you admit it? I can. I *want* you, Angel. I ache from wanting you, but we both know I can't just take you as you implied before, not that I would. Rape isn't my style, but at least I can admit what I want."

Furious heat crept up her neck and flooded her face. He smiled, but she planned to wipe that cocky grin off his arrogant face.

"Maybe so, Bret," she said, barely containing her outrage, "but *you're* not anything *I* want. What *I* want I can never have again because it's gone. Dead. And *you're* not man enough to fill the gap. What you don't seem to understand is," she persisted in the same vicious undertone, "if I'd wanted *you*, I would've had you by now."

She thrust him away with unexpected violence and gazed at him hotly as he returned her stare. Shocked by her fury and her undignified display of it, she glanced around to find they were alone on the deck.

Tears of frustration stung her eyes, but with nothing more to say and a desperate need to get far away from him, Angel turned and hurried past him to the doors at the other end of the deck. Holding back tears, she dashed into the dining hall without another word.

BRET STAYED WHERE HE WAS for some time, leaning his elbows against the railing and trying to cool off.

Angel's words had hurt, but he didn't believe them. He'd known too many women to mistake the spark in her eyes for anything but desire, though the idea that she thought so lowly of him rankled.

He regretted what he'd done, but the dustup was inevitable. He shook his head and shoved his hands into his pockets. Sometimes they were like oil and water, and other times, the attraction was so strong it felt as if nothing would tear them apart. All he had wanted to do was dance with her, to hold her close and see her smile. And what did he do instead? He made her cry.

Again.

Guilt charred his stomach. *When am I going to learn to stay away from her?*

He didn't want to get involved. All he wanted was some physical release, some passionate human contact. *Yeah, good luck with that.*

He wouldn't find any satisfaction tonight. No way would he go back to Kristine, and Jake would be after his hide if he saw Angel crying. His safest option was to remain outside, take a walk, and think. He needed to make his regular check of the grounds anyway, to make sure there were no other uninvited visitors. Bret still didn't know who the person was he had chased through the late-night shadows two months ago, and he hadn't found any hint of their return either. Maybe he'd scared them off, but then, maybe they were just biding their time. Either way, his nightly inspections were intended to make sure they didn't catch him off guard or harm anyone or anything inside the homestead walls.

The cool night breeze brushed his face, and he sighed as he pushed away from the railing and went to the stairs. With long strides, he stepped off the deck and headed through the garden, his mind still on Angel and the jumble of emotions burning through him as he disappeared into the darkness.

8

JAKE SAT CHATTING WITH DEAN, Michelle, Theo, and Peggy when he spotted Angel hurrying down the hall to the other side of the house. She seemed distraught as she rushed out and that sense of dread he'd felt as he watched Bret lead her onto the deck had returned. Worried about what may have happened, Jake excused himself from the conversation and followed Angel.

He found her sitting on the sofa in the living room in front of the enormous picture window overlooking the dooryard. Stars twinkled in the velvety night sky and the moon gave the white buildings a haunted glow, casting shadows around the structures, distorting their features. In front of the beautiful yet eerie scene, Angel perched on the edge of the elegant, cream-colored sofa, her face in her hands, and her forearms resting on her knees. She made no sound to indicate she was crying, but he knew she was troubled. He went over to her and put a consoling hand on her shoulder.

She shrugged him off. "Please don't, Jake. I'm all right."

"Are you sure? You don't look all right."

"Yes," she replied and ruined her aplomb with a sniff, brushing her face as she sat up, though she still didn't meet his gaze. Jake took a seat on the hand carved coffee table facing her.

Clasping his hands and bracing his forearms on his legs, he peered into her face. "What happened?"

"Nothing important," she told him with a harsh laugh. "A little truth, that's all."

Sensing she needed to say more, he sat and waited for her to speak.

"You and Monica are lucky," she mumbled.

"How so?"

"You found each other in this disaster of a society."

"I can't argue with you there."

"I miss it."

"Miss what?"

"The way things used to be," she muttered, still not looking at him, "not so screwed up like they are now. I miss being loved by someone I care about." She lifted her head and her eyes were as big and blue as a clear summer sky, yet filled with sadness. "Do you understand?"

"Yeah, I do."

"You know I love you, Jake," she reached out to rest her hand over his clasped ones, "but it isn't the same."

"I know," he said, taking her hand in both of his, "but I don't understand. What brought this on? Was it memories or did Bret do something to upset you?"

She lifted questioning eyes to his.

"I saw him waltz you out onto the deck," Jake explained. "Neither of you looked very happy."

She smiled at him and nodded. "A little of both, I guess." She stared at their joined hands. "Bret is mercilessly blunt sometimes...cruel even."

Jake's body tensed, afraid of her response when he asked, "Did he harm you?"

She smiled at him again. "No, it wasn't Bret's fault. This time it was my own doing. It's just that... I guess I keep hoping there's more to him than what he shows, but he seems to go out of his way to disappoint me."

"There *is* more to him. He's just become an expert at hiding who he really is."

"Why would he want to do that?"

"His life's been...hard," Jake told her slowly, remembering Monica suggesting a short while ago that he should tell Angel more about Bret. He hadn't agreed at the time, but now he thought she'd been right. He sighed. "After Bret's father died, his uncle did a real number on him."

"He didn't tell me much about his uncle," Angel said softly. "Only that they didn't get along, but I got the impression that their relationship was a lot worse than an inability to communicate."

"Yeah," Jake said, his mind drifting into the past, "much worse. Vince tormented him daily. He used to beat Bret bloody for no other reason than he could. Bret was only a kid when they first moved in with Vince, barely twelve years old; he had no chance against a full-grown man, and Vince liked to make sure Bret knew he was powerless."

"Why?"

"Well, Bret thinks it's because Vince hated his brother...half-brother, Anthony."

"Anthony was Bret's father?"

"Yes."

"And what do you think?"

"I think he's right. Some of the things Vince said to him hinted at a rift between Bret's father and Vince, but..." He paused as if considering something and then the direction of his comment diverted. "Vince would use any excuse to hurt Bret, to let him know how truly defenseless and despised he really was."

"AND NO ONE NOTICED?" Angel asked, surprised that not one person ever tried to help the boy Bret had been—a teacher, a counselor, his mother, *someone.*

"There were people who questioned what happened to him," Jake said, "but Bret wouldn't tell them the truth. He'd say he had gotten into a fight or an accident. When he actually got into public brawls with other boys, people stopped asking and presumed he was a troublemaker. And he did nothing to discourage their assumptions. Personally, I think he was too proud and that he feared he and his mother would have nowhere else to go if anything happened to Vince. He was protecting his mom the best way he knew how, but I didn't figure most of this out until later."

"When you two became friends?"

"We didn't become friends until almost a year later, but I still saw the marks Vince left on him," Jake said. "Like everyone else, I thought Bret liked to fight—he certainly had the attitude for it. I was an angry young man myself when he came along."

"Angry?" Angel asked, unable to picture Jake in that light.

"Yeah. You remember that I told you my mom passed away when I was young?"

Angel nodded.

"Well, I met Bret shortly after and I didn't have the patience for a smart-ass little kid. I thought I was tough and had a moral reason to be pissed at the world. When Bret showed up with his cocky attitude and a huge chip on his shoulder, I disliked him instantly, and the feeling was mutual. We used to kick it up before we both got thrown into kiddie jail." Jake stopped to peer over at her. "Inside is where we became friends. I learned about Vince's physical abuse soon after... About all the rest too."

"The rest?"

Jake shifted as if uncomfortable with the topic. "Vince told him things. Lies to make Bret doubt his identity and self-worth. Things that made him mistrust his mother. He'd been working on Bret for over a year before I met the old bastard. *That's* where Bret's hard side comes from, but underneath his rough exterior, he's hurting and doesn't want anyone to know."

"Why? He hasn't done anything wrong. Why would he need to hide?"

"Because he thinks if someone discovered his secrets, they would use them against him. He keeps everyone at arm's length to protect what he keeps hidden. I don't think he could take being hurt like that again. Not after Amy."

"She's the one who betrayed him, right?" Angel asked, remembering bits and pieces she'd heard from both men. "The one who captured you?"

"Yes," Jake said. "I think Bret loved her, at least, as much as he was able to. He let her in and she destroyed him. That's another reason he is the way he is. I'm not trying to defend what he does. I just want you to understand him. He's a good man, he has a good heart, but he suppresses his natural tendencies and his gentler side because of his past."

Angel nodded, understanding why Bret reacted so brutishly sometimes. It broke her heart to envision him as a little boy— beaten for no reason, his safety and security gone, with nowhere to go, and no one he could rely on. There wasn't a single person he trusted to comfort him or to tell him he had value. Tears burned in her eyes as she realized Bret had spent most of his life protecting himself, which made making friends difficult. He'd had no one *but* himself and he had been so young. Then to be betrayed by a woman he risked his heart to trust and care for… No wonder he was so angry!

"That's too bad," Angel murmured through the lump of pity clogging her throat. "I know what that kind of isolation and hurt can be like. It's devastating."

"Yeah," Jake agreed. "He has a habit of taking his issues out on the people around him, even if it's undeserved."

"I'm okay, Jake," she told him, understanding his meaning. She squeezed his hands reassuringly before she pulled out of his grasp and smiled at him. "It isn't Bret's fault I can't leave the past behind. I'm just as guilty of carrying a chip on my shoulder as he may be."

"But you don't try to hurt people because of it," Jake countered. "Bret does. He tries to push everyone away, including me."

"I'm sure I've done the same at one time or another, Jake," she said with a sad grin, thinking of Monica and her own desire to keep her past and her heart secreted away. She stood. "Try not to be too hard on him. I think you're more important to him than you realize."

Jake got to his feet and reached out to embrace her in a brotherly hug.

"You're too nice sometimes, Angel," he told her as she hugged him back. "You don't have to put up with his crap. I've known him a long time and I love him, but I love you too and I don't want you hurt either."

Blinking back unshed tears, she pulled back and gazed up into his handsome face. Playing the little sister he thought of her as, she smirked, reached up, and tugged on his goatee. Her smile widened at the stern expression he gave her, trying not to grin in return.

"I know you want to protect me, Jake—protect the both of us—but you can't do it all the time."

"You sound like Monica," he grumbled, dropping his arms and stepping away.

"You should listen to her," Angel said, tucking her hand through his elbow. "Let's go back." She tugged at his arm. "I think I'd like that dance with you now."

He grinned and tapped her hand on his forearm as he led her down the hall to rejoin the party.

* * *

Bret leaned against the bunkhouse wall in the shadows of the overhang, watching Angel and Jake through the huge front window of the main house. They were sitting in the warm light of an oil lamp, talking. A worried frown crinkled Jake's brow, but Bret couldn't see Angel's face. By the thunderhead blanketing Jake's expression, he could easily guess the topic of their conversation. Bret groaned, wondering if Angel shed any tears while she related the hurtful things he'd said to her on the deck.

"The cave," he heard himself say as his mind replayed their last conversation. His accusation was a low blow and even as he said the words, she had stiffened in his arms. He'd wanted to upset her, to make her experience the shame and humiliation of being toyed with and discarded. But instead of fighting and trying to escape when he'd kissed her, she'd melted in his arms like butter left too long in the sun.

Stunned by her response, he'd pulled back and stared into her eyes, doubting himself and his interpretation of her words. For a moment, he thought she might pull him back down for another kiss. Then suspicion and anger set in once more and he accused her of leading him on.

He groaned again and scuffed his boot against the deck's wooden planks. He shouldn't have gotten so angry, shouldn't have pushed her to the point of tears. He didn't mean to make her cry, but she'd gotten under his skin and burned like an itch he couldn't scratch.

Bret stared through the main house's front window at the two people sitting together, stupidly wishing he had acted differently. He wanted to be the one at Angel's side, not standing outside observing her with another man while loneliness tore at him.

All at once, Jake stood and pulled Angel into a long, intimate-looking hug. Every muscle in Bret's body tightened. His hands clenched into fists and jerked out of his pockets to hang at his sides as he pushed away from the wall. Every instinct in him was ready to do battle, but he suppressed the urge to rush inside and smash his best friend's face in.

Bret forced himself to take a long, deep breath and then

another as Jake and Angel left the room arm in arm. This was a new experience for him, this all-out, fierce possessiveness. Angel didn't belong to him. He had no reason to feel threatened. He didn't have cause to be jealous of anyone, least of all Jake. Over all the years they'd been friends, not once did they fight over a woman, and Bret never envied Jake's successes with them. But now, it seemed to happen on a regular basis and Bret didn't like the feeling one bit.

Angel may find him attractive, but she didn't want him. Definitely not in the same sense or with the same intensity that he wanted her. Maybe this internal turmoil would pass if he could just get laid, then he could get back to his normal self.

He just had one problem. He didn't want anyone but Angel.

His mind turned to Kristine, but he dismissed the thought immediately. He had already burned that bridge and he would not go back.

It wouldn't be enough, anyway...

He stuffed his fists into the pockets of his slacks as he realized something more. He owed Angel an apology. The way he'd confronted her earlier, saying cruel things to hurt her, wasn't entirely her fault. He was only supposed to dance with her, make her smile, and enjoy her party. Dancing with her was all he had wanted to do, but that had gone all wrong—no thanks to him. He needed to make up for his rude behavior and he thought, maybe, he could. Stepping away from the bunkhouse wall, he strolled toward the rear garden, heading back to the party.

9

BRET TOOK HIS TIME getting around the house, head down, hands jammed in his pants pockets, his brain turning over his interactions with Angel. As he neared the back deck, raised voices cut through the darkness. Lost in thought, they hadn't registered until he was almost on top of them, but a hint of hostility finally alerted him to possible danger. Upon hearing Kristine's voice, the potential threat became a certainty. He stopped in the shadows and peered at the two people facing each other on the back deck.

"What do you mean, it's his choice?" Kristine demanded.

"Exactly what I said." Bret recognized Angel's voice and her annoyance was plain in the stress she placed on each word. "If he wants to spend the night with you, the choice is entirely up to him."

"You don't have a problem disappointing your guests?"

The hair on the back of Bret's neck stood on end. They had to be talking about him and his breeding services.

"Things don't work that way here, Kristine," Angel's reply came out like a tired sigh. "You should know that. Monica doesn't work that way either. Besides, you were not invited as a guest. You're an escort for my guest, which does not give you privileges, even if there were any."

"Why did you call him away?"

"What?" Angle sounded confused by Kristine's sudden change of direction.

"Why did you send for him when you did? If you had no intention of sharing him, then why did you let me waste so much time seducing him?"

Angel's expression—which Bret could only just make out—should've sent Kristine running, but she stood her ground.

"I do not *share* my breeders, Kristine." Her tone, dry and dangerous, lightened slightly with her next comment. "As I keep telling you, if they wish to spend time with someone, they have the right to make that decision themselves."

"And he planned to stay with me tonight," Kristine's heated reply matched the belligerent glare in her eyes, "until *you* called him away for a dance. Then he was no longer interested."

"I did not call him for anything."

"He *told* me you did. Right before he danced with you!"

"Then he... He was mistaken."

Bret noticed Angel's hesitation. At least she hadn't claimed he'd lied. *Is punishment required when a slave lies to a woman?* The thought tightened his shoulders.

"So, I have leave to take him?"

A surge of dread hit Bret and a chill snaked up his spine. *What does she mean, 'take him'?*

"If he wants you to."

"So, if he says no, you'll let him get away with it?" Kristine was apparently appalled by the idea. "What's the point of having breeders if you don't use them?"

"Let me be clear, Kristine." Angel enunciated her words with slow, forceful, distinction. "It is *his choice!*" She gained speed as she continued, "If you do anything to him he does not want you to do and I learn of it, whether he tells me himself or not, I will punish *you*, not him."

"You would do that?" Kristine sounded scandalized. "Take a man's word over mine?"

"Yes, I would, because I trust my people. And because, as I've told you several times, it's his choice!" Angel stepped past Kristine, intending to go back inside, but Kristine's next words stopped her cold.

"Are you jealous?"

Angel turned to confront the other woman. The moonlight and dim lanterns illuminating the deck made her face clearly visible to Bret.

"Of what precisely?" she asked in a disturbingly cool voice.

"Of me with him. Other than owning him, do you have another claim on him? Is that why you're so unwilling to let him go?"

Angel's expression hardened and the hair on the back of Bret's neck stood on end again. She looked dangerously cold and ready to rend Kristine limb from limb.

"Is that what it's going to take with you?" Angel's voice dropped and turned ice-cold as she slowly advanced on Kristine's position.

Realizing she had pushed too far, Kristine retreated, one step at a time before the maelstrom of Angel's sudden fury.

"Fine, if that's what it takes..." Angel went on in that same freezing tone and her eyes blazed as she continued her verbal assault. "Yes! *He is mine*! No! You cannot have him! Not now. Not later. Not *ever*! If you lay one hand on him, if you go near him again, I will personally drag you off my property and take my restitution from your hide. Do you understand me?"

Kristine, having been backed up against the deck railing, nodded.

Angel never touched her.

"Great, now let me make my meaning *crystal* clear so there is no room for interpretation. *Stay away* from Bret Masters. This is the only warning I will give. Do you understand?" Kristine nodded again, but Angel shouted at her to speak up.

"Ye-Yes, I understand," Kristine stammered. "I won't go near him again."

"See that you don't." Angel spun on her heel and went inside, her back ramrod straight and her head high.

Kristine stood on the deck, visibly shaken. She paced for a minute before she realized someone was approaching and then turned to gape at the newcomer. Bret almost laughed at the startled terror in her wide, brown eyes when she recognized him. She squeaked, spun on her heel, and ran inside.

Well, at least I won't have to worry about her anymore, he thought with a short chuckle as he ascended the back porch steps, but other questions plagued his mind.

Did Angel mean what she said? Or was it a consequence of Kristine's badgering? How *did* he feel about Angel claiming him as hers? A part of him bristled to be labeled as chattel, but another jolted with excitement at the prospect of what her words promised. Then he remembered the ruthless glare she turned on Kristine. He had seen Angel hurt, mad, sad, smiling, joking, and terrified, but never anything as ferocious as the harshness she'd unleashed on Kristine. A chill swept down his spine at her ability to change so rapidly and so completely.

Was this what Esther had meant when she said Angel had a temper?

Angel had been furious with him on several occasions, but this was different. If she reacted to another woman so harshly, what did that mean for him or any of them?

Why did he even consider trusting her? He knew better. Guilt still pricked him for the hurtful things he'd said, but his self-protective shell had slid back into place and he'd gained some perspective. *Yes, I want her—who wouldn't, she's so damn cute—but she doesn't want me.*

He shook his head. It didn't matter. He wasn't about to fall under her spell, not now or ever.

But you already have...

He hung his head, knowing that little voice was partially

correct. He also knew couldn't trust her, but like the shock of a cold shower, Bret suddenly realize he wanted to. When he held her and she returned his kisses—when the world and its pain receded and reality narrowed down to just the two of them—he desperately wanted to believe she was everything she seemed. But there were too many questions, too much she was hiding, too many similarities to others who'd broken his heart before.

Maybe they could find a way not to always be at odds with each other.

Yeah, right, if I stopped panting after her like a horny teenager, you mean? he asked that hopeful side of himself as he crossed to the French doors. He stood in the doorway regarding the guests. His eyes landed on Angel dancing with Jake, smiling and chatting as they moved across the floor. Bret sucked in air through his nose and frowned, annoyed to see them together. Still, he forced his balled-up fists to relax and reminded himself that she was not his, but it did little good. Dragging his gaze from the couple, he surveyed the rest of the room, vainly attempting to ignore the tumult inside him.

He wondered what had happened to the woman Jake was supposedly involved with—the lovely blonde Bret first met in the foyer after he and Angel had returned.

So, this was the woman that had Jake wanting to live as a slave, he'd thought when Jake had introduced Monica Avery. Bret's curiosity about her now, and the answers she might afford—like was she the only woman in Jake's life? And if so, who still had Angel's heart?—spurred him to search her out. He located her at the table where she, Angel, and Jake had eaten dinner, and found that she was watching him. She gave him a soft smile and her head tilted as she continued to gaze his way as if assessing him.

Is she checking me out, or is she curious too?

All the talk around the ranch said Monica and Angel were close. Maybe she could give him some insight into the woman he found so confusing.

"May I join you?" he requested politely once he'd reached Monica's chair.

"Of course you may, Bret." Her voice was low and melodic, pleasantly feminine, and her hazel eyes twinkled. Unsure what the merry glimmer meant, Bret pondered whether he might be making a mistake, but he sat beside her anyway. He loosened his tie and released the topmost button of his shirt. Then he leaned forward, rested his elbows on his spread knees, and clasped his hands between them, unsure what to say next.

"Are you enjoying the party?" Monica asked when he sat mutely staring at the floor.

"Yes, I am," he replied, meeting her twinkling scrutiny once more. "Angel seemed pleased."

"Yes, she did." Monica seemed pleased herself.

"She said she was surprised. While we were dancing, she told me." He averted his gaze, inwardly rolling his eyes at his awkward small talk.

Monica smiled. "Hmm… Good to know. Thank you for that, by the way."

He frowned, confused, and turned back to her. "For what?"

"For getting her to dance. Jake said you could persuade her to do it."

"Did he?"

"Yes. He also said you were very good at it."

"At what?" He was having trouble concentrating. His eyes kept drifting to the crowded floor. Another song had started, and Jake still held Angel as they picked up the new rhythm.

Monica chuckled. "Dancing."

"Oh, yeah?" he responded, dragging his attention back to the blonde next to him. "Well, I can't take all the credit. I had lessons when I was young."

"Really?" Amazement colored her face. "Angel did too, but she rarely dances anymore. I think it brings back bad memories."

"How so?"

"I believe her father was a dancer when he was young, but he died long ago."

"I see." That explained the obvious talent he recognized in Angel's abilities, rusty though they were.

"So, who encouraged you?" Monica asked. "To learn to dance when you were young, I mean."

He glanced at her and the hesitation that always came when talking about Ruby tightened his chest. After studying Monica's politely curious expression, he sighed and shrugged. "My mother, and my dad backed her up. So, I learned to dance." He didn't mention that it had been a great way to meet girls and had caused him more than a little trouble with jealous boyfriends in high school.

"Well, you're still very talented," Monica said, and he peered at her suspiciously. She laughed at the question on his face. "I saw you dancing with Angel. Don't read so much into it."

Bret fell silent, digesting her words while they watched the couples on the floor. He got the feeling this woman was friendly but too forthright to be subtle. She didn't give the impression of trying to impress him, though she possessed the physical assets to try. She lounged back in her chair, hands on her crossed knees as she watched the crowd of dancers, and occasionally smiled at him, wholly at ease. He found her complete lack of interest in flirting with him refreshing, and he thought he might like her.

"Have you known Angel long?" he asked.

"Yes, I have. We met just before she bought this ranch, in fact, almost," Monica paused, calculating in her head, "seven years ago. She helped me get my place started too."

"Has she always been so…" He paused, unsure how to ask what he wanted to know and not really certain what that was either. The muddle in his mind must've shown on his face, because Monica giggled.

"Confusing?" she asked. "Difficult, distant, secretive,

frustrating?"

He smiled sheepishly.

"Angel is all of those things," she told him, "and so much more. Kind of like you."

His mistrustful glance made her scoff. "Don't be so suspicious. Jake talked about you a lot after I got to know him. I almost feel like I know you too."

"What exactly did he say?" Jake was privy to most of Bret's secrets and if he'd shared them with this woman, Angel might know them too. An icy prickly tickled his spine at the thought.

"He said you don't trust easily," Monica said, "and you especially don't trust women."

"Can you blame me?" he asked a little defensively. She was definitely direct. "Look at what you all have done to us."

She tilted her head. "Is your current situation so unbearable?"

He frowned. "Would you like to be bought and sold like an animal? Be at the mercy of another person's whims? Be beaten or starved or worse?"

"No, but has any of that happened to you here?"

He sat back in the chair, crossed his arms over his chest, and didn't reply.

She smiled. "I'm glad you didn't try to convince me it had. I would've had to call you a liar. Don't be angry," she said when his eyes narrowed again. "I don't mean any disrespect. I'm only saying that living with Angel is far better than your alternative would've been. I was at the auction. I know who wanted you."

Bret looked away. He knew who wanted him too.

"I heard what she did to you after the auction," Monica murmured, referring to Darla Cain. "I'm sorry."

He glanced at her. "Thanks."

"Angel felt bad about it too."

"Why? She didn't do it."

"She felt responsible. Angel and Darla are not friends. They barely tolerate each other. Angel made her look bad in front of a large audience and stole her prize. Darla took out her frustration on you."

An uncomplicated explanation, but Bret wasn't sure he believed it.

She must've read his thoughts on his face again. "You don't know Angel very well, do you?"

He shook his head.

"I would've thought after eight months you'd have learned a little bit, at least."

He stared at her mutely.

"If you'd tried," she continued, "you would've learned that Angel has a big heart." When he still did not respond, Monica continued, sounding almost as if she were scolding a wayward child. "She started this place to help people, to give them, to give *you,* some semblance of a normal life. She encouraged others to follow her lead and, thanks to her efforts, there are several sanctuaries like this one scattered among the torture chambers of others. Many of us would've lacked the courage to stand up to them. If not for Angel's daring, things would be a lot worse around here."

"Sanctuaries?" Derision coated his words. "You call prison a sanctuary?"

"It's an exceptionally unrestricted and comfortable prison. Tell me, Bret, do you enjoy what you do here, riding and working the land? Even just a little?"

"Yeah, I suppose so, but that doesn't mean I'm free."

"No, but you're not abused either. There are other places you wouldn't be allowed outside a cell for weeks just for asking a simple question. Compared to that or to wandering around the wilds cold, hungry, and afraid all the time, this is paradise."

Bret chuckled. "I guess putting it that way does make this place sound pretty good."

"I'm not trying to be right." Monica leaned toward him, her

eyes earnest as she gazed into his. "I'm asking you to give this place a chance. Jake and Angel both care about what happens to you. Maybe for different reasons, but they do just the same, and I care about them. I know you can be stubborn…"

His eyes narrowed again.

"Don't glare at me, Bret," she scolded. "You know it's true. You can also be rash. I don't blame you for wanting to be free, but you should appreciate, better than most, how hard life is on your own in the wild. Isn't having a little security for once worthwhile? Can you at least try to make life here work? Not only for you, but for Jake too?"

He didn't answer. A few minutes passed in silence while Bret watched Angel and considered her friend's words.

"She's fond of *you* too."

Monica's statement surprised him, not only for its suddenness but also for its meaning. He frowned.

"Angel does care about you," Monica said. "It's not in her *not* to care."

He nodded, speculating the hazards of this woman guessing the strength of his attraction to Angel. "Are you fishing?" he asked, peeking over at her.

"Maybe a little." She gave him a small smile. "Look, Bret, fundamentally, I think you're a decent guy, but you have issues…"

He chuckled. "Well, thanks…I guess."

"You know what I mean. I like you, at least the you I know through Jake, and I think we could be friends. At least, I hope so, if you'll let us."

"What kind of friends are you thinking?" Wary about her meaning, he glared a challenge at her.

She rolled her eyes and sighed. "My God, you're suspicious," she said and sighed. "*Friends*. As in, we keep each other's secrets. Just friends."

He looked away and watched the dancers again, his arms still crossed over his chest. "And what kind of secrets do you want me to keep?"

"Well, like the fact that I'm in love with your best friend."

Bret's eyes swung to meet hers, shocked by her frankness. He recognized the olive branch she'd offered but didn't understand why she extended it.

"What?" Mock surprise painted her face when she caught his startled expression. "You didn't know?"

"I've heard things," he said as he turned his attention back to the couples on the floor, purposely avoiding Angel and Jake.

"Hopefully, you heard them here...?"

Her query drew another silent questioning glance from Bret.

"Having our relationship become common knowledge outside these walls or mine would be dangerous for Jake and devastating for me."

"Why?"

"Hasn't Jake told you anything?"

"Yeah, he's told me a little, but why don't you enlighten me?"

Her gaze turned serious. "Angel and I... We've made some powerful enemies defying the others with our practices. They would like nothing better than to discover a weakness they could exploit. Jake would be my weakness."

Again, she surprised him with her honesty.

He stared across the room, more questions dancing through his mind. "I see."

"Bret?" The way she said his name required him to meet her gaze. "What we've built isn't as strong as it appears. There are still laws we must be wary of and people, other women, we must fear. None of us are as safe as we'd like to pretend."

Her words troubled him. Like most other slaves, he knew almost nothing about their legal structure, but what she said didn't make sense. They all owned slaves, what did it matter if one Mistress' actions differed from another? As far as he was concerned, they were all guilty.

Getting back to her earlier comments, he asked, "What do

you expect from me?"

"Not a thing," she said. "Just remember, if you need something, you can trust me."

He snorted. "You'll forgive me if I don't rush into putting your offer to the test."

"No need," Monica said, taking a sip of her wine, clearly unruffled by his cynicism, "as long as you remember the door is always open."

The song ended and Jake ushered Angel back toward their table. She was smiling at him as they walked, but when she glanced at the table where Bret sat with Monica, Angel stopped in her tracks and her smile vanished. She said something to Jake and then rushed away, blending into the crowd of dancers as they started up again, apparently heading for the kitchen. Bret refocused his attention on Jake and suddenly wished he could escape as well.

Jake's hazel eyes were blazing.

This'll be unpleasant.

Monica glanced between the two men and, noticing the tension gathering between them, excused herself to go find Angel.

Jake took her chair, still glaring at Bret.

"Out with it, Jake," Bret said as soon as his friend sat down, wanting this over with as quickly as possible. "I can see you're upset about something. What did I do now?"

"What *did* you do?"

"You're going to have to be more specific."

Jake growled at Bret's sarcasm. "You do realize the whole purpose of getting her to dance was to make her happy, right? Not make her cry?" Jake barked, still glowering at his friend. "What did you say to her?"

"Basically, I told her she's a tease," Bret said, avoiding his friend's scrutiny.

"What!" Jake shouted, nearly jumping out of his chair. Taking several deep breaths, he regained control and when he spoke again, his volume was closer to normal. "How could you say something like that? She's not—"

"Look, Jake," Bret interrupted, "there are things you may not understand about your precious Angel." Jake's eyes narrowed, but Bret didn't let his friend's anger sway him. "Then again, you may just want to keep them to yourself."

Jake shook his head, but Bret held up his hand to stop Jake from interjecting.

"Either way," Bret said, "I don't want to talk about it. I say what I think and that's what I did."

"Too bad you didn't shut up long enough to get her opinion of you," Jake said, getting to his feet. "And out of respect for our friendship, I won't give you mine right now." He started to move away, but Bret's next question stopped him.

"What do you mean, 'her opinion'?" He deliberately didn't ask for Jake's.

"You think she hates you, don't you?"

"I know she does. She told me so."

"After you said or did something to hurt her." Jake tilted his head, his eyes narrowing. "What happened this afternoon?"

Bret didn't respond.

"Something happened." Jake's voice implied he knew more than he should. "Your knuckles are scraped up. They weren't like that this morning."

Bret clenched his hands, noticing a small cut on one knuckle where Angel's attacker's tooth had caught him and other reddish abrasions. He relaxed his hands and moved them out of sight. He glanced at his friend and shook his head.

"Nothing happened," he lied, calling Jake's bluff. "I knocked my hand against a rock. She had an accident and fell into the river. Nothing more."

"And you had nothing to do with her *accident*?" Jake obviously didn't believe him.

"No, Jake," he said patiently, annoyed that he must tolerate his friend's grilling for Angel's sake. But he'd given his word, and he would keep it. "I may not care much for her, but I wouldn't hurt her."

"Are you sure?"

Bret's back straightened with indignation. "Of course, I'm sure!"

Jake stared down at him, his expression unreadable. Then he seemed to relax.

"Angel doesn't hate you, Bret."

Bret shrugged.

"She cares about what happens to you. Her concern isn't just an act."

"So I keep hearing."

"Then when will you start to listen?" Jake sounded frustrated. "When are you going to stop keeping people out? You've got to let someone else in. I won't always be around."

"I hadn't seen you in five years, Jake," Bret said wryly. "Do you honestly think I won't survive without you now?"

"That isn't what I'm saying."

"Then get to it!"

"I'll always be your friend, Bret," Jake said with an earnestness that tugged at Bret's heart, "no matter how much of an ass you make of yourself."

Bret smirked but didn't interrupt.

"But if you never learn to make more friends, you'll live a very lonely life."

"Not if there are women around." He winked and Jake rolled his eyes, releasing an aggravated sigh.

"You're impossible," Jake said as he turned to leave. "Someday you'll be totally alone, and then you'll wish you hadn't alienated everyone who could've helped you."

"Yeah, yeah." Bret glared at his friend's back as he walked away and fought the twinge of guilt once again rising inside. "Sure, Angel cares," he muttered to himself, "but because of you, Jake, not me."

10

ANGEL SAT ALONE at the piano in the corner, staring at the ivory keys. In the empty room behind her, chairs sat askew from tables littered here and there with debris from the party, waiting for the cleanup crew to finish in the morning. To her right, all three sets of French doors were open to the cool evening breeze and the scents of the late summer night drifted into the room.

She'd been sitting here, contemplating her evening, for some time, trying to exorcize the ache in her chest that never seemed to leave her. Unwanted recollections dazzled her brain. Like vivid oil paints splattered in disarray over canvas, memories were thrown into the sharp relief of her desperate reality.

Staring at the ebony and ivory keys, the urge to press her fingers to them, to draw out the beauty of their sounds, tugged at her heartstrings. The sad melody inside her ripped at her soul and burned her hands with its need to be released. Unable to resist, she placed her slim hands on the keys and began the haunting sonata that had been floating through her tormented mind.

She lost track of everything else, put her whole being into

the song, and the world drifted away as her hands performed. Surprised at how well the ability came back to her, she relaxed into the music and her fingers instinctively glided over the keys. As she neared the end, the tears of mourning for everything she could not change finally returned. She played the last chord and then slowly placed her hands in her lap as she hung her head and allowed the tears to fall.

"That was very nice. I didn't know you could play."

The sound of his voice startled her, and her head snapped up. She avoided looking at him as she brushed her face and had to swallow the lump in her throat before her vocal cords would work.

"You never asked," she replied, sitting stiffly, those damn butterflies in her stomach brushing against the rueful ache in her chest.

"I'm sorry if I startled you," Bret said, coming closer as he spoke.

"I thought I was alone. I don't usually play for an audience."

"I heard the music," he explained, stepping up next to the piano and leaning against its side. "I'm right down the hall. I thought I'd see who was playing."

Angel glanced at him but said nothing. He'd lost his jacket and tie somewhere since leaving the party an hour before. He still wore his white dress shirt and black slacks, and his hair was mussed as if he had run his fingers through it several times. With his dress shirt untucked and the top three buttons undone, the soft whorls of black hair adorning his bronzed chest peeked at her through the open V. Standing in his stocking feet, his hands tucked into his pants pockets, he looked gorgeous, as usual, and a surge of longing burgeoned in her belly, searing out the anxiety that was blooming right along with it.

Reaching for her forgotten glass of wine on the piano top, Angel took a quick sip.

Why must he look so damn good? she thought, forcing her

eyes back to the ivories.

Angel felt his eyes on her, his intense regard was unnerving and made her hot and itchy in ways she didn't want to consider. She wanted him to leave. She wanted him to stay. *Be honest,* a small voice in her mind said. *You just want* him*!*

She swallowed another sip of wine to clear the lump of panic in her throat and set it aside once again.

"What do you want, Bret?" She made her voice cold as she peered up him.

"I was thinking," he said slowly, "we didn't finish our dance. I thought…maybe we could try again now."

"Oh, no." She chuckled bitterly, shaking her head. "I don't think so. I've had enough of your games for one night. Whatever you want will have to wait until tomorrow." She slid across the bench, planning to leave as quickly and with as much dignity as possible, but he stopped her with a gentle hand on her shoulder.

"Wait…"

She glared at his hand, annoyed with her body's sudden heating and the tingles that flashed over her skin. Lifting her frown to his face, she let her irritation show, hoping to chase him away. To her surprise, it worked. He removed his hand and a wave of relief washed over her—and more than a little regret too. Then he sat down beside her and she stiffened once more. With his back to the piano and his hands in his lap, the bench was just wide enough to accommodate them both, but he was too close for comfort. Her runaway body was far too aware of his hip and thigh pressed against her hip and thigh, his bicep brushing her arm, the radiant heat of his body, his musky scent filling her nose and dazzling her brain.

I should just leave. Just get up and walk out!

She stayed.

When she turned her best glare on him, intent on breaking the spell he had on her, the tenderness in his eyes melted some of the ice she'd built up against him. Her shoulders slumped slightly and she sighed. *What is it about him?*

"No games," he said, "just a dance. One dance. With you. That's all."

She snorted and shook her head; reaching for her wineglass, she took another quick drink, seeking courage, but knowing she'd never find it there. Her anger had forsaken her, and she felt herself weakening, almost willingly, under the powerful attraction drawing her to him.

"No," she grumbled after she swallowed. She wouldn't meet his eyes—she couldn't if she wanted to survive this encounter with what was left of her heart.

"You're not being fair, Angel."

Her gaze snapped to his. "*I'm* not...?" Stunned by his audacity, she was momentarily at a loss for words.

"Yes, *you're* not," he replied. "If you'll recall, I was only dancing with you, trying to be pleasant. You're the one who played games with me."

"What're you talking about?" She knew very well what she had done, but she didn't want to admit her cattiness to him.

"You knew how I would react when you said what you did. Why did you do it?"

"Why didn't you leave with Kristine?" She wanted to change the subject, but questions about Kristine were not what she meant to blurt out—even if she did want to know.

"After what you said?" He barked a bitter laugh. "What did you expect?"

That was not true. Kristine had said he lost interest before he danced with Angel.

"Oh, please." Angel rolled her eyes. "As if anything I've ever said to you has made you change your mind. You always do exactly what you want."

"No," he muttered staring at the floor, "not always."

She wasn't sure what that meant, and she didn't want to ask. Instead, she remained mute and tilted her head to toss a glare his way.

"You purposely baited me," he accused, pinning her with his arresting green eyes. "Why?"

The confusion and sincerity she read in his gaze mesmerized her.

Swallowing, she stared back at him. *Why did I do that again?*

Oh, yeah. Kristine...

She could not tell him she had been so ridiculously jealous that all she wanted to do was strike out. She would've preferred hurting Kristine—she had definitely enjoyed ordering that woman to stay away from Bret—but she'd tried to hurt him instead. He would never accept that her comment had been innocent. What could she say that he would believe?

Damn it! Why do I let him get to me?

He sat, waiting for her to reply, his stare so intense she could not turn away. Nothing came to her, until, from out of nowhere, the answer popped into her head.

"Because you threatened me." She put every ounce of frustration she could muster into her reply. "You scared the bejesus out of me in the barn and before that, you were antagonizing me on purpose! You corner me whenever we're alone, force yourself on me, you completely ignore everything I say, and constantly accuse me of playing games with you, even when I'm only trying to help. Why should I *not* bait you at least once?"

He held her gaze for a moment more and then dropped his eyes to the floor.

"As I remember it," he said as he turned his head toward her again, "you enjoyed my kisses."

Her frown deepened. "That's all you got out of what I just said?" She snorted with derision. "Unbelievable!"

Her glass in hand, she slid off the bench and stood to walk past him. His big hand on her forearm stopped her. She glared at the brown hand on her bare skin and thought of shaking him off, but her body wouldn't move.

"I'm sorry, Angel," he said softly and lifted his green eyes to hers. She stared at him, not believing her ears.

"For what specifically?" she snapped, too dazed by his words, his warm hand on her arm, and the rueful expression on his face to think straight.

"For threatening you and for scaring you... I wasn't trying to hurt you. I didn't want that, I just..." He stopped and stared up at her, his eyes unreadable. He glanced away for a moment, his hand still holding her in place. When his gaze returned to hers, his brows had drawn down. His expression, now full of honesty and need, reached inside her, wrapped firmly around her heart, and squeezed. "I'm sorry for all of it." He genuinely sounded apologetic, then his tone changed. "But I'm not sorry I kissed you. Not for any of the moments I've shared with you, except that you don't seem to appreciate them the way I do. That, I *do* regret."

She shook her head, not to negate what he'd said, but because he bewildered her. *What the hell was he saying?*

"Forgive me?" he asked. "I can't promise to be perfect, to not tease you or try to kiss you again, but for the rest, I am truly sorry."

"*You* are *apologizing*?"

"Yes."

"Are you *sick*?"

He laughed and his eyes twinkled at her. "You can blame the wine."

"I see." She was still vexed, but her walls were crumbling.

"I do mean it," he said quietly. "Will you accept it?"

She looked down at him, his palm burning her arm where he held her and experienced the same overwhelming yearning just for him. A wave of giddiness assaulted her. She already knew the answer he waited to hear, but she couldn't make herself speak.

He is so good-looking, she thought, bedazzled, and didn't suffer the same sense of dread she typically experienced when her mind traveled in that vein. Instead, excitement shivered through her, exhilaration at having him sitting on the piano bench with his hand on her arm, gazing up at her expectantly. The possibilities opened by his presence bloomed in her addled brain.

"Yes," she whispered, "I forgive you," but she couldn't resist a little mockery, "this time."

He smiled a soft, sexy smile that melted what remained of her resolve. He released her arm and stood, his closeness stopping her breath. Holding out his hand, he asked, "Dance with me?"

She couldn't help but stare up into his eyes. They fascinated her, the deep green framed by thick, black lashes, the way they locked on her and held her immobile. He looked exceedingly tender in that moment, almost vulnerable.

She abruptly remembered to breathe.

"There's no music," she mumbled, still mesmerized by his nearness and his gaze.

"I can fix that." He winked and in two sock-footed steps, he reached the piano. He flicked on the stereo sitting on top of the instrument and spent a little time skipping through songs. Angel took the opportunity while his back was turned to set the half-full wineglass on a nearby table. As she did so, she heard sultry music start to play, its hushed tones filling the quiet room. He returned to where she waited with a prowling grace that made her heart speed up. He gazed down at her for a moment, then held out his hand, and said in a low voice, "May I have this dance?"

She glanced at his hand before meeting his arresting eyes and a thrill washed over her. A sense of erotic adventure touched her to the core, sending a flush to her cheeks and a smile to her lips. All because this outrageously gorgeous, sometimes perilously sweet, totally irritating, yet kind man wanted to dance with *her*. She wanted nothing more than to pull him close, to be in his arms again, but a niggling doubt made her pause.

"Please," he breathed, even as his eyes pleaded with her to accept, "don't make me beg."

She smiled at him. "Never," she said softly and took his hand. Electric tingles shot through her arm as his fingers closed over hers and he smiled. He led her out to the floor then turned and pulled her into his arms. He moved with the music and she followed, keeping up with every step and gazing up at his handsome face, a secretive curve to her lips.

He spun her around and her world swirled, but she kept up with his lead all the same.

"You've done this before," he teased.

"A time or two." She grinned and the butterflies took flight, soaring through her belly as her excitement and terror at being alone with him again took hold. Their eyes were riveted on each other. Her free hand slipped to the back of his neck and he pulled her closer. When he released her other hand to place both of his arms around her, her second hand slid up to rest on his shoulder and her body molded itself against his. Staring into his too-handsome face, she took in every perfect feature from the shape of his chiseled lips to the straight black brows slashing over his striking green eyes, and the tiny lines that crinkled at their edges when he smiled—just like he was doing now.

"God, you're handsome," she murmured as her hand brushed his cheek.

A strange rush of emotions played across his face as she dragged her nails through the stubble along his jaw and then placed her palm against his cheek. His body tensed and she pulled herself closer. She liked being in his arms, the solid length of him towering over her, the heat of his body engulfing her. He made her feel small and feminine, and she liked that too.

Somewhere in her head, a voice screamed at her to pull away, to run, but the will to obey the warning was beyond her now. The warmth and smell of him were more inebriating than alcohol. Something held her there. Something beyond the strength in his long arms. Something far stronger bound her to him, bonded them together as they moved to the music as one body. They weren't really dancing anymore but swaying, holding each other close. Angel, irresistibly drawn to him, never wanted to let go. There were dozens of reasons this couldn't work between them, even more reasons she should walk away, but right now, in this moment, all that mattered was this man holding her and the way he made her feel by simply dancing.

Monica's words came back to her. *I want you to let someone in, give yourself permission to be happy... If you let yourself open up, maybe it will help you start to heal.*

That's what I'll do. She would let Bret in. He might help. Maybe something good would come of it. She was on the verge of letting him in anyway. Why not take the next step?

Another warning niggled in the back of her mind, a fuzzy sensation of danger, but she ignored it. She wanted this!

BRET FOUGHT A SIMILAR BATTLE. He saw the vulnerability in her azure eyes and he felt the connection pull them together, but he feared he would drive her away, hurt her again, if he acted on it. He wanted the softness of her skin against his, to hear her whisper his name because she chose to, not because he took the opportunity she didn't realize she presented in a moment of weakness.

Her hand still rested against his cheek, her thumb slowly swept back and forth along his cheekbone as she stared up at him, her eyes soft and promising. The nearness of her body, pressed wantonly against him, coupled with the look in her eyes and the way she touched him, tested the limits of his self-control. He wanted her, he'd known that for some time, but he would not force her. It was up to her to let him know what she wanted.

Her hand moved on his face and her thumb traced a seductive path over his lips in an affectionate motion that made his heart skip a beat. She was so different from the other women who had passed through his life. They had all been deliberate, motivated, and sometimes blatant in their attempts to seduce him. He had always despised those women and their games, as much as he hated the lies he'd been stupid enough to believe.

Angel didn't seem to realize what she was doing. Not that she didn't know she was touching him, but her actions felt unpracticed, genuine. She was different, and he couldn't help but feel captivated by that difference. He wondered if she was actually as sweet as she seemed. Did she want him? Or just to use his body?

At this point, he asked himself, *does it really matter?*

11

ANGEL'S EYES DRIFTED CLOSED and she released a contented sigh. Her hands slowly slid down his arms as she leaned back over his hold on her waist. The farther her body curved, the more her hips and thighs pushed into his, and her breasts swelled precariously toward the edges of her low-cut gown.

"Oh, God," Bret groaned as her hands fell away from him to dangle over her head. She could feel his stare as she stretched, luxuriating in the hard planes of his body, his strong hands holding her, and her obvious effect on him. She could feel the evidence of it pressing against her belly, hear it in the way his breath caught in his throat—and she loved it. Loved that she could affect him that way and with so little effort.

"Come on, Angel," he said as he lifted her upward, his hands slowly guiding her until she lay her cheek against his chest. Holding her close, his fingers splayed over her back, her head pillowed on his shoulder, and her hands at his waist—his heart beating heavy against her breast, even more evidence that she excited him.

And that knowledge excited her.

She stepped away and flattened her palms over his belly,

studying his face as her fingers slid over the firm wall of his chest. Her hands dipped greedily beneath his soft cotton dress shirt and repeated the movement. She smiled when his eyes closed and his jaw clenched as she continued her assault on his restraint. The etched lines around his eyes and mouth as he struggled to hold back told her she was winning.

She skimmed her nails over his flat nipples and was delighted when they hardened under her fingers. He exhaled roughly and reached up to press her palms against his chest, stopping their scorching progress over his flesh. Her gaze flashed to his and found his eyes burning down at her. His lips parted as he sucked in air and color rode high on his cheeks.

"Do you know what you're doing?" he asked hoarsely as she drew her hands from beneath his top and out of his grip. She gazed up at him and smiled as she began to unbutton his shirt.

"Yes," she said as she removed the last button, "and no." Her hands slipped inside and her nails raked lightly downward over the soft mat of hair on his chest, following it as it tapered to a thin line that disappeared into his slacks. She tucked the tips of her fingers into the waistband, sliding them out to his hips then back to center. His belly tightened and he gasped with her teasing. The sense of sexual power she enjoyed at provoking such a response in him made her daring to the extreme.

Her head spun with an inebriation that was all Bret. She could not deny how much she wanted him. Nothing mattered right now but this man. How looking at him, caressing him, and experiencing his erotic responses made her dizzy with need.

She wanted more!

She scrutinized his face again as she skimmed her nails back up over his chest, intent on making him as lust-driven as she was. An immense thrill tightened her belly as air hissed through his teeth and she saw his eyes burst into green flame that seemed to leap out to stroke her. Once more, he grabbed her wrists, pressing her hands flat against his heaving chest, stilling her movements. He released a ragged breath as his hooded eyes bored into hers.

"You don't want to do this," he rasped.

He was trembling beneath her palms as she stared up at him. Her lips curved upward. "Do you know my mind better than I do?"

"No, but…"

"But what?"

"You're drunk, Angel."

"No, I'm not."

"You don't want to do this," he said, trying once more. "Not like this."

Angel didn't reply as she tugged her hands free. He closed his eyes and inhaled a deep, shuddering breath as his arms dropped to his sides, letting her do what she would. Sensing his capitulation, she reached up and pushed his unfastened shirt open so his shoulders were exposed and, holding the garment wide, she took in his masculine beauty.

His skin was bronzed from days of hard work in the sun. The play of shadows over the solid angles and planes of his well-built body made her mouth water. She marveled at how his physique had returned to its prior athletic form after the ill-treatment he'd suffered, making her proud of him in a way she couldn't explain. He was all long, lean muscle, strong and virile and so damn beautiful. He was the most gorgeous, the most stubborn, the most intriguing man she had ever met, and she yearned to have his sun-darkened flesh warm hers.

You shouldn't be doing this, her lust-dazed mind warned, but she was too far gone to listen to anything but her need for him.

Taking in every small detail, her eyes caught on a thin line running along his ribs. It was light, almost nonexistent. If she hadn't known the mark was there, she would have missed the scar left by Darla's whip. Angel traced the line with the tips of her fingers and a surge of relief washed through her. The woman's cruelty could have marred him worse. Those on his back would be about the same and she was grateful he wouldn't have to carry that blatant sign of slavery and mutilation for the rest of his life.

Without thinking, she brushed her cheek against the scar and his muscles constricted. When she pressed her lips to the same spot in a feather-light kiss and her tongue flicked out to sample his skin, his breath rasped in his throat and he groaned as if in pain. She looked up, suddenly anxious.

He stood unmoving, watching her. His eyes were dark green and burned with a fiery light that threatened to consume her. Another thrill rocketed through her at what she read in his gaze. She slid her hands up over his broad shoulders and dislodged his shirt from its precarious perch.

He allowed it to slither down his arms to the floor.

"Angel..." His voice was a hoarse croak as his hands shot up to encircle her wrists for a third time. "Angel, you need to stop."

"No, Bret. *You* need to listen. You accused me earlier of not knowing what I wanted." Her hands still trapped against his chest, she leaned toward him, letting him take her weight as her hands slipped up to his shoulders and she brought herself closer. "But I do know what I want." She raised up on her toes so her lips could reach his and she kissed him, a light brush of his mouth, before she drew back an inch and gazed into his emerald eyes. "Tonight," she whispered, "right now, I know exactly what I want. I want to be held. To be kissed. To be loved...by you, Bret. I want you."

She kissed him again, caressing his lips with hers, taunting him, daring him to hold back, which he did for as long as he could. He stood like a stone as she pressed herself against him, her hands gripping his shoulders, her breasts searing into his chest, and he let her kiss him.

HE SHOULD STOP HER, should walk away, but he couldn't. Her nearness and the words she'd just said—the words he so desperately wanted to hear—rooted him in place. When she uttered those words, a surge of molten desire exploded within him and charred his uncertainty into dust.

Her tongue, tracing the line of his compressed lips, begging for entry, was all he could stand. He moved so quickly she didn't have time to avoid him as he grabbed her by the shoulders and held her away from him. He stared down at her for a moment, her eyes riveted by his.

"Say it again," he growled.

Her slow smile made his heart stutter. "I want you, Bret."

Before any other thought entered his mind, he crushed her against him and slanted his mouth across hers almost brutally in his need to possess it. She didn't object, in fact, her response was almost as wild. Her arms entwined around his neck, kissing him back with a passion that rocked him. He slid one hand down her back, over her hip, to her leg, and then under the shimmery material of her dress to the silky-smooth skin of her thigh. His palm skimmed upward to her buttocks, gripping its roundness, pulling her more fully against him, while the other hand swept up her back to stroke the bare skin along her spine to her neck. She shivered and pressed into him. Everything about her was so soft and she smelled so sweet, like the bloom of new spring. He couldn't get enough.

He kissed a path from her lips to her cheek, and then down to the sensitive column of her neck. She moaned and leaned heavily on him. Easing the strap of her dress over her shoulder, he ran a chain of hot kisses across her delicate collarbone and back again. Then he pulled the second strap of her dress down her arm and kissed her other shoulder, longing to taste all of her.

Angel tangled her hands in his hair and held him to her as his fingers pushed her dress down. The glistening material fell to the floor and puddled at her feet in a shimmering black cloud.

His hand cupped the lushness of her breast and the mound bulged upward, nearly spilling its bounty from her garment. His tongue slid across the seam between cloth and flesh and a tremor passed through her.

"Bret," she breathed, and he lifted his head as her eyes fluttered open. Blue languid pools gazed up at him with an unrelenting heat that sizzled over his flesh. "We can't do this…not here."

Tension clenched his belly in a vise, afraid for a moment she would push him away again, but her last words eased his worry and he smiled.

"No problem," he replied, his voice low and husky with desire. In one swift motion, he grabbed his shirt and her dress off the floor, and then, hooking her legs behind the knee, he lifted her into the air. Looking down at her cradled in his arms, something tender and dangerous touched his heart. The old voice of warning rumbled from the back of his mind, but he ignored it and smiled again. She'd said the words and her eyes were saying them again right now. She wanted him, and he was tired of denying himself. Tonight, he would forget about the past, forget all the lies and the heartache. She was giving him a chance, and he wanted nothing more than to take it. He bent his head and kissed her tempting lips as he carried her from the dining hall.

Not sure if Jake would return to his bed before the night was over and believing Angel would be more comfortable in her room, Bret headed for the stairs.

12

ANGEL CLUNG TO BRET as he took the stairs two at a time, then hurried down the hall to kick open Angel's bedroom door. Once inside, he did the same to close it and then leaned back, his heart thumping against her breast. Burying her face in the curve of his neck, she inhaled his musky sent, soaked in the heat and strength of his body as his chest expanded with each heaving breath. He filled her senses to overload. Too drunk on him to think too much, she let wild anticipation and all-out desire guide her actions.

Her fingers fluttered through the short hair at his nape, brushed slowly over the curve of his ear, rasped along the stubble on his jaw, and she felt him shudder. She wanted to run her hands all over his bare flesh, to taste his salty skin, to draw the same glorious emotions out of him as he did to her. She wanted him to *feel* the same as she did, to bring more to their coupling than just his body.

Thanks to Jake's revelations earlier, Angel understood Bret a little better, but she feared his wariness would prevent him from opening up, even during the intimate act they were about to share.

Would he allow himself to care for her?

Does he? And if he does…does she really want him to?

A distant part of her knew that getting closer to Bret—finding out if her fantasies were anything like reality—as wonderful as that prospect seemed, could also be disastrous. Despite what she'd learned from Jake, deep down she knew all too well that Bret might use her—as she had heard he'd used Sara Barrett—to gain the freedom he so fiercely desired.

So then, why do I still want him so much? Why, after almost seven years, was this stubborn, cautious man the one who woke her feminine yearnings?

She pushed all the doubts out of her mind and snuggled closer to him. Right now, none of that mattered. Passion and need thrummed through her veins, overriding even her most sacred promises; she simply couldn't resist. Tonight, she would take anything Bret offered to quench the burning, relentless ache she had for him. Somewhere in the back of her fuzzy mind, a warning about her lack of restraint still buzzed, but the need she'd been fighting for months had taken control, and the only one who could stop her hunger was Bret himself.

His arms tightened around her and he pushed away from the door, his stocking feet making little sound as he crossed the hardwood floor. She sighed as she lifted her head to stare up at him. The look of raw lust and open need she read in his expression halted her breath. Time seemed to stretch as he halted beside her huge four-poster bed, his gaze never leaving hers and she barely breathed. *Would he back out now?*

She was not a tall woman, nor was she light, but being held so closely and carried with such ease made her feel like a tiny, fragile doll. The way his eyes delved into hers made her feel wanted, desired, and more feminine than she ever had in her life. She bit her lip and an ache clenched deep within her. His gaze dropped to her mouth and she felt his arms tense around her.

One moment they were staring into each other's eyes, anticipation and his nearness turning her insides to molten goo, and the next, Bret reached down, jerked back the blankets, set her down on the mattress, and straightened, all without breaking eye contact.

She licked her lips waiting for him to join her and his eyes locked on the small movement. Their normal jade-green color had darkened to emerald. He brushed his fingers across her cheek, his thumb tracing the path her tongue had just taken, and she nuzzled her face into his palm. He hesitated, and doubt flashed across his face.

"Please," she whispered as her desperate fingers bunched in the soft cotton of his slacks, "don't leave."

His hand lingered on her face and a muscle twitched in his jaw.

"I'm not going anywhere," he said in a low, raspy voice and she smiled as her hands relaxed, though she didn't release him.

Moonlight filtered through the unshaded French doors on either side of the bed, making his eyes gleam as they roamed over her face, her bosom, traveled the length of her body, and back again. He seemed to be memorizing every curve, but he looked severe rather than amorous and, still, she sensed his uncertainty.

Taking her cue from him, she let her eyes sweep over him in bold appreciation. She took in the broad shoulders and chest, all sinewy, sculpted muscle; the flat belly; narrow hips; and, on impulse, her hand slipped around the back of one long leg. She gazed up into his flushed face while her hand continued its leisurely path. She loved the tenseness beneath the gentle pressure of her palm and the way his eyes darkened further as she slowly stroked upward. Her fingers slid across his thigh but paused near the top as her eyes drifted to the part of him that made him male. In the pale moonlight, she saw the prominence there, outlined in the smooth black material of his slacks. Before she could reconsider her actions, her fingers skimmed over it. He groaned, low in his throat, and tremble beneath her hands, but he didn't stop her.

Encouraged, she flattened her palm over the hot firmness, enjoying the intimacy he allowed her. He shuddered as her fingers tightened around him and he moaned again. His fingers clenched and dropped away from her cheek and he inhaled harshly.

Her breath caught at that pained sound and her hand automatically retreated before she froze. Had she hurt him somehow? Upset him? An anxious fist gripped her heart as she searched his face.

With his head thrown back, eyelids closed, his hands balled into fists at his side, he appeared to be in distress. His breathing was ragged, and she feared she had gone too far. But when he lowered his chin and met her gaze, the uncertainty she sensed in him before no longer lingered in his eyes. In its place was a burning hunger that stopped her breath.

His hand reached out, touched the back of hers where it hung mere inches from his groin, and pressed it over him once more. He covered her hand with his and held it there as his voracious eyes stared down into hers.

"Don't stop," he murmured. "Touch me...wherever you like." His hand dropped away.

Angel gazed up at him, transfixed. His hard, hot member pulsed through the thin fabric beneath her fingers and every cell in her body responded in kind. Her mouth went dry and everything tingled as heat surged through her and settled into a burning torrent between her thighs. That this stubborn, private man—who hated to be trifled with and was always on his guard—would give her permission to do as she liked with him was an aphrodisiac to her already racing libido. The tightness in her belly broadened and mashed her wits to mush. If any restraint had remained in her, this flood of runaway lust washed it away.

She turned her body toward him, her knees straddling his legs. Her second hand slid up his opposite thigh as the first continued to caress him through the smooth, black cotton of his slacks. All at once, she wanted to tear the barrier away from his glorious body. She wanted him naked. She wanted to touch his bare, burning flesh.

With shaky hands, she fumbled with the button of his slacks until it came loose with a jerk. Slowly, she lowered the zipper, then lifted her head and found him watching her. He made no move to stop her; in fact, the green fire in his eyes encouraged her to continue. Emboldened, she gripped the fabric on either side of his thighs and tugged. The smooth material slid from his narrow hips and long legs to pool around his ankles.

His boxer-briefs were some dark color she couldn't make out in the low light, but she admired the way they hugged him in all the right places as she ran her hands along his legs. The crispness of his leg-hairs tickled her palms and she marveled at the warmth of his hard flesh. Then her eyes caught a long, thin line on his thigh and she froze. The mark where her attacker's blade had cut him was a darker slash in the dimness. The grim reminder of that incident—of the mean-eyed man's cruel hands crawling all over her skin as his tongue invaded her mouth— made her shiver and she wished Bret would touch her. She wanted him to wipe away those memories, but she knew that wasn't the only reason.

She wanted Bret. It seemed now as if she had always wanted him.

Gently, she brushed her fingers over the incision on his thigh; even in the faint light, she could see healing had already begun. His muscles twitched beneath her gentle touch, but he made no other sound or movement.

She shuddered. *He could have been killed!*

Remembering how he had held her, kissed her, comforted her under the bright summer sun melted her heart a little more while warming her blood all over again. Lifting her eyes to his face, she pushed the unwanted memories away, and concentrated wholly on this man and this moment. Her hands skimmed upward over his taut hamstrings until her fingers splayed over his cotton-covered buttocks. She pulled herself toward him. His hot hardness nestled into her cleavage and she used the contact to her advantage, watching his face as she shifted her body so her softness stroked him while her hands clutched him to her. His jaw clenched as her fingers kneaded the tight muscles of his backside. Still, he raised no hand to touch her. The fierce desperation to have his hands on her spurred her on.

She pressed her open mouth along the firm, fiery heat of his erection, nibbling at the throbbing shaft in quick little bites. She heard him groan as if something pained him, but she didn't stop, hoping to drive him mad with lust. She wanted to make him crazy—as crazy for her as she was for him.

Without warning, his hands grasped her shoulders, heaved her up off the bed, and into his arms where, finally, he kissed her. His tongue dashed inside her waiting mouth, stroking her, fanning the flames of her desire. He tasted of wine and smelled of outside, soap, and that unmistakable manly scent she associated with Bret.

She moaned into his mouth and leaned into him, her arms sliding over his shoulders, clasping him to her as she returned his kiss. She loved the feel of his arms around her, holding her in his secure embrace. She stroked the back of his neck, dragging her nails through the short, smooth hair at his nape while he cradled her head on his shoulder and consumed her mouth. Angel shifted her body, grinding her hips against his and, wanting so much more, she pressed into him harder.

His arms tightened around her and then he released her. A soft whimper of complaint burst from her lips at his retreat. A moment later, a gasp replaced it as he swept her legs out from under her and lifted her off the floor. She hugged his neck, marveling at his strength. She'd already surrendered to him, but the tender way he looked down into her eyes made her heart and body clench in unison.

He gently settled her on the bed, a pillow beneath her head, before he joined her. They lay on their sides facing each other, his arms encircling her waist, and their bodies molded together. He bent his head to kiss her again, this time slowly and with an earnest passion that made her ache even more.

His lips lingered on hers and then descended over her chin to the sensitive column of her neck, blazing a path to her breasts. She arched her back in silent offering as he cupped one generous mound until the rosy crest nearly escaped the confines of her corset top. He kissed the tempting curve, ran his tongue along the seam, dipped into her cleavage, and then back again. Attempting to brush the offending garment out of his way, his whisker-covered chin scrapped against her skin setting off shots of unexpected lightning along her nerve endings. Her nipples hardened and she gasped at the mixture of his smooth tongue and the gentle rasp of his rapidly returning beard.

"The dress is too tight," she whispered, her fingers clutching his hair, "and your face is too scratchy.

He pulled back to examine her bosom. "You're right," he said. "Your breast is all red." He bent his head and placed another quick kiss on the offended flesh then pulled back and flashed her a grin. "Sorry about that. Let's try something different."

Raining kisses along the upper curve of her tingling breast, he reached for her zipper. The metallic sound of metal teeth releasing their hold sent a thrill of excitement down her spine. She shivered as cool night air and Bret's warm fingers caressed her naked back. His hand returned to her breast, cupping its weight until the pink peak burst free from the clingy fabric. His tongue, twirling round the throbbing tip, made her groan as he sucked her hardened nipple into the searing cave of his mouth. He nibbled the sensitive point, tugging at it with his teeth, being both gentle and demanding, and sending fireworks shooting through her, swirling round and round until they settled between her thighs. Her fingers fisted in his hair as she clasped him against her. Her body heated and arched against his. With one hand splayed out over her backside, he held her close as she wiggled against him, desperate to feel his hot flesh against every inch of her.

Oh, God, please... Bret, get these clothes off me, she silently pleaded as she held him to her breast.

"Yes," she muttered. "Yes, yes, yes!"

On her back, her underdress remained pushed down around her middle and Bret, braced on his elbows, hovered over her, tantalizing first one swollen, needy nipple and then the other with the delights of his mouth and fingers. His hand moved down her side, leaving a trail of sparks in its wake. Calloused fingers slid up the inside of her thigh. *Oh, please hurry, Bret, she silently begged. Please touch me, please!* Her needy body trembled, and heat suffused every inch of her as her legs spread in anxious anticipation. She wanted him so much that nothing else mattered. Nothing else was important, only Bret holding her, kissing her, making her feel like the woman she once was... No. Better than she once was. This feeling inside her, this warmth and heat and longing, this desire to hold and protect, to give him everything, every part of herself, was so much more than she'd ever experienced before. She had to have him. She wanted to have him inside her, filling her, wiping away every dark memory, every unshed tear. She didn't know how, but instinctively, she felt certain that he was the man to do it.

Propped over her, one hand inching ever so slowly up her thigh, making her whimper and squirm, Bret's mouth returned to her lips. His tongue played with hers and she dug her nails into his shoulders, skimmed over his hard biceps, to grip his arm.

"Hurry," she whispered into his mouth. "Touch me...higher."

He chuckled at her brazen demand and she felt the vibration all the way to her toes. God, she loved his laugh!

"Not yet," he replied, his deep, slightly unsteady voice low yet promising.

The kiss intensified and she ran her hands over the flexing muscles of his back. She traced the sensuous line of his spine, down and then up, while he tempted her tongue to come out and play. She moaned her pleasure, but his kiss hadn't distracted her completely. She still wanted more.

One of his knees nestled between her legs and she lifted her hips to press the neediest part of her along the warm, solidness of his thigh. He removed his hand from her leg and she whimpered against his lips. He chuckled again and frustration drove her nails into his skin.

"Easy, darlin'," he said between slow, sultry kisses. "I'm not going anywhere."

Her grip loosened and she forgot her disappointment when he brought his knee closer to the apex of her thighs. His satin-over-steel limb slid over the searing central core of her desire. The abrasion of his body hair set off hot sparks sizzling and tickling her tender flesh. Her breath caught as her nails raked gently down his ribs, seeking the part of him she wanted most.

He gasped as her fingers brushed his shaft. Grinning, she reached for him, pleased she could affect him with such a simple touch, and wanting to affect him more. But before she could take him into her hand, he pulled out of her grasp, and the warmth of his wonderful body abruptly vanished.

13

ANGEL MOANED IN PROTEST as he rolled off the bed and came to his feet. Much cooler air caressed her still-damp-from-his-mouth breasts, causing her to shiver. She turned her head and peered up at him. "What are you doing?" she asked in a husky voice she barely recognized.

He didn't reply, only stood staring down at her. A moonbeam slanting into the room cast a silver halo around his gorgeous body. It gave him the appearance of Zeus, the god of Greek mythology, descended from Mount Olympus to visit her boudoir. She bit her lip and sucked in a long breath, squirming under his intense gaze. He had been her fantasy for so long, only this time, he was real and so much more than she'd ever dreamed. She had never imagined he would have vulnerabilities that cut as deep as her own, or that she would feel this deep-seated need to shelter him from that pain. How she was supposed to do that, she wasn't sure, but knowing that didn't make her feel it any less.

The angle of illumination benefited Bret's vision more than hers, but Angel appreciated every shadow-cut line. She dropped her arms to her sides as she gazed up at him, admiring the rapid rise and fall of his impressive chest and the barely visible protruding bulge at the front of his boxer-briefs. She didn't hide from him. She wanted him to look at her, but more, she wanted him to *want* her. She let him stare and gave him an inviting smile, wishing she could better make out his expression.

His eyes drifted hungrily over her body and she glanced down at herself. The remainder of her dress had been bunched around her waist and hips, leaving her breasts with their dusky-rose tips and the full length of her thighs naked to his sight. Her skin gleamed in the half-light of the moon and, to her eyes, she looked wanton and sexy lying there with her legs splayed slightly and her secret charms on display. She wondered if Bret felt the same. She looked up and met his intense gaze but couldn't make out his expression clearly. He seemed to be waiting for something, or, maybe, he was having second thoughts. He had pulled away rather abruptly. Her stomach tightened with dread, but she wasn't about to give up. Gathering her courage, she reached over and ran her fingers over the hot bulge between his thighs. He inhaled sharply and she bit her lip again, pleased with his response.

"Come back to bed, Bret," she said, her tone soft and inviting.

His hands fisted at his sides and he turned to look at her bedroom door.

Not about to let him change his mind, not now, she closed her hand over him and squeezed lightly, stroking him, encouraging him to stay.

His head snapped around and his narrowed eyes bore into her face. "Are you sure about this?"

Her tongue felt dry and too big for her mouth.

She was sure, but she was afraid too. Another warning buzzed in her brain, but she refused to listen.

Never taking her eyes from his face, she whispered, "Yes."

He made a sound deep in his throat, then tucked his thumbs under the elastic of his boxer-brief, and swiftly skinned them down his legs. He kicked them away and her gaze fell on his jutting erection. Long and thick and webbed with bluish veins, it pointed directly at her as if choosing her for its next meal. The odd thought sent a thrill of anticipation down her spine and made her mouth water. She licked her lips eager to taste him, all of him.

He stood motionless, letting her hungry eyes have their fill. When she met his gaze again, he smiled as if he had enjoyed the way she visually devoured him.

Crawling back onto the bed, he straddled her body. Staring into her eyes, he sat back on his heels and her stomach tightened as calloused fingers slid over her belly and ribs, arousing and tickling as they slowly inched toward her breasts. He smiled when she giggled, and her heart fluttered at the tenderness of his expression. He looked so young, so innocent. Jake's words passed through her mind. *Bret was only a kid when they first moved in with Vince, barely twelve-years-old... Vince would use any excuse to hurt Bret, to let him know how truly defenseless and despised he really was...*

How much of Bret's childhood had been stolen from him? A vise gripped her heart at the thought. Tonight she would sooth his hurt, hold him, and let him know that he wasn't alone.

Her eyes fluttered closed and her back arched as he cupped her breasts in his large hands. She inhaled and felt them swell in his palms, longing for more of his touch. His thumbs brushed over the sensitive tips, teasing, taunting. She felt him move and then the moist heat of his mouth sucked first one nipple into his mouth and then the other. A gasp of pleasure parted her lips, but before she could do anything more, her wadded-up dress was yanked down over her body, along with her lacy black panties. Bret tossed the tangled mess onto the floor as his eyes wandered over her, burning where they touched—and they touched her *everywhere.*

His gaze fell on the heels still secured to her small feet and grinned.

Seeing his appreciative look, she murmured, "You can leave them on."

He glanced at her. "No," he said, shaking his head. "I want you bare to my touch...everywhere."

Hot prickles danced over her skin at his response.

Kneeling at her feet, Bret lifted one foot, unbuckled the strap around her ankle, and slipped the shoe from her foot. Tossing the pump aside, it landed with a short series of thumps on the hardwood floor. She moaned as his strong hands massaged her sore feet. Her eyes widened when he brought her foot to his mouth and kissed the delicate arch, but then a tingle shot through her body from the butterfly-soft contact. He placed her foot back on the sheets and repeated his actions on the other, all the way down to kissing her foot. Based on their social stations—and how he clearly felt about being a slave—she wondered if he saw the irony in his actions, but she wasn't about to risk angering him to ask.

When he finished with her feet, he kissed her ankle, calf, knee, and then her inner thigh, his keen gaze studying her face through it all. She squirmed as he neared the apex of her legs, shy insecurity stealing over her. She wanted him to kiss her, to follow the route he had traveled, but almost seven years had passed since she'd trusted anyone enough to kiss her *there*, since she allowed anyone near her like this.

Yes, she wanted him—*God, how she wanted him*—but he wanted his freedom. *Could this be his most recent attempt to get it?* Despite the desire threatening to overwhelm her, the sudden thought made her wary. Instinctively, her legs squeezed together, and he pulled back.

"Angel?" The doubt and concern in his voice made her throat go tight and scratchy.

Staring at the ceiling, she tried to breathe as a new fear stuck her. Because she had used the idea of this man to ease her loneliness and to avoid other, more painful memories, had she confused her attraction to him with the affection she felt for someone else? Is that why she'd let this go so far? She didn't want to look at him, afraid of what—of whom—she would see. Would he have green eyes or blue? Black hair or dirty blond? Her lids closed and she took a deep breath.

"Angel, look at me."

She couldn't resist his soft yet demanding drawl. Her eyelids fluttered open and met the bottomless green pools of his gaze across the bare expanse of her body. Raw desire lay in the emerald pools, but she also saw confusion and something more, something deeper.

An almost imperceptible frown darkened his handsome face. "Do you still want me, Angel?" he asked, and she heard the note of hurt in his voice. It made the achy lump in her throat worse.

She stared at him in stunned silence. A part of her knew he was giving her a chance to back out, but a bigger part—the visceral part—didn't want that.

Did she?

Her head spun with desire and doubt. She closed her eyes and took another deep breath. She tried to think clearly, to formulate the correct response, the one she knew she should give.

"Yes." Her eyes popped opened in surprise. That was not what she'd intended to say. She exhaled in a rush, panicking, and met his intense regard. Her body, hot and tingly from his touch, vibrated with need and her heart thumped at the look of uncertainty on his face. She couldn't hurt him again, and she didn't want to stop. She'll probably pay for it tomorrow, but tonight she needed him as much as his eyes said he needed her. "Yes!" she said again, a little louder this time.

He grinned at her, clearly pleased by her response. "Then open your legs for me," he purred, and she heard the smile in his voice. "Let me do this right." He ran his palms over her thighs and she closed her eyes again. She filled her lungs and exhaled in a long, slow breath, only to inhale again. He pressed his lips to her hip, nibbled seductively across her belly and then, with a final whimper of surrender, she gave in.

His stubbled cheek rasped along her sensitive flesh and she shivered from the sheer exhilaration of his face nuzzling her skin. Desire won the short-lived battle inside her as his lips drifted to the quaking heart of her yearning and he kissed that too. He licked, sucked, devoured her, savoring the part of her that cried just for him. She moaned and her hands knotted in the sheets. Branding her with his tongue, his hand slid beneath her backside, tilting her pelvis and lifting her, opening her fully to the heat of his mouth. Her fingers tangled in his hair, holding him to her as he spread her legs to take her with his mouth.

Angel's head thrashed on the pillow and she moaned with pleasure, everything in her tightening, drawing inward in rapid, ever-increasing ripples. Instinctually, she rocked her hips into his mouth, wanting more of his heat, more of the exciting sensations of his talented tongue. He felt so good; she never wanted him to stop. He slid one long finger inside her, then two, and every sense she had centered on what he was doing to her. She moaned, tightened her grip on his short hair, every cell in her body in tune to him and the rhythm his mouth and hand.

"Oh, Bret!" she cried as an explosion of sizzling sparks crashed through her like a tidal wave, flooding her senses until she felt as if she were floating in the clouds. Pleasure rippled through her as he caressed her through the last of her orgasm, gradually slowing until she lay motionless and gasping. He lifted his head and she released her grip on his hair, and she sighed, feeling utterly spent but so incredibly alive.

This act of passion was wonderful but her body, though thrumming like a plucked harp string in the aftermath of his oral symphony, remained unfulfilled. She should be sated after the long play he put her through, but something was still missing.

His lips on her thigh drew her attention and she looked down at him. Something about the contrast between his sun-bronzed skin and the paleness of her limbs was electrifying. She watched him, mesmerized by the clean, chiseled lines of his face as he dallied over her bellybutton. He kissed that too, peering at her as he did and then grinned, his teeth flashing white in the shadows.

"My turn," he said with a crooked smile that made her heart flutter and melt. Then he moved, chest to chest, his thighs between hers, as his hands and mouth roamed over every inch of her. Angel relished each glorious moment, her body coming alive again.

He drove her wild, beyond her earlier craving for him, beyond thought or fear. She needed him! She needed what he could give her, wanted it from him and no one else, but she wanted more than sex. She wanted him to care. She wanted his heart.

A small fraction of her brain knew what she wanted wasn't possible. He would never allow it. The thought hurt, so she shoved it away and let his touch work its wonders, let Bret become her world once more.

His mouth made a slow trail of kisses down her neck to her breasts, teasing her taut, tender nipples with his tongue and teeth, even as his hand slipped between her legs. His finger moved over the small quivering nub that his tongue had exhaustively explored only minutes before, until she once again throbbed and whimpered, and longed for the rest of him. Warmth spiraled through her at his gentle motions, then his fingers dipped lower, slid inside her, in and out, over and over, in a slow, persistent beat. Her heart hammered in her chest. Her blood pounded in her ears. Her hands gripped his shoulders and her nails dug into his flesh, but he never ceased the seductive ebb and flow of his hand.

She moaned and her pelvis lifted in time with each stroke of his fingers. This was only the start of what she was missing, of what she wanted. What she *needed.* She surged against his hand, gasping, her nails now raking at his back.

The sudden hot wetness over her breast as he drew the peak into his mouth brought another shocked gasp and an exhale of satisfaction from her throat. His teeth nipped one aching reddish-brown tip, the sensation shooting sparks through her body.

"Oh, God, Bret!" she cried, arching her back and raising her breasts in offering. His breath was hot on her skin and his ragged breathing matched her own. Her hands tangled in his hair again, holding him to her as if he might disappear if she were to let him go. Unrelenting, his lips lavished attention on the rosy-tipped peaks, moving from one to the other until she ached from and for his touch. He was driving her insane again, drawing her further into his sensuous trap. His fingers moved inexorably between her legs, bringing her closer to the moment she waited for, the moment she would regret.

Hours seemed to pass before he removed his hand, and, though she writhed from his ministrations, her body was eager for more. She whimpered at the loss of his fingers, panting as she pressed into the warm, steely strength of his thigh. He shifted until he lay with his hip on the bed, one leg thrown over both of hers, and his much larger body pressing her into the mattress. She wrapped her arms around his neck with a sigh. She loved the heavy weight of him, her breasts being crushed against his broad chest, his hot, pulsating shaft nestled on her thigh, so close, and yet, so far from the part of her that wept in want for him.

One arm around her waist held her to him, the other slid through her hair, dislodging the pins that once held up her long curls. He draped her ebony tresses over the white pillowcase in a fan, his calloused fingers combing them out in gentle strokes. A look of wonder mixed with lust permeated his expression, and though she longed for the rest of him, she didn't want to break the spell. When he finally met her passion-drunken gaze, he stared for the longest time. There was so much emotion in his eyes, so much Angel wished she understood but didn't dare ask—not now, anyway. He brushed his fingers softly over her cheek and lowered his head. He kissed her as if he was starving for her, as if she filled a need he'd never been able to satisfy, and she reciprocated. The kiss ended when he lifted himself away from her. Her hands slid down his bulging arms, and she murmured a complaint, afraid he would leave her again.

Kneeling between her thighs, he positioned his body over hers, and with one arm braced on either side of her head, he peered at her through the darkness. The look on his moonlit face surprised her. Insecurity and naked vulnerability—he would normally never allow to show—spilled from his beautiful eyes. Hesitation stiffened his body and she realized he shared her fears. He was just as nervous about what they were doing and where their action would lead as she was.

She wanted to console him, to let him know she didn't want to hurt him, but doing so would be as good as admitting he had revealed too much. That would send him bolting for the door. Instead, she decided to share her fears with him.

Reaching up, she placed her hands on his whiskered cheeks and a guarded wall seemed to slam down over his face. She gave him a timid smile. Her chest tightened with fear for what she was about to say and struggled with the words. But she persevered, more afraid of his retreat than exposing her heart.

"Don't hurt me, Bret. Please… Not today."

He stared down at her for some time, unmoving, his face no longer revealing any of his thoughts. Angel held her breath and prayed he accepted her plea as the gift she'd intended it to be.

His hips settled into the cradle of her thighs as he lowered his body onto his elbows. His mouth mere inches from hers, his breath feathered her cheek as her arms twined around his neck once more, welcoming him. His hands caught in her hair, testing its texture with his long fingers and releasing a hint of its lilac scent. She could make out every curve of his face, see the tension in his jaw, the green flame in his eyes, and waited expectantly for him to answer her plea.

He fixed her with a hard expression and disappointment crushed her heart.

"Not today," he murmured and dropped his head, giving her no time to respond. Their lips met in a fiery blaze that made her head spin, and the regret that had filled her moments before turned to joy.

Tasting herself on his tongue mingled with the essence of Bret was a strange yet seductive flavor, and in a heartbeat, she returned his kiss with wholehearted zeal. He angled his body until he lay hard and insistent between her thighs. She clung to him, her hips lifting toward his, begging him, telling him without words what she wanted.

With one swift motion and more care than she could fathom in that moment, he pushed inside her, filled her, stretched her, and she groaned at the pure bliss of having him hot and pulsing within.

He echoed her moan of pleasure and held himself buried inside her. Heat poured off his trembling body, then his arms slipped around her and his weight pressed her down. He all at once conquered her mouth and laid claim to her body in prefect concert, eliciting a moan of sheer pleasure from her. He filled her, stretched her, waking her body in ways she'd forgotten, and she loved it. He drew back inch by slow inch and drove in, again and again, penetrating deep with each forceful plunge. His easy, precise pace grew into a fervent rhythm drubbing between her spread thighs. His urgent need to drive the long, hot part of him into her darkest regions pushed her legs wider. His throbbing length slid in and out, seducing her body, heating her blood, and setting every nerve to tingling.

Still, she wanted more!

He moved over her, propelling everything away, until no room remained for anything else. Nothing but Bret and what he was doing to her, *with* her. Driving her mad with carnal delights, pushing her beyond the boundaries of the sad reality she'd been living, Angel gloried in the overwhelming sensations of his hard body and the musky scent of Bret all around her.

BRET UNDERSTOOD EVERYTHING Angel's body tried to tell him from the start. He'd held back at first, but she'd convinced him—in several ways—that she wanted him. Hell, she hadn't needed to try very hard. He'd wanted this, wanted her, for months.

His initial restraint in the dining hall had been torture—the urge to thrust between her thighs far greater than he remembered it being with anyone else. Living off the land for years while hiding from the Raiders meant that long sexual abstinences were nothing new for him. Still, that lack didn't explain his inexplicable craving only for Angel. He needed the release, but as her moans of pleasure poured over and through him, wrapping around his heart and washing away his fear, he discovered he not only wanted her, he wanted her to enjoy this act of passion as much as he would. He'd held off his own gratification to increase hers, to please her completely.

Now she matched his pace, lunging her hips into each of his thrusts with a strength of body and will he had never experienced. She writhed beneath him with an erotic enchantment that exhilarated him, amazing him with her response to his every kiss, every touch, every plunge of his hips with a power that nearly rivaled his own, and despite his surprise, he loved it! He loved everything about her from her small, shapely form and full rosy lips, to her long, silky curls and big, innocent blue eyes. In another time, he would have fallen madly in love with her, but that was long ago and far from here. For now, all he would consider was this moment and how she felt in his arms. He'd deal with the fallout later.

She moaned and his lips covered hers once more. Her tongue darted into his mouth to taunt his to come out and play. The inferno inside him flared up to an unparalleled degree. All thought burned away as his unleashed desire took control. His arms tightened around her, crushing her to his chest, and he plunged into her with renewed vigor. Her nails dug into his back as her body arched into him and he smiled as his name fell repeatedly from her lips. Then the well inside him burst and he groaned as pleasure rocketed through him.

Time seemed to stand still as if nothing else existed but this act between them. No past, no future, only now, and the ecstasy of passion and forgetfulness.

Angel cried out in joy mixed with what sounded like despair, and his fear that everything would be the same—him a slave and her, his Mistress—settled in Bret's stomach like lead weight.

Or would *it all be the same?* He attempted to squelch the hopeful thought, remembering the heartache hope had caused him before, but it refused to completely leave him. She had said she wanted him, acted as if she meant it. Maybe this time *would* be different.

Bret muted her cry with his mouth and tasted a hint of saltiness. He wondered if perspiration or tears caused the flavor. An instant anxious moment of regret stabbed through his chest, but her amorous response to his lips on hers banished the stinging pain. Her legs wrapped around his waist, drawing him closer as they continued to move in unison, but all too soon they slowed to a stop, both heaving in the aftermath of their exertion.

He couldn't help one last slow, tantalizing kiss.

It had been over a year since he'd been with a woman and longer since he performed the act with anyone he truly desired. Angel surpassed his fondest memory. So much so, the need to have her again, at that very moment, stirred within him, but he would wait. They had all the time in the world now, and they were both exhausted from their long day together and the evening's festivities. Even as the thoughts passed through his mind, he sensed her slip away from him, the emotional tide of passion rushing back out to sea.

She shuddered, and he braced himself over her. "Are you all right?"

She wouldn't meet his gaze and remained quiet. Unexpectedly, a feeling of inadequacy filled him, and he feared he was responsible for her seeming disappointment.

"I'm fine," she whispered, turning her shinning eyes back to him. "I just... I wanted to stay lost for a little while longer. I didn't want to come back here. Back to reality, I mean."

He understood. Reality, for the both of them, held only grief. He rolled onto the bed and drew her alongside him.

"I know," he muttered, smoothing her hair and holding her close. For a long time, they lay together, saying nothing, until Bret finally broke the stillness. "Angel, are you really all right?"

"Yes," she replied, her voice small and soft.

Something tightened around his heart and made it hard to breathe. Bret didn't believe her, but he didn't want to push her either. Not now at least.

The grandfather clock near the door chimed once, signaling the first hour after midnight. Neither of them noticed one day passing into the next amidst the heat of their passion.

Bret smiled. "Happy birthday," he said, and Angel looked up at him.

"Thank you," she replied and snuggled more closely against him with her head pillowed on his shoulder and his arm wrapped around her. She yawned sleepily.

He reached down and pulled the sheet up over them as her leg draped over his. Soon, he heard her even breathing and knew she had fallen asleep. A warm feeling of happiness bloomed inside him for the first time in a very long time. He didn't know if the joy he felt would last, but a small part of him hoped it would.

Something was decidedly different about Angel, he'd already admitted that much to himself, and he couldn't help anticipating a better future for them both. Pessimism raised its ugly head once more, but this time, he crushed it viciously. Jake had told him to trust her and, now, after this, he would. She had trusted him, had finally admitted she wanted him. There was no more reason to hold back.

Tomorrow would start a new chapter in his life. He prayed it was as wonderful as her words implied and his hopeful heart predicted.

To Be Continued...

*   *   *

Thank you for reading *Masters' Mistress*. Angel and Bret's story continues in *Masters' Escape: The Angel Eyes Series Book 2* scheduled to be release in 2021 (if not earlier). There's a lot more to this story and so many twists and turn. I hope you'll be back to experience it all.

If you enjoyed this story please help me reach other interested readers by leaving a review on Amazon. Reviews are so important to Indie authors and I would love to read yours.

And if you're looking forward to what happens next in this story, just turn the page for a sneak peek of *Masters' Escape*.

*   *   *

Masters' Escape

The Angel Eyes Series Book 2

THE ESCAPE

1

BRET MASTERS STORMED into the dark, one-room apartment he shared with his best friend Jake Nichols and slammed the door behind him. Pent-up fury roared through his veins and pounded in his ears. He wanted to break something, tear it apart piece by piece with his bare hands. But that wouldn't make him feel any better, and it wouldn't solve his dilemma.

As he'd made his way downstairs, his chest tightened until he could hardly breathe. Now, raking trembling hands through his raven-black hair, Bret glanced around and discovered himself alone with the enormous weight of his hurt and anger. He stared at his roommate's undisturbed bed and felt another level of pressure inside his ribs, building like a volcano about to erupt. It took him less than five seconds to guess why Jake was not lying there asleep. The thought of his friend enjoying the warm company of a willing partner pricked Bret's already soaring temper.

"What the *hell* are you doing in here?" Angel's high-pitched demand from only minutes ago rang inside Bret's mind. He tried to ignore it, but the memory wouldn't leave, replaying the whole conversation in painful detail.

"I was invited," he had replied as the smile slid off his face and a pang of foreboding clamped like a vise around his vulnerable heart.

For a moment, she'd actually looked confused as her wide-eyed gaze traveled over his naked body and settled on the white bedsheet draped low over his hips. She shook her head in denial. "I wouldn't have done that." Her voice was adamant, but her eyes, when they snapped back to his, told a different story.

"Well, darlin'," he had drawled—disappointed but unwilling to give in so easily—as he lay on his side and grinned, "I hate to break it to you, but you did. Maybe not in so many words, but the meaning was the same."

She squeezed her eyes closed, shutting him out as crimson stained her cheeks, clearly regretting what had happened between them.

Remembering that conversation brought a growl rumbling through his constricted throat. His fisted fingers pulled at his short-cropped hair in frustration, but a heartbeat later, he let his arms fall to his sides with a resigned sigh. It was probably better that Jake wasn't there to witness his exasperated display. Jake would undoubtedly want to know why Bret was so upset and that wasn't something he would willingly discuss. Whether Bret revealed the soft-feeling, sweet-smelling, curly-haired cause of his displeasure or not, the subject would eventually lead to an argument, and he didn't want Jake to become an inadvertent target.

He wasn't angry with Jake; he was furious and utterly disappointed with himself.

Once again, he'd trusted the wrong woman; believed that the beyond-the-physical-connection he'd felt with Angel was mutual. It sure seemed that way last night, right up to the point when she'd fallen asleep in his arms.

He should've known better than to allow hope to grow

inside him—that particular sentiment had always been his downfall.

"You're an idiot," he told himself as he quickly stripped out of the white dress shirt and black slacks he'd worn to Angel's birthday party the night before. He wadded up the clothes and tossed them onto the heap near the door. Then, still fuming, he crawled into the cool sheets of his bed to attempt another hour or two of sleep. Laying on his back with one hand tucked under his head and the other flat on his chest, he reminisced about the wonders of the previous evening. But even that was tainted by this morning's gut-wrenching disappointment.

"Why did you come back to the dining hall last night?" she had asked when her shinning eyes finally met his again. "Why couldn't you just stay away?"

He lifted one shoulder in an indifferent shrug. "I heard someone playing the piano. I didn't know it was you."

She looked away, her jaw clenched and her body curved inward defensively. "Why did you apologize?" she asked without meeting his gaze.

He'd blinked in surprise. Did she think he was so cold that causing someone pain didn't affect him? "Because I felt I should, and you accepted."

"And the dance?" she prompted, pinning him again with her wary blue-gray stare.

"It was your birthday, and you looked sad, disappointed even. I just wanted to make you smile."

She huffed and turned away, dismissing him. "You need to leave before anyone sees you."

Even though a part of him had suspected it was coming, that statement had hit him like a slap to the face—not to mention what it did to his stubborn pride.

"What?" He had tried to laugh it off. "Are you actually throwing me out?"

Her lips thinned. "Yes."

"Angel," he started and reached for her hand, intent on

soothing whatever troubled her, but she pulled away and scowled at him.

"Get out! I don't want you here. I don't *need* you here." Her expression softened suddenly, and her eyes seemed to plead with him. "Please…just leave."

"So, that's how it is?" he asked as the hope he'd felt only a few hours before dwindled and burned to dust under the white-hot fury that burst to life inside him.

Pain. Women always caused him pain. Why did he keep believing it could be different?

"What does that mean?"

"You got what you wanted, and now you're throwing me out?" He scoffed, "I thought you didn't use your breeders?"

"I don't."

"You sure as hell did last night!"

She glared at him.

"What's wrong?" he asked spitefully. "Did you get tired of using your old breeders and decided to play with your new toy?"

"That's not what happened."

"Isn't it?" He sat up. Bending one knee, he draped a forearm across it and met her frown with his own.

Angel's eyes had followed the sheet as it slipped downward and puddled in his lap. Appreciation and something like fear or disgust passed over her face. Not that he cared what she thought of him…not anymore.

"No!" she replied, yanking her eyes back to his.

"Then what did happen?"

She paused and seemed to slump as she shrugged. "You seduced me."

He barked a short, sardonic laugh. "Oh, no, honey. *You* seduced *me!*"

Angel sighed and surprised him with an affirming nod. "I shouldn't have done that. You should've stopped me."

"I tried." He chuckled dryly. "Several times."

"You should've tried harder."

"I did, but you were insistent. Good God, how much restraint do you think I have? I knew you wanted me, there's no denying that. I just didn't expect such a passionate response to a simple kiss."

"What kiss?"

His eyes shifted from her gaze to her lips and back again. She had wanted him, badly. Why was she still denying it? "You know what kiss."

With a slight shift of her head, she had tried to refute his statement, but Bret wouldn't have that.

He locked her with a hard stare and leaned in closer. "Maybe I should remind you…"

"Please don't," she'd squeaked and scooted a little farther away. "Please go, Bret. This can't happen again, and no one can know."

"Why?" he asked, hurt infusing his words. "Am I so below you that being with me is an embarrassment?"

She sighed and shook her head. "It's not that."

"Then what is it, Angel?"

It took her a minute to answer, but when she did, she seemed to be holding something back.

"I've made a lot of enemies," she said, then explained that, with the current laws, her adversaries could take him from her. If those women learned of what had happened between them last night, their attempts to acquire him would only increase. "And when they get their hands on you—and they will with your temper—they'll hurt you to force me to do what they want. If that happened, they'd gain more power than I could ever overcome without an all-out civil war. I can't do that, Bret. I can't!"

He frowned at her for a long minute, weighing her answer and searching her face. When he saw the telltale flicker in her pretty azure eyes, he knew the truth. *She's not telling me something.*

"That's bullshit," he said as he kicked the sheet off and got to his feet, spurred as much by her response as by his own internal demons.

"I don't understand," she said, confusion plain on her face. "You got what you wanted, so why are you so upset?"

He stopped in the middle of pulling up his underwear to glance at her before jerking the garment into place. With his hands on his hips and his slacks clenched in his fist, he directed a furious scowl at her. "Exactly what is it you think I wanted?"

"Last night you told me you wanted to sleep with me. You got what you wanted. So what do you have to be angry about?"

He gave a short, humorless laugh. "And you think that's all I wanted?"

She lowered her chin in an almost imperceptible nod.

He snorted and shook his head as disappointment tightened his chest. "You don't think much of me, do you?"

"That's not true," she said as he jerked on his slacks. "I am…fond of you."

"Fond?" He laughed again, derisively this time. "That's one way to describe it, though not very accurate."

"What are you talking about?"

"You *used* me, Angel." His voice was harsh as he fastened the closure on his slacks and zipped them up. "You had an itch you needed scratched and there I was, a stupid, horny bastard you could easily seduce because I told you what I wanted." His voice had held a sad and sour note as he snatched his shirt off the floor. "Well, ma'am," he'd drawled with a mocking bow and a gallant wave of his hand, "I'm glad to have been of service, but I'll be off now."

When she'd fallen asleep in his arms, hope for something better—for a future with Angel by his side—had spread through his chest like an out of control wildfire. Then she'd smashed all those idiotic dreams and his heart along with them. Her rejection burned in his brain, his belly, his heart. Now, he lay in his room with a crushing weight on his chest, unable to sleep.

Last night she'd given every indication of wanting more than just a one-night stand. Even before that, she'd melted at his touch and practically went up in flames every time he kissed her. And last night...

God, he groaned as the memories danced through his mind, *last night she'd nearly had me begging!*

Despite everything—her rejection and lies about protecting him from enemies he had yet to ascertain—he still wanted her. He couldn't deny it, not when just the thought of her soft, silky body, warm and yielding beneath him, heated his blood and brought his body to rigid awareness.

What the hell happened? He clenched his fist and slammed it against the mattress in pure frustration. Everything she'd said and done the night before told Bret that more lay hidden beneath her cool outer shell, just waiting for him to discover it. Everything from her reaction to his touch to her admission that she wanted him had been enough to set them both on fire. But this morning, the minute she realized he was warming the bed beside her, she turned to ice. Still, her gaze had lingered on his body as he jerked on his clothes. He knew she was attracted to him. He knew she wanted him, but apparently, she didn't want more from him than the use of his body. His heart squeezed tight. *Just like all the others.*

Last night he'd told himself it didn't matter.

This morning was a different story.

Her actions had flayed him deeply and it had gotten worse when he tried to leave.

For a second, when she'd stopped his hasty departure at her bedroom door, he'd thought maybe she regretted throwing him out. But she'd smashed that hope too.

"I need to know you're not going to talk about this," she'd said in a quiet rush. "You can't, not with anyone, not even Jake."

Happy best described his state of mind when he fell asleep

with Angel in his arms—a sentiment he hadn't experienced for a very long time. It shocked him that her cold dismissal after such a wonderful night could hurt as badly as it did. He rubbed at the raw ache in his chest, not wanting to admit that it had anything to do with Angel. His heart was too well protected for that, but even so, he had to admit that she'd cut him deeply—deeper than anyone had before—and the lonely idiot he was, still wanted her.

At her unequivocal final rejection, his uncle's voice, as it often did, had begun to taunt him in his head. *See, boy, no woman'll want you for anything but a good fuck!*

On the heels of that old insult, memories of the last woman he had once loved to distraction slammed into his mind like an old Mac truck. Right before everything in his already sorry life went totally wrong, Amy Hensford had uttered hurtful words that sounded too much like the ones Uncle Vince had once tormented him with.

Lying in bed now, thinking back, Bret could recall everything about that early morning when Amy had shown her true colors over five years ago.

The cool chill of the mountain air, the dark shadows of the evergreens surrounding their camp, the Raiders with their whips in hand, and he and Jake on their knees. Bret remembered it all, including the sharp twinge in his heart when, out of the corner of his eye, he'd seen Jake's worried glance. Right then, he'd desperately wanted to apologize for all those times he'd refused to listen to Jake's warnings about Amy, to find some way to save his friend from the result of his terrible error in judgment. But he couldn't. The Raiders would make them both into slaves and it was all his fault. *God, Jake, I'm so sorry...*

He wanted to roar and rage—physically manifest the hurt, resentment, and fury inside him—but that would do no good. They were outnumbered and all he could do was harden himself and wait for an opening.

The Raiders had attacked their camp in the early morning hours. Anger and disbelief had been his first reaction as horses had galloped into the mountain meadow where they'd been sleeping. He hadn't wanted to believe Amy had betrayed them—betrayed him. *There must be some mistake,* he'd stupidly thought as he knelt on the cold ground beside Jake. But once the other women began to congratulate Amy on her "catch," Bret realized his mistake and his heart shattered.

"Why did you betray me?" Bret had asked, completely stunned by what Amy had done.

Mirth had twinkled in Amy's dark eyes as she laughed in his face. "You're a sappy fool, Bret," she said, giggling as Bret stared up at her in shock. "I don't care for you. I never did. I just liked your looks. Your talents in bed were quite a pleasing surprise. Both are qualities that'll increase your price at auction. Though I'll hate to lose access to your..." her eyes had drifted over his body, assessing his worth and making Bret's skin crawl, "exceptional assets, I might get lucky in that regard."

She touched his face with a greedy caress and his breath caught in his throat. For a brief moment, hope that it had all been a very bad joke had bloomed inside him. Then his stomach roiled, sickened by how much her touch affected him, even after her betrayal, but then his anger rekindled and the tender feelings disappeared.

When he pulled away, she smiled at him. "You do have such a pretty face, but no brains in your head," she said and then chuckled at his fulminating look. She told him that no woman would want him now...no self-respecting, decent woman anyway. Then she taunted him with the threat of making him a slave and that terrible possibility had awakened his fury.

A growl had ripped from his chest as he surged to his feet, all his animosity focused on Amy. To his surprise, Jake and several others had joined him. During the fray, Bret lost all track of Jake. He'd been looking for him among the others fighting for their freedom when Amy struck at Bret, nearly sinking a long-bladed knife into his back. Instead, she landed a glancing blow that left a long shallow gash. As he rolled away, he saw someone had tackled her, but in the dim pre-dawn light, he didn't recognize his savior and there'd been no time to dwell on it.

"Run!" he'd shouted at the others as he made his own escape, while praying Jake would hear his shouts and race for the trees.

Bret had retreated to their predetermined rendezvous point to wait for Jake. Hours crawled by, a day, but Jake never showed. Too late, he realized Jake had been his savior. That once again, Jake had saved his life without thought for his own. If Bret had known—which he still felt he should have—he would never have left Jake. His stomach cramped at the thought of the horrors his friend must've had faced. If he had known Jake was the man who'd taken Amy down, Bret wanted to believe that he'd have risked becoming a slave himself before condemning Jake to that fate.

Bret lost everything that day, including his self-respect. All because he'd wanted a woman's love so desperately that he'd ignored all the warning signs and Jake's better judgment.

He had promised himself he would never be that naive again.

But he *did* do it again—with his eyes wide open this time. Now, he suffered the heartache of being wrong once more. His stupidity made him furious. Not only with Angel, but himself as well, and he'd reacted accordingly by storming out of the room. Well, he would've stormed out if she hadn't stopped him with her demand for his silence.

He had tried to be snide, to pretend her wanting to forget everything that had happened between them didn't hurt like severing a limb, but the pain was far worse than that, deeper and more damning.

"Bret, please..."

He had frowned and looked away, unable to meet Angel's pleading gaze and struggling to contain the burst of rage that struck him. His eyes fell on the big four-poster bed where they'd spent a substantial portion of the night making love. She wanted to pretend their coupling had never happened, but that was impossible, at least for him. Something happened between them that went beyond the physical. He'd felt the connection and had thought she did too, but then, he'd been wrong before.

Unable to block out the emotions crashing through him, he'd closed his eyes and shook his head. *God dammit! Why do I keep doing this to myself?*

Standing beside Angel's bedroom door staring at her bed, he had gathered the tatters of his defenses back around his wounded heart. When he'd met Angel's worried gaze once more, the hurt and anger became more acute. He didn't believe she was concerned for him, but he could be nothing less than who he was. So, he had reassured her that no one else would ever know—at least not from him—and escaped her room as fast as she would let him.

Their relationship had drastically changed over the last twenty-four hours. Instead of having a delicate truce of amicability, they were now lovers, something Angel—and himself, if he was honest—was unprepared to accept.

Now, still laying on his back in his bed, he barked a mirthless chuckle as he remembered telling himself that getting laid would make him feel better.

"Yeah, right," he murmured into the darkness. His situation was anything but better. If anything, his discomfort and dissatisfaction were a thousand times worse.

He wanted to be angry with her, and he was, but he was far angrier with himself. Did he honestly expect her to react differently to their unexpected union merely because of some mind-blowing sex? From the day he'd arrived, she'd treated him kindly but remained aloof. Why would that change now?

My God, I'm an idiot! he thought bitterly, turning onto his side, punching his pillow into a ball, and planting his head in the middle. *I let her use me and enjoyed it as much as she did!*

At least until she threw him out.

I've got to get away from her.

The thought gave him pause.

Do I really want to run? Now? A part of him leaped at the idea, but the deeper part, though bleeding and sore from Angel's rejection, hesitated. What if he was wrong about her? What about the others he'd grown attached to here? What about Jake? Those questions gave him pause, until his hard side—the one that sounded like his hated uncle's voice—reminded him of Angel's rebuff and his ribs constricted with remembered pain.

He didn't have a choice. If he stayed now, she truly would own him and he couldn't accept that. He would not be her toy, regardless of how much he wanted her. No matter how different she may be otherwise. Not now that he knew she looked at him not as a man, but as a slave—a breeder to give her pleasure, not someone with whom to share her life. Her story about the laws and being afraid for him was just that, a story to keep him quiet and coming back for more. He wouldn't play that game.

Hardening his heart, the way he should have kept it, he began to rebuild the protective battlements he'd lowered just for her. He would run, and not even Angel's soft skin or the haunting scent of lilacs that followed her would stop him this time. As soon as the opportunity arose, he would escape and never look back.

*　　*　　*

Look for the rest of this captivating continuing-story
in Book 3, *Masters' Escape*.
Scheduled for release in 2021 if not sooner.

ABOUT THE AUTHOR

Jamie was born and raised in the wonderful Pacific Northwest and she has always wanted to be a storyteller. As a child and young adult, she spent countless hours dreaming up stories to entertain herself and her friends. She kept long-running, developing stories in her head for years, knowing someday she would write them all down.

She still has many stories still floating around the back of her cluttered mind (and haunting her hard drive as well). She hopes they will all make their way out into the world for your enjoyment someday (soon)!

She still lives in Pacific Northwest with her family and her fur-babies.

You can learn more about Jamie and her books on her website: www.thejamieschulz.com

And you can follow her on her social media pages:
Facebook (@TheJamieSchulz)
Twitter (@TheJamieSchulz)
Instagram (@thejamieschulz)
Jamie's Amazon Page
Goodreads4554
BookBub

ACKNOWLEDGMENTS

I'd like to say a special Thank You to my official editors Donna Kelley and Silvia Curry. I'd also like to thank all my beta readers and proofreaders, as well as my family and friends. Thanks, once again, to Sam and TJ, the Facebook groups, Miss N., Bryan Cohen, Dario Herrera and everyone else!

Made in the USA
Middletown, DE
13 November 2020